BETROTHED

'I shall wed you,' he said.

'You are asking me to wed you?'

'No,' he said. 'I am telling you. It must be so.'

She nodded slowly. 'Aye, I believe it must.'

They stared at each other soberly until John gave a sudden shout of joy and swung her off the ground, so that the skirt of her gown floated behind her and she complained that she grew dizzy. He put her back on her feet and held her gently, close against his heart and stroked her hair. She gave herself up to the rhythm of his breathing as his chest rose and fell and she wanted the moment to last forever.

The Heron Saga 1
The Rich Earth

PAMELA OLDFIELD

WARNER BOOKS

A Warner Book

First published in Great Britain in 1980 by
Macdonald Futura Publishers Ltd
Published by Sphere Books 1986
Reprinted 1987, 1988
Reprinted by Warner Books in 1992

Copyright © 1980 by Pamela Oldfield

ISBN 0 7221 6508 0

Printed and bound in Great Britain by
Cox & Wyman Ltd, Reading, Berkshire

Warner Books
A Division of
Little, Brown and Company (UK) Limited
165 Great Dover Street
London SE1 4YA

For Phyllis Hunt

While researching this novel I read many fine books. My thanks to the staffs of the County Library, Maidstone and Westcountry Studies Library, Exeter, for helping me to find them.

CHAPTER ONE

1468 Yorkshire

One of the ewes bleated and then another. Through the short springy turf they felt the thunder of approaching hoofbeats. The shepherd, asleep in the lee of a rock, raised his head but before he could struggle to his feet the horse was upon him. It jumped the rock in a spray of torn earth, scattering the terrified sheep in all directions then galloped into the mist and out of sight, its rider hallooing like one possessed. The old man shook his fist at the retreating figure and then collapsed into a fit of coughing which racked his frail consumptive frame and shortened his breath.

'The devil take him and all his kind!' he muttered angrily. Slightly mollified to see that his flock was returning of its own volition, he crept back under his rock like an insect returning to the shelter of its stone.

The cause of his disturbed rest, oblivious to his existence, rode at full pelt for another mile before slowing his horse to a walking pace. He was an attractive young man, promised to be handsome with his hard blue eyes, well-shaped nose and thin lips above a strong chin. Not a face for laughter. The head was set on the narrow neck with an arrogance exceptional in one of his meagre years. His lean body was muscular from a childhood spent riding, swimming and wrestling. His arms and legs were long, his hips narrow. A fine catch in fact for any young woman, but John Kendal had other ideas.

He was the second youngest son of Hannah and Edwin Kendal a flourishing Yorkshire family grown wealthy on the export of cloth and enjoying the favour of the reigning King, Edward the Fourth. A Yorkist King had ruled

7

England for seven years and John was content. He had lost three brothers to the cause and still felt their loss keenly. His attention was momentarily turned to his mount, as it shied nervously at the appearance of a woodcock bursting from the scant cover ahead of them and thrusting its way upward. A faint smile touched his lips as he patted the horse's neck.

'Rest easy,' he urged. 'Tis not the first time you have seen a woodcock nor will it be the last, though I dare swear they are a rare sight in the streets of London!'

He rode on his excitement increasing as he thought of the prospect ahead of him. He would become the finest gold-smith in London and make his fortune. Then he would return home and buy land of his own and would surprise them yet. He would earn his parents grudging respect and his sister's admiration. His expression softened at the thought of Lydia, his eldest and well beloved sister who alone had shown him affection. His mother's love was reserved for the three sons she had given to the Yorkist cause. They had died gloriously. John did not intend to die. He would live gloriously.

This day's journey was the first step towards his goal. He imagined with satisfaction the look on his mother's face when she found the note he had left, and realized he had fled the nest without even a farewell. Throwing back his head, he laughed aloud for joy and, urging his horse into a gallop, raced on towards the highway, heading south towards his future.

Henry Sheldryke glanced down at the milky-brown water as it raced past his horse's legs.

'A ford!' he snorted, his expression sour. 'They said t'would be a ford! Tis more like a raging torrent'.

He tried again to urge the horse deeper into the water, flapping at the reins and digging his heels into its plump

8

sides. The horse neighed shrilly, shook his head from side to side but did not move forward.

'Useless creature,' Henry grumbled. 'I shall have a complaint to make at that last post on my return. They shall hear a large piece of my mind. The nag's not biddable and the river's not fordable. They think wrongly if they think to cheat Henry Sheldyke and that's a fact. Oh, they shall hear from me again!'

And at length, thought Elizabeth, trying to hide her delight at her uncle's discomfiture. It did not concern her that they would now be late at the smithy where they were to join their travelling party. She was in no haste to finish the journey and hoped for many such setbacks, for every hour's delay was an hour's freedom gained. At the end of the journey marriage awaited. Marriage to an old man and a lifetime's boredom. The idea had little appeal and she was glad enough to sit her horse patiently and watch her uncle's ill temper grow as he finally gave up his attempt to cross the flooded river and turned back for the bank.

'A pox on them all,' he said and Elizabeth raised her eyebrows in mock disapproval at the words. 'We had best ride downstream a while.'

'Or upstream,' said Elizabeth.

He hesitated as she had known he would.

'We must find another fording place or else a bridge,' he told her.

She laughed. 'If tis anything like the last bridge we shall end by swimming the river,' she said and he nodded mournfully for the local people were notoriously lax in their observance of the rules and highways and bridges were badly neglected – the former overgrown with hedges where a cut-throat could hide with ease; the latter rotted away or cannibalized by the poor in search of firewood. They rode on in silence along the side of the river in search of a place where they might safely cross but were out of luck.

'Perhaps we shall miss our party and have to wait over for another,' suggested Elizabeth. 'It would be less tiring for you and, for my part, I care not. One day or the next – it matters not.'

But her uncle would not hear of it, assuring her that Daniel was eager to see his betrothed and an extra day added to the journey most certainly *would* matter.

'He shall not be disappointed if I have my way,' he said firmly and Elizabeth's hopes of a postponement were effectively dashed.

She rode on in pensive mood. Daniel Heron was older than her uncle by three years and had been recently widowed. Her uncle and aunt had been honest with her. He is elderly, they told her, and suffers with his bladder having a tendency to stones, but he is a sober and devout Catholic and has a considerable fortune. They had answered her questions with equal honestly: No, he is not tall. No, he is not a handsome man but no, not ugly either. He had buried two wives and no, he had no children by either of them, 'So he will want heirs,' she had said, shuddering inwardly at the prospect. Yes, they agreed. He would want heirs!

She glanced sideways at the old man beside her. The hair under the velvet cap was thin and grey, the blue eyes faded. His neck was long and scrawny and no longer fitted snugly into the collar of his coat. Would Daniel look this way? She sighed. Most certainly he would, she thought, or if not worse for he was three years older.

Her uncle's hands clutching the reins were gnarled and spotted with brown and the swollen knuckles gleamed in contrast. She shuddered again, imagining the pale bony legs and wasted body. And she must lie beside such a man and call him 'my sweet lord' and listen to his words of love. Sweet heaven! He would peck her cheek with dry kisses and . . . .

Her horse stumbled against a stone and, with the jolt, she determinedly put Daniel Heron out of her mind. She would not spoil her journey by anticipating her fate.

'There is someone up ahead!' she cried suddenly. 'He is

halfway across the river. It must be shallower there. Call to him, Uncle. We may need his help.'

Her uncle cupped his hand to his mouth and shouted, 'Hello, there! You ahead! Will you wait for us?'

'Aye,' came the answer and Elizabeth's spirits rose as they drew nearer, and she made out the slim figure of a young man. Halfway across the river, he sat at ease as the muddy current swirled round his stirrups, his horse rolling his eyes in terror at the water tugging at its legs.

'We've been trying to cross for some time,' began Elizabeth eagerly, but her uncle frowned and motioned her to silence.

'We've been trying to cross,' he told the young man, 'but the river's in flood as you know. Is it safe there, do you think, for my niece and me to attempt a crossing? Our horses are useless nags and it is obviously very deep.'

'Allow me to help you,' said John, although he was not pleased at the interruption of his solitude. A scrawny young girl and an old man were not his idea of interesting companions. He decided he would bear with them until they reached the rest of the party, and then 'lose' them and find more congenial company. He turned his horse with difficulty and urged it back to the bank where Elizabeth waited with her uncle. On first impression she was as he had expected, a thin body under the wool gown with a small pale face. The woollen stuff of her gown was good enough, but the gown itself was poorly designed and the cut skimpy. No rings graced the hands, and she wore no jewellery save for a rosary of amber beads. But the grey eyes burned with an intensity that surprised him. He gave her a brief nod and the merest hint of a smile, so that she read his indifference and flushed with disappointment. What had he to be so superior about, she asked herself. He was no more than a boy, his face soft and downy as a peach and no manners to speak of!

'I'd best cross first,' said her uncle. 'Then this young man can . . . .'

'John Kendal' he announced.

'Ah, yes, yes, the proprieties must be observed. This is my niece, Elizabeth Sheldyke, and I'm Henry of the same name. Now, if I cross first . . . .'

John leaned forward without more ado and took the rein from him. He tugged the reluctant animal into the river and Elizabeth watched them as they moved slowly into deepening water. The water in mid-stream covered their boots, and she laughed aloud to see her uncle trying to keep his dry, leaning back on the saddle, his feet raised high on either side of the horse's neck. They eventually reached the far side and her uncle waved an encouraging hand to dispel any fears she might have of the crossing. She had none, however. Her only fear was that she might somehow make a fool of herself in front of their young escort. She clamped her lips shut and urged her horse into the water while he was still only halfway across. She would show him that she at least did not need his help.

'Elizabeth, wait!' shouted her uncle, but she ignored him.

Her horse laid his ears back and tossed his head uneasily as the cold water swirled against his belly. Out of the corner of her eye she saw the young man watching her, but could not read the expression on his face. Then her horse lost his footing and she was thrown forward.

'Elizabeth!' screamed her uncle. John still seemed yards away, but struggled to reach her. Terrified, but refusing to show it, she clung to the saddle as he reached out his hand to take the reins from her, noting the pallor of her face and the fear in her eyes.

'Thank you, no!' she told him through gritted teeth, and held the reins out of his reach.

'You might well have drowned,' he told her in a low voice so that her uncle might not hear.

'But I didn't', she said, sharply.

He put out his hand again for the rein, but she slapped

12

it sharply with her own – then immediately regretted the childish action.

'No,' she said again and was annoyed to see the corners of his mouth turn down in a grim smile. Why, she asked herself, was she behaving so foolishly and why being so stubborn? The young man merely offered a helping hand. Why could she not accept the offer graciously? Now the water crept up over her ankles, soaking the hem of her gown, but she made no effort to keep dry; merely urged her horse steadily across the river, while he kept pace with her in case of further accident.

Once on the far bank, her uncle began to remonstrate with her for her reckless independence but John, seeing the colour burning in her cheeks, intervened on her behalf.

'All that matters is that we are all safely across,' he said placatingly. 'We should press on. We have delayed long enough and the rest of the party will be growing impatient.'

Elizabeth flashed him a look that held reluctant gratitude and was surprised to receive a brief wink which her uncle missed. She relaxed a little and laughed lightly.

'Last one to the crossroads buys the lunchtime ale!' she challenged and, taking advantage of their surprise, nudged her horse into a canter and sped off, leaving her companions to exchange bemused looks. John watched her for a moment, then spurred his horse after her, passing her easily to wait quietly triumphant at the crossroads.

Henry 'tut-tutted' to himself at the forward behaviour of his niece, and followed more soberly, wondering, not for the first time, how his old friend Daniel would survive such a young and tempestuous wife!

By the time they reached the smithy, the sun was directly overhead. Henry Sheldyke dismounted, gratefully tethered his horse and settled himself comfortably under a large chestnut tree which spread a welcome shade over much of the courtyard. The rest of the party hailed them cheerfully making no comment on the lateness of their arrival, for the recent rains had swollen all the rivers and most of their fellow travellers had experienced similar delays. Now that the sun shone they were content to be out of the saddle. Some sat gossiping and joking, the rest wandered about, glad of the chance to stretch their legs. Two friars were due to join them and had not yet put in an appearance. When they did, they would bring the number in the party to fourteen. The smithy was a convenient assembly point. Horses were available for those who needed to change mounts. Ale could be bought from the blacksmith's wife, and she always had a batch of newly baked pies for any who wanted them. John, who had left home empty-handed and without breakfast, purchased a vegetable pasty and bit hungrily into the warm crust, while Elizabeth unwrapped the cold boiled pork and fresh wholemeal bread her aunt had packed for them.

John sat talking with two young men of his own age and Elizabeth found herself surreptitiously watching him while she ate. Declining to share her uncle's shade, she sat on a low rail to which some of the horses were tethered, and wondered how she could win back his interest. It would not be easy. He was obviously enjoying his companions stories, for they laughed uproariously from time to time and appeared quite unaware of her existence. She took a mouthful of ale and bit into the pork hungrily, for the fresh air and early start to the journey had sharpened her appetite. How, she wondered, did one go about attracting the attention of young men? She had no previous experience to guide her. Orphaned at the age of seven, she and her young brother, Andrew, had been sent to their elderly aunt and uncle whose own children had left home and married. They had shouldered their unexpected burden with resignation and had looked after their welfare and education as well as they were able. Elizabeth had learned household management from her aunt, the teachings of the

Bible from her uncle, and French and a little Latin from the chantry priest in the village. For her part, she had proved herself dutiful and intelligent with an enquiring mind and lively imagination. Unfortunately, her aunt and uncle had exhausted their finances on dowries for their own six children and had very little with which to endow Elizabeth and Andrew. Since a prestigious marriage was not possible, they had done the best they could, and had arranged Elizabeth's betrothal to Daniel Heron, a man who owned a large estate in Devon and had made his money from the rich tin deposits for which the area was famous. Later, when Elizabeth was married, Andrew would become a novice at nearby Harben Priory. Daniel Heron would contribute a small sum of money to this end and Henry Sheldyke a somewhat smaller sum. At first, Elizabeth had demurred. Later she had complained bitterly but to no avail. The wedding would take place and she was on her way south.

Now laughing, she shooed off the large, but friendly mongrel dog who appeared from behind the smithy and began to ingratiate himself with anyone who had anything edible.

'You shall have none of my pork,' she told him, 'for my need is greater! If you are hungry, go catch a coney, you idle object.'

One of John's companions tossed him a scrap of bread and he pounced on it gratefully and gulped it down. The dog cast a reproachful look in Elizabeth's direction, and attached himself lovingly to the three young men.

'Did she refuse you, then?' teased John. 'Mayhap she has a cold heart. A wise old dog bewares such women!'

They laughed and Elizabeth glanced anxiously towards her uncle. She noticed his head had lolled on to his chest and his velvet cap was now lying in his lap as he dozed. Relieved, she laughed also.

'And mayhap I do not waste the warmth of my heart on stray dogs!' she said.

15

'Oh, she has a warm heart,' said the young man on John's right.

He was short and stocky with a mass of tight curls and a round good-humoured face. 'Who do you save it for?' he went on. 'Am I eligible, do you think? I hunger for affection.'

'But he hungers for food more,' said John. 'He has wolfed two pasties in the time it takes to wink an eye. I dare swear he has hollow legs!'

Elizabeth's eyes sparkled. Life was suddenly becoming more interesting. Here she was bandying words with three presentable young men. The prospect had seemed impossible twenty-four hours before.

The dog decided to give her another chance. He sprang over and sat up on his hind legs, begging. 'Oh, very well,' she laughed. 'I cannot resist those brown eyes,' and she tossed him a piece of pork fat. The young man on John's left now knelt down and hung his hands in an imitation of the dog.

'Can you resist *my* brown eyes?' he asked. 'Toss me a crumb of comfort, sweet lady, ere I pine away.'

John gave him a friendly push which sent him falling sideways. 'Do not heed him,' he told Elizabeth. 'He lies in his teeth!'

'I do not!' protested his friend.

'That you do,' cried John. 'For your eyes are not brown. They are as blue as a periwinkle.'

Another traveller, overhearing this exchange, joined in. She was a large, shapeless woman on her way to her grandson's baptism. 'Don't you listen to 'em, my duck,' she called to Elizabeth. 'They're all the same, men. Greet you laughing and leave you weeping. There's nought to choose between them and that mongrel – except the dog's better looking.'

A great roar of laughter greeted this sally from people around them, but before the lads could argue their defence, the two friars appeared and more greetings were exchanged.

'We are late,' said the elder of the two, 'and our apologies to you all. But my horse is gone lame and we have come at a snail's pace these last five miles. We'd have gone faster if I'd carried the horse!'

'You are come to the right place then,' said the blacksmith, emerging from the smithy at the sound of their approach. His face was shining with sweat and he wiped it with the back of a huge forearm as he spoke. 'Bring the animal in and young Martin will have a look at it. If needs be, you can take another — Martin!' he roared. 'Move yourself lad, and see to the good friar's horse.'

A smaller version of the smith appeared, obviously one of his sons. He helped the friar dismount and then led the animal into the forge. The noise of the friar's arrival had woken Elizabeth's uncle, and he now settled his cap firmly on his balding head and glanced round for his niece.

'Ah, there you are, child,' he said. 'I believe I dozed off. The ride has tired me. Are we leaving, then?'

'No, no,' she reassured him. 'The friars have arrived and one has problems with his mount, but the smith is attending to him. We shall not leave yet awhile.'

'Good,' he said. 'Then I shall close my eyes again and – Oh, get away,' he cried to the dog, who, hearing a new voice, had trotted over and now stood hopefully beside him, wagging his tail. 'Go, you scruffy animal! I do not want you. Shoo!'

Elizabeth stood up and straightened her gown, brushing down the back of it where she had sat on the wooden rail. She then wandered over to the door of the smithy and looked inside. It seemed dark in contrast to the sunlit yard but, as her eyes grew accustomed to the gloom, she could make out the hearth glowing dully at the back of the room. An old man stood behind it working the large leather bellows which brought the fire up to the required redness whenever necessary. Now, he waited while the boy, Mar-

17

tin, removed a shoe from the hind leg of the friar's horse. Seeing Elizabeth, the lad grinned cheerfully.

'You may come in, if you've a mind,' he remarked, 'I won't bite.'

Laughing, Elizabeth accepted his invitation and entered the darkened room. She stood at his side, keeping a respectful distance between herself and the horse, a large piebald with rolling eyes. The boy tossed the old shoe on to a pile of sawdust in the corner and reached for another from a hook on the wall. Lifting the horse's foot, he tried the shoe for size and nodded with satisfaction. He held the shoe in the coals for several minutes to heat it, watching Elizabeth meantime with an unashamed admiration which went to her head like wine. Finally, she became embarrassed by his steady stare and looked curiously round her, unable to meet his gaze any longer.

Beyond the hearth there was a large tank of water for cooling the metal. Various tools and implements hung along one side. Overhead, more tools hung from hooks on the beam and a large lantern took pride of place in the centre of the roof space. Tongs, pliers, hammers seemed to be everywhere; but Martin reached out confidently for each new tool, and it was always ready to hand. He took the shoe from the fire, rested it on the anvil and gave it a few blows with a hammer. Then, he seated it against the horse's hoof and Elizabeth stepped back hurriedly as a cloud of smoke rose from it gasping as she trod on to someone's foot and two strong arms encircled her waist.

'You are no lightweight!' said a voice. 'I have a crushed toe to prove it.'

'I'm sorry,' she apologized, twisting free and turning to see the young man with the blue eyes. 'I didn't know you were there.'

'Don't apologize,' he said. 'It was my pleasure.'

'Your pleasure to have a crushed toe?'

'To have it crushed by so charming a lady,' he said but

with a grin which belied the serious tone of his voice. 'My name is Francis, but you may call me Frank.'

'Thank you, kind sir,' said Elizabeth cheekily. 'My name is Elizabeth and you may call me Elizabeth but please take your arms from my waist.'

'And if I don't?' he asked.

'I think you will,' she replied firmly.

He put his lips close to her ear whispering, 'One kiss secures your release!'

Even while she struggled for a suitably scathing retort, she almost longed to accept his offer. She had never been kissed, and the future which stretched before her would contain only the kisses of an old man. Yet here was an attractive young man anxious for her lips. It was all so sudden, quite unexpected – and utterly tempting. But as she hesitated, John appeared beside them. Francis dropped his arms to his side and they all turned their attentions to the friar's horse. The smith's son, playing up to the audience, gave a fine demonstration of the art of shoeing a horse. He cooled the shoe in the water, gripped the hoof between his knees and began to hammer in the nails with quick sure blows.

A disturbance in the yard heralded the arrival of a farmer leading two oxen, and they were soon at the stable door of the smithy, the beasts lowing anxiously. Hastily, Elizabeth and her companions moved back to give them plenty of room, and after a moment or two, John and Francis strolled back to rejoin their companion.

Elizabeth walked in the opposite direction and found herself in a small orchard at the rear of the smithy. About a dozen small fruit trees grew in rows at the end of which two beehives stood against the wattle fence. Slowly, she crossed the grass to the nearest apple tree and, ducking under it, stood with her face among the delicate pink blossom which hung in heavy, scented clusters among the pale green leaves. Closing her eyes, she breathed in the fragrance, willing her heart to cease its foolish fluttering and her mind to stop its whirling. You are a betrothed woman, she reminded herself. You have no right to be dallying with strange young men. But her heart argued rebelliously that every young girl should taste excitement at least once in her life and it was springtime, with the sun shining and her blood racing through her body. She opened her eyes and looked up to the blue sky which framed the confusion of apple blossom around her head. It was breathtakingly beautiful – almost too beautiful to bear, for its glory assaulted her senses and brought tears to her eyes. Bees droned and fumbled among the flowers and somewhere a lark sang. It was too perfect. With a sigh she sank to her knees and leaned back against the rough trunk. Idly, she plucked a clover leaf from the grass and counted its leaves. Only three. She pursed her lips and searched for another.

'No luck?'

She looked up as John Kendal smiled down at her, with that wry half-crooked smile she had noticed earlier.

'Take it,' she offered, holding out the clover. 'But you may be only three-quarters lucky. There is one leaf missing.'

'Three-quarters lucky!' he teased. 'And what do I do when my luck runs out?'

'I suppose you must rely on your own endeavours,' she said as he helped her to her feet.

He picked a tiny sprig of blossom and bowing slightly, offered it to her. 'In fair exchange,' he said, 'although I doubt it will bring you luck.'

'It gives me pleasure,' said Elizabeth, cradling it in her hand. 'I think we can ask no more of it. My thanks.'

'Did he kiss you?' John asked abruptly.

'You shouldn't ask,' she challenged, flustered. 'It is of no....'

'Because they had a wager,' he said.

Elizabeth's cheeks burned as she stammered out a denial.

'They meant no insult,' he confirmed. 'It was in jest. Please don't look so distressed.'

She was silent for a while, then said, 'Why did you tell me?'

He shrugged. 'I'm not certain,' he confessed. 'Perhaps I think you are too good to be kissed for such a reason.'

'For what reason should a woman be kissed?' she asked looking straight into his eyes.

He did not look away but returned her look squarely. 'Because she is an attractive woman and a man finds her desirable,' he said.

She looked down at the blossom in her hand without answering.

'Your uncle tells me you are about to be wed,' he said.

'That's true,' she replied wretchedly.

'Your husband will kiss you for the right reason,' said John.

She shook her head and unbidden tears sprang to her eyes once more.

'He is an old man,' she whispered. 'An old man. Perhaps . . . . ' She broke off suddenly

'Perhaps?' he prompted.

She studied the ground, as the toe of her shoe searched among the blades of grass for the elusive four-leaved clover, but did not answer.

John looked at the fresh young face, the eyes downcast, and saw the humiliation in the curve of her thin shoulders. He pitied the girl her bleak future, comparing it unfavourably with his own. She glanced up at him and the long lashes only partly hid the unshed tears.

'Perhaps you wanted him to kiss you,' he said gently, but Elizabeth turned her face away and remained silent, struggling with her conflicting desires. On the one hand, to preserve her modesty and on the other, to know the joy of one kiss from young lips.

'He wanted to kiss me,' she said defiantly, but her lips trembled.

'I don't doubt it' he confirmed.

'Why should he wish it?' she asked. Her voice was low, but there was a desperation in the tone that did not escape him.

'Turn round and face me and I will tell you,' he commanded, gently.

She did so and he was surprised to see the faint flush of colour which his words had brought to her cheeks. The grey eyes looked into his and he hesitated, aware of the importance of the moment to her. He took one of her hands in his and studied the slender fingers and well-kept nails. Inexplicably, the moment held more for him than he had realized as they stood together beneath the blossom, patterned by the sunlight.

'You have beautiful eyes,' he said and her lips parted with the thrill of her first compliment. 'You are comely and . . .' he hesitated, lost for words. The girl was no beauty but the fine features could well improve, rounded out with the softness a few more years would bring. She had scarcely parted with childhood and yet must assume the ways and manners of a wife. He picked up a strand of her heavy silken hair and put it to his lips. 'And silken chestnut hair,' he said. 'I do not doubt he wanted to kiss you.'

Suddenly a question hung between them. Did *he* want to kiss her? Neither spoke, although Elizabeth longed for the words and he longed to answer 'Aye'. Her throat had gone dry and she felt a fierce yearning that distressed her in its intensity. She saw his eyes darken and he moved imperceptibly nearer, the strand of hair still held in his hand.

'*I* want to kiss you,' he said abruptly, and she nodded not trusting herself to speak.

His arms went round her, he placed his lips on hers and she closed her eyes against their sweetness. John felt the increasing passion in her kiss and, lifting her from the

22

ground, held her slim body against his own. When at last he set her on her feet again, they were both silent, slightly breathless.

'Your future husband is to be envied,' he said softly, marvelling at the change in her. Her eyes glowed, a bright colour burned in her cheeks and the parted lips were sensuous. Her breathing came faster and she was about to reply when her uncle came into the orchard in search of her. Hastily, they moved apart.

'I'm here, Uncle,' she called, her eyes never leaving John's face, wanting to imprint its image on her memory for ever.

Henry Sheldyke looked uneasy when he saw them together, but said nothing. They then returned to the yard for the sudden end to the hammering signalled the resumption of their journey. The two of them spoke occasionally during the long ride south, but her uncle saw that they were never alone again. Finally, their ways parted – John towards London, Elizabeth to Devon.

But a year later, on her wedding night, the faded blossom from the apple tree lay hidden beneath her pillow.

CHAPTER TWO

1480 London

With a muttered oath John set down the goblet on which
he was working, returned the scriber to its place in the rack
on the wall, and rubbed his eyes tiredly. He looked across
at Mark and grinned.

'Tell me, Mark,' he begged. 'Tell me how it is to have
a good night's sleep. Tis so long since I had one I swear I
cannot remember!'

Mark looked up and laughed. 'What did I tell you but
you would not heed but must off and wed the girl! Wed in
haste and repent at leisure, I said. You might still be a
bachelor gay like myself.'

'Hold your gloating,' said John. 'Just tell me how it is.'
He shook the pitcher hopefully and poured himself the last
half mug of ale.

'T'will only torment you to hear it,' said Mark.

'Tell me nonetheless,' said John, 'and let me suffer.'

'Why, then you lie in bed and tis very quiet,' Mark told
him, 'with hardly a sound, maybe now and then wheels on
the cobbles and the shouting of the watch, maybe an owl
hooting — on a bad night, that is!'

'Sweet joy!'

' . . . so, your prayers well said, your eyelids flutter
and close and you slip away gently into a delightful
dream . . . .'

'You can spare me that!' John interrupted. 'I know your
dreams of old — all earth and lust.'

Mark shrugged. 'Tis your loss!' he said.

'You were slipping away.'

'Aye — gently and deliciously — and you lie relaxed and
warm, hearing the house creak and settle, the mouse

pattering in the wainscot, the dog grunting in his sleep
.... and then your mind whirls into unconsciousness
and you're asleep; and *stay* asleep, hour upon hour, until
the birds sing sweetly in the eaves to ....'

'Stop, stop! It is all too lyrical,' cried John. 'You are
right, it does torment me.'

'And which little lamb woke you last night?'

''Twas neither. For once the babes slept right through.
But Bet was restless, tossing and turning and so hot it is like
sleeping with a live coal! She is so near her time and bigger
than ever. She cannot lie comfortably and must have me rub
her back where it aches; and then it is a few sips of ale for
her throat is dry, and then a walk round the bed to ease the
cramp in her leg!'

'You parents pay a heavy price,' said Mark. 'I'll take
good care not to suffer a like fate. I love my freedom and
to sleep at nights. But enough of such a morbid subject.
Surely 'tis dinner time, my stomach tells me that my
throat's been cut! I wouldn't refuse a pasty if the old
fellow's there today. Let's get along to The Tabard.'

Tossing their aprons behind the door, the two men
stepped out into the sunlit yard, turning their faces
upwards to the sun like animals freed from a cage.

'I have done so little work this morning,' John confessed.
'The scriber seems to have a mind of its own and will not
follow the course I have designed for it!'

They walked through the alley into the narrow street.
The midday sun shone directly down and the houses close
on either side cast little or no shade. The midday crowds
surged backwards and forwards, intent upon their lunch or
a browse among the stalls: old men sat over their dice on
the doorsteps: children ran and tumbled, shouted at by-
passing riders and were constantly at risk from the horses
who picked their way nervously along the cobbles. A lost
hoop bounced and rolled to a halt against John's leg and he
handed it back to the little girl who ran bawling in search
of it.

A group of young apprentices argued amiably and pushed each other around, to the annoyance of sober matrons and dignified merchants. A 'blind' flower-seller squinted hopefully at John, but he shook his head at the proffered posy. Mark, however, in his open-hearted way, bought a small bunch of yellow rosebuds and presented them to John. 'For Bet,' he said, 'with my love.'

'She can do without that,' John laughed. 'She has had mine and see where it's put her!'

Cheered by this not very witty remark, John pushed his way past the juggler whose audience effectively blocked the street and they finally reached the inn.

'And a right daisy I shall look going in with these,' said John as he tucked the flowers into his belt.

As usual, on Fridays an old man stood outside The Tabard with a tray of fresh hot pies and pasties. He was well liked, for the pies were always fresh. John and Mark bought one each and, leaning against the sunlit wall of the inn, ate slowly and with enjoyment. A wagon passed loaded with faggots and then a lady, carried by in a litter, glanced their way. Mark whistled admiringly and received in acknowledgement the slightest flutter of graceful fingers.

'Did you see that?' he demanded. 'Reckon I've a chance there? I swear she winked her eye.'

'A speck of dust in it, more like,' said John. 'If the lady so much as sneezed you would see in it an invitation to her bed!'

He pushed the last morsel of pie into his mouth and wiped his lips on the back of his hand. Seizing his friend by the collar, he kicked open the door. They stood to one side as two men reeled past and fell, still fighting, into the gutter.

'A shilling on the lad in the scarlet hose,' cried Mark who dearly loved a wager. Laughing John declined and dragged him, still protesting, into the inn.

The sound of the bursting pea pods soothed Bet's mind but

did nothing to help her wretched body. Her golden-red hair under its neat cap prickled with the heat, a few stray wisps golden-red clinging to her moist forehead. She was small, almost mouselike, with eyes like brown buttons. Sometimes John called her 'his little mouse'. Her body now was rounded by the child she carried and her bare arms were dusky from the sun and her face generously sprinkled with tiny freckles. She worked methodically, taking a full pod from the trug on her right, emptying it into the bowl in her lap and tossing the empty pod into the basket on her left. She had had little or no sleep the night before and now her back ached intolerably. She felt gross, unattractive and defeated. The baby she carried felt monstrously large and was incredibly active, racking her at all times of the day and night with sharp little jabs, that made her draw in her breath or cry out in pain. Now it happened again, and she clutched at her side defensively as though to protect it from the attacker within. Still, for a time at least, the other children were off hand. Dorothy had taken them, with her own new baby, to visit their grandmother and Bet was thankful, much as she loved them, for the respite from their constant demands upon her energies.

The form on which she sat was hard and uncomfortable, but John had rigged up an awning for her across one corner of the courtyard and she sat in its welcome shade, glad of what little air there was. Her shoes lay beside her, for it was pleasant to feel the warm dusty flagstones under her bare feet. The last pea pod dropped into the basket and she set down the bowl, leaning back against the wall of the house, wriggling her toes. She thought of Dorothy, her sister, and the new baby girl. Secretly she hoped for another daughter, but it would never do to let John know. He had set his heart on a family of boys and little fat Catherine had been a disappointment to him. He was fond of her, but Bet knew that Stephen was the favourite. She thought of her husband and her eyes softened with pride. Already he was making a name for himself as a goldsmith. It was true he had a

27

natural talent for the work, but he had worked hard during the long apprenticeship and had seen off a great many candles studying well into the nights, allowing himself little time for pleasure or relaxation. She remembered how proud he had been when he finished his indentures and his nervousness when he went before the Guild for his final examination. 'The finest this year,' the warden had said, and for John, these few words were recompense enough.

Already people came from all over London asking for him by name, and Nathan was so pleased and boasted of him to his friends. They are like father and son, she thought fondly, for the old man was a favourite of hers. John would become famous — of that she had no doubt. It was only a matter of time. People would come from the far corners of the land; from France even, and Holland. And John, a wealthy man, would realize his ambition. To return north and buy land. 'Aye, you will do it, John,' she whispered. 'You can and you will!'

It was a happy marriage despite the inauspicious start and the disapproval. A slight frown crossed her face at the memory of that angry letter from Hannah, and its effect upon her husband. Yet, it was all true. John had married beneath him. She, Bet, had no dowry and brought nothing to the union except an unborn child and that not even John's! He had brought disgrace on the family name; the words leapt into her mind as clearly as they had leapt from the page when she had first read them, in Hannah's dark, bold script. A useless creature and a graceless wretch. Perhaps it was so, yet John had stood firm by his impulsive proposal and she made him happy in her own way. That much she knew, and it gave her satisfaction.

They had been married nearly three years with rarely an angry word. Bet still loved him as she had done on her wedding day. Sighing she stretched her feet. They were dusty but comfortable. She looked at her hands – the fingers small and neat, now stained a little from the green pea pods. If she had the energy she would get up. There was washing to be done but the thought of it dismayed her, so she remained where she was. The baby kicked again. 'All in good time,' she whispered smiling and ran her hand gently over the spot. Which little limb was it, she wondered? A leg or an arm or the head butting impatiently? She considered . . . hardly a head. Too small and sharp. She closed her eyes and her thoughts drifted, becoming confused . . . disjointed . . . She was almost asleep when the first pain came, piercingly sharp but mercifully brief. Gasping with the shock she straightened up. It wasn't possible. The baby wasn't due for another three weeks. She waited breathlessly. Nothing happened. Perhaps she was mistaken. It was a different pain, she told herself. But then it came again, less sharp but more lasting — and quite distinctive. 'I'm starting!' she told herself. 'I'm starting the baby!'

Her voice held a mixture of joy and fear. She stood up clumsily, then sat down again. 'Don't panic, Bettina,' she said sternly. 'There is no need. You are not a novice at this game!' But her heart would not cease its fluttering and she stood up once more. As calmly as she could, she picked up the empty trug and the bowl of peas and hurried into the house. The trug she returned to its hook, and the peas, covered with muslin, went into the larder.

In spite of her determination to be calm, she moved distractedly about the kitchen and then, for no reason that she understood, went to her bedchamber and, took up a small hand mirror. 'You're starting,' she told her reflection, watching the lips move as she spoke. Then came another pain — a fiercer pain that finally left her panting for breath. The mirror had dropped from her hand. Bending with difficulty, she picked it up. A crack ran across it. Her torn reflection stared back reproachfully and a small cold fear touched her heart as she dropped it hastily on to the bed. 'I must fetch someone', she told herself.

But who to fetch? Her mother lived some distance away and her neighbour was away. It would have to be John.

With trembling fingers she took a coin from the purse that hung at her belt and half ran into the street.

Beckoning urgently, she called the first urchin that passed, and pressed the coin into his grimy hand. 'This is for you,' she said. 'You must run to Gutter Lane. To Nathan Byrnes, the goldsmith, and ask for John.'

He was staring at her, impressed with her size.

'Do you hear me?' she demanded. 'Are you listening to me?'

'Aye,' he replied.

'Then tell me back what I have said.'

He looked at his shoes for assistance, but none was forthcoming. He shook his head.

'Don't rightly recall,' he said.

'Then listen again, you johnny,' she said 'And don't stare so. You've seen a woman in child afore now, I'll warrant. You're to find Nathan Byrnes in Gutter Lane and ask . . .'

'For John' he interrupted triumphantly.

She nodded approvingly. 'And say it's Bet and the babe is on the way!'

The boy's eyes widened but he said nothing.

'Now be off—'.

She stopped, abruptly, one hand across her body, the other clinging to the door jamb, her knuckles clenched and white. 'Sweet Mother of God!' she cried. 'Go and run all the way.'

He nodded, but still stood fascinated until she gave him an urgent shove. As soon as he had gone, she closed the door and bending her head began to pray. Half way through, she hurried to fill a kettle and hung it over the fire which had been lit earlier for the washing.

The pains came at regular intervals, closer and closer and still John did not appear. Bet lay on the bed, then got up again. She seized a broom and began to sweep out the kitchen, then changed her mind and began to sort the washing. Sweat streamed from her face and she tried once more to pray.

'Holy Mother, help me, I beg you . . . Do not leave me thus alone but comfort me and make me brave . . . I am so afraid, Sweet Mary, so terribly afraid . . .' The tears rushed to her eyes and ran saltily into her mouth. She licked them away.

The contractions grew stronger. She had had two children and was not unfamiliar with the procedures of childbirth, but now panic emptied her mind. Experience told her that the birth was near. Nothing was ready. Making her way upstairs she found an old blanket and threw it across the bed and found clean linen for the cradle.

'We must send word to Dorothy,' she told herself, her voice reassuringly normal. 'The children must stay with their grandmother overnight.' Unfastening her gown, she stepped out of it leaving only her kirtle. Her feet still bare, she lay down on the bed. Turning on to her side she stuffed the corner of the pillow into her mouth to muffle her groans, for the sound of her own pain frightened her. Thus she lay, eyes tightly closed to shut out the fear, and waited desperately for John.

Barely twenty minutes later, John took the stairs two at a time and rushed into the bedroom. Bet lay on the bed in a state of near exhaustion. The waters had broken and the lower half of the bed was soaking wet. Her face was streaked with tears and she was very pale. She had bitten her lower lip in an effort to suppress her screams of pain and the pillow was smeared with blood. Taking her hands in his, John fought down the panic which rose in his own breast at the thought of what was to come.

'I came as quickly as I could,' he told her. 'And Miriam will be here directly. Nathan has gone in search of her.'

Miriam was Nathan's wife and had acted as midwife when Catherine was born. Bet nodded as she clung to John's hands.

31

'I am done with the first pains,' she told him in great agitation. 'I wanted to bear down but was afraid. I think I must . . .' she told him through clenched teeth and he nodded without understanding.

'Help me turn on to my back,' she asked and almost immediately was bearing down strongly. It seemed an age before she relaxed again. 'There, that one is over,' she told him and smiled reassuringly.

'I was feeling it with you!' he declared. 'Now tell me what I must do to help.'

'There is water heating on the fire,' she told him, 'and I would dearly love a cool drink, but John, I beg you do not be gone too long.'

'I promise,' he said, 'I will be back directly.'

He returned a few moments later with a pitcher of hot water and a glass of orange juice, freshly squeezed.

Time passed and Miriam did not arrive although John, stationed at the window, positively willed her appearance. Bet's body, having produced two babies within three years, was working efficiently and the final stage of the birth was reached without complications. At last she felt the searing sensation that heralded the child's head and prewarned, John's hands waited to receive it. Bet held her breath as the small body began to emerge.

'It has gold hair!' John told her. 'A fine head of gold hair!'

With a wriggle the tiny shoulders freed themselves and the rest of the body slithered into the daylight. Bet saw the delight in his eyes and knew she had a son.

'Dear God!' he whispered. 'Oh dear God . . .'

Bet stared up at him, unable to believe it was safely over. Tears streamed down his face and dropped on to the baby, who now kicked strongly and began to cry.

'A boy,' said John, 'with gold hair . . .' Then with an effort, 'What must I do now?'

'We must cut the cord,' said Bet, 'but first let me hold

our new son.' John handed the baby to her. He was purplish and here and there flecked with smears of blood.

'Messy little lad!' she smiled. 'But never mind. You shall soon be as spruce as a sparrow.' She kissed the damp head and John looking down at them, choked with pride; but before he could speak there was a shout from downstairs.

'I'm here, my chickens,' called Miriam, 'Sorry to have been so long but I was at my sister's and Nathan, the old fool, had clean forgot —'.

'You are too late!' John cried as she hurried breathless into the room.

'The baby is here and all's well. Tis a boy and.....'

'What?' she cried, 'here already and without my help! What next? And me running halfway across London on these poor old legs and missed all the excitement. Well, where is the little pet, then? Ah! What a bonny little lad. And the spitten image of his father, and such fair hair. It will curl later, I do believe....'

John and Bet exchanged amused glances. None of their children had curly hair, but it was Miriam's dearest wish that they should.

Capably, she took charge and the cord was soon cut, the infant bathed, wrapped in a clean cloth and laid in his cradle. John was despatched to make some tea and while he was downstairs Bet complained that she wanted to bear down again. They waited for the afterbirth to come away, but the pains increased. Suddenly Bet realized she was expelling, not the afterbirth, but another child. And within minutes a twin boy was born, the cord looped tightly round his neck. While Miriam released him and coaxed him back to life, Bet began to bleed. John returning with tea, found Miriam in some agitation, attending to a second child; while she watched hopefully for signs that the bleeding was going to stop. It seemed it was not.

'I'm all fingers and thumbs here,' Miriam told him, 'and cannot be spared for the moment. Run down and put together this certain remedy. She is in need of strengthening and I swear this will not fail. Take a dram of cinnamon and pound it well, add a pinch or two of dried mint and infuse with white wine.'

The delight John should have felt at the discovery of his newest son was overshadowed by his anxiety for his wife. The bleeding increased and the 'certain remedy' did nothing to help. They watched fearfully as Bet grew weaker. Made drowsy by the wine she slept fitfully, but her breathing was shallow, her face grey. Finally Miriam abandoned her pretence that 'all would be well' and urged John to run to the apothecary for help. John, however, was reluctant to leave his wife and it was agreed that Miriam should go instead. John remained by the bedside, Bet's hands held tightly in his own. The two boys cried lustily from time to time, but John was no longer aware of their existence and heard nothing. The blood, encroaching over the bedding on which she lay, appeared at last as a bright scarlet token on the sheet which covered her; a token which, as it spread, drained the young life away.

When Miriam returned with the apothecary in attendance, John's head was pressed against the body of his wife. The drooping yellow rosebuds lay on the pillow by her head. He looked up slowly and his face was haggard. The tears which had come so readily before to greet his first son, now held back, refusing relief to the pent up anguish in his heart.

Mark knocked at the door, waited, then knocked again. Receiving no answer, he pressed his face up to the window shielding his eyes from the sunlight reflected there. There was no sign of John so he made his way round to the back of the house. Surprised to find it open he went in.

'John?' he called. ''Tis me, Mark. Where are you hiding yourself?'

Upstairs the bed frame creaked and Mark took the stairs

two at a time. John lay face down on the bed, his arms encircling his head. Mark stood awkwardly beside him. He looked around at the small bare room.

All signs of the birth and death had been scrupulously removed. While Mark tried desperately to think of something to say, John rolled slowly over.

'Tis all mine,' he said. 'The whole bed is mine. Such a terrible truth! And I cannot rid myself of the words. They go round and round in my brain. The whole bed is mine.'

Mark stared at him perplexed. John propped himself on one elbow. His eyes were dry but his face was grey.

'Am I crazed?' he asked Mark. 'All that I think is that I have the bed to myself.'

Mark sat gingerly on the edge of the bed. 'Your mind is disordered,' he said. ''Tis bound to be. You are shocked. It takes folk in various ways.'

John nodded.

'I came to say,' Mark began, 'I came to tell you how sorry — ' his voice trailed into silence and John nodded again.

'I know it,' he said.

'Where are the children?' asked Mark.

'All with Bet's mother.'

'Have you eaten?'

'No.'

'You should. You should feed grief.'

'I cannot.'

'Well, I haven't eaten and I'm nigh on starved!' said Mark as heartily as he could manage. 'So what say you keep an old friend company?'

But John had rolled on to his back and lay staring at the ceiling. He didn't answer and Mark stood up, and crossed to look out of the window.

'You must not stay here alone,' said Mark anxiously, ''tis bad for the spirits . . . . ' He tried a new line of approach. 'The new babes,' he asked, 'are they thriving?'

'Aye.'

'Good. Two bonny boys I hear. And are they named yet?'

'Matthew and William.'

'Can you tell them apart?'

'Aye. One lad's bigger.'

'So—you're a father of four. You must be very . . . .' He broke off suddenly, the word 'proud' unsaid. 'Forgive me,' he said. 'You must be grieving. I'm that sorry, John, and can't string the words together to tell you.'

John blinked rapidly and his lips trembled.

'Come out with me, John.'

'I'm cold,' he said. 'So cold. Tis as tho' my heart is cold and it spreads all over me. I lay here this afternoon – after they had all gone – and the sweat poured off me.'

'Twas a scorching afternoon!'

'Aye, but I was cold inside. Does that make sense?'

Standing up, he smoothed the rumpled coverlet.

'Where is she?' Mark asked, in spite of himself.

'Nathan has her. He will see to everything. He's a good man.'

'He is.'

John looked at the bed critically. 'She never could abide a rumpled bed,' he said with the faintest hint of a smile at the memory. 'Woe betide the children if they jumped on to it.'

Mark searched for words, but they evaded him.

'I'll watch you eat,' said John.

'That you won't! If you won't eat then we'll walk.'

And they went out together into the soft evening.

An hour later, they sat on the embankment steps watching the Thames swirl at their feet. The water was calm, but when a boat passed the wake would ripple towards them, slapping at the steps and splashing their shoes with muddy droplets.

John tossed a pebble into the water and followed it with another.

'Do you know what hurts?' he said. 'Tis passing all those people two by two. Husbands and wives, sweethearts and lovers — what a thing, eh? It is a physical hurt. Can you understand that?'

'Maybe not, John. I have never been "with" anybody for long enough to feel that we belong. You know me!'

'I do that! But for me not to belong to anyone . . . . ' He shrugged helplessly 'I feel lost!'

'Tis natural enough. In a way I envy you.'

'Envy me?'

'You have lost something that I've never had.'

'Then find yourself a lass and wed her, Mark.'

It was Mark's turn to shrug.

'I am not the type to wed,' he said. 'Love them and leave them!'

'You are cynical beyond your years!'

'You won't stay lone, John. You will wed again in time.'

'Not I.'

'You are the type that weds, and your chickens need a hen!'

'I will not have a wife if I can't have Bet, and will have no more children if they can't be hers.'

Mark was silenced by the intensity of the words and the look on John's face.

Behind them, a queue was forming for the ferry which was approaching, propelled skilfully and speedily towards the steps. John pulled his friend to his feet.

'We had best eat,' he said. 'I am deafened by the sound of your hunger, rumbling like thunder in that paunch of yours!'

Mark patted his generous girth fondly. 'Looks well on me, I've been told,' he laughed.

'The wench lied!' said John. 'Come. Let's eat.'

He laid a hand briefly on Mark's shoulder in a rare

gesture of affection and then followed him back up the steps in search of food.

CHAPTER THREE

1481 – Devon

Daniel Heron lay at rest peacefully and forever. Eyes closed, arms folded on his chest, he slept like a baby on four inches of bran and his crib was a coffin. A white cap covered his head and was tied beneath his chin. He wore a long white shift which was turned up at the bottom to enclose his feet, and narrow white ribbons fastened the neck and cuffs. His wife stood beside him, looking down at the man with whom she had shared her life for the past twelve years. The sight of his familiar face, now composed in death, moved her not at all. She looked at the small triangular beak of a nose and the soft girlish mouth, pursed even in death, and time passed away as she waited for the first stirrings of emotion that would preface her grief. There were none. Though she concentrated her mind on her loss, she felt only indifference. Surely she should miss him – should feel frightened and alone. Whatever his faults, he had given her a home and security. Guiltily, she recalled how bitterly she had wept at the death of her beloved father. Elizabeth Heron was no stranger to grief, so why no tears for Daniel, her departed husband?

'Perhaps I didn't love you,' she whispered and thought the candle flicked in reproach. 'I don't think I did although I tried, indeed I tried. Please say that you forgive me.' She put out a hand and stroked his face with a curious finger.

The flesh, yielding slightly, was neither warm nor cold. 'And you didn't love me,' she said withdrawing her hand. 'Oh no, you didn't,' she said as though he argued with her. 'I was a decoration for your home. Aye, that's the truth of it. You didn't love me, you didn't even know the real me.

39

But mayhap you couldn't. You were a cold man, Daniel.'
Searching her conscience, she wondered if this was quite
fair. 'You couldn't help it,' she conceded slowly. 'You had
no love left to give. No love and no passion . . . . And now
it's all over.'

She scooped a handful of bran and let the fine brown
husks trickle through her fingers. Some of them found their
way into the pristine folds of his gown and she flicked them
out hastily as Della, her maid, called her from the far end
of the hall.

'Ma'am, your brother's coming across the lawn and
Martha be weeping fit to burst for the biscuits are burnt
and . . . .'

'Della! Hush yourself child, in the presence of the
dead!'

The young girl appeared round the screen which separated Daniel's lying-in from the rest of the room. She was
barely twelve but cheerfully dutiful, with tousled hair and
a wide mouth that was always smiling. She clapped her
hand to her mouth and darted a quick look at her late master
to see if he had registered her lack of respect.

'Now tell it again,' said Elizabeth. 'Andrew is here?'

The girl nodded. 'And the biscuits are burnt and Martha
be . . . .'

'I know!' said Elizabeth wearily. 'Pay no heed to it, but
ask her to make haste and bake a fresh batch.'

Della nodded, turned away, but then turned back, and
smoothing the new black gown asked, 'Does black become
me, ma'am?'

Elizabeth smiled. 'You look well enough in it,' she said,
'but remember the gloves, they are in the chest at the foot
of my bed, and brush your hair. It's tousled as ever.'

'Biscuits, gloves, hair,' Della repeated.

'Oh, and Jacob, Della. Have you seen him? Is he
ready?'

The girl giggled. 'Been ready this past hour,' she said,
'and looks like a blackened bean pole in them clothes.'

40

'Mind that you don't tell him so,' said Elizabeth. 'And remind Martha to keep the marchpane out of the sunlight or it will go sticky and there will be more tears. Now, off with you and make haste. If Andrew is here, then it is almost time and the others will be arriving.'

Della cast a last look at her late master. She and the other servants had looked to their fill at him before Elizabeth had risen, and the still body no longer held any terrors for her.

'He looks peaceful, ma'am, don't he,' she commented.

Elizabeth nodded. 'Very peaceful,' she agreed. 'Now off you go. Andrew is come.'

Obediently, Della hurried off muttering 'Biscuits, gloves, hair' to herself and Elizabeth crossed the room to greet her brother, the hem of her gown rustling softly across the fresh straw that covered the floor.

Andrew, her younger brother, was twenty years old. The dark cloth of his habit accentuated the pale blond hair, but his face and hands were tanned from work in the priory gardens, and his eyes were a startling blue.

'Sweet sister, forgive me', he said, holding out his arms in greeting. 'I meant to come earlier and offer my assistance but was delayed by the sub-prior, no less, who must needs learn the fate of his precious salmon and was halfway through a favourite recipe before I could free myself. How goes everything? You look well.'

'Thank you,' she said, kissing him lightly. 'And the salmon is indeed a fine one and I saw to its preparation myself. The old man will find no cause for complaint. It was generous of him and I have written so.'

'Is anyone else arrived?'

'No. You are the first.'

'And you, how do you feel?'

She sighed. 'Still nothing,' she admitted. 'I want to grieve for him but I cannot. The tears will not come. I ask myself what it was all about, these past twelve years. It must mean something to me and yet I feel so empty. I look and I look on him and he is both familiar and a stranger to me. I tried to be a good wife.'

'I don't doubt but you were,' he answered. 'And no doubt he was a good husband — in his own way.'

She nodded slowly. 'Aye.' she agreed. 'In his own way.'

There was a clatter of hooves in the courtyard and Andrew gave her hand a small but reassuring squeeze.

'They are arriving,' he said and Della appeared once more, waving her gloved hands triumphantly for Elizabeth's approval.

'They're here ma'am,' she informed. ''Tis Mistress Ruth, and her husband and an old fella.'

'I'm coming,' said Elizabeth.

Unnoticed, Rufus, the elderly hound, had sneaked into the hall and now sat in a patch of sunlight and began to scratch. As an indignant Della chased him out, Elizabeth went forward to greet her guests.

Forty minutes later and only ten minutes late, the formal procession left the house. The sun had dropped behind the trees along the ridge to the west of Ashburton and cast long shadows over the land. Daniel Heron's funeral procession was all that he had wished it to be. It was led by six poor men of the parish hired for the occasion. Dressed in black, their faces set in earnest expressions, they preceded the coffin with burning torches which flickered dully in the half-light. Behind them, five male members of the Heron family and Andrew bore the coffin on their shoulders. A group of eight young choristers came next, singing a mournful funeral hymn, mingling their Latin with the muffled sobs of the mourners. The rest of the family followed with friends and acquaintances from the surrounding area and finally the servants and thirty-two tinners, a total which equalled Daniel's sixty-nine years.

Almost all were in black, and those that were not fluttered with black ribbons.

The procession moved at the slow pace of those bearing the coffin and they were fortunate, having a quarter of a mile to walk, that the weather had been fine for the past week and the highway was in a reasonable state. They climbed the slight hill and rounded the corner. As they came in sight of the church, the bell ringer was alerted and the passing bell began its ministrations on behalf of Daniel's soul. Elizabeth stumbled suddenly and immediately a hand grasped her elbow, steadying her. She turned in surprise to see Joseph Tucker, their nearest neighbour.

'Will you lean on my arm?' he asked solicitiously.

She hesitated, then shook her head.

'I think it would not be seemly,' she whispered, 'but thank you for your concern.'

Father Benedict walked to meet them with Father Marryat the chantry priest close behind him. The procession halted and the blessing was given. The light was fading rapidly and a cool breeze rustled the cyprus trees beside the newly dug grave to which they were now led. A pile of freshly dug earth littered the grass and Donnell, the gravedigger, leant on his spade and watched the proceedings with a critical and experienced eye.

The mourners gathered around the graveside and the priest began the service.

He had known the Heron family for as long as he could remember, had buried Daniel's father and had attended Daniel for the last eighteen months while he had been bed-ridden. He spoke with sincerity and assurance. The choristers sang again and everyone joined in the two psalms Elizabeth had requested. The bell was silent and the sound of thin voices, accompanied only by the spluttering of the torches, hung eerily in the darkening air. 'Now must I speak to you of life and death, of sound and silence, of love and hate, of heaven and hell . . . .'

Father Benedict's sermons though frequently inspiring,

were notoriously long and this one promised to be even longer. With the encouragement of everyone's rapt attention, he rose to the challenge and was presently engrossed in his theme, his voice rising eloquently, then falling dramatically, to a near whisper.

Elizabeth stole a quick look at Joseph Tucker on the far side of the grave. He stood, hands clasped behind his back, listening to the priest, but as though sensing Elizabeth's interest he glanced towards her and smiled briefly. Ruth, beside Elizabeth, saw the smile and glanced up at Elizabeth's face but her attention was now firmly returned to the priest. The sermon continued. The light faded. The breeze disturbed the torches and lit the faces of all around with an unhealthy glow.

The gravedigger yawned hugely, making no effort to disguise his boredom and the fact that he was being kept from his supper. With an impatient gesture, he thrust the spade well into the earth and turned to prop himself against the trunk of one of the trees, with his back to the proceedings. He considered to himself, for the hundredth time, the folly of such late funerals. 'All for a bit of a show,' he mumbled, 'and twinkling torches and look what happens when it rains? The pesky things are nigh on doused and I can scarce see to fill in the grave by their feeble light . . . and old Benedict ranting on seemingly forever. Likes the sound of his own voice, he does . . . and just as well he has a loud voice for the noise in old Donnell's belly. Would wake old Heron and that would never do,' he added spitefully, recalling how small a tip the old man had given him when he buried his wife, 'and the snow was thick on the ground and the earth rock hard. No, let him sleep on and his bonny young wife'll mebbe take a new husband to her bed as'll do her a sight more good than her last. Ah, there goes the bell again.' He peered round the tree, in time to see the shrouded body taken from its coffin and lowered into the grave.

'And now the widow throws her sprig of rosemary; in it

44

goes. Much good that may do him! And in goes all the rest and now its old Donnell's turn and high time too . . . .'

The gravedigger heaved himself away from the tree, took up his spade and handed it to Elizabeth who threw the first earth into the grave and then handed the spade back to him. For a while, there were no sounds but the tolling of the bell and the sound of falling earth.

Two torch-bearers remained behind to light Donnell's work and the rest accompanied the procession back to the house. At the church gate, Elizabeth turned, and saw the three men intent on their task, tidying the world of the living by disposing of the dead. She thought of her husband's ineffectual body lying helpless under the shower of earth, and was suddenly weeping for pity.

' . . . while still in sweet health, both of mind and body. I write herein of my eventual calling unto God, and the manner of my passing. I beg grace that my friends and loved ones might attend me in my journey to the grave and pray them that be not scandalized should rage or stupidity happen upon me in the extremity of sickness . . . .'

Ruth, Daniel's sister-in-law, paused to wipe away a tear and her husband Samuel, patted her arm consolingly.

'At least he was spared that,' he said, managing with an effort, a respectful tone of voice. It was well known that there had been no love lost between the two brothers.

The small knot of listeners nodded agreement. Ruth took another sip of the spicey burnt wine and resumed her reading in a quavering voice.

' . . . I doe also beseech I should be laid to rest at sundown as is seemly and doe exhort my executors to make provision for such as are necessarie and decent to mie calling; for which I bequeath the sum of ninety pounds to include a memorial of marble, a goode sermon, the tolling of the passing-bell and bread to be given to the poor.'

'Aye. At least he was spared that,' Samuel repeated

piously, glad that he had found something non-committal to offer to the conversation without being judged a hypocrite. His wife, put out by the interruption, gave him a sharp glance and continued in stronger tones.

' . . . and a gift of scarves to the chief mourners and wine and biscuits to my loyal and devoted servants . . . . '

Elizabeth, listening, repressed a rueful smile. She was well aware of the feelings of the servants towards their late master, with his sarcastic tongue and penny-pinching ways. No doubt they would welcome a relaxation in the government of the household. She must guard against too great a leniency or they might take advantage. She looked across the room to the panelled wall under the arched tie beams of the roof, where several of the servants stood together; the girls dutifully red-eyed but growing more talkative with each sip of wine, the men uneasy in their unfamiliar black.

Della caught her eye and smiled briefly, with an instinctive lack of intimacy suited to the occasion. To show familiarity with the new mistress would set her apart from her fellows. She would look forward to a renewal of confidences later. Behind Della, stood old Jacob, ridiculously tall and thin, his shoulders hunched, his head jutting forward on the skinny neck in an effort to appear the same height as other men. Jacob was loyal and devoted, but to the garden. He had dedicated his life to its maintenance and the furtherance of its beauty, tending the straight gravelled paths, the neat square lawns and clipped bushes with a passion which he felt for nothing else. Elizabeth could imagine the scrubbing that had taken place to rid his fingernails of the red Devon soil and the lathering of the white mop of hair that grew more unruly each year. And Martha, the cook, large and red-faced, now composedly receiving compliments on her culinary efforts; while keeping a strict eye on the two young girls she had chosen to act as servers for the great occasion. Rufus, appearing beside her in hopes of cajoling scraps of food from the guests, received a sharp kick which sent him howling back into the passage, where he settled himself on the far side of the door to watch resentfully for another opportunity.

Elizabeth became aware, suddenly, that the wine was going to her head. The scene around her was losing its reality, as though she herself had no part in it. The voices blended with a babble of meaningless sounds; the many and various guests blurred and softened into one amorphous mass of colour. She felt drowsy and detached.

Carefully, she set down her goblet and studied the funeral feast with an attempt at concentration. She must eat something. The wine was reacting on her empty stomach. A bewildering range of foods swam before her. Roasted meats: venison, and capon; baked fish – the plaice from Brixham and the sub-prior's salmon from the fishery at Kilbury; a pyne puff, slightly over cooked but it would pass and a large bowl of cream of almonds, one of Martha's specialities. It was too early for fresh fruit but there was a selection of dried raisins, figs and nuts and the rich marchpane. Only one cask remained of the brown October ale, but there was plenty of cider. They must make do with that.

She took a handful of nuts and chewed without tasting them. Ruth was coming towards her, Daniel's letter rolled in her hands, fresh tears trickling their way down the faded, powdered cheeks.

'He was a goodly, righteous man,' she sobbed. 'A kindly, goodly man. A good son to his parents. May God rest their departed souls; a good husband.'

Not good, Elizabeth corrected her silently. Not really good. An adequate husband, perhaps. Nothing more than that. She took the proffered letter and coughed suddenly, as one of the nuts caught in her throat.

'A goodly, dutiful brother to me,' Ruth lamented, 'and kindly, too. Aye, always kindly . . . .'

Not always kindly, amended Elizabeth. It had not been kind of him to reproach her constantly for her failure to

47

produce an heir. It had not been kindly to raise the matter so frequently when guests were present. Especially not so, since the occasions when she might possibly have conceived were so pitifully few; Daniel being an old man even in middle-age, and an unsuccessful lover on many occasions.

But she nodded her head and murmured sympathetically as she guided the old lady to the window seat, offering her a chicken leg and a glass of ale 'to keep up your strength and spirits'.

Now she spooned some cream of almonds into a bowl, enjoying its bland flavour and smooth texture.

The doors were open at either end of the room and a draught swept through, rustling the black drapes that decorated the walls.

It eddied towards the open log fire and smoke billowed out into the room. Someone's light touch on her arm made her turn and she found Father Marryat beside her, a look of concern on his familiar face.

'You are bearing your loss with fortitude,' he said and she nodded guiltily. This man, if any, might see through her deceit and read in her eyes a lack of grief at Daniel Heron's passing.

He smiled. 'They say it was a fine departure,' he told her. 'The passing-bell was loud enough to drive away the fiercest of devils. I warrant none have dared accost his soul. It is safe in purgatory by now and a few Masses will see it safely on its way to Heaven. I will see to that . . . You'll miss him.' It was more a suggestion than a fact, almost a question.

Elizabeth nodded but didn't meet his eye. He looked at her keenly for a moment. 'We all have our faults,' he said softly, and smiled at the surprise in her eyes. 'We have a hard row to hoe,' he added. 'Some are better gardeners than others. Think on him gently, if you can.'

And he moved on to speak to Jonah, a cousin, and his wife, Cecily, who sat on a form with their five children.

These were arranged in diminishing size, whether by design or accident, Elizabeth could not tell.

Father Marryat was Ruth's 'kindly man', having a great compassion for his fellow men. And goodly. The people of Ashburton were fortunate in their chantry priest. He was more conscientious than most. Masses for the dead entrusted to him would be sung without a doubt. Daniel Heron's soul was in good hands.

'The service went well.'

It was Joseph Tucker.

'Thank you.'

'And the sermon well said.'

'If a little lengthy,' she said, smiling.

'He speaks well on such occasions.'

'Aye, he does.'

'And this fine spread.' He indicated the groaning table. 'The whole occasion does you great credit. Your husband would have been very proud.'

'Thank you.'

Joseph Tucker was an old friend of the family. Considerably younger than Daniel, the two men had both lived most of their lives in Ashburton and a friendly rivalry existed between the two families. There was little to choose between the quality and extent of the two properties and extensive lands, of which the latter were leased out in 'sets' to the men who mined for tin along the eastern slopes of Dartmoor.

'So now we are both alone,' said Joseph. His own wife had died a year earlier leaving him with two children, and he had not re-married although there were plenty of women only too willing to become the second mistress of Maudesly Hall.

Joseph Tucker was an attractive man, tall yet stockily built with fine brown eyes, a dark beard and a wealth of curly black hair. Elizabeth nodded. He looked at her reddened eyes.

'Don't weep for Daniel,' he told her. 'He was a fortunate

49

man. He had a long life, wealth and three beautiful wives. There were many that envied him.'

Uncomfortably aware that other ears were listening to his words, Elizabeth shot him a warning glance but he chose to ignore it.

'I embarrass you,' he said. 'Forgive me. But I must talk to you.'

Elizabeth was startled.

'I cannot leave my guests,' she said.

He looked around. With the tensions of the funeral behind them, everyone was relaxing, as the wine loosened their tongues and the good food comforted their bodies.

'They will not even miss you,' he assured her, his voice low. 'They are deep with their reminiscences. I think you can safely leave them to their own devices.'

Still Elizabeth hesitated.

'Perhaps some other time,' she hedged. 'I am weary from lack of sleep and my head spins.'

'It is the wine,' he said. 'You must eat.'

Despite her protestations, he cut a generous slice from the pyne puff and handed it to her. Then, taking her by the arm, he propelled her gently but firmly across the room, down the broad steps and out into the garden. She found the fresh air soothing and followed him without further argument. He led her to a stone seat which stood beneath a large mulberry tree and she sat down gratefully. It was almost dark, but there was very little breeze and the air was warm. Surprised to realize that she was hungry, Elizabeth took a mouthful of the sweet spicey flan and waited for Joseph to begin. He hesitated, then smiled ruefully.

'I have practised my speech,' he said, 'and now the words have flown my mind. But to speak plainly, — you are now alone and, as Daniel's friend, I want you to know that you can look to me for help at all times.'

'You are very kind,' she said.

And you are very beautiful, he thought, and will be more lonely than you know. His own wife's death had left a coldness in his life, an absence of tenderness. She would miss the frail old man as a child misses a father, or a babe a nurse. Daniel had wed her as a gauche young girl with few graces beside the natural dignity that was an integral part of her character. He had coaxed and led his young bride towards the confidence and poise she now showed, and she would realize only now how much she owed him.

'Daniel spoke to me of his approaching death and wished me to concern myself with your welfare,' he told her. 'I shall take great pleasure in being of service to you. Look on me as a very dear friend.'

The grey eyes that looked into his were dark and large in the pale face. The young girl had grown into a mature and beautiful woman. Since his wife's death, Joseph had become increasingly aware of Elizabeth's qualities and his feelings towards her had lately troubled his conscience. Now, he struggled to keep from his voice any hint of his admiration. This was not the time nor place for such thoughts, and he tried without success to banish them from his mind.

'Thank you, Joseph,' Elizabeth said. 'I consider myself fortunate that I am left well provided for. Poor Daniel.'

Her voice shook slightly. In spite of his failings, his intentions had been kindly. He had spoken to Joseph on her behalf. Had concerned himself for her welfare after his death. Perhaps had cared for her more than she realized.

'You have no need to feel alone,' Joseph told her gently. 'My home is not far from Heron and you will always be a welcome guest.'

'I'll remember,' she said. 'But I fear my extra duties will take up much of my time. There is much to be done and I intend to manage Heron as Daniel would have done.'

'Until your mourning period is over,' he said.

She looked at him squarely. 'Until Heron is prosperous once more.'

'Once more? I don't understand.'

'Heron is no longer prosperous,' she said simply. 'It is

51

worth less now than when I married Daniel. No — .' She held up a hand as he tried to interrupt. 'I mean no disrespect,' she continued, 'but Daniel was old and frail of late and found business matters irksome. I have helped him and I have learned much about the affairs. I mean to use what I have learned to Heron's advantage.'

'But how?' he asked.

Her eyes flashed. 'By taking heed of the Cornish tinners,' she told him excitedly. 'They put us to shame with their new ideas. Streaming will soon be a thing of the past. Supplies of tin are failing.'

'Indeed they are.'

'But only on the surface, Joseph. There is abundant ore under the rocks and we must dig for it. Drive shafts down into the rock and inwards through the hillsides.'

'But to do that will need costly equipment,' he protested.

'Aye, so it will,' she cried, 'and the tinners cannot find such money. A lone tinner can no longer survive. We must regain control of our own lands, organize the tinners and find the money for pit props and ropes, candles and wagons. Oh Joseph, don't you see? This is the time for change. If we don't . . . .' She left the rest of the sentence unfinished and waited breathlessly for his comment.

Joseph shook his head in amazement. 'So the little child bride has become a business woman!' he teased.

Elizabeth nodded. ''Tis a dream I have cherished for nearly three years. I shall devote my energies to restore the Heron fortunes so that one day . . . .'

She broke off suddenly and Joseph interpreted her discomfiture. She had no children. Daniel had left no heirs. Who would inherit the fortunes thus restored. In the silence, she knew that he understood, and her brave speech faltered.

'You will wed again one day,' he told her gently and prayed that he might be the fortunate man. 'You will have children.'

'I hope so,' she said in no more than a whisper. For the first time she had spoken of her childlessness, had put into words a terrible secret doubt.

'Meanwhile you have your dreams,' he said, and the fear lifted from her eyes to be replaced by a strength of purpose of which he had never guessed. Before either of them could speak again Ruth's quavering voice reached them.

'Is that you, Elizabeth? Where are you, my dear? The night air is growing cooler. You will take a chill. Are you alone?'

'She is with me,' said Joseph. 'She is quite safe.'

'But some of the guests are leaving,' Ruth persisted. 'They want to make their farewells.'

'I must go back to the house,' said Elizabeth. 'But once again my thanks for your kindness. I'm coming, Ruth.'

Joseph watched her go and the familiar longing filled him. Then, he shrugged lightly. I must be patient, he thought, and she must have her dreams.

CHAPTER FOUR

A week later

Elizabeth woke at first light and was instantly alert. She looked down at Della who still slept, her thumb in her mouth, in the truckle bed beside her. Leaning over, she lifted a corner of the pillow and smiled to see the rabbit's paw without which the girl declared herself unable to sleep. Such a child still, she thought, but with the body of a young woman!

Throwing back the bedclothes, she slid out on to the sheepskin that served as a rug, and moved round to wake Della.

'Hey, sleepy one!' she cried, 'stir yourself. We have another day, by the Grace of God, so let's be about!'

She gave the girl a little shake and Della opened her eyes. With comprehension came her usual smile, followed by the realization that her thumb was in her mouth. Guiltily she pulled it out and hid it beneath the sheet.

'Suck-a-thumb!' Elizabeth teased. 'You are a real baby-bunting!'

Della opened her mouth to protest but instead rasped soundlessly. With a look of almost comic surprise she put a hand to her throat and tried again. Nothing happened. She swallowed and immediately frowned in discomfort and put both hands to the glands in her neck.

'You are not ill?' demanded Elizabeth, a trifle impatiently.

The girl sat up warily. The effort made her head ache and she clapped a hand to her forehead, screwing up her face.

54

'Della!' protested Elizabeth. 'You cannot do this to me. Not today! Have you forgot where we are going?'

The girl shook her head and stared miserably up at her mistress.

'Are you really out of sorts?' Elizabeth asked telling the young girl's forehead. 'Burning,' she said and sighed with disappointment. 'I shall have to go without you. How very trying of you, Della, to go down with an ague at such a time! But never mind. I shall send Martha up with a quince syrup for your throat.'

The girl tapped her forehead enquiringly.

Elizabeth laughed. 'Della! It seems to me that you delight in your sickness! But you shall have plantain with oil of roses for your head. Will that suffice?'

Della, nodding, tried to give a little groan, but began to cough instead and slid back hurriedly under the blanket. Elizabeth crossed to the tableboard and poured cold water into the large earthenware bowl. She splashed it generously over her skin and towelled herself dry. She rinsed her teeth with cold water and cleaned them with a piece of linen. Then, she threw open the shutters and looked out. There was a heavy mist and the sun, unable to penetrate it, produced only a diffused glow. She therefore dressed warmly, covering her woollen gown with a heavy crimson riding cloak. She gave Della a brisk wave of her hand and went down to the kitchen where Martha, slumped on a stool, leaned on the table, gathering her wits and energies for the demands of the coming day.

Elizabeth explained Della's plight and Martha gave a disparaging sniff to show her opinion of such idleness.

'And we're right out of quince syrup,' she said triumphantly. Elizabeth hesitated. 'Then distilled lavender water,' she said 'That also is of Mercury. I know she does enjoy ill-health, but this time tis no false alarm. The child has an ague and it may lead to something worse. I shall be out for the morning so will have a coddled egg and wine before I go.'

To Martha's dismay, she told her nothing more but hurried outside to find Eric the young stable lad. He stood by the pump rubbing the sleep from his eyes and picking straw from his clothes. He ran his fingers through his hair while Elizabeth spoke to him, in an effort to subdue a mop of tow coloured hair.

'I have business on the moor,' she told him, 'and you must ride with me for Della is sick. Saddle up the roan palfrey for me and the old one for yourself. Oh, and ask Martha for ale and a lump of cheese for your breakfast. And make haste!'

He sped away grinning with delight at the prospect of an unexpected outing. Elizabeth shivered and pulled the hood up over her curls which, free of the usual head-dress, were loosely held by a net. She shivered again, but knew she was not really cold. It was excitement spiced with fear at her own temerity. She momentarily watched the horses at their stable doors tossing their heads and shuffling in anticipation of their morning bran. Elizabeth closed her eyes and a fierce elation seized her.

'So!' she whispered. 'Look your last on Elizabeth, wife of Daniel Heron. This is Elizabeth Heron, mistress of the Manor! A new Elizabeth with new dreams! Wild and wonderful dreams!'

She flung out her arms and spun round on the cobbles, her cloak billowing round her until it swirled itself round her long slim legs, then unwrapping itself again. The horses watched composedly, only the twitching of their ears betraying their interest. Opening her eyes, she stared round at her audience.

'Do you hear me?' she demanded. 'Don't you believe me? Oh, you just wait and see. I tell you I have dreams!' Covering her face with her hands she breathed deeply while her heart hammered under her ribs. 'You'll see,' she whispered again. 'You'll all see!'

Shortly afterwards, Martha and Jacob watched them depart.

'Whatever is she about?' asked Martha. 'Traipsing off at this hour with none but young Eric to keep her company. To the moor, he tells me. I wouldn't wonder if the master's death ain't addled her brain.'

Jacob shook his head. 'No fear of that,' he said. 'She's got her head screwed on the right way. Sharp as a needle, that one, if you ask me.'

'I don't,' snapped Martha. 'For what do the likes of you know of folks' brains. Carrots and onions — maybe even a flower or two; but folks' brains never! And what am I to tell Master Tucker when he calls? That his fancy has took off with Eric and not a word as to when she'll be back. Huh!'

She glanced at Jacob. Silenced by the look in her eye, he merely shrugged and cut himself another piece of cheese.

At the end of the lane Elizabeth reigned in and waited impatiently for Eric to catch up with her. Then, she turned her mount eastward and skirting the town, they headed towards the moor.

As they journeyed on, the sky grew lighter and the track narrower until it rose steeply and they found themselves leaving the mist below them. Glancing back, they could see the town submerged in a white sea, only the church towers visible, glinting in the sunlight. Eric, burning with curiosity, stole a look at the face of his mistress and wondered whether he dare ask the purpose of their journey. As if reading his thoughts, Elizabeth turned to him smiling.

'Tis no great mystery,' she said. 'We go in search of Will Retter.'

The boy's eyes widened. 'And do you know where he is?' he asked.

Elizabeth shook her head. 'No, but I know one who might. His name is Luke Rydd and we've a fair distance to cover. So prod that idle nag of yours, Eric, and we shall make better time.'

Luke Rydd, crouching beside the stream, did not raise his eyes from the muddy water in the bowl between his knees to acknowledge Elizabeth and Eric's arrival. Rhythmically, he rocked the bowl from side to side, separating the soft red earth from the fine gravel. Elizabeth and Eric dismounted and waited, holding the horses, reluctant to disturb him. He leaned over the stream and poured off the reddened water, stirring the stony residue with his finger. Then, he refilled the bowl and began to rock it once more. Elizabeth and Eric exchanged glances. She handed him the reins of her horse and moved forward to kneel beside the grizzled tinner.

'Tis Elizabeth Heron,' she announced. 'I'm looking for Will Retter and I'm told you may know where he is.'

'Oh, aye,' he said.

'Can you help me?'

He frowned and scooped up a handful of gravel and examined it with a practised eye.

'I might,' he said. 'And again, I might not.'

'Oh!'

She looked at the impassive face and wondered whether he was being insolent. Perhaps this taciturn behaviour was normal to him.

'May I?' she asked, holding out a hand towards the bowl.

He nodded and she picked out a few of the small, sharp grains and rolled them between finger and thumb.

'Tin ore?' she asked.

'Aye.'

'See here, Eric,' she called to the boy. 'This is the ore. The stuff that fortunes are made of!'

Rydd grunted, an apology for a laugh, but he held out the bowl for Eric's inspection.

'My grandfather was a tinner,' the boy volunteered.

Rydd eyed him with interest. 'Was?' he asked.

58

'He's dead long since.'

'Oh, and your father?'

'He's a fisherman.'

'How come?'

'Grandfather lost all his money and Father wouldn't follow.'

'Aye.' The man nodded his understanding and glanced up at Elizabeth. 'That's the way of it,' he said. 'It makes or breaks you.'

But he had mellowed a little towards them and, beckoning the boy to the water's edge, he pointed out the deposits of earth among the rocks that made up the bed of the stream.

He plunged his arm into the shallow water and scooped up a handful. A few larger fragments came up with the soil and he examined these with a critical eye, then nodded.

'Washed down from higher up the moor,' he told him.

Now that they had caught the old man's attention, Elizabeth sought to keep it.

'And what happens next?' she asked.

'Break it up and crush it,' he informed, 'with this.' And he pointed to a large mortar, nine inches deep and twelve inches across, and a heavy wooden pestle banded with iron. Elizabeth lifted the latter and grimaced at its weight. Then she looked the old man straight in the eyes.

'And the ore?' she asked. 'They say it dwindles and can't be found.'

He gave her a sharp look. 'Tis there, right enough,' he said, 'but reaching it, that's the trouble. There's no lack of it but tis getting it out. Under the ground and inside the rock, that's where tis now. What lies on the surface for easy picking, that's nigh all gone. That's dwindling, right enough. But the tin's still there in plenty, you can be sure on that.'

She nodded, satisfied. 'And then what happens?' she asked, reverting to their previous topic.

59

He indicated the pannier which stood some feet away. It was filled almost to the brim with bags of ore. Behind it a pony, tethered to a stake, grazed half-heartedly. Strapped to its back was a second pannier and an assortment of bulging bags and bundles.

'That lot goes to young Cobbett at the blowing house,' he said, 'for smelting and that's where I'm going. If you've a mind to come along, I should, for I hear young Cobbert has seen Will Retter and might be able to put you on the right road.'

So, shortly after, the three of them set off: Rydd walking ahead leading his loaded pony, while Elizabeth and Eric followed. The journey was longer than they expected and almost without conversation. Eric was becoming aware of his empty stomach and Elizabeth was immersed in her own thoughts.

The blowing house proved to be a small building on the edge of the river. This latter had been adapted and deepened, so that the water level dropped about twelve feet over a distance of eighty yards and finally flowed past a small water wheel.

Tom Cobbett came out to greet them and Elizabeth begged permission to explore while he, Eric and Rydd unloaded the pony. Inside the building she could see the large bellows made of wood and leather which were powered by the water wheel. The unloading completed, Tom Cobbett hastened to make her a more courteous welcome; offering them each a mug of ale which they accepted gratefully. The furnace gave off a mighty heat, for another tinner had arrived earlier and now waited for his ore to be smelted.

Elizabeth watched, fascinated, as the molten tin ran down on to the grooved stone which channelled it into rectangular moulds, where the tin would cool and shrink until it could be safely lifted.

'Will Retter?' Tom Cobbett repeated. 'Aye, I've seen him. Not more'n a week since. Up at the moor house he is, out along the ridge, though I'll wager you'll not get a word out of 'im for he's as sullen as the very devil these days and won't thank you for a visit. Not so much as a civil word did we get. Not that we expected nothing more knowing how it is with him, like.'

'Doesn't he work at all?' Elizabeth asked, dismayed. 'How does he live?'

Tom Cobbett shrugged. 'From hand to mouth, and tis a wonder he survives. Berries, I reckon, a rabbit mebbe, or a bird.'

'Mebbe a fish,' Eric suggested, eager to take part in the conversation, but Elizabeth gave him a warning look which effectively silenced him.

Tom Cobbett shook his head. 'Tis a pity,' he said. 'A pity to see a fine man laid so low. A mortal shame and that's a fact.'

Thanking them once more for their help, she motioned Eric back to the horses and waiting only to receive directions, soon joined him. It was all taking longer than she had anticipated. Now the sun was overhead and they had had nothing to eat since breakfast. Nor were they likely to eat for some time yet. The prospect ahead of her was daunting and her earlier confidence and enthusiasm were beginning to wane. I won't give up, she told herself grimly. Not now that I am so near. The wretched man cannot eat me, so why do I quake so. He can either say 'Yea' or 'Nay' and there's an end to it. And please Sweet Mother, let it be 'Yea', for without him my dreams will remain but fancies. I must have Will Retter. I must! And I will! Unknowingly she spoke the last few words aloud and with passion.

Ahead of them a bank of dark cloud blew in from the west, and they rode on in silence to meet the rain.

Will Retter was well known the length and breadth of Dartmoor as one of the most successful tin miners in Devon. Envied by many and hated by some; yet he was respected by all for his knowledge. He had been a hard working, hard drinking man and many a man had suffered

61

a beating at his hands. But it was Will Retter's boast that what he didn't know about tin could be written on his thumb nail with room to spare, and what he didn't know about mining the ore was best forgotten.

As a boy he had worked at his father's blowing house to which the local miners brought their ore for smelting. But as soon as he had saved enough money from his meagre allowance to lease a plot of land, he had gone his own way. At the age of fourteen, he had ignored both his mother's tears and his father's threats and left home. With a confidence rare in one so young, he had chosen for his first 'set' a parcel of Heron land, dismissed by the rest of the tinners as unlikely to yield enough ore to cover the year's leasing fee. They had settled back comfortably to await his downfall.

Well aware of this, Will had marked out the boundaries of his land and walked every inch of it. Head bent, eyes fixed on the stony furze-covered ground beneath his feet, he would pause occasionally and kneel, scrubbing among the lichens for loose stones and rocks which he examined carefully. A stream ran through his land on its way to the River Dart. This he paddled the extent of the shallow water course, reaching down to pluck up the gravel that littered the stream's bed. After a week, he was familiar with his ground and knew every contour and the small variety of its vegetation. At last he lay face downwards, feeling his own ground beneath him, then rolled on to his back to watch the interminable grey clouds which scudded across the sky bringing a constant threat of rain. He stood up, sighed deeply and moved on. A kind Fate patronized him. Within an hour he had found ore. The tinners' amusement changed to grudging admiration.

It was a rich find, and Retter's fame spread. Others flocked to the surrounding area, but with less success. Intuitively, he had chosen the richest lode and he mined it for four years, amassing a small fortune as he did so. He married and fathered three sons. His family rarely saw him but they lived in a style that few could emulate.

When his lease expired, he moved on again, breaking new ground, this time to the west of the town on Tucker's land. Again, he chose correctly and there was a rush to follow him. He was what men called a 'natural' with an affinity for the rich granite with which he worked.

The peak of his career came with his election to the tinners parliament which met at intervals on Crocken Tor. Scarcely had he achieved this crowning of his success when Fate, ever capricious, withdrew her favours. His family perished one black night in a blaze which engulfed their house and that of their neighbour. Next the lode of ore failed unaccountably and the strain took its toll of his emotions. He began to drink heavily and his judgement became blurred. He made a false choice and leased a piece of barren ground. Everything he had owned was lost in the fire and he replaced nothing, preferring to live a rough and incredibly meagre existence high on the moor where none dared approach him, for his temper had worsened and he was unpredictable and frequently violent.

Now he lay in the moor house. There were no windows and the door was securely barred. The only light came through the eaves, between the rough stone walls and crudely turfed roof. He opened his eyes. His ears had picked up the sound of approaching horses. He crossed to the door and put his eye to a crack in the wood. A lad on an elderly pony and a woman! He watched as she slipped easily from the saddle and tossed the reins to her companion. The riding cloak flattered her tall slim figure and the hood had slipped back to reveal a mass of dark auburn curls loosely held in a white net.

It was raining heavily, but she seemed unaware of it. She moved towards the door and her step was purposeful. At the door she stopped, her fingers feeling the edges for a means of opening it. There was none, so she rapped loudly upon it.

'Will Retter!' she called authoritatively. ''Tis Elizabeth Heron. I wish to speak with you.'

He made no answer. She knocked again, calling his name, a sharpness in her tone. Silence greeted her and she hammered on the door with her clenched fist.

'I know you're in there,' she called. 'Are you awake, Will Retter? I would speak with you.'

At last he unbarred the door and pulled it open.

His attitude was both defensive and aggressive, like an animal at bay. His light brown animal eyes held dark flecks under heavy eyebrows, his nose was slightly hooked, his face beaten brown by the weather. Dark thinning hair lay smoothly over his head, but gave way to a curly beard which did nothing to hide the strong jutting jaw. He wore a leather jerkin and rough woollen hose.

He met Elizabeth's startled gaze with an unflinching stare. So this was Elizabeth Heron, mistress of the Manor. There was a sensual magnetism about her which reduced her, in his eyes, to Elizabeth the woman. Neither spoke until the spell was broken by the startled whinny from one of the horses, as a small bird took fright from the gorse and fluttered upwards with a shrill cry. Elizabeth spoke quickly.

'I'm Elizabeth Heron,' she said with a lack of confidence that was new to her. 'I have a matter to discuss with you. Are you willing?'

He eyed her with an indifference that was almost arrogance.

'Likely not,' he said at last and she felt her cheeks burn. He stood with his weight on one leg, one arm against the jamb of the door. His legs were well-shaped, his body lean and there was nothing in his manner or bearing to suggest shame at the straits in which she now found him, or in which he found himself.

Fighting down her irritation, she tried again. 'What I have to say is of importance to us both,' she told him. 'I need your help. I have certain plans for which I need the help of an experienced tinner. I have made enquiries and your name was given to me, not once, but many times.'

'Is that so?' he said his tone mocking the little speech.

'What do you say?' she asked.

'I say no,' he said flatly.

Elizabeth stared at him, at a loss to know how to continue. She could not imagine any line of approach that would appeal to this man. She could certainly not bully him and she doubted whether he was receptive to a reasoned argument. Nor could she appeal to his better nature for she doubted he had one! Perhaps she could buy his co-operation.

'I promise you would find it worth your while, at least to give me a hearing,' she said.

'You think you can buy me?' he said and she flushed angrily.

'Not you,' she replied firmly. 'Your experience, yes. I want to buy your knowledge and your advice. I need your help and I wish it given willingly and at a fair price. I can see you are a proud man,' she said her tone softening.

Retter raised his eyebrows but said nothing. He watched her steadily. He seemed to be considering her suggestion and for that, at least, she was thankful. She glanced back suddenly at Eric. He had unrolled a blanket which hung by his saddle and now wrapped himself in it as a protection from the rain. Elizabeth decided that he must stay where he was. The only shelter for miles was the tiny moor house and she had no intention of allowing his keen young ears to overhear any discussion that might take place between herself and this difficult man.

'What do you say?' she asked again.

'You'd best come inside,' he said and stepped back to let her pass. There was no furniture in the moor house and dirty straw covered the floor. In one corner there was a stack of turf and brushwood and a few cooking pots.

'Take a seat,' he mocked.

'Do you never have a fire?' she asked him, shivering.

'When there's food to cook,' he said.

'But to keep yourself warm?'

'I'm warm enough.'

He turned to stare out through the doorway. 'Is that your son?'

'My stable lad.'

He glanced at her over his shoulder.

'Any of your own?' he asked, casting her a knowing glance.

She shook her head. By his look she felt intuitively that he had assessed her age, considered the fact that she was childless and concluded she was barren. The thought, humiliated her.

He turned away again and the silence lengthened between them.

'I don't know if you are aware,' she began, 'that my husband, Daniel, had been ailing for some years. There has been no one attending to the property or land. Now he's dead, I'm assuming that responsibility. We have a deal of land, I believe several thousand acres, most of it rich in tin but most of it leased out to tinners.'

'Get to the point,' he said brusquely.

'We are losing money and I mean to do something about it.'

He turned round. 'What will you do?'

She sneezed suddenly and shivered again.

'I'll knock up a bit of a fire,' he said immediately scraping some of the straw into a pile in the bare, sooty area that served as a hearth. He tossed on a few twigs and a bundle of furze and soon had a small but smoky fire underway. There was no chimney and the smoke hung in eddies below the roof so that her eyes smarted painfully. The sneezing was replaced by a fit of coughing, but she accepted the fire as a friendly overture and thanked him courteously.

They stood on opposite sides of the fire and Elizabeth tried to pick up the thread of her explanation.

'You'll have heard of Sir William Godolphin,' she said

and he nodded. 'He is forming his own company,' she informed him bluntly. 'I want to do the same.'

Retter made a small sound that was somewhere between amusement and disbelief.

'I don't speak rashly,' she said. 'I've considered well and my plans are made. You are part of them, if you've a mind to be.'

'And these plans?'

Elizabeth, wet and cold though she was, took heart. The man was not as unapproachable as she had expected. He had invited her into his 'home' and was at least prepared to listen to her.

Cautiously, she began. 'There is still tin to be found on Dartmoor,' she said. 'I think we have so far plucked only what was readily found. Men have streamed along the rivers and at the rock face. Now we must search below the ground and beyond the rock face! Sink shafts into the earth and tunnel into the hillside.' She paused and took the ensuing silence to be one of agreement. 'I own this land,' she continued 'I do not choose to sit back while the tinners give up for want of organization. The time has come for change.'

'Most of them lack money,' he reminded her. 'They are poor men. They know they must dig and tunnel. But how? They need timber, ropes, candles. Would you become another money lender? Is that the way of it?'

'No!' she cried. 'That is not the way. I have no wish to lend Heron money to a disorganized rabble! I intend to invest it in a well organized company. I want you to help me form one. I need your help, Will Retter. That's why I'm here.'

She had grown passionate once more and her flashing eyes and ringing tone inspired him momentarily. Briefly, she saw in his eyes an echo of her own feeling — a passion for the land and the, ore imprisoned within it. Then his face hardened.

'And what of old Tucker?' he asked suddenly. 'They say you'll wed the man.'

She stiffened.

'I may well wed him,' but twould make no difference to your position. I give you my word.'

'But the land is already leased out,' he said.

'I do not intend to renew them nor offer new ones. Gradually the land will revert to me, to us.'

'Twill never work. Tinners won't work for a woman.'

'But they would work for you,' she said.

He shook his head.

'They would,' she insisted. 'You have their respect.'

'They would never give up their independence.'

'Master tinners could work on tribute,' she said, 'or take shares in the mine. Labourers could be paid a daily rate, say four pounds yearly, and be contracted to us. Or be paid half in money, half in tin. Tis possible, Will. I know it is.'

Unwittingly she had used his first time. Even now she was unaware that she had done so. But to Will Retter the word hung in the air above all the rest and he read and re-read it there. The sound of his name spoken by a woman, and such a woman, moved him incredibly.

'Say it is possible, I beg you!' she cried, and now there was a note of desperation in her voice. He looked at her and saw the ambition and the need which he alone could fulfil. But more than that, he saw the woman behind the ambition from her weakness to her strength.

'It would be impossible!' he cried and saw her face crumple into incredulity. Even while he cursed his folly and searched for a way to soften his impetuous words, she was turning her face away. Half-blinded by unshed tears, she pushed past his restraining hand and stumbled out of the door. She was half way back to the horses when he called.

'Wait!'

She turned immediately and looked at him, but did not

68

retrace her steps. Her face was streaked with tears and her lips trembled, but she held her head high. She would not plead. Since she stood her ground so resolutely, he moved towards her, coming to a stop a few feet away.

'You want me then?' he asked, his voice low.

'You can name your price!' she said, unable to believe this change of heart.

'Shares in the mine,' he said, and she nodded but his expression did not change.

'Is it "Aye"?' she asked.

She stared into the pale animal eyes and heard his breathing quicken. He made no sound and seconds passed. Will Retter saw the expression in her grey eyes harden as she faced the possibility of a refusal. What would she do, he wondered. She would not plead, he was sure of that. Yet he held the key to her cherished ambition. Almost as though she read his thoughts she said, 'I need you, Will.'

She had deliberately used his first name. Now they were two equals. A man and a woman. He drew in his breath sharply, reluctant to take his eyes from her. There was something magnetic about her that held his senses captive. Not her beauty, not her dignity. He searched his mind for the right word.

'Tis the nature of the beast,' he muttered at last, unaware that he spoke aloud.

Still Elizabeth waited, not daring to speak lest anything she said might sway him from her purpose. Will Retter knew suddenly what he wanted. He wanted to touch this woman, feel her warmth. Abruptly he raised his hand and her eyes flinched and her body stiffened, her senses alerted like an animal sensing danger. Gently he reached forward. A strand of her hair clung damply to her cheek and he brushed it back with fingers that were rough and calloused. Then he drew a long, shuddering breath and said 'Aye'.

CHAPTER FIVE

1483 London

Although it was a fine day, the houses met so closely above their heads that no sunlight reached them and they rode in shadow. Joseph led the way, followed by Elizabeth with a wide-eyed Della bringing up the rear. It was the girl's first trip to London and she was determined not to miss any detail that might impress the other staff on her return home. It was also the first time she had ridden and she was tired, her muscles ached intolerably from the strain of remaining in the saddle. But her pains were forgotten now as she looked about her. They had come through Exeter and Salisbury on route from Ashburton, but those two towns paled into insignificance beside the wonders of London.

Never had Della seen so many houses in so small a space, or so many people. The noise was unbelievable; shouting children, pleading beggars, the cries of the street sellers with their trays of pies, baskets of fish or bunches of flowers. Carts rumbled clumsily along the street, horses slithered on the slimy ill-kept cobbles, men and women clattered to and fro on their wooden pattens. Women chatted on doorsteps while babes in arms bawled lustily for their attention.

Even overhead neighbours exchanged items of gossip and occasionally emptied slops out of the window on to the head of unfortunate passers-by who did not move fast enough at the warning shout of 'Gardez l'eau'.

Groups of apprentices roamed the streets and many appreciative glances and winks came Della's way to her great delight and embarrassment.

Progress, though interesting, was necessarily slow. A wagon load of firewood filled the narrow street blocking their passage, while street rakers were busy pulling the muck into heaps, throwing it into carts for eventual disposal outside the city limits. A dancing bear showed off his tricks to a large crowd which gave way reluctantly to Joseph and Elizabeth who now rode abreast of him, for fear they should be separated by the crush of people. Della was urged to 'keep close' and was glad to do so.

At length they turned off into a side street and Joseph beckoned one of the many urchins who ran alongside, hopefully offering their services in return for a coin or two.

'Do you know a Nathan Byrnes?' asked Joseph. 'A working goldsmith under the sign of the Gold Plumes.'

Elizabeth's birthday was imminent and Joseph planned the purchase of a ring as his gift to her. Not a betrothal ring, for Elizabeth's dreams were well on the way to becoming reality and success had made her independent. She knew that Joseph loved her. She had seen it in his eyes and knew that a word from her was all that kept them apart. She was fond of him and had great respect for the man. He was attractive and would be the ideal partner. Why she hesitated she did not know. Or would not admit. For secretly she still nursed a fear that she was barren and that a second marriage would prove it to herself and the world.

Now, as he spoke to the lad, showing him the goldsmith's trade card, she studied Joseph covertly. The green and gold suited him well. The face was handsome, the voice rang with an unstated authority. He knew how to sit a horse and was at ease in the unfamiliar surroundings. He carried his years well, was fit and intelligent. Joseph Tucker would make her an excellent husband and she would be greatly envied in the neighbourhood. 'But will you give me a child?' she beseeched him wordlessly. 'Can you — can any man? Only make me with child, Joseph, and I swear I will be a good wife to you so long as I draw breath! I'll spin and sew and weave, and fill your stomach with good food. I'll be thrifty and wise. I'll keep the accounts, and reprove the servants. I'll warm your heart and your bed to your infinite satisfaction . . . . only give me a child, Joseph I beg you!'

He turned suddenly and caught sight of her earnest expression. 'What is it?' he asked.

'Nothing. I am thinking,' she said, 'that the street smells increase with each visit. Thank Heavens we need visit London only once a year!'

Each year the bulk of their household provisions were fetched from London and the expedition lasted well over a week. Visits to tailors and dressmakers were included in the itinerary, as were any necessary business calls or visits to friends. The trip provided a welcome if exhausting break in the year's routine and was eagerly anticipated.

The young lad screwed up his face in an effort to concentrate. 'I know a Lynche,' he said. 'A German. He's under a Golden Plume, or maybe it's a Golden Lion. No, I think it's a . . . . '

'It's Byrnes we're looking for,' said Joseph.

'I know a Purdie under the Golden Grasshopper, but I think that's in Lombard Street.'

'Do you or don't you know Nathan Byrnes in Gutter Lane?'

'I know Gutter Lane,' said the boy.

'This is Gutter Lane,' said Joseph impatiently.

'No, sir. Gutter Lane's a turning off this street. I do know Gutter Lane. Follow me.'

And he led the way importantly, fiercely elbowing a passage through the throng of people with loud shouts and a fine disregard for his own well-being; for many were the cuffs he earned in return from irate passers-by. More by good luck than good judgements they stopped outside a small shop. A counter jutted out into the street and inside they could see the gold painted walls and a table covered with a red cloth. Outside, a painted sign hung above the counter, depicting three gold plumes and various items of jewellery and bearing Nathan Byrnes name in large ornate letters embellished with flowers and ribbons. Joseph tossed the lad a few groats, which he caught skilfully before disappearing once more into the crowd. They dismounted and Della was left holding the horses while Joseph led Elizabeth into the shop.

As Nathan Byrnes hurried forward into the shop to greet them, Mark put his head round the curtain for a quick glimpse. He whistled admiringly under his breath and John's mouth twitched into one of his rare smiles.

'God's truth!' said Mark. 'I wouldn't say "No" to that one warming my bed on a cold night! Two of everything and all in the right places! Take a look for yourself if you don't believe me.'

'I believe you,' said John, disinterestedly.

'Aren't you even going to take a look?'

'No.'

Mark snorted his disgust at his friend's lack of interest, and gave himself the satisfaction of a further look before returning to his bench.

'I despair of you,' he told John, sadly. 'Here am I combing the city for you and only offering the very best, and you won't even do me the honour of a quick glance. I tell you she is beautiful.'

John straightened up from the locket on which he was working and rubbed the back of his neck to ease the muscles. His eyes were heavy from lack of sleep, the children had been fretful in the night, and he had only just recovered from a bad chill. He took the locket to the far corner of the room and held it carefully against the felt covered drum of the buffing machine, working it up to the required speed with the foot treadle.

Mark lowered the shank of a half-made ring into a dish of 'pickle' and changed his line of attack.

'Perhaps I shall pursue this one myself,' he mused. 'I like them tall.'

John laughed. 'You like them short, too,' he said. 'And fat and thin, and old and young.'

'Not old!'

'As long as they breathe!'

'You do me an injustice!' protested Mark, laughing. 'But this one maybe I will add to my collection.'

He withdrew the shank, examined it critically, and rinsed it.

The sound of voices reached them from the shop and John looked up at his friend in mock dismay.

'Is that a man's voice I hear?' he asked. 'I thought she was available! A fine friend you are! The lady has a husband. Am I to run him through with my sword then and carry off the widow?'

'Calm yourself and listen. I have a plan, John. She is not his wife, only betrothed.'

'Only! Then they're as good as wed! Don't waste my time, lad. I've no energy to spare for your crack-brained plans. If I want a wench I shall choose my own, and without your help! At the moment I am weary from lack of sleep and . . . .'

'What ails you is too much sleep,' said Mark. 'Too much sleep and not enough exercise! Spare her one glance, my friend. I swear you won't regret it.'

'Sweet God, but you persist!' cried John in exasperation. 'Then I will have a look and will I then be allowed to get on with my work?'

Mark grinned, quite unabashed by his friend's apparent disinterest, and watched as he crossed to the doorway and drew the curtain slightly to one side. Elizabeth's back was towards him but then she half-turned to speak to Joseph and he saw the arrogant toss of the delicate head in its neat cap and fine veiling. He heard her light laugh in response to one of Nathan's comments and noted the slim hand as it reached up to tuck a stray hair behind the small ear. And then to his dismay, she suddenly turned and caught sight of him, spying on them from behind the curtain, like a cheeky schoolboy. He was aware of the amusement in her eyes and hastily replaced the curtain, cursing himself and Mark!

'Was I right?' asked Mark, eagerly.

'Go to Hell!' said John. Returning to his bench, he picked up the locket and taking up a small garnet, reached for the flux.

Nathan Byrnes, with his back to the doorway, saw the look on Elizabeth's face and turned in time to see the curtain fall back into place.

He laughed. 'Please forgive the prying eyes,' he said. 'I dare say t'was Mark, my youngest apprentice. He has a natural curiosity for the world and its master, but he's a promising lad in his last year.'

'How many apprentices do you have?' Joseph asked.

'Only Mark. John, my right hand man, is finished his apprenticeship two years since and is a fine craftsman. He is already making a name for himself. His gold on silver can scarce be bettered.'

'Much credit to you, then,' Elizabeth remarked.

Nathan shook his head. 'You cannot make a silk purse from a sow's ear,' he reminded them. 'The lad has a natural talent, a great natural ability. I have merely fostered it. If a lad's no leaning for it, then I can teach 'til Kingdom come to no avail! John has a feeling for it.'

'And the younger one, Mark is it?' questioned Joseph.

'Aye, Mark. Well, he's got it, but he needs to work at it. Too many distractions at present. He'd be out wenching every night if he had his way, begging your pardon, ma'am,' he said hastily, 'but John's more dedicated. A quieter lad all told. Lost his first wife and won't take a second. Took it harder than most. A pity, a great pity.'

He shook his head and they fell silent.

'And he is to make this ring?' said Joseph.

'Aye. If you're wanting it so immediate, for I shan't be back from Bath until the middle of next month. I go for the waters twice a year for my aches and pains. Does me a deal of good. So come into the workshop and talk with him.'

He swept the curtain aside and led the way into the small room behind the shop. The whitewashed walls contained only one window, but a door to the back yard stood open to let in the light. A wooden bench ran along two sides of the room and on this a variety of tools, trays, boxes and bowls competed for space. Several jerkins and an apron hung against a third wall and a small table held the remains of their lunch: a dish of soft cheese, a crust of dark brown bread and a jug. The stone floor was strewn with the usual rushes and an acrid smell of burning hung in the air.

Mark looked round eagerly at their entrance, but John's blond head remained stubbornly bent over his work. Mark sprang off his stool and offered it to Elizabeth but she declined it with thanks.

'I've a customer for you, John,' Nathan declared.

John put down the locket and turned towards them. The introductions were made. He shook hands with Joseph and then turned to Elizabeth. He did not smile and there was no expression in the dark blue eyes. His hand was cool on hers and to her surprise Elizabeth trembled at his touch. Quickly, she withdrew her hand, smiled briefly and turned to Joseph who was describing the design he had in mind for the proposed ring.

The old man held up his hand. 'I'll leave you with John,' he told them. 'I have a visit to make to Lord Denny. Mark, keep an eye on the shop until I return. Sir, madam, your good servant until we meet again.' He left them and Mark reluctantly removed himself to the shop.

Elizabeth changed her mind and sat down on the stool Mark had offered, while John made a few sketches for a design. She shook her head at Joseph's suggestion that as an interested party she should take part in the discussions, pretending that she felt a little faint and preferred to sit.

'Perhaps a little ale,' said John and he took up an earthenware cup, wiped its rim on a cloth and filled it from the jug.

'Thank you,' she said.

She took it, sipped it carefully, clasping her hands round its rough surface to steady them. Now her heart beat faster and a strange elation seized her. Amazed at the reaction of her body to this man, she allowed herself to stare at him unashamedly as his charcoal skipped across the page in a series of deft strokes. There was something familiar about him. He was handsome, tall and slim and he was proud! It was written all over him, in the movements of his head, in the tone of his voice. Nathan Byrnes was right. This man was no ordinary goldsmith. He had a superior talent and knew it. And he was no ordinary man. Elizabeth could vouch for that! Her swirling emotions told her so. Almost timidly, she looked at his face. The head was well shaped. Under the small round cap the pale hair, brushed and gleaming, reached almost to his shoulders in the current fashion. His nose was large enough to be attractive on a man, and straight. The mouth, beneath the heavy moustache, was thin and emphasized the almost grim set of his narrow jaw. She sipped again at the ale and wondered if he had drunk from the same cup. He wore short leather boots, dark blue hose and a short grey doublet which laced across the front. Elizabeth, a little calmer, swallowed down the last of the ale and set the cup down on the bench beside her. Joseph glanced round.

'Are you recovered?' he asked and she nodded.

John gave her a quick look and the lack of interest in his eyes was like a blow. She forced herself to look away, fingering the small tools and instruments that lay within her reach, trying to quell the inexplicable feeling of vulnerability that was taking hold of her. Almost angrily, she took a deep breath, then another. A small glass dish filled with clear liquid caught her attention and she reached a hand towards it.

'Don't touch that!'

His voice cut across the air like a knife blade and Elizabeth jumped.

'I'm sorry,' she said, surprised and embarrassed by the

abrupt command. Joseph looked from Elizabeth to John.

'There's no call to bark at her like that,' he said, sharply.

'I'm sorry,' said John, 'but that is what we call "pickle".'

'Pickle?' echoed Joseph.

John nodded. 'A mixture of sulphuric acid and water. We use it to clean the oxide from the metal. It's dangerous stuff. You could have scarred yourself,' he told Elizabeth. 'I didn't mean to frighten you but see here . . . .'

He dipped a finger into his mug and allowed one small drop of ale to fall into the 'pickle'. There was an immediate and violent reaction, as droplets of acid spat upwards. Elizabeth watched in alarm.

'I see,' she said simply. 'Then I must thank you for your vigilance.' But he had turned away and was once more engrossed in his discussion with Joseph.

Now that his back was towards her, Elizabeth allowed herself another look at him and became aware, as she did so, that their discussion was developing into an argument. Joseph, it seemed, had decided on a green stone and had selected a fluorite from those offered. John explained that the stone was too soft for a ring and suggested a tourmaline.

'Too soft?' Joseph argued. 'How can that be? You offer it with the other stones and when I choose it you say it is not suitable. Why, then, do you offer it?'

'It is suitable for other items,' said John evenly. 'It is suitable for a pendant or ear-rings. They do not receive the same amount of friction as a ring. A hand is in constant motion, in touch with other objects. The tourmaline is a hard gem. The flourite is not.'

'But I prefer the fluorite,' Joseph insisted. 'It has a better colour.'

'The colour always deepens when it is in its setting,' said John. 'The tourmaline will look deeper.'

78

'Are you saying you will not use the stone I have chosen?'

'I do not advise it.'

'And if I insist?'

Hastily Elizabeth slid from the stool. 'May I look at the stones?' she asked. Joseph hesitated, reluctant to give ground, but John put a small green stone into each of her hands. She looked at them carefully, but could see very little difference. Joseph was watching her anxiously and she felt a sympathy for this man who was to be her husband. It would be more sensible to choose the harder stone, but Joseph's pride was obviously at stake. John turned away to consult his sketches with a convincing show of indifference.

'They are both beautiful,' said Elizabeth. She caught Joseph's eye and he glanced almost imperceptibly towards the left hand.

'I think I prefer this one,' said Elizabeth.

'You have chosen the fluorite' said Joseph. 'Good. You are quite happy with it?'

Elizabeth smiled and nodded and his dark eyes softened at the sight of the sweet familiar face as he patted her hand affectionately. She returned to her stool and listened incredulously as they began another argument about the desirability of piercing as a method of decorating the shank.

When it was finally resolved, Joseph announced that they were ready to leave. They made their farewells and went through into the shop where Mark was sitting on the counter, swinging his legs and whistling cheerfully. He leapt up and made a charming bow towards Elizabeth, his eyes catching hers boldly as he straightened up so that she laughed in spite of herself.

'Then I will call back tomorrow afternoon for your estimate,' Joseph repeated when they regained the street.

John nodded politely and turned back into the shop

without another glance.

'You are very quiet, Beth,' said Joseph, 'and I swear you haven't heard a word I've said these last five minutes!'

Guiltily, Elizabeth looked at him across the table of the inn where they were lodged. Even now, she did not know what he had said to her and he repeated his words for her benefit.

'Your thoughts are miles away,' he added, 'where are they?'

'I don't rightly know,' Elizabeth lied. 'I wonder where the meat has got to. It is taking an incredible time.'

'Still hunting the beast, most like!' joked a man beside her to the amusement of the company nearby.

The table seated ten travellers and was laid somewhat haphazardly with knives, spoons and wooden trenchers in which large thick slices of coarse bread awaited the stew. An ornate pewter salt cellar held pride of place in the middle of the trestle table. A dish of stewed plums and a bowl of soft cheese were almost empty, and they were making short work of a custard tart. Whatever came to the table was hailed with enthusiasm and devoured with speed.

'Hey Annie! Stir your stumps, my pretty,' cried a young man. 'Either bring on the pot or give us a kiss for I'm starved of affection as well as food!'

Annie, daughter of the house, gave him a playful slap for his impudence, but he caught her arm and pulled her down on to his lap. She screamed and wriggled, rather unconvincingly, but finally allowed herself to be kissed on the ear at the moment when her mother appeared with a steaming iron pot which she dumped in the middle of the table. Annie scrambled to her feet and seizing a ladle, began to scoop a portion of meat and vegetables into each trencher.

'Takes after her mother, does Annie!' quipped the

irrepressible young man. 'Cheeks like peaches I'm told, tho' never been lucky enough to see 'em!'

He received a friendly clout on the side of his head and Elizabeth, catching Della's eye, smiled. It was impossible not to relax in the boisterous atmosphere, although after the meal they would retire to bed, to avoid the last hour when the men would be drunk, and the talk bawdy.

The venison was cooked with herbs and mushrooms and there was ale to wash it down and a quince pasty to follow. Elizabeth, Della and Joseph, hungry after a day of shopping and sight seeing, enjoyed the food and the talk that followed; which was mainly of Richard the Third's forthcoming coronation and the preparations for it.

'A third King Richard,' said Joseph. 'And let's hope he loves the people.'

'Enough to cut these scurrilous taxes!' cried an old man at the far end of the table. 'Else folks won't afford to eat for that's what 'twill come to afore long. Look at this coronation. Tis costing a rare fortune, and whose purses will it be coming out of? Ask yourselves that!'

'He's right,' said Annie, the dripping ladle poised over Joseph's bread. 'Have you seen all them stands they're knocking up for people to sit on? With wood the price it is! Not to mention all the decorations for the streets, all them gold and silver trimmings! And all new harness for the horses. They say there's not a yard of purple cloth or gold braid left in the city. And every goldsmith's working night and day to get all done that due.'

This last reference sent Elizabeth's thought circling back to her meeting with John. She pictured once more the cold blue eyes, the tight set of the mouth, the exact sound of his voice and felt both confused and elated. Why was she so strangely disturbed by a man with whom she had barely exchanged a dozen words? It didn't make sense and never would. She and Joseph would return to Devon and she would never see him again. The ring would follow in due course, and she would wear it for Joseph.

Joseph reached across with the pitcher of ale and refilled her mug and then his own. She smiled her thanks and drank deeply. A burst of laughter greeted someone's comment and Elizabeth joined in although the joke had escaped her. Watching Joseph, she saw that the ale was loosening his tongue and she smiled. He would tell a good joke. Men liked him. He was a man's man . . . and John, what sort of man was he? Why had the touch of his hand and the nearness of his body affected her so that she could think of nothing and no one else? She looked at Joseph, his head was thrown back, the mouth, wide open in laughter. Would he give her the child she craved? Would John? The traitorous words echoed round her mind. But Joseph was leaning over to her.

'Your ring size!' he said. 'The wretched fellow forgot to measure your finger.'

'Aye, so he did,' said Elizabeth. 'And I forgot also. How very foolish.'

She spooned another mouthful of vegetables into her mouth, but a faint hope sprang up in her heart. Had he been so affected by their meeting that he had forgotten such a necessary part of the proceedings?

'You had best call in again tomorrow,' Joseph advised. 'Go in the morning while I am at the solicitors. You can take Della with you.'

She nodded, and hoped no one heard the thumping of her heart.

Joseph smiled across at her. 'You are weary,' he said, and came round to help her to her feet.

'It's been a long day,' she confirmed, as they made their way up the narrow wooden stairs to the communal bedchamber. He saw her installed, then left her to sleep, returning to the company below for another hour of good humour and the usual eager exchange of news.

'Ma'am, wake up! Tis well past eight!' Della pulled back

the bed drapes and opened the shutters. The myriad sounds of early morning London filled the room and Elizabeth stirred in her sleep.

'Ma'am! Tis gone eight, — I heard the chimes!'

'Gone eight?' muttered Elizabeth, rubbing her eyes. She propped herself on one elbow and tried to think. 'But I asked you to call me at seven.'

'The master told me to let you be, ma'am. Said you was . . . .'

'He is *not* the master yet, Della,' said Elizabeth. 'How many times do I have to tell you. Is there any hot water brought up?'

'Yes, ma'am, but 'tis gone cold long since.'

'Then run down for some more, please, and what is the weather doing?'

'A mite cool, ma'am.'

'Then put out the blue damask. I have to go back to the goldsmith and you must come with me. Mister Tucker has to go to the solicitors and I – '

'He's already on his way, ma'am, an hour since.'

Elizabeth looked at her in dismay.

'An hour! Then hustle, Della! He may not be there long and we must be gone!'

And she threw back the covers and slid hurriedly out of bed.

In spite of her good intentions, it was nearly an hour before she was once more in Gutter Lane. This time they tethered the horses outside and went into the shop. The goldsmith greeted her warmly and laughed when she explained the reason for her visit.

'Forgot to measure your finger! Well, there's a thing! The lad will forget his own head! You go through into the workshop, you'll find him there.'

Elizabeth going in, passed Mark coming out. He had seen Della and decided to make himself known. Thus Elizabeth, with her chaperone detained in the next room, found herself quite alone with John for the first time. She

83

expected him to be working on her ring, but he was otherwise engaged. She stood without speaking for a few moments, watching, reluctant to disturb him and happy to watch the large capable hands about their delicate business. He had coiled a heavy gold wire round a narrow metal rod, to form a close spring. Now he took a finely bladed saw and cut along the upper side. The cut coil became small links. He brushed the links into a small pile and tipped them into a cone of paper for safe keeping. Only when that was done did he acknowledge Elizabeth's presence.

'What is it?' he asked abruptly and without smiling. The woman annoyed him. Disturbed him and annoyed him.

'You didn't measure my finger,' she told him. 'Joseph suggested I should call in this morning.'

'Hold out your hand,' John said cutting her explanation short and picking up a scrap of wire. He twisted the wire expertly round her finger until Elizabeth judged it comfortable.

'And now will it come off over the knuckle?' he asked and eased it gently off with no trouble at all. Smiling briefly he gave a little nod of dismissal.

'Tis all taken care of,' he said and turned back to the bench.

Elizabeth, thus summarily dismissed, felt her face burn with sudden colour. Such insolence! Angry words rose to her lips but she forced them back. It really would not do to antagonize him. Perhaps he had intended no slight. Perhaps it was merely his manner. She found herself making excuses for him, unwilling to leave. He looked up, saw that she was still there, and his eyes showed her that he understood the reason. Mortified, Elizabeth said 'Do you show all your customers such disrespect?' She had intended it as a mild rebuke, but it sounded harsher and she noticed his mouth tighten. His blue eyes were suddenly much colder than she remembered.

'I did not intend you any disrespect,' he said. 'You must forgive me.'

She said unsteadily, miserably aware that she was making the situation worse. 'Mayhap I have offended you in some way?'

'I don't think so.'

'Then you dislike all women?'

'I am not aware of such a dislike.'

They eyed each other across the small room and Elizabeth knew instinctively that the next few seconds were crucial. Each recognized the other's pride. At last, she said, desperately, 'I have changed my mind about the stone, I'd like you to use the tourmaline.'

The words hung in the air, a peace offering. Slowly, his expression relaxed slightly. 'You are well advised,' he said.

She breathed more freely, and managed a faint smile. 'But I think we need not mention it to anyone else.'

'That might be wise.'

'And when will it be finished,' she asked.

'A matter of months,' he told her, 'Mark will most likely be despatched to Devon to deliver it.'

He smiled briefly, but there was some warmth in it. The correct thing for her to do now was to thank him, collect Della and leave. Instead she picked up from the bench the first tool that came to hand and examined it.

'What a strange little hammer,' she commented.

'Not a hammer,' he informed her, 'but a mallet. A rawhide mallet for stretching gold or silver.'

'And this?'

She picked another tool at random, anything to prolong the visit.

'That's a needle file,' he told her, 'and that's a scriber for drawing on metals.'

Gently, he took the instruments from her trembling fingers and returned them to the bench and held her hand in the palm of his own, studying the slender fingers and well manicured nails. Then he looked up.

'I was discourteous,' he admitted. 'I'm sorry.'

She nodded, unable to speak and he released her hand.

There was a sudden shrill scream from Della, followed by a rush of footsteps and a flurry of thumps and curses. Mark appeared in the doorway, a triumphant grin on his face, holding a dead rat by the tail.

'That makes thirty-one!' he told John, 'and your maid, ma'am, is near to swooning! One would think she had never seen a rat before!'

It was obviously time to go home.

That night, Elizabeth sat up in bed, her eyes suddenly open wide. The word Kendal rang in her ears as clearly as if someone had spoken it. 'John Kendal!' she whispered. 'The boy on the journey down. It is the same man. It must be!'

Della, asleep beside her, stirred and opened her eyes.

'What is it, ma'am?' she mumbled, hazy with sleep. 'Are you ailing?'

'No, Della,' said Elizabeth. 'I've never felt better! Go back to sleep.'

The girl turned over, closed her eyes and was soon asleep.

Elizabeth lay down but remained wide awake, a rapt expression on her face, her mind busy with this new discovery. Not until the early hours of the morning did she finally sleep.

CHAPTER SIX

A groan went up from the crowd as the first mastiff was hurled upwards with a shrill whine of fear. The small body reached twenty feet or more, before falling back upon the hard dry earth of the small arena. John watched the scene before him, but his mind and emotions were elsewhere. A cry went up – 'The neck is broke!' and the dog's owner ran forward.

As soon as it was evident that the dog was indeed dead, wagers were met and fresh ones exchanged in a discordant babble of voices. After the various transactions were over, the next man prepared to release his dog, a pale coloured long-haired mongrel. He held it by the ears as, barking furiously, it strained towards the black bull which stood at the full extent of the rope that tethered it. The bull's left foreleg was badly torn and a steady trickle of blood mingled with the sand.

A butcher beside John cupped his hands to his mouth and shouted, 'Let's have it, then!' and John glanced at him with distaste. The man was dirty, his cheeks were veined with scarlet, his breath reeked. The hands cupping the mouth were large and bore several fresh sores and half-healed scabs. Grinning at John, he said, 'That little tyke's a winner, a sworn winner. Clings closer than a leech he does. It's sensational to see. You just watch.'

John turned from him as a roar greeted the second dog's release. It ran forward and circled the bull who turned to keep sight of it. The dog crouched low as he moved nearer, out-manoeuvring the bull that strove to hook a horn under his belly for a toss.

'Hold him!' roared the crowd, as the dog leapt suddenly for the bull's muzzle; but the animal jerked his head and the dog merely tore out a piece of flesh. He sprang back as the bull's sheathed horn scraped the ground ineffectually and the dog's owner stepped forward to urge him on with shouts of encouragement.

John watched the two animals as they nervously circled each other, but in his mind's eye he saw Elizabeth. He saw the intense grey eyes and the long slim neck. He heard again the tone of her voice, the small nod of the head.

He drew a deep sigh and her name echoed again and again. Hellfire! he asked himself angrily. Why could he not rid himself of this image? It haunted him, waking or sleeping. He had grown irritable over the past week and was no longer able to concentrate on his work. He had not even started on the ring and Nathan Byrnes grew impatient. He had quarrelled briefly with Mark for the first time in their long friendship and although they were now on amicable terms again, the incident had troubled him more than he cared to admit.

Another shout from the crowd jerked his mind back to the present and he searched the crowd once more for a glimpse of Mark who had arranged to meet him. There was no sign of him, so he turned back to the baiting in time to see the dog hanging from the bull's neck, as the cumbersome beast threw himself from side to side in a vain attempt to dislodge him. Blood spattered the ground and ran into the dog's pale coat.

'What did I tell you?' cried the butcher triumphantly grinning to reveal a row of discoloured, broken teeth.

John closed his eyes but opened them immediately as Mark's voice said, 'Ah, they're parting them!'

'Oh, you're here then,' said John, a trifle ungraciously.

'In the flesh,' said Mark cheerily. 'So eat that, and tell me what I have missed.' He put a large pear into his friend's hand.

'I'm not hungry,' said John, but he took a bite nonetheless and wiped the juice from his chin with the back of his hand.

Mark eyed him severely as he bit off and spat out the stem from his own pear. 'You haven't been hungry for a week past! What ails you, John, as if I don't know!'

'Then if you know, I'll hold my peace,' said John, sourly, and finishing off the pear in several massive bites, he tossed the core over his head into the crowd.

The man on his left nudged him delightedly and pointed to the bull where the dog still hung tenaciously. 'Didn't I say twas a winner?' he demanded. 'Didn't I tell you. Ah, no!'

With a supreme effort, the bull flung the dog into the air but before the body could hit the ground, three or four men reached out with staves and poles and placing them one across the other, broke the dog's fall. As soon as he regained his footing, however, the dog was at the bull's throat once more and would not be dislodged. It finally needed two men to hold off the bull, while the dog's owner prised the dog's jaws apart with a stick and removed it, still snapping and struggling, amid cheers from the delighted crowd.

'I've seen enough,' said John, 'and smelt enough! This cup-shottern old fool beside me stinks of sour ale and Lord knows what else. The place sickens me today.'

Mark shrugged without answering and followed him up the steps and back into the street.

'Have you been home?' asked Mark.

John shook his head. 'I walked by the river.'

They turned their steps northward without further deliberation.

'Let's go back to my room for a game of dice,' said Mark. 'Tis my turn to relieve you of some more silver if my memory serves me aright. You had a run of luck Thursday last and emptied my purse.'

'Twas skill,' said John, 'not luck.'

'Is that so?' said Mark. 'I notice it is always poor luck when you lose!'

'You talk like a true friend!'

'None truer.'

Mark lodged above a saddler's not far from the Golden Plume. There he was well-fed and cared for by Mistress Hannow, an elderly but still cheerful widow. His room was small and lit by one small window. It was sparsely furnished with a pallet bed, a chest, a couple of stools and a shelf. A small trestle table held a bowl and water jug for washing purposes. The old wood floor was stained and spotted with candle grease, but a new orange stuck with cloves hung from a ribbon in the window. John seeing this last object, laughed.

'Not another pomander!' he teased. 'So the foolish maid still fancies your horrible self!'

'Aye, and will wed me if I don't watch out!'

'Ella wears her heart on her sleeve,' said John.

'And her thoughts are writ large in her eyes!' said Mark. 'You wouldn't care for a small round woman, would you? She has cold feet but a warm heart!'

'I wouldn't rob you,' said John laughingly.

'Tis true,' Mark said. 'You wouldn't, for I should only let her go for a large consideration. She can cook, so she swears, and makes a nifty pomander as you see.'

Thus restored to a moderate good humour, they settled down to a game of dice but after a few wins, John tossed the dice on to the chest.

'I'm sorry', he said, 'I've no mind for the game today, not even winning!' He pushed a hand through his hair distractedly and sighed.

Mark refilled his mug as well as John's and said, abruptly, 'So what will you do about the wench? Tis obvious she is on your mind.'

'I wish I knew,' said John. 'She has taken over my thoughts so that I cannot call my soul my own. I think of nothing else but despise myself for it and that's the truth.'

'But why despise yourself,' Mark protested. 'She is a desirable woman.'

'And betrothed to another!'

'Not so! The ring is a birthday gift, nothing more.'

'I shall forget her,' he said.

Mark laughed and deciding he had said enough on the subject, took himself downstairs to charm some bread and cheese out of Mistress Hannow for their supper.

'I shall forget her,' said John again. 'Elizabeth Heron is not the woman for me.'

Nathan Byrnes, coming downstairs into the shop next morning, was pleased to see that John was at work on the ring at last. The gold strip was gently hammered into a circle and a collar was made in which to seat the stone. The fluorite was seated and when John began to whistle, halfway through the afternoon, Mark knew that he was himself again.

A week later, Elizabeth sat at the trestle surrounded by the remains of her meal. She had eaten well, too well in fact, and her goblet stood half- full of beaujolais. She stared into the dying fire. Her back was straight and she held her head high. She had ridden home from London unusually silent and had thrown herself into her work, filling her days to the last minute and refusing to spare herself. She slept badly and looked tired. Now she lifted the goblet and drained it. The logs shifted suddenly in a shower of sparks and she jumped nervously. Specks of burnt wood ash floated above the fire and the dogs moved hurriedly back, looking at it reproachfully. She heard a rustle at the far end of the hall as Will Retter lifted the curtain.

'Please,' she told him, 'come and warm yourself. The night is chill.'

He crossed the room.

'Shall I mend your fire?' he asked and she nodded and watched as he raked the embers into a blaze and threw on two more logs. The dogs, after welcoming him, settled down again by the fire and closed their eyes.

'I would I were a dog,' he joked. ''Tis not such a bad life, coddled and fed and pride of place by the hearth!'

She smiled agreement and he noted the change in her, for this was their first meeting since her trip to London. He did not gossip with the servants and knew nothing of the state of mind of the mistress of Heron Manor. He stretched his hands out to the fire and wondered about her.

'Was it a good trip?' he asked.

'Good enough.'

'And how is the fair but sinful city?'

'It smells,' she said, 'and tis intolerably crowded. The streets are filthier than ever and the people boors.'

He laughed. 'So you were not impressed?'

She sighed and smiled. 'The river is as beautiful as ever,' she admitted. 'I cannot find fault with that. Will you take some wine? Martha can bring us another flagon.'

But Will shook his head.

'Some ale, then?'

He thanked her, and she crossed to the doorway and called for Martha to bring some. As she walked back to the fire, he had a chance to study her. She wore a green gown trimmed with white and her hair was enclosed in a white net. Her body was slim, virginal almost despite her years, and the beautiful hands were ringless. Why did she remain alone, he wondered. Why not put the man out of his misery?

Joseph Tucker was the ideal match and had been so for several years past. Small wonder that people gossiped about them. They invited rumour and encouraged speculation. He saw that her face was thinner and the light was gone from her eyes.

'The journey to London is always tiring,' he suggested and she looked at him sharply but made no answer. She needs another husband, he thought, and an armful of children. That way she would become a woman. This brave solitary life was no way for such a woman. He recalled that day on the moor when he had touched her. That day had changed his life and he was grateful for the respect in the men's eyes and deference in their voices. He was growing old and did not need a woman, but still he felt drawn to her by some deep magnetism. All his endeavours were for her alone.

'Is there much to discuss?' asked Elizabeth. 'I confess I am weary and out of humour.'

He shrugged. 'No more than usual,' he said. 'But we can leave some matters until you are more yourself.'

He produced a bundle of bills and papers and began to sort them into a semblance of order.

'What of the Cullworthy claim?' she asked. 'Do they go further with it?'

'I fear so,' he said. 'They insist they will bring it to court.'

'They have more money than sense, then.'

'Aye, they do. They say we take all their water for our leet, to the ruin of their crop and livestock.'

'And do we?'

'Aye, but tis legal. We are entitled to it. We do no wrong in the eyes of the law.'

'But will the court uphold us?'

'Tis to be hoped so for their sakes!' he said grimly. 'They will have me to reckon with else! What is a stannary court for if not to uphold its tinners?'

She laughed. 'I envy you your trusting nature,' she told him. 'I think we may do better out of court. Is there not a farm between us and the Cullworthy's? Could we not argue that we take but half the water and they the rest?'

'It won't stand up in court,' he said. 'The farm belongs to the Cullworthy's and the tenants will say that they too have no water.'

'Then let them sue!' cried Elizabeth, suddenly irritable. 'Twill cost them time and money and we may yet win the day . . . . And what news of the tinner's parliament?'

'On Crockern Tor as usual.'

Martha came in with a jug of ale and handed him a tankard from the shelf. He thanked her.

'I think that is all, Martha,' said Elizabeth. 'You needn't wait up.'

'Thank you, ma'am.'

She moved heavily across the room and the older dog followed her. Retter drank deeply and set down the tankard.

'These bills,' he said, 'they are mostly the chandlers for rope and the smithy for tools. Much of the wood we use is from our own trees.'

'We are fortunate in that.'

'Aye . . . and I have with me the plan I spoke of, to show where our various bounds lie . . . .'

From the corner of his eye he saw that she stifled a yawn and blinked tiredly. As he talked on, her gaze drifted constantly from the plans to the fire and it was obvious that her thoughts were miles away and not intent upon the problems of Heron mining. Abruptly he gathered up the papers, and she glanced at him in surprise.

'Is that all?' she asked.

He smiled. 'All that you can bear, I daresay,' he said. 'You are tired and should rest. Some of this will keep and I will deal with the rest.'

'Forgive me,' she said. 'I am poor company and you do not have time to waste. You are right. I *should* sleep. Maybe tonight.' When he had gone she buried her face in her hands. The firelight lit the bright auburn hair, so that it glimmered like gold beneath the delicate net. 'Merciful Heavens, what is become of me,' she whispered. 'My thoughts return to him whatever I pretend . . . A plague on the wretched man! I swear I will not dwell on him further . . . Not another thought shall find lodging in my mind!'

Impulsively, she stood up and ran from the room. She left the house by the back door and made her way to the orchard. The cool dark air clung damply to her face and

94

hands and she revelled in its cold touch, for her whole body burned with a confusion of emotions. Restlessly, she walked among the neatly pruned trees until at last the shadows began to soothe her troubled spirit. As she moved from tree to tree, her fingers caressed the rough bark with satisfaction and because of the strangeness of her mood, the moonlight overhead held no fears for her.

Heron Manor stood beside the River Dart, and from the orchard, steps led down to the water's edge. As a young bride, she had hidden herself away below the steps on more occasions than she cared to remember. Not to escape Daniel's temper, but more to escape his vigilance. To escape also the curious eyes of the servants who watched with unabashed interest as the young girl struggled to prove herself both mistress of the house and wife to the elderly master. She had sensed their unspoken pity and had suspected their concealed contempt.

She picked her way carefully down the worn steps and found herself on the low garden which in winter or high tide was often under water. Jacob had therefore done little with the area except to plant a few shrubs, which sprawled untidily for want of attention. Daffodils appeared in the spring and there were violets and primroses growing wild. But bramble and ivy held sway and threatened finally to obscure everything else.

Elizabeth looked round her curiously. It was many years since she had sought sanctuary in this place and she was dismayed to see how wild it had become. The old log was still there, she noted, but of the pillow, there was no sign. Probably rotted away, she thought. As she slowly sat down on the log, now thick with moss, she thought back to the day when she had stolen the pillow. . . .

Daniel had liked to write his letters in bed before going to sleep. He had a special pillow, blue damask with tassels at each end, with which he gave himself extra support for this purpose. When she was first married, Elizabeth longed for the sight of the blue pillow because it meant Daniel would be writing to his sister Ruth, and would not require her unwilling body that night! Only later, when she yearned for a child, did she grow to hate it. For then Daniel used his letter writing as a defence against her requests for love. She had taken the pillow one day and had hidden it under the old log in the lower garden. Daniel had blamed the servants but after an embarrassing scene in which they all denied knowledge of it, the matter had been forgotten. Sighing, Elizabeth walked to the water's edge and knelt down. She looked across to the far side and smiled at the memory of the young man, whom she had once surprised here, swimming naked. His name had long since escaped her memory, but she recalled again the large blue eyes in the baby face, and the shock of straw-coloured hair. His teeth were large and even, his mouth full – and gentle against her own. He had thought her a servant girl, for that morning she had run out in nothing but a shift and she had let him think so. Their meeting in the dawn had been unexpected and quite perfect. They had sat together on the river bank tossing pebbles into the water and he had waded out to gather for her a strand of the small white flowers that grew on the surface of the water, where it slowed into eddies around the rocks. Closing her eyes she could smell the faint perfume of almonds . . . .

Of course, they grew there still. He had wanted to make love to her and she had almost said 'yes', so desperately did she want a child and how was Daniel ever to know? But the dogs had been let out from the house and ran eagerly to seek their mistress, and the moment was lost. She had never seen him again.

The ground sloped down to the water in a confusion of grass and pebbles, and beyond them spiky bunches of water mint thrust up from the water. Leaning out, she picked a spray and held it to her nose, inhaling not only the sharp tangy smell of mint but the memory of the harvesting.

She had been to a party in the village to celebrate the end of the harvesting. Daniel had been invited also but had business to attend to. The fare was homely, bread, cheese, pickles, ale and fruit; but they had eaten long and drank heartily. They had danced until dark, weaving in and out in a long happy chain, tugging themselves and their fellow dancers under the arches, helplessly merry. Elizabeth had seen the looks exchanged as, one by one, the young couples made their excuses and slipped away. When she could bear it no longer, she too had fled home to Daniel, warm and hazy and had told him of the ache within her. Inspired by her eagerness, he had taken her to bed. But he had failed to reach her body and seeing the disappointment in her eyes had wept. Poor Daniel, she thought, but now for him it was all over. For him it was all peace.

Pulling off her flimsy shoes, she dropped them on to the grass and carefully lowered herself into the cold water. Her feet felt cautiously for the smooth rock which she recalled as somewhere nearby and, finding it, was able to stand comfortably upright, holding her skirts knee high to keep them from the water. She smiled in spite of herself, for it was here she had waded on the morning after her wedding. The little maid had brought her here, had first shown her the secret place. Funny little Nan, with her tight tangled curls and eager child-like face. If her mind was not whole, then her heart was. She had shown her young mistress a rare affection.

The wedding night had frightened and distressed Elizabeth, who had come to the marriage bed ill prepared for the sight of her husband's ageing flesh and strange demands. Nan had found her weeping and had comforted her. Had told her how acceptable it all was, had shown her the good side of Daniel's nature and had urged patience and understanding. Poor Nan had known nothing of love for herself, being slow-witted and an object of pity. But her reassuring presence had helped Elizabeth, and then a year later the girl was dead. Taken by a consumption and all for the best some had said, but not Elizabeth. Nan had shared with her the forgotten garden, her own secret escape. And now, it belonged to Elizabeth alone, as she stood in the darkly flowing water and felt the tugging against her legs like wraiths from the past appealing for recognition.

'You'd best come out of there.'

She turned startled to see a man at the bottom of the steps.

'Is that you, Will?' she asked.

'Aye. Now come away out.'

He came forward, picked up her shoes and helped her up the bank. She sat on the log, while he dried her feet as best he could with the hem of her shift. Her feet were swollen with the water and the shoes were suddenly too small.

'What are you doing here?' she asked, as he struggled with them.

'Keeping half an eye on you,' he said and, despairing of making the shoes fit, put them into her hand, lifted her in his arms and carried her up the steps. Her head lay against his shoulder and as they passed through the moonlit orchard, he felt the sudden warmth of her tears. She was a child again in her father's arms. He would comfort her, would set the world right for her.

They went into the house and still she remained close in his arms, safe and warm. He carried her up the stairs but then it was over.

Gently, he set her on her feet outside her chamber door. She didn't speak for the tears flowed still and her hair, escaping from its net, straggled over her shoulders. For a moment, they looked straight into each other's eyes as they had done so many years before. Then, Will nodded as though in confirmation.

'Aye,' he said. 'You'd best wed.' And he turned away without another word.

Elizabeth went into her room but did not close the door until his footsteps ceased to echo on the stairs.

CHAPTER SEVEN

It was nearly eleven o'clock and North Street was already crowded. Jacob, elbowing his way through the throng of people, was met with scowls for he was tall and would obscure the view of those behind him. But he finally wedged himself at the back of the crowd settled down to wait for the day's entertainment.

Jane Pryvett, notorious gossip and scandal monger, had at last been reported to the Portreeve and found guilty. The malicious gossip concerned the matrimonial plans of Elizabeth Heron and Joseph Tucker, and it was for this reason that Jacob had slipped away from his duties to observe her downfall at first hand. Martha and Della would have been conspicuous by their absence, whereas he might be hidden away in the garden and hopefully would not be missed.

A woman in front of Jacob glanced at him, then gave him a longer look.

'Aren't you from up there?' she demanded.

Jacob hesitated. He was a shy man and any attention frightened him.

'From Heron?' she said. 'Aren't you from Heron?'

He nodded warily, and she tutted sympathetically. 'You'll enjoy this then,' she said. 'Venomous little wench is Jane Pryvett and high time she was taught a lesson. I said to my husband, "Tis high time that Jane was taught to mind her words. Too free by far with that tongue." Why she put it round, a month or so back as our Ned had stole a horse! Stole a horse! Holy St Katherine, he could have hanged and him never been near the dratted animal!'

It was Jacob's turn to 'tut' sympathetically, but now there was a disturbance towards the pump and the crowd pressed back to allow the cart with its single occupant to enter. The crowd began to shout and jeer and the woman in front of Jacob, finding her view unsatisfactory squeezed on to the step beside him, so that he clung precariously to the door frame, silently cursing her.

'Oh, look at her!' she cried. 'Dressed up like a dog's dinner. You'd think she was here for a wedding, not a whipping! She's even got a ribbon in her hair, the vain hussy. No shame, some folks, and that's a fact.'

Jane Pryvett was indeed dressed in her finest gown and stood defiantly among her persecutors, hands on hips, her head thrown back. Even now she met taunt with taunt and cursed as fluently as a man.

'I may be here today,' she screamed, 'but tomorrow twill be you, you trollop, or you, you bandy bastard! Aye, and better deserved for I've spoke nothing but the bloody truth and that's why I'm here. Truth hurts, doesn't it! That's what you're afeared of, the whole lousy pack of you.'

Jacob watched in amazement, his quiet soul shattered by the woman's vehemence. Her dark eyes glistened angrily, with her dark hair, curling over her amply rounded shoulders — her large bosom, was enhanced by the low cut of her cheap and gaudy gown. Now a man drummed his fists on the side of the cart and tugged at her skirt.

'Now we shall hear you holler!' he told her. 'Now we shall hear you scream and not before time, you lying slut. Remember me as you name called last summer? Called me Tom o' Bedlam and the like. Told my wife I was crazed in the head!'

'You lying toad!' she cried and spat in his face.

'Liar is it now, you dirty queen! Then there's more toads for several heard you. Aye, I shall enjoy this morning's sport and the sooner they start the better.'

A roar of approval greeted this remark for Jane Pryvett was unpopular everywhere. A constable now climbed into the cart and selecting a rope from a pile in the corner, ordered her to take down the top of her gown.

'Take it down yourself if so be you want it down,' she spat

and a delighted howl went up from the crowd as he slapped her face with the back of his hand.

'Do as you're told, you cheap little trug,' he said, but she put her tongue out and received another blow which knocked her down. He then hauled her to her feet and told her once more to take down her bodice. To the accompaniment of cat calls and ribald comments she did so, blaspheming the while. As soon as she was naked to the waist her hands were tied and a second rope went round her waist.

'Who'll lead her then?' the constable asked and many hands went up.

He chose a loutish man who seized the rope end and Jane Pryvett climbed down from the cart. The crowd moved back hurriedly, for the constable's whip was waiting. Jacob was a sensitive soul and as the whip was raised he closed his eyes, but the woman's shriek and the spectators jubilation told him the first blow had been struck. He opened his eyes to see her led down the street, blood oozing from the first lash to stain the pale skin of her back. The whip fell again and she fell to cursing at the top of her voice. A crowd of boys, released from their lessons to watch the salutary scene, cavorted alongside adding their childish insults to the babble of voices.

The woman beside Jacob slipped down as the crowd surged forward.

'Aren't you coming then?' she asked. 'Don't you want to see it through? She'll faint, more than likely, before they reach the bull ring. The women always do.'

And she darted away and Jacob sighed heavily. The cheers of the crowd faded as the victim reached the street corner and was lost to view. He hesitated. His inclinations were to return home, but he had strict orders from Martha to see all there was to see so that she might enjoy the benefit of his account. He had best go to the bull ring and see the end of it.

North Street was now deserted and he made his way with

101

comparative ease, picking his way between the rubbish and chasing off a mongrel which sprang at him unprovoked from a doorway.

When he'd reached the entrance to the building he propped himself against the wall of a house and took a hunk of cheese from his pocket. Halfway through it, the sounds of the crowd reached him once more, and he stuffed the remainder into his mouth. The streets rapidly filled again and the air was once more rent by the gossip's curses. Jacob flinched as she drew level and his stomach turned at the sight of her, bloodied and torn. She was almost exhausted and only the cruel jerking of the rope kept her on her feet. The constable laid down his whip and she staggered and almost fell. She half turned toward Jacob and a glimmer of recognition burned suddenly in her pale face. The tousled hair dripped blood and it trickled between her breasts. Her face was beaded with sweat and she gasped for breath, one hand clasping her side.

'I know you,' she mouthed, and he recoiled in horror. 'I've seen you. You're from Heron. Come to see the fun, have you? Where's your fine mistress, then? Or was she too squeamish to watch me bleed. Well, you can tell her from me "my thanks!" Tell her about this!' And she turned abruptly, to reveal her hideous back.

'I'm sorry,' Jacob mumbled, but his words seemed only to incense her further.

'A pox on your fine lady of Heron, — and a pox on your Joseph Tucker. May they burn in Hell. May fire . . . ' but before she could say more the ordeal proved too much and she sank to her knees in a dead faint. Water was thrown over her and, her punishment now at an end, a friend rallied round her. Jacob took a last glimpse at her pathetic body being carried away, feet trailing carelessly over the cobbles.

Martha wiped the perspiration from her forehead with the

corner of her apron. Stooping, she hoisted the basket of washing on to her left hip and settled it there. She went out into the yard where two of the girls sat in the sunshine, heads close together, exchanging confidences. Theoretically both were busy, Joan scraping carrots, while Bess polished the salt cellar. Martha halted and glanced down at them.

'Are you two working or prattling?' she asked.

They appeared suddenly bereft of speech and stared up at her guiltily.

'Well?' she demanded. 'Cat got your tongue or something?'

The older girl held up a half-scraped carrot as proof of industry and immediately the other held up the salt cellar.

'Hmm,' grunted Martha. She glanced at the latter and then into the pan which contained the carrots already prepared. 'I shall expect to see a sight more carrots done by the time I get back,' she said, 'and don't make that salt cellar your life's work, Bess! There's a coffer by the mistress's bed. You can clean that while you're in the mood, and the ink-well in the master's study.'

The girls exchanged looks which Martha interpreted correctly. It was three years since Daniel had died and still no master.

'Is the milk skimmed?' Martha asked.

'Aye.'

'And the cheeses turned?'

They nodded.

'Then you come with me, Bess,' said Martha. She switched the basket on to her right hip and crossed the yard, followed obediently by the younger of the girls. They went straight through the kitchen garden, ignoring Jacob who crouched lovingly over some seedlings, and into the orchard. This area of a little under half an acre had received from Jacob the same devotion as the rest of the gardens. Redcurrant bushes stood in rows, picked clean; but there were still plenty of fat gooseberries ripening to a dull red. The strawberries, their leaves turned red and gold, were long since over; the raspberries, too. Now only the trees had anything to offer. Crab apples and quince trees were heavy with fruit and there was a new apple tree brought from Buckfast Abbey, and greatly prized.

The sun, almost overhead, cast circles of shade and Martha chose the nearest one and set down her basket. Taking out the first sheet she shook it vigorously so that it slapped against itself. 'Take an end,' she snapped and obediently Bess caught hold of two of the corners. They pulled the sheet diagonally in one direction and then the other to make it a good square and reduce the creases. Then Bess carried it to a patch of sunlit grass and spread it out to dry. When all the sheets were laid out on the grass, Martha remained behind to deal with the pillowslips, while Bess was sent back to her silver. The girl received no word of thanks, but considered the absence of criticism to be praise enough. When Martha had emptied the basket, she looked round her with satisfaction. It pleased her to see the orchard decorated with the bright white squares. She nodded approvingly at the pillowslips hung over the currant bushes and picked up the basket once more.

Returning to Jacob, she upturned the basket and sat down on it, making herself as comfortable as she could.

'Hot enough for you?' Jacob asked without looking up.

'Too hot by far! And what are you about, then?'

'Pricking out beetroots,' he told her as his long sensitive fingers continued the task, passing the well sieved soil gently around each seedling.

'We could do with some rain,' he said.

'Aye. T'would cool the air,' said Martha, 'so clammy it is, of nights, and can I sleep? I cannot . . . And look at me now! Sweating like a pig.'

She mopped her face again. Jacob worked on steadily

104

until Martha grew tired of waiting for the expected snippet of news.

'Well?' she said. 'So did you see her?'

'Who's that then?' he asked.

'Jane Pryvett, of course!' she growled.

'I did.'

'And?'

He shrugged and pressed in the last seedling. Then he filled the old leather bucket with water, dipped a cloth into it and trickled a generous measure over each plant. Martha bit back the caustic comment which rose to her lips. Antagonizing Jacob would only further delay the account. At last he dropped the cloth into the bucket and lowered himself on to the dry earth beside her.

'So she *was* presented to the court?' she said.

'Aye. By old Tucker.'

Martha's eyes gleamed with righteous satisfaction.

'So!' she said. 'Jane Pryvett has taken a tumble! And tis no more than she deserves. A right cruel tongue, that one, and should have been presented long since! Everyone do say so, you know. Everyone . . . Did she deny it?'

'No. She repeated it at the top of her voice, cool as silk!'

'She never did!'

He nodded. Taking up a small twig he began to push holes in the earth.

'What did she say, then?' asked Martha. 'Tell it me from the beginning.'

Jacob launched reluctantly into a full account of the morning's event, and she listened avidly, nodding approval from time to time. When he had finished she sighed.

'She got no more than was due to her,' she said. 'Though when all's said and done I do wonder what keeps the mistress from naming the day. Joseph Tucker would make her a fine husband, — and she's not getting any younger and no family! I'd jump at the chance of such a man!' She sighed again, 'I reckon that Della knows more'n she pretends. Acting all knowing. I could box her ears.'

Jacob looked up at the sun and then at Martha. 'How come you're not baking?' he asked.

Martha snorted. 'Turned out of me own kitchen, that's why,' she told him. 'There's a visitor coming and my cooking's seemingly not . . . .' 'A visitor?'

'But don't ask me who 'cos I'm not in on the secret. And her ladyship must needs prepare the food herself.'

'In all this heat? What's come over her?'

'I ask myself that,' said Martha darkly, 'but I don't answer meself because I don't know. Leche Lombard she's making.'

'Lesh what?'

'Lombard,' she snorted. 'Some fancy foreign sausage. You should see what it's got in it! Port, dates, raisins and such like. Looks more like a cake, I told her, but she made out she didn't hear me . . . And it's "Fetch me some red wine, Martha", and "Where's the saffron, Martha," Had me buzzing about like a demented blue-bottle, and you can take that smirk off your face!'

'Funny sounding sausage,' he said hastily.

'That's what I thought. Let's hope he's got a strong stomach, whoever he is.'

'Oh, tis a "he", then.'

'Seemingly.'

'Tucker, most like,' he said.

'Mebbe. But why all the fuss . . . unless.'

They looked at each other. 'A special dinner?' he suggested grinning.

Martha considered the possibility and smiled also.

'A celebration!' she said. 'Mebbe that's it! Mebbe she's going to give him her answer at last. I wonder . . . Oh, I do hope so.'

Jacob nodded. 'I reckon that's about it,' he said.

Martha picked up her basket. 'D'you want more ale?' she

asked. 'Give me the flagon and I'll send Bess to fill it for you.'

And taking it, she returned to the house, greatly comforted.

The candlelight flickered as the curtain was lifted. Bess brought in the marchpane and set it down with a flourish and a giggle in the middle of the table. Elizabeth glanced across at Joseph, but if he noted the lover's knot which decorated it he gave no sign.'

'Thank you, Bess,' she said. 'Now you may go to bed. It grows late and you must be up early tomorrow.'

The girl nodded, bobbed her head and withdrew with another giggle.

'What ails her?' Joseph asked accepting a slice of the rich dessert which Elizabeth cut for him.

She laughed and the candlelight sparkled in her large grey eyes. Joseph looked at her admiringly – she couldn't look more beautiful than she did tonight in her new gown – or more desirable. In the three years since Daniel's death he had watched her change from a bold, inexperienced but determined girl, into a mature, confident woman. The determination was still there but it was more controlled, and softened by a new diplomacy. He looked again at the oval face, the full mouth, wide eyes, under the dark fringed lashes, cheeks flushed a delicate pink and saw the intelligence behind the beauty. He felt the vitality behind the graceful movement as she leaned towards him. A single tendril of hair had escaped from the gauze head-dress and he reached across the table and coaxed it back, his fingers stroking the smooth forehead as he did so. She smiled her thanks.

'Your thoughts are far away,' she teased. 'I asked if you enjoyed the marchpane and you do not answer. Poor Martha made it specially when she knew you were coming.'

'It's very good,' he said. 'She spoils me. I have enjoyed the whole meal, and have eaten too well! But my compliments to the cook.'

'Thank you, kind sir,' she said laughing off. 'The lombard sausage was my own creation. I am not without talent.'

'No sane man would suggest you were!' he said.

No one indeed! Elizabeth Heron had proved herself a shrewd and capable business woman with an astuteness secretly envied by many men. In the past three years her dream had become a reality. He marvelled daily at the fixity of purpose which had carried her inexorably towards her goal, and the resilience with which she had faced various problems and disappointments. She had allowed nothing and nobody to stand in her way.

Unerringly, she had chosen as manager the one man who would guarantee the success of her schemes. Once he had agreed terms, the project had gathered such momentum that all who watched, wondered. Between them, she and Retter had planned a skilful operation. As certain lands fell due for renewal, they had offered a share in the company or financial help and expert advice. Gradually, the area under the Heron control had grown and with it the number of men willing to work with them. Plans were drawn up and an overall picture prepared. Discussions were held and the tinners knowledge shared. Timber was purchased, simple machinery designed and built for digging and tunnelling. An attempt was made to ensure the safety of the men and reduce the number of accidents; for there were many. Underground working was a new art and not acquired without mistakes. Elizabeth and Retter made several trips to Cornwall and Godolphin's name became a household word. Men other than tinners were needed, and there was keen competition among carpenters and smiths to take up employment with the Herons, for Elizabeth had a reputation for fairness.

Will Retter, too, had changed, from a man without hope

to the strong, competent man he had once been and he had regained the respect of the community, though some resented or mistrusted the influence he had over Elizabeth Heron. It was true she relied on him to a very large extent, but the partnership was not always a smooth one and there had been several fierce clashes between the two; some resolved to her satisfaction, some to his. It was a working partnership, no one would deny that. There was a bond between them but an intangible one. Joseph accepted it at face value.

Will Retter had never re-married. He owed his resurrection to Elizabeth Heron. Taciturn, ruthless but withdrawn as ever, he now had a purpose in life. That purpose was the furtherance of Elizabeth's dream and he was content to devote his life to it.

'Your new gown becomes you,' Joseph remarked.

'You are very kind.'

'And you are very desirable,' he said. 'Had I not eaten so well I would hurl myself at your feet.'

'But you won't?'

'In faith, I cannot move. No, no!' He held up a protesting hand as she indicated the marchpane. 'No more, I beg you. But please give Martha my thanks.'

She looked across at the man opposite her, the man who might one day be her husband. He had drunk a little too well and his face was flushed, but there was love and sincerity in the brown eyes. He raised his brows quizzically and the familiar gesture touched her heart.

'Three years,' she mused. 'It is a long time.'

'Is it only three?' He said. 'It seems a lifetime!'

'We're celebrating,' she pointed out. 'Did you know that?'

'I wondered,' he said. 'And may I ask what we are celebrating? Is it the realization of your dream?'

She nodded and raised a glass. He raised his also and though his smile was slow and steady, his mind raced along its inevitable track. When should he speak to her of love?

When broach the subject dearest to his heart. He had waited patiently these past three years, had allowed her time for her ambition. Now apparently it was achieved.

'So you have doubled the Heron fortunes!' he teased lightly.

Elizabeth shook her head. 'Not quite,' she admitted, 'but I am well satisfied with the results of my striving. It hasn't been easy.'

'I've watched with the greatest admiration' he told her. And with growing affection, he thought. His love for her had grown daily until she dominated his thoughts and all his future plans included her. Now perhaps, was the time to speak what was in his heart.

'Retter is a good man,' she said, 'I have been fortunate.'

Idly, she swirled the glass and the wine spun hypnotically.

'Elizabeth,' he began and was annoyed to hear the tension in his voice.

She glanced up and there was a hint of wariness in her expression.

'You know, I'm certain, that my feelings towards you are more than one of friendship,' he said, and cursed silently at the coldness of the words. They were not what he had intended.

'I look upon you as a very dear friend,' she said gently. 'In fact, my dearest friend.'

'I'm glad of it.'

He saw that she lowered her eyes suddenly and he was uneasy. Perhaps now was not the time. Was she so thrilled by the realization of her dream that her mind was too full for anything further? Should he delay again or no?

'I have something to say,' he blurted out suddenly, 'which I hope . . . ' He stopped again. She had not raised her eyes. To see the expression in them would be to know all. If only she would look at him.

'Joseph,' she said, 'I am still unsure about – about the future. Still undecided about many things.'

She looked up and his spirits sank. The reserve he dreaded to see was in them.

'I must speak, though,' he rushed on, aware that however hopeless his chances he must know his fate. He could not go on longer in this way. Wanting her as his wife. Longing to care for her, to save her from any harm the world might hold in store for her.

'Please Joseph,' she begged. 'I know what you want to ask of me and I am not ready with an answer. You have waited a long time and I admit freely that I expected to accept the offer you would make me.'

A sudden hope lifted him, but her next words alienated him once more.

'I do not know my own mind yet, Joseph,' she told him. 'I cannot understand the behaviour of my heart. It beats a rhythm, but I cannot dance to its tune. I'm so fond of you. You are a fine man and many women would envy me my place in your affections. Why do I hesitate? I don't know. I only know I cannot wed unless it be whole-hearted. You deserve that of a wife. Until I can be whole-hearted I must say "No" to any offer of love and marriage. From you or any man.'

He shook his head, unable to put his disappointment into words. Then he looked at her directly.

'Is there anyone else?' he asked. 'Forgive me, but I must know.'

Elizabeth sighed and he fancied her eyes were haunted momentarily.

'There was someone, many years ago,' she whispered. 'But now? No, I fear not.' Tears filled her eyes but she blinked them back. 'I don't want to live alone, Joseph, but it must be the right man. Whoever he is.'

His heart ached for her and for himself, also. She rose suddenly and held out her hands.

'Will you forgive me if I retire early,' she said. 'I am suddenly poor company yet would not be discourteous.'

'I understand,' he said. 'I'll take my leave of you until tomorrow. But Elizabeth, I beg you give me some hope. Tell me I may speak to you again on the matter.'

'You may, Joseph,' she said. 'But I may give you the same answer.'

'I'll take my chance on it,' he said, as lightly as he could manage and kissing her hand, let himself out into a night grown unexpectedly chill.

A few days later the sudden clatter of hoofbeats past the window late one evening surprised Elizabeth. She waited for Bess to answer the summons but then, remembered the girl had been sent to bed early. Already her visitor was hammering on the door for admittance.

'I'm coming!' she cried. 'Spare the door, for pity's sake. It has done you no harm!'

On reaching it, she lifted the heavy bar and allowed the door to slowly swing open. The next instant, her hand flew to her throat, a small shocked cry escaping her lips. 'Sweet Mother of god!' she whispered as the colour drained from her face and her legs grew weak under her.

'What sort of welcome is this?' John asked, his voice level, the expression on his face revealing nothing of the emotions that churned within him at the sight of her. He made no move to enter but stood watching her, as a succession of expressions flickered across her face. Elizabeth's senses reeled at the sight of him. The cold pale blue eyes, the tight set of his jaw and the mouth characteristically drawn down at the corners. She thought his face thinner, the high gaunt cheek-bones more noticeable.

'I did not expect you,' she faltered.

'Yet here I am,' he said. 'And likely to stand here all night if you will not ask me in!'

'Please forgive me,' she said. 'I forget my manners.'

She held the door wide, and he walked past her into the house.

'You will want refreshment,' she said. 'I will ask Martha to bring you food and wine.'

'No matter. I'm lodged at the inn,' he said. 'But let me show you the reason for my journey.'

He took a ring from the purse at his belt and held it out for her inspection.

'May I?' she asked and nodding, he dropped it into her outstretched hand. It lay there, perfect in every detail. The green stone cool and crisp, the gold band gleaming warmly.

'It's beautiful,' she whispered and seeing that her hand trembled took it up hastily and tried to slide it on to her finger. To her dismay it would not slide over the knuckle.

'Oh dear,' she said. 'How odd.'

'That is not the finger it was made for,' he told her and she flushed slightly at the amusement in his voice. 'Allow me to help you.'

He took her warm hand in his cold one, and eased the ring on to another finger. Wonderingly, she held out her hand to admire it.

'My deepest thanks,' she said and then, guiltily, 'but shouldn't it go to Joseph Tucker?'

John shook his head. 'His instructions were that it come direct to Heron.'

'Then I must thank him formally tomorrow.'

He nodded calmly, disguising the confusion he felt now that he saw her again. Mark should have brought the ring, he would be spared more easily, but John had asked if he might bring it personally. Something about the woman disturbed and puzzled him, as though a bond existed between them.

'We met once,' she said suddenly, afraid that he would leave, his mission accomplished. 'Not in London, I mean, but earlier. You won't remember.'

'I can't believe I would forget such a meeting,' he said.

'It was a long time ago on our ride. I was . . . . '

'Wait!' he held up his hand. 'You were with your uncle on your way to – why, of course! Heron! The name had a familiar sound and yet I could not place it.'

'I was on my way to be married.'

'And I to be apprenticed!'

She waited. Would he also remember their kiss? He smiled at her. 'It was a long time ago,' she said.

He nodded agreement. 'But in truth I remember the occasion, and the funny scrawny little girl.'

'Funny! Scrawny!' she protested laughing.

He laughed also. 'I was going to say that I remembered the girl but had not recognized the woman.'

The pause lengthened between them. Each had thoughts they longed to express but feared to do so. They were both aware that a parting now would be forever, for there was no reason on earth for them to meet again.

'Strange that Fate should throw us together again,' he said, casually.

'But pleasant,' she said.

'Aye.'

Another silence. Elizabeth's heart began to hammer beneath her ribs and she prayed he would not notice her distress. She searched desperately for some excuse to detain him. Now that she had seen him again the fierce attraction was renewed, even strengthened.

'So now you are a widow,' he said.

Elizabeth nodded. 'And you? Did you marry?'

She waited breathlessly for his answer.

'My wife died,' he said simply.

'I'm sorry.'

They exchanged a long look but neither spoke. Then John said, 'I must be on my way.'

'Do you start back for London tomorrow?'

'Aye.'

They turned towards the door.

'And what do you think of Devon?' she asked desperately. 'Are you impressed?'

He laughed. 'Well enough,' he said, 'but I have found nowhere to equal Yorkshire.'

'Dartmoor is golden in October,' she informed him. 'And the red cliffs at Plymouth, so bold and magestic.'

'You will never convert me,' he laughed.

Outside his horse waited impatiently. He swung himself up into the saddle and Elizabeth stared up at the lithe figure and into the firm strong face.

He looked down into her wide grey eyes. 'God be with you' he said and turned his horse abruptly.

'Don't go,' whispered Elizabeth in spite of herself. 'Please . . . Don't go.'

With a clatter of hooves John reined in, but did not turn to look at her.

'Don't go,' she whispered again and there was an agony of longing in her voice that pierced his soul.

Still he hesitated, knowing full well that if he stayed it would be forever. It would be the end of his ambitions, the end of his return home. He would be exiled forever in a 'foreign land'. If he looked on her again, he was lost. He spurred his horse angrily and it leapt forward. But at Elizabeth's strangled cry he reined in once more. Turning his horse he slid suddenly from the saddle and Elizabeth ran into his arms. He covered her face and hair with kisses and uttered the bitter sweet words of love for which she had always longed, but never expected to hear from him. Unable, indeed unwilling to resist, she gave herself up completely to the passion of his embrace, glorying in the feel of his body hard against her own. He pulled off her head-dress and snatched greedily at her hair as it fell loose around her shoulders. He held her so closely she was almost unable to breathe and Elizabeth, the cool competent mistress of Heron Manor was drowned in an overwhelming passion that she had never before known. Every nerve in

115

her body was aware of his nearness and tingled with a strange chemistry that blended with his and fused them into one being. Suddenly there was nothing else in the world for her but the sound of his breathing and her own heart-beat.

'John . . . John,' she whispered. 'Oh my love, I wanted you so. I knew how it would be like this. The way it is . . . kiss me again. Hold me . . . Oh my dear heart. I can scarcely breathe. My joy. Such joy. It fills me, chokes me . . .'

And she clung to him passionately, terrified to release him, unable to draw back from his embrace, yet crushed by the strength of the arms which held her to him. Time ceased to exist. She had no idea how long they stood there, but at last she let her arms fall to her sides and shook her head wonderingly to stay his kisses.

'What are we doing?' she whispered. 'Are we bewitched?'

He made no answer and she looked at the man whose image had haunted her day and night since her return from London.

'You are thinner,' she said, placing a hand on the side of his face. 'But you are here, and I am content.'

He released her and held her at arm's length and the blue eyes were no longer cold but burning with emotion and desire. The cool night air did little to quell the fever in their bodies.

Abruptly his expression changed.

'I shall wed you,' he said. 'There is nought else for it.'

'You are asking me to wed you?'

'No,' he said. 'I am telling you. It must be so.'

She nodded slowly, 'Aye, I believe it must.'

They stared at each other soberly until John gave a sudden shout of joy and swung her off the ground, so that the skirt of her gown floated behind her and she complained that she grew dizzy. He put her back on her feet and held her gently, close against his heart and stroked her hair. She gave herself up to the rhythm of his breathing as his chest rose and fell and she wanted the moment to last forever.

When his horse had been led away by a sleepy Eric, Elizabeth led the way back into the house and rang for Martha. The old woman looked curiously at the stranger and at her mistress's radiant face. Elizabeth smiled brilliantly. 'We have news for you, Martha and tis good news. We shall need a flagon of wine and you shall help us celebrate.'

'News?' echoed Martha and she looked at John.

'We are to be wed,' he told her simply.

'Wed!' gasped Martha.

'Aye,' he said. 'How are you with pastry, Martha?'

She opened her mouth to reply but he gave her no time. 'We shall call the banns and there will be a feast to prepare.'

'Martha is a first-rate cook,' said Elizabeth.

'Then I'm in luck!' cried John. 'I'm very partial to jugged hare and venison pastry and the children like gingerbread and . . . .'

'The children?' gasped Martha.

Elizabeth stared at him and a small panic seized her. Overnight her life was changing dramatically and she prayed she was ready for it.

'Aye, children,' laughed John a little later, as he poured the wine. 'They will return with me, and Dorothy, my sister-in-law will come with us for a few weeks, to help them settle.'

He glanced at Elizabeth for her approval and she nodded. She marvelled at his confidence.

'They will liven up the place,' he said. 'A girl and three boys, Martha. What do you say to that, eh?'

While Martha expressed her delight, Elizabeth looked at John with a mixture of joy and grudging respect. He was showing himself master of the situation. She, Elizabeth, was playing a supporting role. It was a new sensation and she savoured it curiously, analysing her reaction to it. In one way she almost resented the ease with which he had made himself at home. In another, she was thankful that he had taken the initiative. Yet it was *her* house. Martha was *her* servant . . . . No, not any more. They would all be his. Even in this moment of rejoicing she felt a sense of loss, a small pricking of regret.

But they were raising their goblets in a toast. 'To the future Elizabeth Kendal!' said John and the eyes that met hers held a hint of triumph.

'Aye, and the new master!' cried Martha downing her wine in one gulp and already longing for morning so that she could recount the night's events.

Elizabeth sipped her wine and her eyes never left John's face.

'This is a hard man who will not be dominated,' she told herself 'and I love him.' His goblet touched hers and the nearness of his body quickened her own.

'But I am strong too,' she pleaded with him wordlessly. 'And I must stay true to myself!'

The following day, John rode back to London to wind up his affairs. He would return with his four children, Dorothy, and her daughter. Meanwhile, the household plunged into a frenzy of preparation. The banns were arranged and most of the Heron household appeared in church the following Sunday to hear them read for the first time. A buzz of surprise and excitement rose from the rest of the congregation, who had been anticipating a wedding but expected to hear Joseph Tucker named, instead of a stranger from London. Joseph had not been to Heron and though Elizabeth hoped that they could eventually continue as friends, she respected his present need for privacy.

She turned her thoughts to the hundred-and-one matters requiring her attention. Father Marryat was consulted, bridesmaids and brideknights were chosen, four of each. Mark Lessor, as John's closest friend, was to be chief brideknight. Since Elizabeth had no sisters of her own,

Dorothy was invited to fill the office of chief bridesmaid. Little Catherine Kendal would be another. Della, to her immense satisfaction, would be a third and Blanche Tucker the fourth. The knights would be Joseph Tucker's son and Andrew would attend as a guest. The sub-prior of Buckfast Abbey had also agreed to attend. Nathan Byrnes was asked if he would carry the bride cup and, accepting with delight, wrote that he 'deemed it an honour and a privilege to do so!' His wife would not be able to travel down as her health had deteriorated, but she 'sent her love and the blessing of Sweet Mary to the happy couple'. Accommodation was the next problem, but eventually solved. Close friends would stay at Heron. John and Mark would lodge overnight in Harben Priory and the rest must fend for themselves in the various inns and taverns to be found in the town.

Martha pored over a succession of household rolls in an attempt to discover the finest recipes. She intended the wedding feast should be the grandest that Ashburton had ever seen and her temper grew shorter as the great day drew nearer. Bess, Sue and Della kept a respectful distance from her meaty right hand, as the occasional clouting of an ear seemed to afford her some relief.

Elizabeth and Della rode into Exeter to purchase new clothes for the wedding. Elizabeth sought out a silk mercer and Della went in search of the pedlar; pushing her way through the crowds until her sharp ears caught a line of the familiar jingle:

> Will you buy any tape,
> Or a lace for your cape,
> My dainty duck, my dear – a
> Any silk, any thread.
> Any toys for your head.
> Of the newest and finest wear – a –

The pedlar's face lit up at the sight of a customer and he

jumped down from his box and delved into his pack, determined that she should not leave empty-handed.

'What is to be, dear heart?' he flattered. 'A mirror all the way from Venice or a packet of pins? Or a silver thimble? Oh, too big for your dainty finger? Then here's a brooch, solid gold unless I'm a monkey on a stick which I ain't! Or a lace cap?' Della told him of the approaching wedding which pleased him immensely and he pulled out all his best finery for her inspection.

She indulged herself and bought a necklace of amber beads and the pedlar, well satisfied, gave her a large wink and threw in a yard of cheap lace which made her the happiest girl in town!

Gifts began to arrive from those friends and relations unable to attend the wedding. A pair of silver candlesticks from John's parents, a dozen spoons, a small carved chest and a bale of grey satin. There were five bushels of wheat and six hens! A copper warming pan with a carved handle, a pair of pillows edged with hand-made lace and a small barrel of gascon wine. Elizabeth was happy as she had every right to be. She was still young, still beautiful and was soon to marry a man she adored and time was running out. The day dawned at last with bright sunshine and only a scattering of clouds.

The woman in the tree belched softly and giggled. She peered through the boughs with eyes that refused to focus properly, shook her head and took another drink from the leather bottle in her lap. Her body fitted comfortably into the forked trunk and her bare legs swung carelessly, toes brushing the tips of the tall grass that grew unchecked in the neglected corner of the churchyard. From the tree she had a perfect view of the south door outside which the wedding would be conducted, a fact well known to the local children. She had wrested her vantage point from two of them by the strength of her arm and the sharpness of her tongue. Now she sat firmly ensconced and noted the arrival of the first wedding guests.

'Ah, there's the young Tucker, treacherous whelp! What cares he if his father's jilted, eh? What cares he if the tongues arc wagging? Not a groat, I'll wager, so long as he can dress up fit for a king! I'd give him brideknight if he was son to me!'

She shook the leatherjack, listening with her head on one side and, reassured to learn it was still half-full, took another gulp.

'And the sub-prior of Buckfast, no less!' she went on. 'We are honoured, your Holiness, and no mistake. But only a *sub*-Prior? The Prior's busy elsewhere, no doubt, and sends his kind regrets. Pah!'

She spat contemptuously and slapped at a fly on her leg, splashing a few drops of ale as she did so. Cursing roundly, she brushed the drops from the coarse wool of her kirtle and finally glanced up again in time to see the arrival of Nathan Byrnes.

'Now who's that tubby old fellow,' she mused. 'Carrying the bride cup and grinning all over his stupid face. Grin while you may, old man, for I'll wipe the smile from your face before I'm done with you. Ah, they've a fine shock coming. A fine shock . . . whip Jane Pryvett would they and call me a liar! They don't miscall me and get away with it. I don't take kindly to their sort and that's a fact. Just look at 'em, prancing and preening! Oh, Lord, what a sight! Look at that Della. A primped up servant, and looks it. Every inch of her, ribbons in her hair and I don't know what else! God's eyes! What a rabble. There's none of 'em worth a farthing!'

Scowling, she tilted the ale and drank deeply. For all her brave words she felt in need of the false courage that alcohol gave her. For weeks she had waited for this moment, plotting and planning and now nothing was going to rob her of her revenge.

It was becoming difficult for her to see with so many

121

people flocking into the churchyard. Half the population of Ashburton seemed to have turned out to watch the wedding, including a number of beggars and cripples who now mingled with the crowds, but who would gather at the north porch when the ceremony ended, to crave alms.

Now John arrived, resplendent in russet velvet, a favour of rose and blue ribbons in his hat. With him were the bridesmaids in rose pink gowns and ribbons to match. Some carrying posies of summer flowers, the others bride-cakes for the wine. After a slight delay, Elizabeth arrived with Mark Lessor and the rest of the brideknights, all wearing rose and blue ribbons fastened on their sleeves with sprigs of rosemary. Finally Nathan Byrnes took his place carrying the be-ribboned bride cup of sweet wine.

Jane Pryvett drained the last of the ale and dropped the empty leatherjack into the nettles. She wiped the back of her hand over her mouth and scrambled clumsily down from her perch. Her expression was grim.

'Now Mistress Elizabeth,' she muttered threateningly. 'We'll see if you remember me!' And she moved forward to mingle with the crowd and bide her time. As soon as all the guests were present, the priest appeared and greeted them with a cheerful smile. The wedding contract was read and returned. It was then John's turn to repeat his vows which he did in a low voice, his eyes fixed on Elizabeth's face. The wedding ring was hallowed and sprinkled with holy water while the prayer was said: *'Then maker and conserver of mankind, giver of spiritual grace, and granter of eternal Salvation, send thy blessing upon this ring that she which shall wear it may be crowned with the virtue of heavenly defence, and that it may profit her to eternal Salvation through our Lord.'*

John placed the ring on Elizabeth's finger. As he did so he felt the trembling of her hand and pressed her fingers with his own. Her eyes met his as he made his promise: *'With this ring I thee wed, and with gold and silver I thee serve, with my body I thee worship and with all my wordly chattels I thee honour....*'

His voice was low for her ears alone, but when Elizabeth spoke her nervousness vanished and she spoke clearly, in clear tones so that all might hear: '*I, Elizabeth Heron, take thee, John Kendal, to my wedded husband, to have and to hold, for fairer for fouler, for better for worse, for richer for poorer, in sickness and in health to be meek and obedient til death us do part if Holy Church it will order and thereto I plight my troth.*'

The priest was about to declare them man and wife when there was a commotion in the crowd and all heads turned as Jane Pryvett's voice rang out.

'So I was gossiping, was I? Making mischief, they said. But I were right, seemingly.' With a triumphant laugh, she began to push through the startled crowd. Hands reached out to restrain her, but she fought them off fiercely and struggled nearer to the wedding group.

'What 'ave you to say now, then, you as had me whipped til me back was bloody and every word I uttered as true as God's name!'

The crowd murmured but there was no denying the woman spoke the truth. She had been falsely punished. Elizabeth Heron had not wed Joseph Tucker and here was justification of the wretched woman's prophesy! Elizabeth paled and John glanced to her for enlightenment but before she could speak, the woman had reached them and stood hands on hips, glaring defiance. She pointed an accusing finger at John.

'You ain't Joseph Tucker,' she said, and her words slurred. 'I've heard about you, you're from London. Whipped I was from the pump to the bull ring.' She stopped abruptly as Will Retter appeared beside her and clamped a large hand over her mouth.

'And whipped you will be again if I have my way!' he said, and lifting her up he threw her over his shoulder, despite her beating fists, and kicking legs.

'A curse on the whole bloody pack of you!' she screamed. 'And a curse on Heron. May God punish you and yours. Whipped I was and bled for you . . .'

'Hold your tongue!' cried Retter, 'or you'll feel my hand across that loud mouth of yours.'

Elizabeth ran after him.

'Don't hurt her, Will,' she begged. 'The wretched woman speaks the truth.'

He nodded briefly.

The crowd parted to let him pass and he carried her to the far side of the churchyard and dumped her unceremoniously against the church wall. He held a massive fist in front of her face and she was silent at last. Elizabeth, trembling, resumed her place. Visibly shaken by this interruption, the priest proceeded, hurriedly declaring John and Elizabeth man and wife, he led the wedding party into the church to celebrate High Mass.

Then, it was time to hallow the wine cup and they all moved into the Lady Chapel, where the bride-cakes were broken and eaten after first dipping them into the wine. The people outside now grew impatient and crowded into the room to add their good wishes, and the ugly incident outside was not mentioned again.

'Make way for the bride and groom!' cried Mark and somehow cleared a passage for them. Outside, those waiting for alms set up a new hullabuloo of cheers, entreaties and a few groans. Mark tossed money among them, and, shouting and laughing and adding to the general excitement, they scurried about after the coins which rolled in all directions.

'Kiss the bride! Kiss the bride!' roared the crowd and smiling broadly, John did so, drawing Elizabeth gently towards him and kissing her full on the lips. The tenderness in his eyes brought tears to her own and for a moment she clung to him fiercely.

John lifted her face. 'No tears, Elizabeth,' he whispered and she smiled and blinked them back, unable to trust herself to speak, for she was sure such exquisite joy could not last, and she must enjoy it while she may.

A small band waited at the church gate, pipes, flutes and a hurdy-gurdy, and they struck up a lively tune and played with great enthusiasm, making up in volume for what they lacked in style. They played the happy couple through the streets of Ashburton which were lined with smiling well-wishers. Flowers were thrown in their path and petals fell around them like snow. At last they left the town and climbed the hill to Heron where crossed swords had been placed over the front door to bring them luck. In the great hall, four table boards held the five course wedding feast and everyone sat down with a hearty appetite; while outside in the courtyard the band played on, with an occasional pause for the quenching of thirsts. Martha had excelled herself but now declared she was 'all of a flutter' from the unaccustomed walking and could eat nothing! Nathan Byrnes settled her with a mug of cider and left her to 'come to herself' as she requested. It was veritable feast. There was a large boar's head and brawn, venison, swan and roasted pig. A custard shaped like a lamb, bore the motto — *I meekly into you am sent To dwell with you and be ever present* and a large sponge cake resembling an angel declared: *Thanks be to God for this feast.*

There were trout, eels, plaice and salmon; cheeses and hot bread; a pyne-puff, a marchpane, syllabub, a mountain of crystallised fruits and finally the bride-cakes, piled on top of each other like platters and bearing the motto: *God did decree our unity.*

Ale and wine were plentiful and the guests grew merry. To round off the meal, the bride-cakes were cut and all received a small portion which was eaten with a rich sweet aquavite. This was served in a small silver cup and passed round in a token of friendship.

The priest said the Latin and the youngsters were then allowed to hurry outside where various entertainments had been planned, the adults remained seated in a pleasant haze of goodwill and a reluctance to do anything more energetic than talk.

Delighted screams from outside sent Della rushing to the window. 'They're playing Barley Break in the orchard,' she cried, forgetting her new-found dignity in the role of bridesmaid, and picking up her skirts she ran out to join them.

The children then flocked to the meadow behind the orchard where the men from the village were to take part in 'Scramble for the pig'. A large pig had been well soaped and lathered and the young men formed a circle round it. One after the other they tried to catch and hold it, rolling and tumbling and hollering their disappointments to the amusement of all who watched.

By this time, the musicians had eaten their fill and were striking up a dance in which old and young alike could take part. John and Elizabeth led the way outside and others followed. The youngsters were put to bed and the dancing continued until the light faded. Finally Elizabeth and John left the remaining dancers and slipped away back to the house. They glanced in at the four children who slept together in a large bed, their faces relaxed in sleep.

'You must be very proud of them,' Elizabeth whispered, wistfully aware that there was a large part of John's life to which she would always be a stranger.

'Don't fret,' he said, 'they will love you as much as I do.'

'Oh, John, I hope so,' she said and her sigh was heartfelt.

In their own room, John and Elizabeth undressed, comfortably free from the embarrassment that traditionally afflicts a bride and groom, since both had been married before. Elizabeth was first to slip between the sheets, the linen cool to her flesh. She watched John, marvelling at the firm young body. A mental picture of Daniel floated up from her subconscious for comparison, but she resisted it.

John blew out the candle, closed the bed drapes and slipped under the sheet and into her arms.

'And are you happy, John?' she asked.

'I am.'

'Please God, I shall presently make you more so.'

He laughed softly.

'I don't doubt it,' he said. 'Your Della, in the next room, is she a sound sleeper?'

'She is that! She goes out like a snuffed candle that must be re-lit each morning.'

'My way is not the silent way,' he said. 'I like to cry my joy aloud. And you?'

She was puzzled and didn't answer.

'Your joy?' he prompted. 'Shall you cry it aloud. If you are lost for words kisses will do. One kiss for "Aye" or two for "No".'

Elizabeth kissed him, then twice, then a third time.

'Three kisses?'

'Three for "I know not",' she told him. 'I have never known joy.' She thought of the ineffective fumbling of her husband and sighed.

For a moment he was silent then said gently, 'Then I will teach you, and it will be my pleasure to do so. I swear you will soon learn. My body is an eager tutor.'

She laughed. 'And you have in your arms an eager scholar!' she said. 'None more so!'

'Then we'll waste no more time on words,' he said. 'Here beginneth the first lesson!'

His lips found hers in the darkness. His hand caressed her face, slid down over her shoulders and moved up again to her chin and then fell slowly, slowly to her breasts.

CHAPTER EIGHT

'Mama! Mama!'

Catherine's shrill voice echoed across the garden as she fled towards the house, pursued by Stephen who trailed behind him a still fluttering butterfly on the end of a thread. 'Mama. Tell him no! Mama!'

The word still fell strangely on Elizabeth's ears. Mama! She was their Mama! The thought thrilled her anew as she hurried to the window in answer to the heartfelt cry. She, Elizabeth Heron, had a family. Overnight her life had altered dramatically and the last three months had opened up a new world to her. She had been a business woman, now she was also a mother. A mother to John's children! The idea was as sweet as life itself. Elizabeth adored her new husband and adored his children. *Her* children now, she reminded herself as Catherine, now nearly five years old, hurtled into the room, her face wet with tears.

'Tell him he mustn't, Mama,' she begged, wrapping her arms round Elizabeth's knees in a passionate embrace. 'Tell him no. It's cruel.'

Rashly Stephen had followed her inside, and now stood defiantly in the doorway, the butterfly held captive in his hands.

'Tis not!' he shouted, his small oval face red with anger.

'Tis so, then,' cried Catherine. 'And Dorothy says you . . . .'

'She's not here any more,' the boy reminded her. 'She's gone to London and I *can* do it so.'

Dorothy had indeed returned to London once the children had settled into their new home. Elizabeth had regretted the loss of her company, but had longed to have

128

the children all to herself; for while Dorothy stayed she had prior claim on their affections.

Elizabeth held out her hand. 'Show me the butterfly, my pet,' she said, and he came forward reluctantly and opened his palm. A large tortoiseshell butterfly lay crushed but still fluttering. Catherine gave a little scream and hit Stephen on the back with her fist.

'You've broken it,' she cried, fresh tears springing to her eyes. 'You've hurted it and now its dead. I'm going to tell Papa.' Stephen raised his free hand to return the blow but, seeing Elizabeth's face, thought better of it.

'Children! Please, I beg you!' said Elizabeth. 'Show me, Stephen, what have you done to it?'

'He pierced it with a needle!' cried his sister. 'He pierced it through and through with a needle and thread and he never will let it go again, for ever and . . . . '

'I *can* pin butterfiles,' Stephen told Elizabeth earnestly. 'It gives them no pain.'

'I think it does,' Elizabeth began, but he interrupted her with, 'Papa let's me pin butterflies. Retter lets me pin butterflies. Eric lets me.'

Elizabeth hesitated. It was true men were less squeamish than women and it was possible that John allowed it. Even as she hesitated, Catherine seized her chance and snatching the thread from Stephen's hand, she raced out of the room with the unfortunate butterfly closely followed by Stephen who roared horribly and uttered all manner of wild threats with which to punish Catherine when he caught her. Elizabeth sighed and picked up her sewing once more. Was all childhood a series of battles to be fought, she mused. Was her own that way? She did not recall that each day had been such a bewildering succession of highs and lows, joy and pain, love and hate.

She finished the flower and cut the thread and reached for another colour. As she did so, Martha appeared smiling broadly followed by the twins. Their faces beamed, their eyes shone with excitement. They each carried something hidden behind their backs and Elizabeth, prompted by a wink from Martha, looked suitably puzzled and laid down her sewing.

'What's happening?' she asked them. 'I smell secrets in the air!'

The two little boys laughed delightedly and Matthew said, 'We've been helping Martha to make the....'

'Don't tell her. She must close her eyes!' William cried.

Elizabeth did as she was bid and Martha said, 'Hold out your hands.'

Elizabeth gave a cry excitement as a small, still-warm pie was put into each hand. She opened her eyes and looked at the pies and then at the twins who had cost poor Bet her life. How proud she would have been thought Elizabeth, charmed as usual by the two small faces, so unlike each other, yet inseparable. One blond head and one dark. William, like his father, Matthew an echo from the past, a reminder of Bet. And yet, Elizabeth felt no resentment towards the woman who had shared so many years of John's life and given him four children. Death stalked them all and a man must take more wives than one and a woman more husbands. At least John now had a family even if she was unable to give him more children. A cloud passed over her face as the familiar fear crept into her happiness, but she put the thought from her. Of course she would bear him a child. She would not consider any other possibility...

'Mutton pies!' they chanted and Elizabeth declared that she had just been wishing for a mutton pie.

'Two,' William corrected her quickly.

'Oh, two is better than one,' she agreed.

'And aren't I to get one then?' cried Martha, a look of dismay on her face.

The twins exchanged worried glances and then William said, 'Mama will give you one,' and Elizabeth agreed.

Martha laughed. 'I never knew it could take so long to bake a few pies,' she said. 'Little fingers everywhere and so much help! But I love it, bless them. Twas a good day when you wed the master, and that's a fact!'

But Elizabeth, with a mouthful of mutton pie, could only nod her endorsement of the statement.

At that moment, a shout from the garden warned of John's arrival home and the twins rushed headlong from the room, the pies forgotten. The two women laughed.

'They love their father,' said Martha. 'There's no doubting that.'

'I love him, too,' said Elizabeth, and brushing the crumbs from her mouth, she followed the twins out of the room.

John stood at the stable door speaking with Eric while four children and two dogs clamoured for attention. Elizabeth watched them for a moment, the twins chattering of their mutton pies, Catherine complaining of Stephen's butterfly and Stephen, silent, a little apart. Not discreetly removing himself from any possible retribution, but waiting resignedly for the outcome of her betrayal. Then John turned. He handed the reins to Eric and slapped the horse's rump.

'So,' he cried. 'What have you chicks been up to while I was away? Nothing good, I warrant. I never knew such chicks for getting into mischief.'

He scooped Catherine into his arms and swung her round until she squealed. Putting her back on the ground, he reached for Stephen but the little boy took a step backward out of his reach and John swooped on the twins instead. He tucked one under each arm and shook them until they begged delightedly for mercy and Catherine hopped up and down crying, 'Do it to me, Papa! Do it to me!'

Glancing up, John caught sight of Elizabeth and smiled.

'What shall I do with these two porkers?' he asked. 'Mayhap we should have roast pork for dinner, and Catherine shall be the apple sauce!'

'Yes, Yes!' cried Catherine. 'But what shall Stephen be?'

'Stephen?' said John, setting down the twins and regarding him with a critical eye. 'Now let me think . . . Ah, I have it. Stephen shall be the roasted parsnips, all golden and crisp. How will that be, eh?' He held out his arms to his oldest son but once again the boy retreated, his eyes dark in his serious face. John glanced to Elizabeth for enlightenment and she shook her head very slightly.

'I shall be the parsnips,' Elizabeth told them, 'but woe betide any who eat me for I shall be tough!'

She came forward and into John's arms and the children exchanged amused looks as they kissed. John had remained alone for so long that a woman behaving as a wife was still a novelty in their experience.

'How went the day?' she asked John, as they walked back to the house.

'Well enough,' he said. Elizabeth fought down her rising impatience. 'Well enough is no answer,' she implored. 'Was he helpful on the question of the shaft? Is our proposed figure a reasonable depth? What experience does he have and will he share it?'

John frowned a little at her persistence. 'Godolphin is a wily bird,' he began. 'There's very little he doesn't know and few tricks he hasn't tried. But we'll speak more of it later when we are on our own. And you? What news since I left Heron?'

She sighed. Always the same answer, she reflected. 'We'll speak more of it later'. But they rarely did. It was as though she were relegated to the role of wife and mother in everyone's eyes but her own.

'You have only been gone three days,' she reminded him. 'The earth shook and the sky rained silver pieces. Apart from that, nothing has happened.'

He laughed also and picking up a stick threw it for the dogs who bounded after it, pursued by the children. 'No other news?' he asked as casually as he could manage.

Elizabeth hesitated, crying inwardly. 'Not *that* question! Dear, John. Not *that* question again. So innocently put, yet so deep with meaning.' She knew exactly what it meant and what her answer should be. 'Yes, John. The bleeding is delayed. I think I am with child'. That is what he wanted to hear — what she longed to say, but couldn't for there was no delay and she was not with child.

'I think not,' she said as lightly as possible. 'Stephen has been pinning butterflies and Catherine is out of countenance with him.'

'Hence the dark looks and cool welcome,' he said.

'He does not intend any hurt,' she said hastily, flying as usual to the boy's defence. 'I think he feared a reprimand from you and he shrinks from your displeasure. He loves you as deeply as the others.'

John was silent. It grieved him that his son did not show him affection in the same way as Catherine and the twins. But now he put aside his disappointment and smiled at Elizabeth.

'But have you missed me?' he asked. 'Have your waking hours been filled with melancholy? Have you wept nightly into your pillow for wanting me beside you? In short, have you missed your husband?'

'God knows how much!' she told him truthfully. 'I wondered what Godolphin's charms can be compared with mine!'

He laughed as she had hoped he would.

'Never fear on that score,' he said. 'The man is not as bonny as you and the beard distracts me!'

He tightened his arm round her and she leant happily against him, feeling the rhythmic movement of his hip as he walked, enjoying the pressure of his fingers as they gripped her arm. She had missed him. She always did. He was often away on business in their own county, or, as on this last occasion, as far as Cornwall. He had thrown himself wholeheartedly into his new role as master of Heron and Elizabeth, equally involved with the children, had gladly

133

surrendered most of the work. He had spent the first month with Retter, learning from him as much as he could of the wild Dartmoor which was to be his life. They had ridden off at dawn each day and covered large areas of country. Retter had shown him the ore, explained the way it was mined, introduced him to the tinners. He had discussed the development which had taken place over the past three years under Elizabeth's control and the plans they had made for the future. John found him a first-rate teacher. Retter found the new master intelligent and enthusiastic. A healthy respect developed between the two men, in which there was no place for rivalry.

Elizabeth, becoming aware of this was satisfied, yet her satisfaction was tinged with a kind of envy. There was no room, she felt, for a woman in their relationship. She almost felt a smouldering of resentment. For so long it had been just herself and Retter — she did not easily relinquish her position. They went up the steps into the house and dogs and children followed them in. Martha ran from the kitchen to greet them, a letter rolled in her hand.

'Tis come from London,' she told them and with cries of delight, they all crowded into the hall to learn the latest news.

Greetings to you, John and to your wife, Elizabeth in friendship and love John read *from your chief bride-knight Mark in the Year of Grace 1483, with fine hopes that you are in good health and the children thriving also in the air of the West Country. Three days since I would fain have joined you there, for London is become more hazardous and I sport a fine dark eye to prove it. I fell foul of a band of apprentices who wanted more space than I would give them and fell to arguing with one of them, a right roaring boy, who took a dislike to the colour of my eye and offered to change it for me. I gave him the merest nick with my dag, but he took it unkindly and leapt at me as though he would tear the flesh from my bones. The outcome is I have a broke finger and coloured eye. So nearly did you lose a friend!'*

'Poor Mark,' said Elizabeth.

John laid down the letter, laughing ruefully. 'Your heart is too soft,' he told her. 'Save your sympathy for those who need it.'

'And who shall that be?' she asked.

'Why for your husband,' he told her.

'And do you deserve sympathy?' she asked.

'I do most surely, sweet wife!' he replied. 'I have ridden far and am desperately weary. I have not breakfasted and my belly calls for sustenance.'

'Stop, I cannot bear this catalogue of woes!' she cried. 'You have earned my sympathy and more. Martha shall serve the meal on the instant and you shall sleep after if you've a mind. But first will you not finish Mark's letter?'

He tilted her face to his own and kissed her lips lightly, then scanned the letter again.

> *You must know, John, that the fair Ella is still desirous of hauling me to the church door but I put up a brave fight in defence of my freedom! The wench despairs of winning me with pomanders and is taken to baking me pies. Yesterday a tasty veal pasty and a week since it was an apple dumpling. I grow fat on so much love!'*

'Who is this Ella?' asked Elizabeth.

'His beloved Ella? Oh, the simple girl plans to wed him, but Mark has other ideas. They have played this game of cat and mouse for nearly two years, but Mark will never wed. He loves his freedom more than life itself. Poor Ella. She will . . . .'

'It's poor Ella, is it?' asked Elizabeth. 'So, who has the soft heart now?'

135

John laughed affectionately. 'You are too quick by far,' he told her. 'A woman should know her place, but let me finish. He says . . . .

Do you recall the plate I worked for Mistress Bryonwell? I delivered it to her house on Tuesday last and she showed me a very fine book. It has above fifty pages in it of best paper and is bound in leather of a green hue and richly tooled in gold. She told me it was of great value which I well believe and am determined to own such a book before I die. Now I must make an end to this scribbling for the candle is almost spent and I must to bed. May the Trinity hold you in its keeping. Your affectionate friend. And he adds a line – I unseal this letter to pen greetings from Nathan and his good wife. Now I close in haste to catch the messenger.

He sighed.

'And does it make you sick at heart for your old life?' she asked.

He shook his head drawing the little family towards him. 'All I want is with me now,' he said, 'within the compass of my arms.'

The following day, John developed a chill and Elizabeth insisted that he stay in bed. His temperature rose, his head ached and although he protested half-heartedly, he was glad enough to rest. Elizabeth put the children to bed and wondered how to spend her evening. She could check the household accounts. She could write a letter to her aunt and uncle. Or she could speak to Martha about Bess. The girl was lazy and occasionally insolent. If she didn't improve she must be replaced. She sighed. None of these pursuits appealed and as Rufus appeared suddenly to put his head in her lap, she thought of a better way to pass the next hour. She would ride out towards the coast and Rufus should accompany her. Since her marriage she had neglected to ride and yet the exercise and fresh air improved her health and spirits.

'Listen for the children, Della,' she told the girl, 'and wake the master and see that he takes his draught within the hour. I shall ride for a while, but will be back before dark. Tell him where I am gone.'

Within minutes Eric was leading one of the horses out of the stable, and helping her to mount.

'Thank you,' she said and turning the horse expertly with a light movement of the reins, she rode out on to the highway. Rufus ran beside, ahead and behind her, excited at this unexpected adventure. She smiled as she watched him nosing into rabbit holes and hurrying purposefully among the dense brambles. Once he put up a bird which rose squawking and startled the horse, but finally he disappeared in pursuit of a rabbit and didn't come back. Elizabeth rode at an easy pace along familiar paths.

She let her mind dwell on the children and her eyes softened. The twins, such robust little boys and so devoted to each other. Catherine, all sweetness and so affectionate. And Stephen. She sighed as she pictured him, his face serious, rarely laughing. What was it that set him apart from the others, she mused? They gave their love so fully but he held back, reluctant to show affection. Only to his beloved Catherine did he occasionally unbend. To her he brought small gifts, a bird's egg or a peacock's feather. Was he jealous, she wondered, of the younger boys. She sighed and her thoughts switched to John. Pray God tis only a chill, she whispered fervently and smiled at his pretended reluctance to admit his weakness. He was a proud man, yet he had given up his ambition to wed her. Now, he had made Heron his own. Did he ever yearn still for the land where he was born. Did he regret the final break with Yorkshire?. Did he still think of his home? They had not visited and yet he wrote often and his mother, delighted at the dramatic improvement in his fortune, replied warmly. John must bring his new bride to meet the family. She would be very welcome. Elizabeth was enthusiastic but somehow there was no time and John always delayed the journey. There was no time for anything but Heron and the mines. She should be thankful, she told herself, that he applied himself so wholeheartedly to her inheritance, and yet a small unease filled her as she dwelt on her own diminished role in Heron affairs. More and more John made decisions, acting on Retter's recommendations, it is true, but without consultation with her. After so many years of passionate involvement, she found it difficult to accept her less than major role and the only disagreements to date had been on that subject. She was now a wife and mother, John argued, and could not be expected to burden herself with problems of mining which he and Retter could deal with. Elizabeth could not accept his reasoning. How, she countered, could he expect her to give up everything she had held most dear and take no further interest. It was not possible. Heron was never out of her mind.

The light had all but faded when a shout interrupted her line of thought. Joseph Tucker rode towards her and she raised a nervous hand in greeting. Since the wedding, he had stayed away from Heron and although she regretted the unspoken rift between them, she understood how he must feel and sympathized with him.

'Forgive me,' he said. 'I bring news of a disturbance.'

'A disturbance?' she questioned, alarmed.

He nodded. 'Word has just come from Dartmouth that the fishermen are moving again in an unfriendly mood.'

'Ah, not again!' she cried. 'That age old grievance will never be settled! The King grants us the right, but still the fishers must kick against it. Do they think we silt their river for pleasure or to do them down! Such narrowness of spirit! Such ignorance is unforgivable!' Her lips tightened at the memory of past harrassments from the inhabitants of the estuary town. For years bad feeling had festered between tinners and fishermen over the tinners right to disturb the

138

river bed in the necessary pursuit of their work. Large amounts of red soil released annually into the river and streams found its way eventually to the river mouth. Here the swiftly flowing river slowed down as the river bed widened and the red soil was deposited. The gradual build up of the river bed hampered the passage of the boats. It was a constant source of trouble which had now flared up again.

'And how many are they this time?' she asked.

He shrugged. 'They say forty or fifty,' he answered, 'and they have sworn to burn Ashburton.'

'Burn us!' her voice rose angrily. 'We shall see if so much as a spark reaches us! Are your own men roused?'

'Aye. My bailiff is out now.'

'Then I will do the same. Retter shall find as many men as he can. Come.'

They called at Retter's cottage instructing him to gather some men. Then, they rode south as fast as they could. On the way they passed several groups of mounted men and more on foot; all heading for Dartmouth and all eager for a fight. The tinners were wild, lawless men at the best of times, but given a righteous cause, they were in their element. Now they were defending their homes and loved ones and could not tangle with the enemy fast enough! They had a reputation for ferocity equal to none, and were always eager to prove themselves worthy of it. It was almost nightfall and ahead of them in the darkness a burning thatch lit up the surrounding country like a beacon. They could make out the figures of men moving in the firelight.

'Looting, I don't doubt,' said Elizabeth grimly. 'We will give them looting when we catch up with them!'

Word had spread and more men joined them. Some carried clubs or staves, others knives. They reached the burning cottage. In the bright glow of the flames they made out three men and a woman, who struggled to douse the fire which had already devoured a third of the thatch. Joseph shouted to some of their followers to assist them but Elizabeth noticed, without surprise, that his words went unheeded. There was not one tinner who could give up the prospect of the forthcoming fight.

Joseph turned to Elizabeth. 'Where are the devils who did that?' he shouted. 'Why have we not passed them on the road if they make for Ashburton?'

'Maybe they are few and in advance of their fellows and hid at the sight of us,' she cried. 'We could scarely miss them otherwise.'

Her guess proved correct. Within minutes they reached a small hamlet and ran suddenly into the main body of their adversaries and a confusion of yells and blows burst upon the air.

Elizabeth's horse leapt to one side, as a rider beside her was thrown heavily and fell against them. Miraculously she was not unseated and watched helplessly as the two men grappled beneath the legs of her horse. To her left, she saw Joseph bring the flat of his sword down on a bare head and saw the man fall, stunned by the force of the blow. Nearly a hundred men now fought in the confines of the narrow street between the small cottages; and around and about them faces appeared briefly at the windows, as shutters were pulled shut. Their reproaches were drowned by the thudding of hooves, the exchange of blows and loud shouts of aggression and pain. Elizabeth had only a knife with her, one which she carried tucked into the saddle for defence against cut throats on the highway. Now she snatched it from its hiding place but hesitated to use it. She had never used it and recoiled from the idea of injuring another human being. Yet, as the fighting intensified, she accepted reluctantly that she might have need of it.

'Elizabeth!'

It was Joseph, now separated from her by the width of the street. His warning cry came too late as a bloodied face leered up at her and a hand clutched her ankle and tried to wrest her foot from the stirrup.

140

'Oh no you don't!' she hissed and brought her knife down without a moment's hesitation. It missed its mark, however, for the man anticipating the blow caught her wrist and jerked her from her horse. She gave a scream that was half fear, half anger and lashed out at him wildly. His face, contorted with rage, was close to hers and she could smell the ale on his breath. He threw her back against the wall of a house and the breath was knocked from her body. As he twisted her wrist, the knife fell to the ground and instinctively she began to pray, her trembling lips moving soundlessly. Then, from out of the darkness Will Retter appeared, his horse driving a path through the flailing arms like a scythe through waving corn. He was at her side and putting an arm round her, lifted her bodily on to her own horse, while another tinner held it for her.

'Get out of here, for the love of God!' he cried. 'John will be here directly and will flay me if any harm has come to you.' And he slapped her horse's rump so violently that the terrified animal sprang forward, scattering men to right and left.

Seconds later, she was beyond the worst of it, patting her horse's neck with a trembling hand in an effort to calm him. But her own distress, far from being alleviated, was suddenly increased. A terrible coldness had seized her, with Will Retter's mention of John. With slowly dawning horror she realized what she had done; — she had acted as Mistress of Heron, riding on with Joseph without a thought for John. Dear God! He would never forgive her. She sat her horse like a statue — the fishermen and tinners forgotten.

Even as she sat there, a lone horseman galloped up and John was beside her. His face was pale with rage and he could barely trust himself to speak.

'Are they ahead?' he asked and she nodded, dumbly.

Without another word or glance, he spurred his horse and galloped in pursuit. She remained where she was, numb with fear and remorse. He would never understand.

She sat on, while ahead the fight continued. She could see the lights of the burning torches and hear the cries of anger as the men battled on for their rights in the only way they knew. But Elizabeth, wrapped in her own private misery, had lost interest in the outcome. She knew, as they all knew, that the tinners would carry the day. They always did. The fishermen would run before the onslaught of men who tore their living from the wild moor. They would put up a strong resistance, the fishermen, and they would feel their honour satisfied for a time; but she did not doubt they would lose the day.

Turning her horse, she rode slowly home, black with despair. Back at Heron she undressed and sat on the bed to await John's return.

Hours later, she heard him come in. The front door slammed and he took the stairs two at a time. He stood in the doorway, his chest heaving as he gulped huge breaths. The candlelight shone softly and his haggard face wore an expression she had never seen before. The face of a man betrayed. She opened her mouth to speak his name but could not utter a word. Blood trickled down his face from a gash above his eye but he seemed unaware of it. He rubbed his eyes tiredly with the back of his hand, smearing it further.

Still she dared not speak. At last he shook his head wonderingly.

'Have you any idea,' he began, his voice ominously low, 'how it feels to arrive last at a fight? How it feels to ride into a battle behind your own men? Can you possibly know what that does to a man?' He held up a warning hand as she made a move towards him. 'Stay away from me, for God's sake, Elizabeth, for I swear before God I have never tasted such humiliation as I did tonight. In God's name!' he burst out suddenly, 'why did you do it? How could you?'

'John, I beg you listen,' she began but suddenly he was towering over her, his face terrible.

'No,' he said softly. 'I will not listen because there is nothing you can say to justify what you have done to me tonight. Did you think to protect me, was that it? That a goldsmith cannot fight his own battles but must....'

'I thought nothing!' cried Elizabeth desperately. 'That was my only fault. My mind turned only on Joseph's news. I acted as tho' I was alone, before I had you with me. As tho' I still had to act for myself. I forgot.'

'Forgot?'

The word rang in her ears and then his fist struck the side of her face knocking her backwards on to the floor where she lay half stunned, terrified of this stranger she had married.

'So you forgot,' he repeated bitterly. 'You forgot that I am your husband. Forgot that I am part of Heron. Forgot that these last three months I have lived Heron, breathed Heron, aye – loved Heron! And I would have fought for it, died for it if needs be. But you would deny me the chance! You must ride out like Jeanne D'Arc. That is the extent of your love for me, is it? That is what I gave up my ambition for and buried myself in this God forsaken county. For your sake only and this is how you repay me! Oh, dear God! I still cannot believe it.'

He covered his face with his hands and Elizabeth found herself sobbing uncontrollably. Not for herself, but for the fearful wrong she had done the man she loved. The terrible truth filled her mind to the exclusion of all else; nothing she could do or say could alter the deed. And he would never forgive her. She would never forgive herself! Ignoring her, he leant against the window, staring out with unseeing eyes. He turned suddenly.

'I shall go back home,' he said. 'A Kendal has no place here. I'm not needed.'

'John! Oh, sweet Heaven. No, John. No!' she begged, struggling to her feet, panic-stricken. 'Don't talk that way,

I beg you . . . my dearest John, I adore you. You know I do . . . don't talk of leaving. I cannot bear it.'

He shook his head. Desperately she snatched at his arms pulling him towards her, holding him in her arms. Trying to control the trembling in her voice, trying to speak reasonably.

'Wait until the morning, John,' she begged. 'Won't you wait. Just until the morning? Let me bathe your face, it bleeds . . . it bleeds . . . Oh, God. What can I say . . . . ?'

She broke down once more into passionate weeping, aware that nothing she said would alter his resolution. He would not sleep with her that night. Maybe he would never sleep with her again! Abandoning hope, she flung herself on to the bed, drowning in misery, arms outstretched, her hair flowing across the coverlet.

She heard the sound of his buckle as his belt hit the floor and turned over and stared at him in disbelief.

'Oh, never fear,' he told her, his voice like ice. 'I'm going. But first I'm going to say "Goodbye" to my wife . . . .'

His body, crashing down on to hers, knocked all the breath from her lungs so that she gasped struggling for air.

He tried to enter her, but the shift she wore hampered him. With an oath he tore the gown from her body and thrust into her with a sound that was part love, part hate and with such force that she uttered a thin scream of pain. He clutched her head close to his chest, muffling her cries and her world shrank to the size of their two bodies locked in conflict . . . . After the final convulsion, he lay beside her for a moment or two then flung out of the room with a wild cry.

'John!' she screamed. 'Don't go! Don't . . . John! John . . . ' but his footsteps echoed as he ran down the stairs and the door slammed behind him.

Martha came rushing to the room, candle in hand.

'Ma'am,' she cried. 'What ails the master? He. Ah my poor lamb!' Her eyes took in the scene, the woman on the bed, crushed and sobbing, the torn shift on the floor. Setting down the candle, she sat on the bed and took Elizabeth into her arms, smoothing her hair, wet with perspiration and gently wiping her face still shaken with tears.

'I never would have believed it, not of the master!' she muttered. 'A hard man, aye, but not to treat a woman so . . . there, there . . . . Tis all done with now . . . Weep if you must for there's nought so healing for a broken spirit . . . Hush, my dear. You'm safe now and I shall bathe you presently and you shall have a sleeping draught . . . .'

Her comforting, familiar voice droned on and Elizabeth's distress slowly grew less. Her sobbing stopped at last and she put a trembling hand to rub away the tears. The candle flickered revealing her face, blotched and swollen.

'Ah dear, what a sight, what a pitiful sight . . .' said Martha. 'Barely three months and tis come to this! I can scarce credit it but there you are.'

'He was hurt,' Elizabeth said. 'There was a gash on his face from the fight. Did he go out again, Martha? His face was bleeding . . .'

'Then tis no more than he deserves!' said Martha.

'No, he did no wrong,' protested Elizabeth. 'I was at fault so grievously at fault. Oh, you do not know the man as I do. His pride . . . I did him a great wrong and he had punished me.'

'You've never wronged him!'

'I did, Martha, I did! I wonder where he has gone? My poor John. Pray God he will come back . . .'

Elizabeth fell to weeping again and Martha deemed it time to 'put her to rights' and hurried downstairs to fetch warm water and towels. She bathed Elizabeth's aching body and helped her into a clean shift. Then, she mixed a strong sleeping draught which Elizabeth drank willingly enough, for though comforted in body, her mind was in a turmoil and she longed for oblivion.

Martha wished her a sound sleep, and returned to her own room where Della now sat up in bed waiting for her.

'What ails the mistress?' she asked wide-eyed.

'Nought for your ears.' Martha told her. 'Back under the covers with you or you'll overlay in the morning.'

'And tis Corpus Christi!' the girl reminded her.

'Corpus Christi? Lord, so it is,' agreed Martha. 'It'd flown right out of me head .... Corpus Christi .... Ah me. She'll not feel like celebrating, poor lamb.'

'Why not?' asked Della.

'Because I say so!' snapped Martha. 'Now one word more from you and you'll feel the back of my hand.'

It was no idle threat. Della slid hurriedly under her blanket and an uneasy silence fell. Outside on the moor, a fox barked a warning as John's horse thundered past in the darkness and night came at last to Heron.

As Matins drew to a close and the last organ notes filled the church, those members of the congregation nearest to the doors began to slip away. When the service ended, the procession of Corpus Christi would gather in the church-yard for the parade through the streets, and there was fierce competition for the most advantageous positions from which to watch it. Elizabeth, at the front of the church, was forced to wait until the rest of the congregation had left. Della looked at her anxiously. Martha had told her that Elizabeth was 'not rightly herself' and warned the girl to keep an eye on her. Della took her responsibility very seriously. She was aware, too, of the interest aroused in the congregation by the fact that John was not with them for the Corpus Christi service. In answer to several whispered enquiries. Elizabeth had said he was delayed on 'an urgent matter', but the girl sensed that they were not entirely convinced. Elizabeth was very pale and drawn and was obviously relieved when the service ended. Della held Stephen's hand and Elizabeth held Catherine's, but the twins had been left at home with Martha and would be brought down later to share in the excitement.

Corpus Christi Day loomed large in the town's calendar and preparations had been in hand for several months. Three plays would be performed on stages newly erected in the church and there would be the usual gathering of pedlars, street musicians and side shows, so that the town took on the air of a vast fair.

'You look poorly, ma'am,' said Della.

'I'm well enough,' Elizabeth answered. But she could not hide the misery in her eyes, and Della was glad when the church emptied and they were able to follow everyone else outside. The two children jumped around asking countless questions and Della was kept busy trying to answer them. Elizabeth's eye searched the crowd for a glimpse of John although she hardly expected to see him there. But if not, then where was he? He had not returned to Heron and his horse was missing from the stable. No. She was too proud to make enquiries. As they walked through the churchyard to the gate she prayed — 'Holy Mary, protect him from all harm . . . . soften his heart, I beseech you . . . forgive me my wrongdoing which was not meant . . . bring him back to me — She longed for the sight of his lean frame and the blond arrogant head and a fierce panic seized her that she might never see him again. Closing her eyes, she willed herself to be calm and forget such wild notions.

'Ma'am?' Della looked at her anxiously, but Elizabeth merely shook her head to discourage further questions. She caught sight of Joseph Tucker ahead of them and turned aside, but he had seen them and waved a hand in greeting. She saw that it was heavily bandaged.

'Sir!' cried Della, wide-eyed. 'You're wounded.'

He laughed. 'A souvenir of last night's encounter,' he said. 'But well-earned for there's several in Dartmouth this day with bloody heads as won't count me their friend! But how is John? He fought well last night. You'd have been proud of him.'

'The master?' cried Della turning to Elizabeth. 'Is the master hurt? Martha said nought of it.'

'He suffered a bad cut,' said Joseph. 'That much I saw but we were soon separated in the melee. I noticed he was not in church and hoped he didn't suffer worse. It was fierce while it lasted but mercifully none was killed, though they fear Ned Luckins may lose his eye and that's bad.'

Della glanced at Elizabeth for further enlightenment but none was forth-coming and the look in her mistress's eye discouraged a direct question.

Stephen tugged at her hand, impatiently. 'Where is the procession?' he wanted to know. 'Why isn't it come? I want to see the banners. Martha said there would be banners and . . . .'

'I can't see,' wailed Catherine not to be outdone and the crowd had indeed drifted in front of them blocking their view of the street.

'Shall I take them to the horse trough, ma'am?' suggested Della who was put out to discover that she would not be able to see either, in spite of her superior height.

'They could stand on the rim of it and see fine from there.'

'I doubt such a vantage place will still be free,' said Elizabeth. 'Push a way to the front with them, Della, but don't loose their hands. Make haste for I hear the music.'

They were just in time, for at that moment the procession came into sight round the corner. They were led by the choir and priests chanting psalms. The priest followed them bearing the Host and behind him the Portreeve led the long succession of Guilds, each turned out in force with banners and full insignia which made a brave and colourful glow. Every Guild has its own music makers, and the procession flowed through the town on a wave of sound to

148

the accompaniment of the cries of the crowd as they recognized and greeted friends and relatives among the marching men. There were frequent stops to 'elevate the Host' wherever an altar had been placed. At each one the Sanctus bell was rung, everyone knelt and a short Mass sung. The altars, provided by householders, consisted of a table bearing a crucifix, candles and were decorated with flowers and greenery. The procession was thus a slow affair, as it wound its way through the admiring crowds and back to the church where the next part of the festivities were to take place. As soon as the tail of the procession had passed, the crowd melted away back to the church for the first play. By this time, Martha had joined Elizabeth with the twins and suggested that she might wish to return home. She hesitated. Joseph gave her a keen glance and saw for the first time how subdued she was and wondered at the cause.

'My mount is at the Blue Boar,' he told her. 'If you wish to go home I will take you.'

His brown eyes were full of concern and she lowered her eyes, embarrassed. Until the previous evening he had stayed away from her and now, feeling particularly vulnerable, she found the thought of his familiar gentleness more than she could bear. She almost wanted to hold out her arms and be enclosed protectively in his. But his offer remained unanswered. Did she want to go home to an empty house? Every minute would be an hour, alone with her fears. Or would John be there, waiting to make up the quarrel? Intuition told her that he would not. No, time would pass more quickly in the church where the plays would provide welcome distractions.

'I'll stay awhile, thank you,' she said.

At that moment, Blanche, Joseph's daughter, joined them. She was a pretty girl, already a favourite with the children. They immediately began to argue as to who should hold her hand as the end of the procession passed and they all moved once more in the direction of the church.

They were just in time to settle themselves when the curtains were parted and three stages were revealed, one above the other, with Heaven at the top. Here, quantities of white muslin were bunched together to form clouds against a bright blue backcloth with God seated on a gold throne flanked by two angels. The middle stage was strewn with boughs and rocks to represent Earth, while Hell, the bottom stage, contained two large jaws hung with red cloth from which smoke issued at intervals. Catherine gave a shriek of fear whenever this happened but finally, enjoying it, insisted Joseph lift her up to enable her to see more clearly. The play was about to begin and a small boy stepped forward and held up his hand for silence, and declared: –

> 'Within our stage's narrow bound
> The whole Creation circles round
> Each soul with measured haste is driven
> Through this wide earth to Hell or Heaven.'

A mixture of groans and cheers greeted this introduction and he withdrew smiling self consciously to the wings. Now a white robed God stood up and directed the Creation, ordering the release of various small creatures on to Earth: three cats, a dog, a rabbit and several pigeons. These scattered hastily into the audience amid shrieks and laughter and were eventually captured and returned to the stage. One of the angels then stepped forward: –

> 'So God Almighty does create
> With bounteous gifts this earthly state.
> A paradise to man is given
> And Eve from his own rib is riven.'

Adam then appeared and strolled around Earth admiring the scenery and finally lay down to sleep. God then descended a ladder to the middle stage and produced a huge bone from beneath Adam's sleeping figure. With a great deal of hand-waving Eve was produced, making a spectacular entrance through a trap-door on to the stage, to wake Adam with a kiss and a touch of her hand.

The play proceeded and, faced with the abounding enthusiasm on stage and the children's increasing delight in the proceedings, Elizabeth found her desperation fading. She was too sensitive, she reasoned with herself. Too anxious by far. She must wear a smile lest she come suddenly face to face with him. Which by God's mercy she hoped she would before too long! An old woman made her way through the crowd selling nuts and raisins and Joseph brought some for the children. Cries and jeers from the audience greeted the arrival of the Devil who sprang through the jaws of Hell, accompanied by an excess of smoke and a shower of sparks. He came complete with red stockings and tail and wore a goatskin over his body and horns on his head. He leaped menacingly around the stage, shook his fist at the audience and then turned his attention to Adam and Eve in their earthly paradise. Pointing dramatically upwards he intoned:-

'See now, I end this state of earthly joy
Eve shall be tempted by an artful ploy
And Adam too, must taste the bitter gall
As from this perfect state of grace they fall.
And evermore shall earth's narration tell
How Adam and his Eve were led astray by Hell....'

He then clapped his hands and a lesser devil appeared on Earth and hung a large red apple on one of the boughs. The audience screamed loud and long to draw Adam's attention to this deed, but he turned a deaf ear and Eve was duly persuaded by the Devil himself to taste the forbidden fruit. As soon as she took the first bite the Jaws of Hell were filled with gleeful devils congratulating each other on their

151

master's success. Adam then tasted the apple amid cheers from Hell and groans from the audience.

Catherine, her arms securely locked round Joseph's neck, watched wide-eyed and open-mouthed, enjoying the thrills from the safety of his arms. From Heaven an angel now descended the ladder and, wielding a large stick, drove Adam and Eve out of the Garden. There were a few boos here and one bold spark threw a handful of nuts at the angel, but was swiftly reminded of the proprieties by a thump on the side of his head from a more virtuous neighbour. The musicians struck up briefly and the curtain fell to tumultuous applause at the end of Act One. Now a roaring trade was done by the ale-wives and pedlars of various foodstuffs.

Surreptitiously, Elizabeth scanned the faces of the crowd, but failed to see her husband. She saw and acknowledged several acquaintances but was careful not to hold their eyes for too long lest they make their way through the press of people to enquire after John. It suddenly occured to her that he may well have spent the night at the moor-house and she was briefly tempted to ride out and see for herself. But commonsense prevailed with her returning confidence. If he was not there, she would waste precious time during which he might return to Heron in search of her. She would not go. But she longed to see him. Longed for the estrangement to be at an end. Longed to be reassured once more of his love for her and to convince him of hers.

Suddenly a small boy tugged at her skirt.

'What is it?' she asked.

The boy mumbled something shyly, his head well down to avoid the interested stares from Elizabeth's own children.

'I cannot hear such a thin voice,' smiled Elizabeth. 'I beg you speak up, little one.'

The boy raised large grey eyes. 'There's a gentleman would speak with you,' he repeated.

For a moment Elizabeth looked at him without comprehension, then her heart began to race.

'A gentleman?' she asked. 'Where is this gentleman?'

The boy pointed outside and Elizabeth turned quickly to Martha.

'I think tis John,' she whispered. 'Watch over the children. I must go.'

Beaming, Martha nodded her understanding of the situation.

Elizabeth took the boy's hand and he led her through the church door and out into the churchyard.

'He's under the tree,' he told her.

'Thank you,' said Elizabeth. 'Did he give you something for your errand?' He nodded.

'Then be off.'

The child sped off to spend his money and Elizabeth walked towards the large oak tree on the far side of the churchyard. She tried not to look too disturbed, walking with her head held high, suddenly determined not to let him know the extent of her distress.

He was leaning against the trunk of the oak, his head bent, and she was reminded of Stephen with his crushed butterfly. He must have heard her approach but didn't look up until she was almost beside him. 'I cannot leave you, Elizabeth,' he said simply turning to meet her gaze.

'I'm glad of it,' she said.

He looked away from her wretchedly.

'I love you, John,' she said.

He nodded, then asked. 'Have I hurt you much?'

'No,' she lied.

'And is everyone at the play?'

'Yes. The children are with Martha and Della.'

Instinctively she made no mention of Joseph.

'Then we'll go home,' he said.

CHAPTER NINE

1485

It was quiet in the courtyard. Quiet and still. The sun, almost directly overhead, cast no shadows across the cloisters. There were few sounds, a bee droning disconsolately among flagstones between which no weeds flourished. A small black kitten played with a pebble, patting it, then springing excitedly after it. But then, losing interest in the game it stretched luxuriously upon the warm stone and fell instantly asleep. Fish swam among the lily roots in the pond below the small fountain. Time itself appeared to pause, waiting for the midday hours to ring.

Brother Andrew laid down his quill, sanded the parchment carefully and directed the sand back into the small earthen pot. Then he blew away the sand that still clung to the ink and re-read his list.

	For the monthe of Auguste
Item	Potell of vynegar – ij s
Item	Nyne makrel – xv d
Item	Tallow for candells – vi d
Item	A small swane – iii d
Item	Halfe a porke for salting – xij d
Item	For black clothe – ij s
Item	Treecle for soothynge syrup – x d

He rubbed his eyes and yawned, tapping his mouth politely with the back of his fingers then leafed through a further pile of invoices which lay scattered on the desk in front of him. He selected various items, compared them with his list, and set them on one side, using a large polished pebble as a paper weight. He straightened, screwed up his eyes

154

then blinked them rapidly. He spread the fingers of his left hand and examined the nails and scratched out a stray speck of dirt. Slapping his belly, he mouthed the words 'I'm hollow' and wished the bell would ring. But it didn't, so he picked up another invoice and his quill and bent without enthusiasm to his task.

> Item   Salte – xiiij d
> Item   For shoeing the oxen

He frowned at the receipt.

'Two shillings!' he exclaimed then looked around him guiltily and repeated the phrase in a whisper. 'Why that's two pence more than the last time. That smith is a rogue . . . .'

He wrote down 'ii s' and slipped the account under the pebble. The next item also attracted his attention and he shook his head in disbelief.

'Twas never three shillings for a plaice!' he muttered. 'I'd best ask in the kitchen.'

Glad of an excuse to abandon his book-keeping, he pushed back the stool and stood up. As he crossed the courtyard, his sandals scuffed the ground and the cloth of his habit flapped reassuringly against his legs. The sun shone on the blond head of Elizabeth's young brother as he moved within the bounds of his small world, at peace with himself and God. The kitten still slept and Andrew bent down and tickled her ears, smiling to himself as she burst into loud purring and leaned lovingly against him.

It was hot in the kitchen although all the doors were open to create more draught. Brother Dominic sat by the fire fanning himself with a large rhubarb leaf, while Brother Gregory slipped the skins from newly cooked beetroots. They looked up as Andrew entered and he smiled as he offered the invoice for Brother Gregory's inspection. The old man raised his eyes in exasperation at his own careless-ness and mouthed, 'Pence, Brother Andrew. Three pence!

155

My old brain grows addled,' and tapped his forehead. Andrew grinned and nodded. He glanced round the kitchen hopefully and the two older brothers exchanged amused glances. Andrew's gaze rested on a basket of small loaves and he patted his belly.

'Take one,' whispered the old man.

'My thanks.'

'And carry the rest through to the refectory.'

'I will.'

The young man picked up the basket of bread, slipped one into the pocket of his habit, and left his elders shaking their heads tolerantly at the ways of the young. Instead of crossing the courtyard, he kept to the shady cloisters and walked round two sides of the square. The refectory door stood open, propped back by a leather bottle filled with sand. The long table stood laid for the midday meal and he placed the basket of bread in the centre of it.

Continuing round under the cloisters, he came again to his cell and once inside bit hungrily into the bread. As he did so, the Gabriel bell began to toll and with a muffled exclamation, he filled his mouth, wiped away the crumbs and chewed rapidly.

As if by magic, the courtyard was filled with hurrying feet as the brothers converged for prayers. The courtyard dust settled again as they knelt in the tiny chapel, and the warm air was filled with the sound of voices raised in chant. Shafts of sunlight lit the small chapel and fell across the bowed shoulders of the monks, as they knelt on the hard floor, their knees protected only by the cloth of their habits. Andrew squinted at the broad back of Father Patrick noting the scurf which speckled his shoulders, and was immediately ashamed of his own feeling of superiority.

Andrew was the last brother to join Harben Priory and then only as a special dispensation. Elizabeth had wanted him near when she wed Daniel Heron and they had paid the Prior well for the privilege. He was younger by eleven years than any of the others.

Their thanks and praise paid to God, the monks rose and made their way into the refectory where bread, beetroots and soft cheese awaited them, with jugs of home-made ale. They ate in silence, each ministering to the needs of his neighbour. Andrew preferred the evening meal when one of the brothers would read from the Bible, for much time passed without the luxury of entertainment.

Andrew enjoyed the readings. He loved the variety of their voices: Brother Dominic's high-pitched and rather nasal, the words delivered at great speed; Brother Gregory, slow and resonant, making the most joyous passage sombre; and old Brother Michael, so feeble since his heart failed, that the words tumbled out unrestrainedly and his hearers turned their thoughts elsewhere, while paying him due attention with their eyes. And his own turn! How he revelled in the sound of his own voice, young and clear, struggling to extract the last shades of meaning from the holy words, aiming to hold his fellows enthralled by his rendering of the familiar Latin. He half suspected that they laughed at him, shaking their heads at his vanity, but understanding it, for it struck a long dormant chord in each one of them. He loved the brothers, loved his quiet life.

He pressed a slice of beetroot on to his cheese and lifted it to his mouth. A sigh of contentment welled up in him as his teeth sank through the cold red flesh into the creamy cheese . . . . Brother Dominic nudged him suddenly and jerked his head towards the window. Looking up Andrew saw Elizabeth crossing the courtyard, with little Blanche Tucker. He waved to catch her attention and then, excusing himself from the diners, went out to greet her.

'Elizabeth, greetings. Tis good to see you, and Blanchette also, looking very bonny.'

The young girl grimaced at this diminutive as he knew she would and he tugged playfully at the long plait of hair which hung down one shoulder like a burnished gold rope.

'I know why you grow this hair,' he teased. 'You are not

in truth Blanchette but Ripunzel! One day the prince will climb up your hair and rescue you from the tower!'

Blanche giggled and Elizabeth smiled. 'You put unseemly ideas into her head,' she said, 'and she has enough of them already . . . . ' She lowered her voice, aware that their voices carried in the quiet of the cloisters. 'May we speak privately. I will be brief but I would speak of – that matter.'

He nodded. 'Let's walk in the orchard,' and he led the way through an archway into the grassy area laid with fruit trees. 'See here,' he said proudly, patting the trunk of a slender young tree. 'Tis newly brought from Calais and highly prized. The brothers coddle it as a new born babe!'

Elizabeth laughed politely, but was ill at ease at the delay. He thought she looked thinner and there were shadows under her eyes. Blanche wandered off through the trees towards the beehives and Elizabeth made the most of her opportunity.

'Tis the chart,' she began, 'that you spoke of many weeks ago. Do you recall? The one that Brother Bartholomew keeps.'

'Aye. I recall. You wish a meeting with him?'

She nodded, waving an acknowledgement to Blanche, who had found a small hen coop with a broody hen and wanted Elizabeth to see it.

'As soon as maybe,' she added.

Andrew nodded, looking at her keenly. 'Then all else has failed?' he asked and the look in her eyes was answer enough.

'I have lately taken a potion,' she said, 'which was told Martha by a wise woman at the fair but I cannot keep it down. My stomach throws it back and I am grown weary by it. In truth, Andrew, I am sick at heart and know not where else to turn. You say the chart will work? How certain is it, can you say?'

He hesitated, reluctant to promise too much but not wishing to depress her further.

'It has worked oftimes,' he said, 'so I am told but can say no more. When can you come? It should be after nightfall near, to midnight is recommended. But if you are apprehensive . . . .'

'No, no!,' she assured him quickly. 'If it should be midnight, then I will come at midnight. John will be away Thursday in Tavistock. Will that suit?'

Andrew considered, then nodded. 'Twill do very well,' he said. 'If ought goes amiss I'll send word by one of the servants to give you another date. If not, come to the chapel at midnight on Thursday.'

'And shall you be there also?'

'Aye, if you wish it.'

'I do,' she said.

'Then I'll be there.'

'My thanks, Andrew. I could not wish a better brother.'

'Nor I a dearer sister.'

They looked fondly on each other for there was a strong bond between them. It had been so since they were children, in spite of the difference in their ages.

'Elizabeth!' called Blanche. 'Come quick and see this one little chick. Tis newly hatched.'

'I'm coming!'

She turned to her brother. 'I'll go and see for she'll not rest otherwise.'

'It seems you have a family of five,' said Andrew and she smiled.

'Blanche is no trouble,' she said. 'And the little ones adore her. She is nearly ten years now, and very motherly. Poor Joseph has no attractions with which to tempt her home!'

He looked at her seriously for a moment. 'And you, you are happy enough with John?'

'Aye, but will be happier soon I trust!'

'Ah, the child. To be with child, is that so great a prize for a woman?'

'For this woman it is the greatest prize. I pray your Brother Bartholemew can help me.'

'Come quick, Elizabeth,' cried Blanche again. 'The mother pecks the little one! What must we do? You must come at once!'

'I must go to her,' said Elizabeth. 'And you must return to your meal. I will see you on Thursday just before midnight. God keep you, Andrew.'

She kissed him on the cheek then turned towards Blanche who was watching them impatiently. When she reached the hen coop, the girl looked up curiously, the chick forgotten.

'Why do you kiss a monk?' she asked. 'He's a holy man. Tis a sin for him to kiss a lady.'

Elizabeth laughed. 'Not to receive a small kiss from his own sister,' she said. 'We are kin folk and we love each other.'

'Does he love me?' the girl asked.

'He likes you, I'm sure.'

'But to love me would be a sin?'

'I think not,' said Elizabeth, amused by the girl's persistence. 'You are only a child.'

'And were I grown into a woman? Then it would be a sin?'

Elizabeth laughed. 'I think it would. I cannot rightly say. But come. — What of this unfortunate chick?'

They looked for it but the hen had finally persuaded it to return under her protective wing.

They left the garden and returned home, Blanche chatting on about the chick, to which Elizabeth nodded absent-mindedly, busy with her own thoughts which centred entirely on her forthcoming appointment.

There was soil in his eyes, soil in his nose. He coughed and

160

spluttered; there was red soil in the phlegm. His shoes were full of grit and the dust had found its way under the waistband of his breeches to irritate the skin and make a redness that needed frequent scratching.

The sides of the shaft reared above him like a wide circular chimney and all the way down were spade and pick marks. His marks and Ben's. They had dug the shaft between them. Now Ben was home, with a dose of the flux and he, William, dug on alone with only the lad to shovel the rock, into the leather bucket and shout 'Hulloo' to Jack at the top, who would pull it up and empty it. He sneezed, blew through his nose to clear it, and wiped the mucus on to the back of his hand and then on to his breeches. Taking up his pick once more, he swung it into the red rock under his feet and grunted with satisfaction as it cracked. Another blow and another. Two cracks crossed. Yet another and the piece was loosened and he prised it up. The boy squatted, watching and waiting. William loosened a few more lumps and straightened up.

'Move yourself,' he told the boy sharply. 'Sit on your backside any longer you'll lose the use of your legs!'

The boy scrambled to his feet. He had no wish to incur the man's displeasure. He had felt the pick handle across his back once or twice and didn't relish a third time. He shouted for the bucket and it came swaying, jerking down the shaft, seeming to get larger as it neared the bottom, blotting out the sunlight.

Suddenly a man appeared at the top of the shaft, his body fore-shortened by the distance, his head jutting forward incongruously as he leaned forward to look down.

'William!' A voice called.

'Aye.'

The old tinner looked up, squinting into the light to see who called him. Ah! Twas the master, this Kendal from the wilds of Yorkshire, his speech still foreign to Devon ears, but a fine man by all reports.

'How goes it?' asked John.

161

'We've reached half way, sir.'

'Good. What now, then?'

'A bit of a shelf, sir, like, round the edge then another drop.'

'How far does Retter reckon the second drop?'

'Same again should do it.'

'Good. And Ben. Is he on the mend?'

'Soon will be, sir, but slow, like. He's an old man and the old do take their time.'

'They do,' agreed John, smiling.

The shaft was being dug to match up with another being bored horizontally into the rock face on the edge of the granite escarpment. Below the jutting rock face, a small spring trickled over scree and gorse to feed the larger stream which flowed from east to west, in a shallow bed long since picked clean of tin gravel.

Jack now returned with the empty bucket and lowered it once more. 'Goes down a deal lighter than it comes up,' he joked.

John laughed. 'I'll warrant!'

'Old William down there, he's a grandfather again.'

'He is?'

'Oh, aye. Nineteen all told, so he says.'

'Nineteen!' John leaner over the shaft. 'I hear you've another grandchild, William.'

'Tis so, sir,' cried William. 'Yes, another boy. We grow mostly boys seemingly. My daughter says tis all the ale we drink. Oils our parts, she reckons!'

John laughed and Jack grinned, but his smile was nervous. What would the old fool say next and the master's wife barren or so they all said. Nothing to show for all their bedding these two past or three years. But John had turned from the shaft and now stared upward, his hand shielding his eyes, watching a hawk as it hovered and then dropped seizing its prey in mid-flight. He heard the clang of the pick and the scrape of the boy's shovel. He wondered where Retter was, and asked Jack who didn't know. A small knot of fear formed somewhere inside him. Lately he mistrusted the man. And he mistrusted his wife. She was behaving irrationally and she lied to him. He knew that she lied. She was irritable and tearful and strangely preoccupied. Where was she now, he wondered? And the small fear found a voice – with Retter? Hell fire! It could not be. He wronged her and the man.

'Ho, there!'

Turning, he saw Joseph Tucker dismounting and thought he looked fit for his years. His clothes became him and were well cut of good cloth. Maybe Tucker was the man. Did Elizabeth visit him whenever she disappeared? Or did she really pray, as she affirmed? She had refused the man once to marry a goldsmith! But did she now repent her hasty action? God's name! Such thoughts troubled him lately and gave him no rest.

'Hello there!' He forced a smile as Tucker drew near.

'I've just been to the house,' Joseph informed him, 'hoping to find you or Elizabeth.'

'And wasn't Elizabeth there?'

The question sprang to his lips before he could prevent it and he cursed his stupidity. Now this man knew that he didn't know where Elizabeth was. But at least that meant it wasn't him, and if it wasn't Tucker who kept Elizabeth company? It must be Retter. Suddenly he realized Joseph was speaking to him and he'd missed most of what he'd said.

'My thoughts were elsewhere,' he said, feeling guilty that he had wronged the man in his heart.

'I said I am beginning to think of Blanche's future.'

'Oh . . . aye. They must all be provided for.'

'Have you thought on Stephen yet?' said Joseph falling into step alongside John, leading his horse by the bridle.

John looked at him sharply. 'A boy of six years!' he gasped. 'Have I thought of his marriage, why no. Tis early for that, surely?'

Joseph shook his head. 'Tis never too early for such

163

plans,' he said. 'Believe me. I have had my older boy, Jo, promised these last seven years, to a cousin in Somerset. You'd do well to give the matter some thought. Aye, and Catherine, too.'

John laughed. 'She is but seven!' he said. 'Poor babe. I think we will let her play first before she weds!'

Joseph smiled politely, but persisted with his theme until they reached John's horse and both men remounted.

'I would like it well,' he said, 'if Blanche might wed Stephen. Will you at least consider the advantages of such a match?'

John thought that they would all be on Blanche's side, for she would inherit Heron, but made no immediate reply.

Joseph looked at him anxiously. 'You say you have made no other plans,' he reminded him, 'so will you discuss the matter with Elizabeth?'

John sighed. 'For the present I believe it is too soon,' he said, 'but when we judge it time to think of his future why, by all means we shall consider your daughter.'

And with that, Joseph had to be content.

Elizabeth pulled the hood of her cloak over her head and let herself gently out of the house. She paused at the gate and looked back. The only light at any of the windows was the glimmer of the candle in the children's bedchamber. Stephen was still terrified of the dark and, despite John's express wish to the contrary, Martha permitted him a small light and Elizabeth turned a blind eye to the deception. Now, oddly comforted by the sight and the memory of the four sleeping children, she walked rapidly across the garden, through the quiet orchard and on to the highway. She had decided not to ride, she could go more quietly on foot. Beneath her heavy cloak she clutched a small dagger, one of Daniel's. She hoped not to need it, but to travel at night without a means of defence would be the height of folly.

Ahead of her a small night creature skittered across her path and she froze, her heart beating painfully. A stoat, perhaps, or a rabbit. In the trees to her right she heard the snuffling grunt of a wild pig . . . It seemed an age before she reached the Priory gates and eased them open, praying that they would not creak. They did, but the sound went unheeded except by Andrew who waited for her with a lantern and now came forward to meet her.

'Brave girl!' he said.

'Not so brave,' she told him shakily. 'My heart was in my mouth! Is all well? Do we proceed?'

'It is and we do,' he said. 'Come.'

She followed him through the garden, along the cloisters, now dappled in deep shadows and into the small chapel. Here they were greeted by Brother Bartholomew, his round face pale above the dark habit, his voice low.

'Do not be afraid,' he told her. 'Follow me to the alter.'

'Go on,' said Andrew. 'I will wait here for you.'

She moved forward out of the lantern's light and followed the monk into the darkness. The moonlight slanted in rays through the dark air and their footsteps echoed among the stonework. A single candle burned on the alter, flickering slightly. She kneeled at the altar step and bowed her head, praying, 'Send me a sign, Holy Mother. Have pity on your daughter, Elizabeth'. Then she stood up and Brother Bartholomew handed her a candle which she lit from the first and set beside it so that they shone bravely together, winking on the silver plate and gold chalice cup. The monk motioned to her to kneel once more and he placed a hand on her head and recited in Latin, inviting her to repeat it after him: *O Sancte Andrea effice et bonum pium acquiram virum; hodie mihi ostende quolis sit cui me in uxorum ducere debet. Amen.* Elizabeth repeated this without faltering and he nodded his approval. He knelt beside her

165

and prayed, 'Holy Mary, Mother of God, look kindly on thy child, Elizabeth, who is grown to womanhood and fain would bring forth a child. Bless her, I beseech you and quicken her body that her womb may be fruitful . . . .'

Amen to that, added Elizabeth fervently.

Brother Bartholomew stood again and helped her to rise also. He led the way to a small table which stood below the right hand chancel window. From this he picked up a circular piece of parchment which was divided into twelve sections each representing one month of the year, which was further sub-divided in some way. It was fixed upon a frame by a central pin and a long string hung from the wheel. Elizabeth took hold of the string and tugging it gently, set the wheel spinning on its frame. It came to rest and he peered short-sightedly to see which section was now marked by the string.

'Aha,' he said. 'It augurs well,' and he pointed to the words selected. Elizabeth read with difficulty the small cramped handwriting.

'The seasons of the year incline
For you – tis August twenty-nine'

'August twenty-nine,' she repeated and glanced towards the monk who nodded solemnly.

'But that's tomorrow night!' she said.

'Tis indeed the most propitious night for your union.'

He took the wheel from her trembling fingers and replaced it on the table. Opening a Bible which also lay on the table, he withdrew a small cluster of lavender spikes and gave them to her with instructions to put them under her pillow for seven hours before retiring.

'And now you can go home,' he told her. 'Rest easy in your mind. The deed is well and truly done!'

Catherine, next day, sweated with a high fever and Elizabeth thought fit to call in the doctor. He arrived late in the evening when she had almost despaired.

'Forgive the lateness of my visit,' he said. 'But I have been delayed with the Portreeve's wife who has such a cramp that her head is drawn down to her left shoulder, poor woman ....'

He grasped Elizabeth's hand and she smiled. 'I am glad that you are come,' she said, 'and I trust you will set my mind at ease.'

'She led the way towards the stairs and he followed her.

'Tis your daughter?' he asked and she nodded.

'She has had a fever this past day and night,' she told him, 'and I judged it an ephemer fever and thought it would pass but it grows worse. She came to a sweat but was not cooled by it.'

'No?'

'No. She slept through it and spoke wildly in her sleep.'

'Ah. The fever is in her blood and overheats the brain.'

'And now she complains of pain in her head.'

'Mmm.'

She led the way into the chamber where the four children slept. Della's bed had been moved in with them, and now she rose to her feet to nod to the physician and move the candle nearer to Catherine's bed. The little girl lay in her small bed, weighed down with blankets so that only her eyes and forehead showed, the latter beaded with perspiration. She looked with alarm at the appearance of the doctor, but Elizabeth took her hand and patted it reassuringly.

'Tis only the good doctor,' she said. 'I told you he would come. He will make you well and take the pain from your poor little head.' He stood looking down at the child, then slid a hand under her chin, disturbing the bedclothes as little as possible. Feeling around her neck, he nodded

167

several times in satisfaction, then smiled at her and the smile lit up his lean, almost cadaverous face.

'You singe my fingers!' he teased her and turning to Della said, 'She is like to set the bed afire! Douse her with a bowl of water if she does so!'

Catherine stared at him wide-eyed, but Stephen giggled at the doctor's joke.

'She has sneezed also,' Della volunteered.

The doctor nodded again. 'And your throat?' he asked Catherine. 'Is there any soreness here?' and he pointed to his own throat.

Catherine nodded.

'Mmmm . . . ' he said thoughtfully. 'I think this young lady has the measles, . . . if so then they will all take the infection for it comes of corrupt air and one infects the other.'

'Oh dear!' said Elizabeth and Della rolled her eyes despairingly.

'You will know by tomorrow,' he told them, 'for the spots will appear or may perchance the day after. Who can tell. On no wise let her stand in fresh air or drink anything cold but warm it first. A little chicken or mutton to eat or white fish, and avoid new ale. If the spots are small 'tis the measles, if large and raised 'tis probably the smallpox. If the latter, hang red cloth at the window. Twill aid the healing of the skin.'

He clasped his hands together as he glanced at Elizabeth enquiringly. 'Is there any more you would know of me?'

'I think not,' she said. 'If you send in your account my husband will pay you anon.'

'I thank you,' he said and nodding to Della, followed Elizabeth out of the room.

When they were on the doorstep, he lowered his voice and said, 'And the other matter we spoke of?'

She sighed, 'I have not despaired,' she said.

The doctor hesitated. 'And your husband?' he asked. 'Is he able to — to perform the act of matrimony?'

'Oh yes. The fault lies within me,' she informed him.

'Tis no fault,' he corrected her gently. 'Tis a weakness and can be cured. I am glad you do not despair.'

Elizabeth said suddenly, 'I have been to the Brother Bartholomew at the Priory.'

'Ah, the good monk. Good. Good. Tis well done. And did he give you a day?'

She said self-consciously. 'The twenty-ninth.'

He raised his eyebrows, and again the humour in his eyes lit up his face.

'Tonight!' he repeated. 'Why then, I'll delay you no longer. If the stars are favourable there is much hope, and you must to bed. I shall pray for you.'

'You are very kind.'

She held out her hands and he took them in his own for a moment. He had attended the family for years and was very familiar with Elizabeth's problem. He had suggested all the remedies he knew without success and now, like her, was prepared to put his faith in the stars.

'You must tell me how this matter goes,' he said.

She smiled with sudden eagerness. 'You will be one of the first to know,' she said.

After he had left, she hurried up to see that Della and the children were settled for the night, then made her way to her own chamber where she began careful preparations for the occasion.

John had ridden into Exeter and would be tired on his return. She could not afford to let him sleep! Nor could she tell him why tonight she especially wanted his body. The subject was a delicate one between them and rarely referred to. She must make herself so desirable that he could not resist her. 'Dear John,' she whispered. 'Love me tonight or I think I will die of misery'. Then she smiled sadly at her own foolishness.

From the secret place, the chest by the bed, she took the spray of lavender that Brother Bartholomew had given her and laid it under her pillow. She sprinkled rose petals on to the sheet and covered them with the top sheet so that they might perfume the bed. She was thankful that Della was sleeping elsewhere, for the nights were warm and the bed was stiflingly hot with the curtains pulled. There was water in the pitcher and she poured some into the bowl and splashed her teeth and mouth. She rubbed the former with a mixture of vinegar, rock alum, cinnamon and honey. With fresh water she washed her body, then brushed her hair, one hundred strokes each side, and bit her lips to redden them.

The final question now was where should John find her when he came into the room? Perhaps she should sit up in bed with the Bible, or stand at the window watching the light fade, or sit on the stool brushing her hair. Perhaps she should be naked as for bed, or wear her robe? Dear God, such petty deceptions! No, she would not stoop so low. She would go to bed as usual. Remembering the rose petals, she threw back the covers and was brushing them from the bed when she heard him arrive. Her heart began to pound and she realized that she was shaking. 'Let it be tonight, Sweet Mother of God!' she prayed. 'Help me I beseech you! I must seduce him with sweet words and such caresses that he must take me with passion. Oh, he is here . . . . '

She turned almost guiltily as he came into the room and was tongue-tied. She had so much to say yet none that could be spoken of! Instead of words she held out her arms. He kissed her briefly and sank wearily on to the chest and began to pull off his boots. She knelt to help him.

'The children well?' he asked. It was always his first question.

She chose her words carefully. 'Not well,' she said, 'but not really ill. Catherine's fever had persisted and the doctor thinks . . . . '

'The doctor?'

'Tis not serious,' she insisted. 'Tis probably the measles or the smallpox but twill run its course. Don't go to her!' she said hastily. 'She is asleep. Della is with them.'

'Why the petals?' he asked.

'Oh, the linen smelt stale. Did you dine in Exeter or are you hungry?'

'I dined with a fellow by the name of Bawsley,' he said. 'The solicitor introduced me to him. He is interested in investing in mining, it seems, but knows so little about it, he suggested I should stay the night and return tomorrow! I could not fault his enthusiasm, at least!'

Elizabeth closed her eyes and thanked the Virgin Mary for her intervention. So nearly her carefully laid plans had come to nought! So easily were hopes frustrated and by perfect strangers!

'I'm glad you came home,' she said. 'I have missed you, and the bed looks lonely without you.'

He laughed. 'It looks very good to me right now,' he said. 'God's Nails but I am weary. I thought I would fall asleep in the saddle this last five miles!'

She unlaced the front of his shirt and helped him ease it over his head.

'I'm enjoying the attention,' he told her. 'And will you also take off my breeches for me?'

'If you wish it. You cannot deny I take my wifely duties seriously.'

'I do not deny it. But I ponder the reason. What dreadful sin have you committed that you will soon confess?'

He spoke lightly, but his heart hammered uncomfortably. Did she have something to confess?

She laughed, protesting her innocence.

'Then I will attend to my own breeches,' he told her. 'While you warm the bed for your lord and master. Some say the handsomest man in Devonshire.'

'Oh? And who says so?' she asked, scrambling into the bed and sliding between the sheets.

'Why, I for one. And I'm as good a judge as the next man.'

He blew out the candle and climbed in beside her and sat looking down at her.

'How was your day?' he asked.

'Well enough.'

'Any visitors while I was away?'

'Only the doctor. Why do you ask?'

He shrugged without answering.

'Then enough of this nonsense,' she said. 'You must attend to the serious business of the night.'

'And that is?' he asked.

'Me!'

'Oh! so you take no pity on a weary man who has ...'

'No pity at all. Here I am waiting to please you and satisfy your every desire.'

'So I see.'

She moved into his arms and clung to him, her face against the soft hairs on his chest. It was dark but she knew they were gold, and that above them the shoulders were sprinkled with large freckles. It seemed to her that the sound of her heart was louder than usual and she moved slightly away so that he should not notice and ask the reason. 'The seasons of the year incline, for you tis August twenty-nine. A most propitious night.' And what had the doctor said? If the stars are favourable, there is much hope. He was a clever man. And learned. He wished her well.

Now John's fingers felt their way down her spine.

' – nine, ten, eleven, twelve....'

Her own fingers crept through his hair and round and into his ears.

'fifteen, sixteen ...' 'Tis August twenty-nine and the stars are favourable and he is with me and his fingers will soon lose patience and his desire will take over from the gentleness. Ah, now he holds me at arms length, reaching for my breasts, circling my nipples....'

'What was that?' he said suddenly as downstairs the dogs began to bark.

'Damnation!'

He sat up in bed and she clung to him. 'Don't heed them, my love. Don't listen to them. It is probably a fox in the garden. Oh, John, don't go down. Please don't leave me.'

He sat, one hand raised for her silence while he listened to the sound of the dogs.

'They are alarmed,' he said. ''Tis no mere fox. I will go down and see. Loose your hold of me. I shall be back presently. They will rouse the whole house else!'

He pulled on a robe and went out of the room. A wave of despair swept over her. Would there be any going back or was the spell broken? Had fate conspired against her for some reason that she did not understand?

'Wait for me!' she cried and snatching up her shift, struggled into it as she descended the stairs. He was pulling back the bolts as she reached him. The two dogs leaped frantically at the door hampering him until he shouted at them, cursing, and they fell back offended. The heavy door creaked open and Elizabeth screamed as the body of a man fell through the doorway and crashed on to the floor.

'God's name!' John muttered. 'Quick, fetch a light.'

She moved cautiously through the semi-darkness. In the hall she found a candle and lit it with trembling fingers. Hurrying back to the entrance the flame spluttered and hot wax fell on to her wrist.

'Who is it!' she asked as he took the light from her and held it above the prone figure. Above them from the stairway Martha's anxious face peered down and there were sounds from the nursery.

The man on the floor was a soldier. They could see that much from the heavy sword thrust through his belt.

'Is he dead?' asked Elizabeth.

John shook his head and as if in corroboration, the man stirred and rolled over on to his face groaning.

'Keep back,' said John. 'He may have a sickness and could infect us all.'

She stepped back hastily and put out a warning hand to Martha who now joined them. The man's face was grey in the flickering light, his beard untrimmed. His boots were

173

worn and his clothing ripped in several places. He groaned again and tried to sit up.

'The poor wretch is hurt,' said Martha.

He opened his eyes and looked around him, then put a hand to the back of his head.

'I'm surprised my bloody neck's not broke,' he said.

'Were you attacked?' John asked.

He shook his head.

'Thrown from my fool of a horse!' he said. 'You'd think the animal had never seen a coney before. Up he went and off I came, then off he went like all the demons in Hell were after him. I've promised him a right beating if ever I set eyes on him again!'

John helped the man to his feet and he and Martha guided him into the hall and on to the bench by what was left of the fire. The dogs, growling low in their throats, kept a respectful distance, and watched for a false move.

Martha was sent for some broth and a hunk of cold mutton and Elizabeth retired to the chamber to dress more decorously before coming downstairs again to learn more of the man's story. When she rejoined them, the man was finishing his broth. He took a large bite of meat and handed the empty bowl to Martha.

'That tasted good,' he told her. 'My own mother couldn't do better.'

John, impatient to hear how the man came to them, asked, 'And are you come from a battle?'

'A battle and a half,' he said bitterly. 'We have a new King, my friends!'

'Another?' cried Elizabeth. 'So soon?'

'But what of Richard of York?' asked John, dismayed. 'Is he taken in battle?'

'Not taken, but dead!' he told them and John cursed soundlessly, his face darkening with anger. 'And tis now the turn of a Welshman to ride through London with a crown on his head and the crowds shouting themselves hoarse.'

The man took another bite of the mutton and finishing it off, tossed the bone to the dogs who fought over it noisily.

'A Welshman?' said John. 'Henry Tudor?'

'Henry Tudor aye, and already crowned. Crowned him on the battlefield, they did. It rolled off one head and on to another.'

John turned away and stared unseeingly into the cold hearth. Elizabeth, watching him anxiously, at a loss how to comfort him. Three brothers lost in the Yorkist cause and now Richard was dead.

Martha shook her head. 'I don't know what the Kings are come to,' she said. 'Here today, gone tomorrow. They don't last above a few years nowadays. No little wonder we're all at sixes and sevens and don't know where to run. And what are you doing here?' She demanded as Della appeared in the doorway, reluctant to miss any of the excitement. 'You get off back to the children. You'll hear all that's good for you in the morning.'

'But I've only . . . .'

'But nothing! You get along.'

Reluctantly the girl retreated, but only as far as the stairs. She sat there listening and shivering for the night had grown chill.

'Where was this battle?' John asked.

'Bosworth Field. Know of it?'

'I do,' said John heavily.

Elizabeth said, 'And how do you come to be falling through our doorway so far from Bosworth Field?'

His name was Thomas Ridd, he told them and he was a Plymouth man, returning home. It was all over. The Yorkist army was vanquished. The Yorkist cause lost. They must all make their ways home and be done with fighting. He had intended riding to Plymouth before dark but losing his horse, had finally decided to head for Harben Priory, hoping for hospitality.

'Somehow in the darkness I must have taken a wrong

175

turning,' he said, 'and found you instead. But my strength had all but left me and my head ached. Ah, I thought, when I saw the light. I'll beg a night's shelter from the good monks . . . .'

'I'm no monk!' John said, 'but John Kendal, this is my wife Elizabeth and this is Heron. But you're welcome to a night's shelter. Martha will make you up a bed here by the fire and you shall rest. In the morning you must tell us more of the battle though tis a sorry business. Tis not often we hear such news at first hand.'

A pallet was found and blankets and another candle and the stranger was soon as comfortable as they could make him. Eventually the house fell silent once more.

In the big bed, Elizabeth lay in John's arms as he turned over the events of the past hours. She knew his mind was hopelessly active and his body forgotten. She let him talk. When he had said all that he had to say he fell silent at last. Slowly, she let her hand slide down over his back, into the curve of his waist and on to his narrow hips and buttocks.

'Don't sleep yet,' she whispered. He didn't answer and she slid further into the bed, kissing him as she went. She felt his body move suddenly against her and heard the sharp intake of his breath as body and mind awoke together.

'My mood is gone,' he said. 'This is not the time.'

'But I say it is,' she said. 'My body cries out for you and my mood is unchanged.'

He sighed deeply. 'How will you seduce me from my despair?' he asked.

'Let me try,' she said. 'Richard is dead and nothing will bring him back. But must his death kill our love? Come into my arms and let me console you. There is no more I can do for a man who has lost a King.'

He laughed briefly and turned towards her. 'You have a most persuasive way with words,' he told her. 'You are not easy to resist.'

'Then surrender graciously,' she teased, 'as I mean to do.'

He laughed again and there was more warmth in it. He took his wife into his arms and the nearness of her body comforted his own. Kissing the top of her head he frowned into the darkness. Perhaps it would be tonight. Perhaps he would kindle the elusive flame in her body that would give her the child she craved. He knew, more than she guessed, how much the lack of a child grieved her proud spirit and he understood her sense of failure. Maybe tonight? Suddenly he threw back the covers for they hindered him and she gave a small cry of pleasure as his hands reached out, feeling for her in the darkness.

When it was over she smiled happily and crept back into his arms.

'The twenty-ninth' she murmured, dizzy with weariness and closed her eyes.

John kissed a strand of her hair. 'Tis no longer the twenty-ninth,' he told her, 'but the thirtieth.'

But fortunately for her peace of mind she had fallen asleep.

'Fourteen years the Welshman has been in exile,' said Ridd bitterly. 'Would he had stayed another fourteen and Richard would still live.'

John was silent and the two men stared across the river to the far side where the dogs now wrestled with the stick he had thrown for them. They had crossed the river but were scarely wet for the water was low after a period of drought, and large boulders projecting from the water had provided stepping stones. Mud showed along each bank and the rank smell of dried water-weed hung in the still air. Tiny flies danced above small puddles along each bank, cut off from the main flow by the shallowness of the river. John whistled and the dogs sprang apart, ears pricked, poised for his command. He threw another stick, this time into the river and they plunged in and swam after it.

'It should have gone to us,' said Ridd. 'The day should have been ours but we had poor allies.'

'Who do you speak of?' asked John.

The man shook his head. 'Northumberland and the Stanleys,' he said. 'They hung back to see how it would go. Three thousand men the Stanley's had between them. They could have carried the day. Henry had but five thousand all told! Three thousand! If they had joined us . . . .'

'Did they go with Henry?'

Ridd spat in disgust. 'For a while they did nothing,' he said. 'Tis said Henry invited them to join him, we saw the messenger go down, but they declined. We had the stronger position, too, right from the start. Up on the ridge we were. Ambien Hill they call it. Surrounding them, you could say, on three sides. Looking down on their fires in the night and the sound carrying so that you could hear the horses whinney. Richard reckoned he could hear them saying their prayers!' Ridd laughed. 'It'll take more than prayers to save them, I told him.'

He crouched by the mud and took up a twig. 'Look here and I'll show you how it was.' He drew a horseshoe. 'Here's the ridge.' He drew a few lines at the open end. 'And here's the Welshman on the plain. Back here's the Earl of Northumberland. He was a late starter, too. Curs, the whole pack of them, cowardly curs. Between them and us there's this strip of marshy ground. We can see them. They can see us. Whoa! I don't want a shower!'

He broke off and put up his hands protectively as the wet dogs bounded up and Rufus shook himself violently.

'Hi, Rufus!' cried John. 'Is that the way to treat a guest? Even if he does fall in through our door like a sack of turnips! Stay!'

Reluctantly but immediately, they sank down. 'So we had all the advantages,' said John, 'yet lost the battle.'

'Aye. Soon as they moved, we attacked. Sent over a few

flights and received some. Not me. I was always useless at the butts. I don't see too well,' he laughed. 'I'm a swordsman. Always have been. I like to get in close and see the whites of their eyes. I ask you now, what did the Welshman know about fighting? Precious little. And what didn't Richard know! But the Welshman had his Uncle Jasper, and the Earl of Oxford. Both good men. Very experienced men, and they'd been into exile with him. After the archers we went in, hand to hand. Nothing of note. Then both sides fell back.' He looked up at John and asked, 'Why? Why stop? We should have pressed on. Richard should have pressed right on.' He shook his head and sighed.

As he did so, a girl appeared from beyond the trees on the far side of the river. She hesitated on seeing the two men but then came forward. It was Blanche Tucker. Her long, fair hair was held back from her face by a yellow ribbon which matched her gown.

'Who's this then?' called Ridd. 'A wood nymph?'

She came to the edge of the river and looked at the distance between the bank and the first boulder. The dogs leapt up and barked a welcome and she clapped her hands imperatively to silence them.

'Shall I help you across?' asked John, but she shook her head and jumped lightly on to the boulder, balancing gracefully. The two men watched with pleasure as the girl sprang from one boulder to the next with nervous movements like a young deer. When she reached them they clapped the performance and she blushed.

'I thought it would be low enough today,' she said, addressing her remarks to John. 'I looked each day. Now I have a secret way to visit.'

'Secret?' teased Ridd. 'When we know of it.'

'But you will not tell,' she said earnestly and they laughingly bound themselves to eternal secrecy on the matter.

'Blanche, this is Mister Ridd,' said John, 'and this is Blanche, our neighbour's daughter,'

They shook hands solemnly.

'You will find Catherine in the kitchen with Martha,' John told her and with a last shy smile she hurried past them and up the steps to the garden, followed by the two hounds.

'Please continue,' said John. 'I'd like to know how Richard lost his crown after so short a stay on the throne of England.'

'Short!' echoed Ridd. 'I'll say twas short. He scarce had time to warm the seat! As I say, twas a mistake,' he went on, 'to fall back the way we did, a bad mistake and we paid dearly for it. The Earl of Oxford is no fool. He saw that we hesitated and he brought his men forward again. Really fierce it was, then. Bloody fighting and a lot of good men died.' He shook his head at the memory. 'Still, we took the Duke of Norfolk's son. He'll fetch a pretty price I'll wager.'

'And the Duke?'

'He was killed.'

'So they lost father and son!' said John.

'Aye. But still the Stanley's hung back. Poor wretches. Very hard it must have been knowing what we must think of them. Kept there in safety while good men were dying. If we'd had them early enough . . . . Still, what's the use of ifs and buts! They stayed back and we lost the day.'

'The Stanleys! To sit their horses! I can scarce credit it.'

'Tis the truth,' he said indignantly. 'And the damned irony is that they hung back when they could have saved Richard — then when twas too late, came in for the Welshman!'

'God's truth!'

Ridd shook his head despondently. 'We were sickened. You can imagine. The Stanleys! Ah!' He spat contemptuously. 'Thank God I have never fought for such men . . .'

They were silent for a while.

'I've never fought for the Yorkist cause,' said John. 'Yet have lost three brothers to it. Fine men all of them and loyal.'

Ridd shrugged. 'Tis not to every man's taste,' he said, 'but I like it well enough. There's a companionship in battle that's like nothing else. You meet some fine men. Young Alan, only a lad, well born but no airs and graces. And Douglas,' he laughed at the memory, 'what a fighter he was. Couldn't get to grips with them fast enough for his liking. Had to hold him back like an eager pup on a leash. Good swordsman too. Very good swordsman. Doesn't know what fear is, that one. I wager the hum of arrows is music in his ears!'

'So now you're going home,' said John. 'Bit of a change for you, eh?'

Ridd laughed. 'Oh, not so different. There's battles galore with my wife. Fierce little thing she is. Scratched my face once from here to here!' He drew a line from his right temple down to his neck. 'And throw things! She's got the truest eye I know of in the battlefield. Never misses. If I don't move fast enough, it's wham! Right on the back of my head with whatever comes to hand! If she'd been with us at Bosworth t'would have ended differently!'

He tossed a pebble into the water.

John said, 'So how did Richard die?'

'Oh, aye. Richard.' he said. 'It was a brave attempt. Suddenly charged with his guard right up toward the Welshman, straight as an arrow. I'll wager Henry shook in his shoes seeing them come thundering up to him. But he stood his ground. I'll give him that. He threw down the Red Dragon and killed the standard bearers before they could close up the guard. Might have killed the Welshman too, but that's when the Stanleys decided to move. No one knew who they were going for. They could have carried it for Richard but, no — they came in for Henry. Richard was suddenly felled down from his mount and so many swords flashing it dazzled the eyes!' He sighed. 'That's when Hugh died. Right in close he was, I saw him move in as Richard fell trying to put himself between him and the enemy. Took a mighty blow on the back of his neck. Must have broke his spine. No other mark on him but stone dead. Just a little blood oozing from his mouth when we picked him up. But Richard! I've seen some horrible sights in my time but that was one of the worst. Slashed to pieces, you could say. Slashed to pieces! They stripped his body and slung him over a horse like so much baggage. Ugh!'

He sighed and turned away from the river. Slowly, the two men retraced their steps into the garden.

John frowned. 'So we shall all be taxed to pay for another coronation!' he said.

'Aye, though he's been crowned already!' said Ridd. 'One of the Stanleys put the crown on his head, still warm from Richard's so they say, and up go all the swords like a field of barley and tis "King Harry! King Harry!" and "Long live the King!" Same name as you, the lad, now I think on it. Kendal, – Hugh Kendal. Now there's a ...'

He stopped abruptly as John turned sharply towards him.

'Hugh Kendal? Are you certain of the name?'

'Certain enough,' said Ridd, suddenly uneasy.

'Where was he from, this lad?'

'Not from round these parts,' he said hastily. 'I've got the place on the tip of me tongue but can't ....'

His memory previously so clear, now appeared to fail him as he realized the awful truth. John gripped his arm painfully hard.

'Did he speak of his family?' he insisted. 'Did he name any names? Think, man. Tis no use to pretend. We shall know by and by. Did he speak of brother or sisters?'

'I'd not bring such tidings,' Ridd mumbled uncomfortably. 'Twas the last thing ....'

But John still held his arm and something in the tight line of his jaw prompted Ridd to say, 'He spoke of a Faith. She

182

was, either a sweetheart or a sister. I don't rightly recall!'

'His sister Faith!' said John. 'And in looks?'

'Fairish,' said Ridd. 'Blue eyes.' he looked at John, keenly, as though seeing him for the first time. 'Same shaped face as you. Same cheek-bones.'

John released his arm and stared back across the river.

'That was my nephew,' he said dully. 'We have lost four souls to the Yorkist cause and Richard is no more!'

CHAPTER TEN

1486

They sat side by side, the old man and the boy and watched the horse's rump swaying before them. The wooden seat was cold and they huddled into their clothes, lips chapped by the February weather. The old man's fingers, blue with cold, held the reins loosely, letting the horse have its head. They didn't speak. It was too early for conversation, so they were thrown back on their thoughts. The old man's sole concern was that the wind would drop but the boy wondered what the 'folks' would be like and whether, as sometimes happened, there would be any 'treats', a bun hot from the oven or a hunk of bread dipped in dripping from the meat. Behind them, the wain creaked under its load. Four hundred fathoms of Norfolk reed already bundled five to a fathom. The sedge for the ridging had been delivered the previous day, though what havoc the wind had played with it the old man shuddered to think.

'Did you get enough sways?' he asked and the boy nodded, withholding speech reproachfully. It was too early for conversation. Too dark for it too, for the days were short and it was barely light. He had spent a whole day cutting hazel for the sways, a dreary lonesome job which the boy hated. Today while the old man stripped the first area of its old thatch he would sit and twist the strings from lengths of briar. Another job he hated. He hated all the jobs, he told himself bitterly. At least he hated all the jobs he was allowed to do. He wanted to get up the ladder, tear off the old reed and hurl it to the ground. He wanted to pound the new bundles into shape on the rafters. He wanted to trim off the sedge ends with the big metal shears.

He sniffed as a large drip ran to the end of his nose. Ahead of them a hedge sparrow darted from the scrub at the side of the track swerving and looping in front of the horse and startling it into a flicker of acknowledgement. With it, the old man's thoughts jerked on to a new topic.

'Was you in the market, Saturday?'

'No,' replied the young boy.

'Then you missed summat. The ale wife was hurdled again with a pitcher round her neck.'

'Again?'

'Aye. Second time and before that was the stocks.'

'I saw that.' He laughed at the memory. 'Proper sight she was when the schoolboys was through with her. Eggs and flour and I don't know what else. What she done this time?'

'Same thing,' said the old man. 'Sour ale. Some folk never learn.'

'The hurdle ought to learn her.'

The old man shook his head. 'It won't,' he said. 'Not her sort. They never learn.'

He tightened his hold on the reins and turned the horse along the track leading to Heron.

'We be there,' he said at last. 'And mind your manners.'

'Aye,' said the boy.

The conversation had lightened his mood and he sprang briskly down. He surveyed the courtyard and looked up at the roof with what he hoped was a professional eye for the benefit of anyone who might be watching.

The old man climbed down more slowly and together they moved to the back of the wain. As the first thin beam of sunlight filtered through the trees, they began to unload the reeds.

Half-an-hour later, Martha stepped outside and screamed as the first bundle of the old thatch slithered down and fell into the yard in a hail of dust. Simeon stuffed a fist into his large mouth to stifle his laughter.

'God's nails!' she cried, and shut her eyes tight as she

waited for the dust to settle. Then she opened them and glared at him.

'I *was* coming out to ask if you'd care for a sup of summat,' she told him, 'but you'll not be getting any if you don't take that smirk off your face!'

The boy looked suitably chastened and composed his features hoping that Harry hadn't overheard this rebuke. Martha came further out into the yard and put her hands on her hips surveying the scene with displeasure. There was reed everywhere, bundles and bundles of it, but at least it was neatly stacked. But the sedge for the ridging was another matter. That was loosely tossed into warm brown heaps against the buttery wall, and the fresh February winds now sought out the fluffy seed and scattered it far and wide. Beside the kitchen door was a stack of hazel wands cut into three-foot sways and beside that a tangle of briar awaited conversion. It was to this last, that Simeon applied himself while Martha cast a baleful eye over the proceedings. He sat on his heels and nicked the end of the briar then, holding the knife in his teeth, eased the pliant stem into two strands. He tied the two together at one end and coaxed the two strands round each other so that they formed a string. He reached for another briar as Martha shaded her eyes and called up to the old man.

'Will you take a sup of summat hot, Mr Maskin?' she said, 'and a bite of cake?'

'I will and gladly, thanking you,' he called down.

He didn't turn as he called, for his fingers were fumbling with the next bundle, cutting the sway loose and preparing to drop the reed as soon as Martha was out of the way. But she was in a friendly mood.

'You've a fine bright day for it,' she shouted up.

'Aye, tis that, but a mite too fresh,' he said. 'You'll do well to keep your windows and doors shut against the dust. It finds its way in through even the least little crack.'

Martha was to find this distressingly true throughout the next three weeks, but now she thanked him for his advice and, carefully avoiding the three ladders which spanned the yard and leant against the roof, hurried indoors to act upon it.

Harry Maskin dropped the reed and it burst apart as it hit the ground in a smother of grey dust and mildewed reed. Tucked into his belt he held his legget, a flat square board dotted with flattened horseshoe nails. This and his fifteen-inch needle were the sole tools of his trade. The rest, his craftsmanship, he carried in his head. Slowly he made his way down the ladder. Harry Maskin never hurried. It was not in his nature to do so.

'Lord!' cried Della in her turn, coming into the yard. 'What a mess. Small wonder the mistress has gone on pilgrimage. She's well out of all this. Would she had taken me with her instead of Eric.'

She carried a pitcher of mulled ale and a trencher with two hunks of currant cake.

'How could two of you make such a pother?'

'We practise,' said Simeon pertly and rolled hurriedly sideways to avoid the toe of Della's shoe as she tried to give him a kick for his sauce.

She set down food and drink and gazed around. 'How long will all this be going on?' she asked 'and where's them buckets?'

'Buckets?' said Simeon.

'Aye. They were upturned just there, ready scoured and sweetening overnight.'

She pointed accusingly to the pile of sedge and the thatcher looked at Simeon who reddened.

'I don't rightly recall,' the young boy began.

'Ooh!' cried Della. 'They're never still there, under that lot.' Harry took a large bite of cake. 'Don't fret,' he told her. 'If they be in there, he shall find 'em.'

'Aye, that I will,' Simeon agreed and hastily reached for his share of the cake before it should occur to anyone to withold it as a punishment for his carelessness.

'What's going to happen to all this old straw?' Della asked.

'We shall burn it,' said Harry. 'That'll make a fine bonfire.'

'Oh, the children will enjoy that,' she said.

'Wish we could have it now,' said Simeon. 'I could do with it. I'm fair frozen.'

'You, you're always cold,' said Harry.

'You need some good warm blood in your veins,' Della told him. 'Like me. I never take chill. Hot potato, my ma used to call me.'

'Oh aye,' said Simeon. 'Hot stuff, are you?'

'You could say that!'

'Only got your word for it,' he teased, but she flounced back into the kitchen at a shout from Martha and shut the door.

Some hours later, Simeon found himself inside the kitchen, balanced precariously on a plank between two ladders; but glad to be out of the cold, for the wind had increased and the February sun gave little warmth. Outside on the roof, Harry laid the reeds over the exposed rafters and flattened the lower edges with the legget until it corresponded to the angle of the roof. Then, he pinned it down with a length of hazel and taking a briar from round his neck tied it round the sway in a timber hitch. He then threaded the briar through the eye of the long metal needle and stabbed it through the reeds to the rafters below. There, Simeon took it and the needle was pulled through and plunged in again on the other side of the rafters. Simeon rethreaded the briar and it was drawn to the outside and fastened to the sway with a clove hitch. It was repetitive, even tedious, but it gave him the chance to observe the workings of the kitchen and to cast a wistful eye on Della. Della, conscious of his interest, flounced around the room with a sight more energy than was usual. Martha, well aware of this, held her tongue and made the best possible use of the girl's temporary enthusiasm.

Patiently, Simeon waited his chance and eventually Harry descended to attend to the call of nature, just as Martha was called to the hall to give an eye to the children. Simeon sat astride the plank watching Della scour the pots.

'Nice little job you've got,' he said. 'Peel a few parsnips, sand a few pots.'

Della rounded on him as he had hoped she would, her eyes flashing indignantly.

'Nice little job!' she echoed. 'You've not seen anything! Run off my feet I am, and could well do with another pair of hands. D'you know what I've done this morning?'

'Tell me,' he said, admiring her tousled brown hair and what he could see of her freckled breasts, peeping out above the frill of her woollen dress.

'I've made six beds' she counted the items on her fingers, 'emptied six pots, given the babes their breakfast, cleaned out the ashes, brought in the wood ...'

'Like I said,' he interrupted 'a nice little job!'

She regarded him provocatively. 'Not so nice as yours!' she remarked. 'Standing around, threading a needle! I suppose you're going to be a thatcher, *when* you grow up.'

'When?' he protested. 'I'm already growed. Take my word on it.'

'You call that growed,' she laughed. 'Why, you're nothing but a twig – all skin and bone and your face is as downy as a peach!'

'I'm lean,' he protested.

'Lean?' she mocked, arms akimbo. 'Skinny, I'd say. Where are your muscles?'

He leaned forward, flexing his arm but on the pretext of feeling his biceps, she pulled him, so that he overbalanced and fell off the plank. He scrambled, red-faced, to his feet again, while she rocked with laughter. Harry's irate face peered through the rafters above them.

'Oy!' he shouted. 'Where've you got to, Simeon?'

189

The boy darted towards the ladder. 'I'm coming,' he called then, greatly daring, darted back and snatched a kiss.

'Well, there's a liberty!' Della declared indignantly but secretly delighted. Returning, to her scouring, she decided happily that the thatching, contrary to expectations, promised to be fun!

As he slid thankfully from the broad back of his cob, Eric thought he had never been so cold in his whole life! He wondered how his mistress bore it so stoically. His own fingers were numb and his toes, inside the short leather buskins, were almost devoid of feeling.

'My very bones are cold,' he told her, 'and my teeth chatter. Tis the icy wind. It seeks out the holes in my jerkin and . . . .'

'Holes?' said Elizabeth in surprise.

'My arm holes,' he grinned. 'Thanks be the Lord we are arrived before my blood froze in its veins.'

'We have come far enough,' said Elizabeth. 'Tonight we rest and tomorrow I will go on alone.'

She slipped out of the saddle and handed the rein to the ostler who ran out of the inn at their approach.

'Alone?' said Eric in alarm.

'Aye. You will wait here for me until I return.'

'Oh no, ma'am,' stammered Eric. 'The master told me not to let you out of my sight and I swore on my oath that I . . . .'

'And I tell you I will go on alone,' said Elizabeth, her discomfort sharpening her tone. 'The master is not here and will know only what we tell him, which will be what he wants to hear. But tomorrow I shall go on alone.'

Still arguing, Eric followed her through the archway and into the inn where several men and women warmed themselves at the large fire. He stood stamping his feet and shaking his hands while the host, a corpulent man in his fifties, bustled out rubbing his hands jovially and uttering a welcome.

'Give way at the fire there,' he cried, 'for this good lady, parched and pinched by the cold! And have you come far to be in Canterbury this night?'

'From Ashburton, near Exeter,' she told him, 'but we have made a three day journey of it.'

She smiled gratefully as a space was made for them and the heat of the burning logs comforted their bodies.

'From Exeter, eh!' he cried. 'And not even pilgrimage time.' The two main pilgrimages to the tomb of Thomas Becket were in July and December. Elizabeth and Eric had been lucky to find fellow travellers for the journey in February and it was for this reason that John had insisted Eric accompany her instead of Della as had been proposed orginally.

'I make private pilgrimage,' she told their host and he nodded.

'And wisely done,' he replied, 'for last month you would have been hard put to find a bed, much less a room, in the whole of Canterbury. The town was crammed with folk and no room to swing a cat! Trade's brisk at such times but I like it better when you can walk the streets without being jostled and the town belongs to us as lives here. But my tongue's wagging and you're thirsty. What's your pleasure, ma'am?'

Elizabeth ordered mulled ale for both of them and a capon to share. While they waited for it, they chatted with the other customers and generally made themselves at home. Although it was only early evening, the daylight had gone and the candles were lit. A mangy dog and a kitten shared the hearth, blinking in the firelight. Eric, disturbed by Elizabeth's intention to finish the journey alone, wrestled silently with the problem; but then decided to await inspiration or divine guidance with the dawn and abandoned himself to the pleasures of the evening. He had been charged by John with Elizabeth's safe keeping and was full of importance at the honour done him. He saw that the others treated Elizabeth with respect and basked in the reflected glory. A lady of means making a pilgrimage out of time was an object of interest and speculation. Even he did not know the purpose of her journey. Della had hinted at exchanged confidences but had not seen fit to enlighten the likes of him, merely murmuring about 'women's needs' and tapping the side of her nose meaningfully.

'Oh, she wishes a larger nose!' he had said, deliberately obtuse, and had laughed heartily at his own joke. He smiled still at the memory. But he kept a wary eye on the assorted company.

Trust no one, John had told him. The world is full of rogues and innocent pilgrims are their favourite food! But now the host's wife appeared with their supper and they deserted the fire as the table board was set up for them.

Eric beamed as the hot wine warmed him. Nothing had ever tasted so good, he told Elizabeth.

'I wager the capon will taste better!' she laughed and they each broke off a leg and bit into the pale flesh. It was succulent and still juicy, the skin crisp and scented with wood smoke.

He closed his eyes rapturously and ate quickly to the bone, then tossed it down on to the rushes where the dog and cat now waited patiently for the 'pickings'. Wiping his fingers on the bread, he pulled off the wings leaving the breast for his mistress. Behind him there was a burst of laughter and then a request for a song.

'Ah no,' cried a young man, modestly. 'I've no voice tonight. The frost has been at my chords.'

'Long as that's all it's been at!' cried a wag and there was more laughter, until finally he was persuaded to give them a song and broke into a bawdy ballad about a highwayman and an innkeeper's daughter. Eric stole a look at Elizabeth's face but she kept her eyes on her food.

'You'll be tired,' he said hopefully, and she nodded.

'I'll take to my bed when I've done with eating,' she told

him and he breathed more easily. With his mistress safely out of the way he could settle down to enjoy what promised to be a very lively evening.

As soon as it was light, Elizabeth washed hurriedly and dressed. Eric, sleeping in the hay loft above the horses had been told to wait at the inn for her return around midday. They would then begin their return journey in what was left of the daylight. She had spoken with a confidence she did not feel. Faced with the imminent prospect of her solitary excursion, she felt apprehensive and her stomach churned. But she would not be sick, she told herself. It was only fear that affected her, or perhaps hunger? She had decided to fast until after her visit to the shrine. When she came downstairs, the shutters were still closed and the smell of stale food and wood smoke hung in the air. She had to call a girl from the kitchen to unbolt the door.

'And will you want the ostler, ma'am?' she asked.

Elizabeth shook her head. 'No thank you,' she said. 'I shall walk to the cathedral.'

'Walk, ma'am? But tis nigh on three miles.'

'Be that as it may, I intend to walk.'

The girl pulled back the bolts and opened both halves of the door. Elizabeth thanked her and stepped outside into a grey world touched by a heavy hoar frost. Rime glittered on the gate posts and sparkled on the bare branches of the fig tree which grew in the middle of the yard. She shuddered as the first cold air entered her lungs.

'Tis a raw old morning,' the girl said and Elizabeth smiled ruefully.

'And twill be a raw old day,' she replied, and squaring her shoulders, set off across the cobbled yard, picking her way carefully for the layer of frost made the ground slippery. The girl watched her for a moment then called, 'God be with you, ma'am,' and closing the door, she wondered anxiously what sin Elizabeth could have committed that required her to walk to the shrine of the blessed Saint Thomas alone, and at such an ungodly hour of the day!

The highway had suffered in the December rains. The earth had been churned into mud by the feet of countless pilgrims and the mud had been rutted by cart and wagon wheels and frozen by the January snow. Pedestrians must now pick their way along the verges or walk in the middle of the highway between the ruts.

Elizabeth chose the middle, in order that she might be as far away as possible from the vegetation on either side where an assailant might possibly hide. In her right hand, she clutched a small dagger and made no effort to conceal it lest any think her unarmed and easy prey. There was no sound apart from her own footsteps. The birds were silent and she saw no one. She kept her thoughts on the town ahead of her, silhouetted against the lightening sky and she whispered the words of various prayers to steady her nerves. A rabbit suddenly darted across her path and her heart hammered as it cast a frightened glance in her direction and scuttled erratically towards the safety of the long grass.

She walked thus for maybe half-a-mile before she heard the welcoming jingle of a horse's harness and the rumble of wheels. In her state of nervous isolation, it was a sweet sound and she waved cheerfully to the young driver who reigned in his horse abruptly. He did not often meet with a beautiful woman walking alone and touched his forehead respectfully and with great daring offered her a lift.

'But we're not going in the same direction,' she said, laughing at his impudence.

'Why, then, more's the pity, ma'am,' he said, 'but you watch your step a sight further on when you reach the lepers. Tisn't good for a woman on her own, nor for a man, neither. They be that persistent, poor wretches.'

Elizabeth's heart sank. She had quite forgotten the

presence of the lepers outside the town wall and now recalled with misgiving their reputation.

'I am very early,' she said. 'Mayhap I shall pass through them before they are stirring.'

He laughed shortly.

'And mayhap I am a one legged monkey!' he said. 'You'd not avoid their attentions were it dead of night for their ears are attuned to the sound of silver in a passing purse! You mark my words and take heed, mistress.'

'I will and good-day to you.'

'God be with you,' he replied and sharply tapped his horse causing the cart to lurch forward, one wheel lodging in a deep rut which then set him cursing in no uncertain terms. Elizabeth, unable to help, went on her way.

Sure enough, ten minutes later as she drew near to the first ramshackle dwellings, there were signs of activity. Hesitating, she considered skirting the area but it meant a large detour across rough country. While she was deliberating on the best course of action a figure appeared in the nearest doorway. It wore the shapeless garments which covered lepers from head to toe, an attempt by law to prevent contact of any kind with the unaffected populace. She walked on nervously, aware that if he so wished he could cut across the highway before she could pass him. He took a few steps in her direction and she quickened her pace.

'Alms! Alms!' he called and the words acted as a signal provoking a flurry of activity. Another man appeared and there were more faces at the windows.

'Alms, mistress, for the love of God.'

Taken unawares by her early appearance he had no begging bowl and the hand that reached out towards her had only two fingers and a thumb. The rest were gnarled stumps rotted away by the dread disease that killed by inches. He shuffled his feet and she hastily averted her eyes, unable to look at them.

'Wait!' she called, fumbling in the purse at her waist, and

snatching out a few coins she threw them towards him. As he knelt to gather them, scrabbling in the frozen earth with his pathetic hands, she felt a wave of revulsion sweep through her, leaving her ashamed and sick. 'There but for the grace of God' she thought and yet could not see him as a human-being but as an animal to be avoided.

'Alms!' The cry was taken up on all sides and she saw to her horror that she would shortly be surrounded by the shambling shapeless creatures. She fought back a rising panic that clutched her, making her legs weak, her mind numb.

'Please,' she mumbled soundlessly. 'Please, stay away . . . . Don't come any nearer, I beg you . . . .'

She tossed a handful of coins towards them as far as she could and they, diverted as she had hoped they would be, fought among themselves for the money, pushing and kicking each other out of the way with small fierce cries that were terribly human and touched her heart with a poignancy that brought tears to her eyes.

Running along the highway her tears blinded her and she stumbled on the uneven surface falling headlong with a frightened, despairing cry. Terrified, she lay there as the feet shuffled nearer and the muttering voices grew louder. Without lifting her head she opened her eyes. Hideous feet, some clad only in rags, surrounded her and her stomach heaved. Dear God forbid that any hand reach down to help her! That any of those terrible hands should touch her! She closed her eyes again as a black despair seized her and crushed her almost insensible. It was then that she heard hoofbeats on the road and a voice, reassuringly familiar crying, 'Stand back there! Let me through. Stand back, I say.'

With a surge of relief, she recognized Eric's voice.

'Stand away, you wretches. Can't you see the lady is sick!'

She struggled to her knees and tried to stand, but stepped on the hem of her mantle. Thrown forward, she instinctively threw out her hands to save herself and in so doing felt the cloth of someone's garment as she fell again, the hands clawing at her body as she went down.

'Are you safe, ma'am? Calm yourself. I am here and you are in good hands. Come now. Let me help you.'

His firm young hands lifted her to her feet and through her tears she saw his cheerful face. In no time at all she was safely behind him on the cob's broad back, the mass of lepers dwindled into an indistinguishable group as Canterbury drew them into its comforting environs.

Sobbing but quieter, she clung to the lad's back, her face pressed into the rough leather of his jerkin. The movement of the horse and the sound of its hoofbeats soothed her bruised and battered spirit until at last she lifted her head. Seeing that they were already within the town walls, she cried to Eric to stop.

'I must walk the last mile,' she told him. 'I have sworn it. You must set me down here, Eric.'

But Eric, having saved her from one disaster, had no intention of allowing another and would not stop the horse until they reached the entrance to the church precincts. There he dismounted and helped her to do likewise. She looked at him soberly.

'I owe you much thanks,' she said, 'for disobeying my instructions this morning. I need scarcely tell you how timely your intervention was to me, nor how welcome your face!'

He smiled.

'The master threatens dire punishment if any harm befall you on this journey. I do not choose to sample it, nor could I sit idly by while you may be in danger.'

'Twas fortunate you woke when you did and followed.'

'Twas no fortune but a bribe,' he said, 'to the kitchen wench, to wake me when you left the inn. But now, if you wish, I will wait here while you visit the shrine, or would you have me come in?'

197

She shook her head emphatically. 'Thank you, but no,' she told him. 'You buy yourself something to eat for I warrant you are empty. Meet me here again in . . . .'

She broke off dismayed. Her hand reaching for the purse and found only the cut strings. The purse itself had vanished!

'Dear God!' she burst out, tears springing afresh to her eyes. Those wretches. It must have been the last man as I stumbled.

Eric cursed roundly, calling down the wrath of God on their hapless heads.

'But I have money,' he said. John, it seemed, had foreseen every misfortune! Eric drew a small purse from the lining of his jerkin and Elizabeth breathed a sigh of relief. 'And I thought myself so wise!' she laughed. 'But give me silver for the candle and guard the rest with your life. I will be an hour, no more. Find food for yourself and come back for me later.'

She watched him lead the horse away until they disappeared down a side road and then she turned toward the mighty church. Unremarked, she took off one shoe and then the other and removed her hose. People passed with no more than a shrug. The pilgrim was a strange creature but a common enough sight. With her shoes in her hand, she walked to the church door. The ground was icy but the discomfort to her feet was balm to her spirit. By the time she was inside the church itself her feet throbbed with the cold, but the tiled floor was easier to walk upon.

At last she stood before the shrine and its beauty took her breath away and distracted her momentarily from her purpose. In spite of its size, it was covered with plate of gold thickly encrusted with precious stones: diamonds, rubies, emeralds and sapphires, and glinted richly in the light of the flickering candles which surrounded it. A monk hurried forward to raise the cover of the shrine which was done to the accompaniment of tinkling bells. He pointed to the various bequests with a white wand, but the actual relics of the saint were hidden within and out of sight. Other relics were not so inaccessible and beckoning, the monk then showed her a piece of rock from the Holy Sepulchre, Aaron's rod, a piece of the clay from which Adam was made and the arms from eleven saints. Reluctantly, at his proud insistence, she gazed also on the heads of St Blasins, St Fursaeus and St Austroberta, and a sample of wool profess-edly woven by the Virgin Mary herself completed his 'exhibition'. She thanked him warmly and he departed a disappointed man for she was able only to give him some of the money intended for the purchase of a candle. Alone again, she returned to the shrine and knelt before it.

Closing her eyes, she prayed earnestly: 'Holy St Thomas, whose blood was shed on this cold earth and who rests now with the Lord God on high, hear thy daughter Elizabeth. Be merciful unto me. I do humbly acknowledge all sins whatever they may be . . . . ' Here she paused to consider what she might offer up for his pardon and continued, 'I have been vain and full of pride, have been selfish, and hasty-tempered. I have taken for granted thy bounteous goodness to me and mine, and have acted thoughtlessly and without compassion.' Her thoughts returned to the lepers and she wondered suddenly if they had been sent to test her. If so, she must have failed lamentably! 'Forgive me, I pray you, for my harsh thoughts of those less fortunate than myself and comfort them in their afflictions. I was afraid.'

A small sound behind her interrupted her thoughts and turning round she watched an urchin boy running down the aisle, her shoes in his hand. She gave a despairing moan, half rose then hastily resumed her kneeling posture. 'And now I am brought down before your shrine,' she continued, 'and humbled in your sight. Perchance I may be in a state of grace in your eyes.'

'Mistress, may I disturb your devotions for a moment?' An elderly man smiled down at her. In his hand he held her shoes which he had retrieved from the thief.

'Oh, my thanks,' stammered Elizabeth as he put out a hand to help her up. 'And the lad?'

'I let him go,' he said. 'He was but a child.'

'Thank you. May I know your name, sir?'

'Thomas Attwood of Winchester. And yours?'

'Elizabeth Kendal of Ashburton.'

He smiled briefly. 'The town has rogues aplenty!' he said. 'One must be wary.'

'But some honest citizens like yourself.'

'My pleasure to be of service.'

She held out her hand, he grasped it firmly and took his leave.

On her knees again, she continued her supplication, 'Most Reverend Saint, hear my plea. Grant me a child to gladden our hearts and I will ever give thanks. Thomas!'

Her mind was suddenly filled with a wild hopefulness. The elderly man's name was Thomas and he helped her. It was a sign! St Thomas! And Thomas of Winchester! Or was it merely a coincidence? No. She would take it as a sign from the blessed Saint to whose shrine she had come for help. 'I most humbly thank you for the sign you have given. I am truly forgiven my sins and in a state of blessedness. And you will send me a child, and I will name him Thomas.'

When the prayer was at last concluded she bought a candle and lit it before the main altar. Then, she bought a small pewter badge of Thomas Becket on horseback and pinned it to her mantle.

Eric arriving shortly afterwards, was surprised to see the change in her. Her eyes shone and her voice was steady, and she smiled as she greeted him. He sat at her feet and rubbed them back to life and squeezed the shoes on again.

'If you've blains on your feet,' he chided, 'the master will blame me!'

Elizabeth shook her head. 'No, he will chide no one,' she said. 'Not you. Not me. It has been worth the tribulations. I am full of hope!'

She spoke so fervently that Eric eyed her curiously and together they returned to the inn and later began their journey home, Eric proud that he had safely carried out John's order; Elizabeth in a mood of such exultation that two days of uninterrupted rain did nothing to dispel.

CHAPTER ELEVEN

'Throw the ball to me!' cried Blanche, her arms held high above her head. 'Throw it to me, I say. Oh, you ninny!'

The ball flew wide of William's hands and lodged itself firmly in the branches of one of the young cyprus trees which bordered the lawn. They all ran over to it and watched as Blanche tried to shake it free.

'I told you to throw it to me,' she scolded and Catherine looked suitably crushed. 'We need a stick to poke it free,' Blanche continued. 'All look for a stick.'

Obediently the three younger children began to search. William and Matthew as always stayed close together, but Catherine wandered off on her own, peering under the trees and behind the lavender clumps. She came suddenly upon Jacob who was pruning a small shrub.

'We need a stick,' she told him. 'The ball is lodged in the tree. What are you doing?'

'Making a cock,' he told her proudly. 'See here, that's his tail. And this is his neck and head.'

He stood back and surveyed his handiwork. Catherine also looked at it, but saw only an odd shaped shrub.

'Where are his legs?' she asked.

He laughed. 'Ah, trust you to ask that,' he said. 'Now legs is a very tricky matter. I shall give the matter some thought. But what do you think on it so far, eh?'

The little girl screwed up her face thoughtfully.

'Tis a comely bush,' she said at last and wondered why the old fellow laughed, wheezing asthmatically and slapping his leg.

At that moment, Blanche appeared and finding her in conversation frowned. 'You're not searching,' she said accusingly. 'Have you told Jacob we need a stick?'

The little girl nodded and looked to Jacob for corroboration.

'Show me where it is,' said Jacob, 'and I'll fetch it down. You'll be all over the garden if I don't and doing Lord knows what damage.'

He laid down the shears and followed the children who ran before him impatiently. There was no sign of the twins. Blanche groaned.

'Cathy, be a pet and go find them,' she said. 'We cannot play the game else. They cannot be far and I warrant they will be together. They may be in the orchard.'

Catherine trotted off on her errand, while Jacob reached into the tree and retrieved the ball. He handed it to Blanche and she blew on it to remove the fine brown dust from the tree.

'Don't I get a "thank you" then?' he reminded her.

'Thank you, Jacob,' she said dutifully. And then glancing up at the house, shading his eyes from the sun, he said, 'I reckon the mistress is calling you,' and he pointed to the chamber window from which Elizabeth was leaning.

'Me?' called Blanche and Elizabeth nodded and withdrew.

As Blanche prepared to go to her, Catherine returned towing two reluctant boys who wriggled crossly and complained that they no longer wanted to play with the ball.

'They may go in then,' said Blanche, 'for your mama is calling me and I daresay she will send me to Andrew.'

'I wish I might come to see Andrew,' said Catherine wistfully, but Blanche was very proud of her important position as messenger and did not intend to share it.

As she expected, Elizabeth had a small purse for her to take, but this time she had written a note which was rolled and sealed with wax.

'Take care that no one else sees the note,' she told her, 'and speak only to Andrew. You know where to find him?'

Blanche nodded. 'Tis Tuesday,' she said. 'He'll be about his beloved pottery.'

Elizabeth nodded. 'He is clever with his hands,' she said. Blanche took the money and letter. 'And shall I return?' she asked.

'If you wish. Would you care to take four hours with us? Martha has made a marchpane for John's birthday tomorrow and there was a little left over. She has made a small one for us to eat today.'

Blanche said, 'Then I shall run all the way,' and darted out of the room. She ran down the stairs and out of the house, waving to the children as she passed and calling out assurances as to her return. The year was still young but the sun shone brightly and, wrapped in her cloak, the girl was warm enough. She made her way through the orchard with its stark trees and silent hives and crossed into the stable yard where Eric sat inside the open door of one of the stalls. Behind him a small foal nuzzled its mother.

'Another message?' he cried. 'You should start up in business and make your fortune.'

She laughed. 'And will you make yours, polishing horse brass?'

'Ah, but I shan't be a stable boy all my life,' he said. 'A jockey, that's what I mean to be.'

'You're not small enough,' she said with some truth.

'I shall ride big horses!'

'Then I shan't wager on your winning,' she said peeping past him to see the foal which was nearly two months old and as black as the ace of spades.

'Have they thought of a name for him?' she asked, but he shook his head. 'Then I shall put my wits to work,' she said.

'What wits are those?'

Stumped for a reply she swung away, informing him that she could waste no more time in his company, then running delightedly to escape the rush of feet as he chased her out of the yard.

Skipping down the lane she reached the bridge where, to her surprise, two men were repairing the broken handrail. The law required all men to spend a number of hours on the maintenance of the roads and bridges, but it was impossible to enforce and was frequently ignored. But winter brought with it the usual hazards of swollen rivers and heavy snowfalls and the work became more urgent if the roads were not to become completely impassable, an inconvenience to rich and poor alike.

Recognizing her, they touched their foreheads respectfully as she passed, but she was mindful of Elizabeth's warning and did not speak. She paused only briefly for a glimpse of the milky-brown water which raced and swirled beneath the wooden structure. The power and speed of the current fascinated her, and she would have watched longer had she not been conscious of the interest shown in her. Tearing herself away, she continued up the hill to the Priory which echoed with the sound of the bells, rehearsing a special peal for Ash Wednesday on the following day. And the next week it would be Valentine's Day!

Blanche felt a glow of excitement as she remembered the occasion the previous year when Della had allowed her to share in the drawing of lots. She had written her name on a scrap of paper and Della and Martha had done the same. Jacob, Eric and Retter had been persuaded to join in and added their slips to those of the women. Drawing the lots had produced much laughter.

Della drew Eric and received a large smacking kiss. Martha drew Jacob and received a small, embarrassed bow. Blanche had drawn Retter who had swung her up in the air and declared her the bonniest Valentine he had ever had!

She smiled to herself at the memory and huddled closer into her cloak, as though to preserve the recollection from the February frost. Who would it be this year she wondered. She would cross her fingers and hope for Eric. He was cheeky but at least he was young and maybe he would kiss her! A shiver of anticipation ran through her as she tried to imagine how it would be. He might even give her a gift. They sometimes did, or so Della informed her. Della had once received a scarlet ribbon!

Maybe the young thatcher would draw lots if they were still working on the roof. He was almost handsome in a puny fashion. Not chunky like Eric.

She made her way to the small room where Andrew was, as she expected, bent over a pot. He looked up when she entered and smiled.

'I thought to see you today,' he said. He spoke quietly and Blanche wondered if being so often silent his voice had lost its strength.

'You do not use the wheel today,' she said. 'Why not?'

'I am making a coil pot, see. A long sausage of clay. I wind it round and round and shape it, so.'

She surveyed it critically. ''Tis not so smooth,' she told him. ' 'tis not so messy either!'

'True enough. But what do you bring me today. A letter?'

She held it out but his hands were brown from the clay and he first washed them in a bowl which stood in the corner. Then she handed him both letter and money, 'for the usual supplication' and while he opened the letter, amused herself by treadling the wheel and pretending to shape a non-existent lump of clay.

Greetings to you my dear brother, read Andrew, *from Elizabeth, the day before Ash Wednesday. As you see by this note, we are safely returned from Canterbury. I beg you pray for today with more than usual zeal if that be possible, the reason being that I am of late in such torment of hoping and yet fearing. John speaks no more on the matter, but his heart is heavy and I grieve for him. Therefore I beseech you light me two candles and not one to help your prayers on their way to the Blessed*

*Mary. I am confessed of all my sins and in such a state
of innocence before God that surely I may bear my dear
husband a child. My own prayers will strengthen yours.
May the blessed Trinity take us into safe keeping.
Elizabeth.*

Slowly he re-rolled the letter. He would burn it later. He
tossed up the small purse and caught it again and watched
the girl's slim fair hands shaping the empty air with
confident movements.

'There!' she said. 'What do you think of it?'

'A very fine pot,' he said. 'Tall and . . . .'

'Tis not. Tis short and wide.'

'Ah, so it is.'

'Here,' said Blanche, a spark of mischief in her eyes. 'Tis
for you.' She sliced it free with an invisible wire and
carefully lifted the pot and held it out to him.

'But tis not my birthday.'

'Then tis a Valentine's gift.'

He shook his head again. 'Tis not until next week.'

'Then keep it by until the day. Quick, take it for it grows
heavy!'

Laughing, he reached out for it and as he took it their
fingers touched, unnoticed by him but with a sensation for
her that made her heart pound. She stepped back and
looked at him. His hands clasped round the imaginary pot,
his head thrown back in laughter, a wide mouth with even
white teeth, blond hair. He was not a monk, she realized
suddenly. He was a boy. No, not a boy. He was a young
man and he had touched her. He had accepted her gift.
Suddenly with that brief meeting of hands, Blanche felt the
first flicker of awareness of the body's chemistry. She was
no longer little Blanche Tucker. She was female . . .

She stopped on the way home and leaned on the newly
repaired bridge, watching the water tug and fret at the
supports below her. The marchpane awaited her and the
children's chatter and she knew she couldn't bear it. She

wanted to lie on her bed and let this new emotion take hold of her. Andrew ... Andrew Sheldyke. She studied the hands that had touched his and thought them more beautiful because of it. Abruptly pushing herself away from the rail, she continued her journey towards Heron but once within sight of the house she stopped again, hesitated and turned instead toward home.

Some time later, Eric was sent to enquire after her and Joseph, learning of the matter, was displeased with such a lack of courtesy on her part. She listened in surprise. He still spoke to her as though to a child. Unable to eat, she was judged 'out of sorts and in a poor humour' and sent to bed. Delighted, she lay there undisturbed, staring at the ceiling until she finally fell asleep in the early hours of the morning. She slept with a faint smile on her face. She had come to a decision — Blanche Tucker was in love with Andrew Sheldyke!

The year unrolled its seasons, spring gave way to a golden summer and the corn ripened in the fields. Beyond Heron, England's history continued to unroll. The new King had taken a wife, Elizabeth of York, who now became pregnant within weeks of the ceremony.

Rumour was now widespread that her two brothers had been murdered on Richard's instructions. Certainly they had long since disappeared from the Tower gardens where they had once been seen at play. The King went on a progress to the North to foster more friendly relations in that area, but returned to London within a few months. In June, he and the Queen set off for Winchester where England's heir was to be borne. She was delivered of a son on the twentieth of September and the country rejoiced with the pealing of bells and the singing of *Te Deum Laudamus*.

'A baby prince!' whispered Catherine, her eyes shining. 'And may we see him, Papa? May we see the prince?'

'I fear not, little one,' he said ruffling her hair playfully, 'but we will celebrate. How should you fancy a bonfire, and Martha shall make us some mulled wine.'

'And toasted parsnips?' asked Stephen, and John nodded.

'And toasted parsnips?' said Martha, coming into the room. 'What do I hear about toasted parsnips, young Stephen.'

'We will have a bonfire tonight,' said John. 'To celebrate the news.'

Martha beamed. 'Ah, and what news,' she said. 'A little Prince Arthur. Tis a fine name and well chosen.'

Stephen frowned. Now in his seventh year, he was still withdrawn and lacking confidence. He rarely showed affection, except to Catherine who mothered him like a hen with one little chick.

'Stephen is a fine name, too,' said Catherine kindly.

'A very fine name,' John agreed. 'And so is Matthew and William.'

'Prince Arthur Stephen William Matthew Tudor,' said Blanche. 'That would be a splendid name! And when the Queen has a daughter why then, Princess Blanche Catherine Tudor!'

They all laughed. They sat in the garden in the shade of one of the trees, the girls busy with their spindles, while John read aloud to them and the twins amused themselves with a brightly coloured finch in a small cage. Elizabeth was resting on the bed. She had been unusually restless for several nights and had taken to sleeping in the afternoon.

'But now,' cried John, 'enough of working. Close your book, Stephen, and put away those spindles. If Martha will take the twins then the rest of us shall ride out in search of wood for the bonfire.'

It was quickly settled. William and Matthew were lured into the kitchen with the promise of an apple and a handful

209

of plums, while Stephen ran to the stable to ask Eric to saddle the horses.

'And will Mama come with us?' asked Catherine.

'I think not,' said John. 'She is tired. But she will join us at the bonfire tonight. Of that I am sure.'

They rode out a little later, Catherine behind John, clutching him firmly round the waist. She had recently had a fall from her own pony and did not care to ride alone. Blanche rode a small roan and Stephen the rugged Dartmoor pony which Eric had schooled for him. They rode across country, ignoring the highway, and headed for the large area of common land on the far side of the town where a copse of trees provided a plentiful supply of dead wood. They passed Retter returning from Exeter and stopped to exchange the latest news of the Queen's son.

'And what news of the Queen?' asked John. 'Will she survive the birth?'

'Tis more than likely. A straightforward delivery, they say.'

'Let us hope so. And the christening?'

'All over, but quite a gathering. A strange sight that, I warrant, Lancastrians and Yorkists giving thanks together! An uneasy truce by all accounts! The Earls of Oxford and Derby were there and the de la Poles, not to mention Elizabeth Woodville. She was godmother. But the bells! They say the townsfolk will be deaf for a week!'

'So, twill be the Queen's coronation next,' said John.

'No doubt. There's always something to spend folks money on.'

'I've a mind to see that,' said John thoughtfully. 'Elizabeth might enjoy a trip to London. She is in poor humour these days and a change might be welcome.'

As they rode on, John turned and called after him, 'We are having a bonfire tonight if any youngsters wish to come along,' and Retter promised to pass on the invitation.

Once in among the trees, they dismounted and tied their horses to a low branch, while they collected several large boughs and tied them with a rope. They passed the time of day with one or two villagers who were grazing their pigs amongst what remained of the autumn's acorns. Catherine grew tired of the search for wood and enlisted Stephen's help to fill her skirt with rosehips 'which Martha will make into a jelly'. After an hour, as the light was beginning to fade, they remounted and turned homeward, towing the large bundle of wood behind John's horse. The logs he towed slowed their pace to a walk and, while the children chattered, John's thoughts dwelt on a letter they had received from his sister, Lydia. The wording was cheerful enough but John, reading between the lines, was disturbed by her frequent references to 'some loss of vision' and 'a little difficulty with my sight'. How serious was it, he wondered anxiously, and was anything being done for her? Poor vision, the bane of many people, did not usually trouble the Kendals. They were fortunate in their general health and were not prey to the various inherited disorders that plagued other families. He smiled as he remembered his boyhood boast that his parents were never sick. 'Nor ever like to be' he had added and received a hearty jab with an elbow for his arrogance.

He remembered suddenly Lydia's sudden decision to relinquish their large house to their eldest son and retire to their smaller house in Exeter. She had blamed her husband's failing strength, he was much older than she was, and John had had no reason to believe otherwise. Now, it occurred to him that it may have been her failing sight that prompted the move. Or had they both felt the burden of increasing age and infirmity? He would visit her, he decided. He would speak of it to Elizabeth and they could ride together. Thus easier in his mind, he turned his attention to his son who rode silently beside him.

'You do not look happy, Stephen,' he said patiently. 'What troubles you today?'

The little boy scowled. 'There is no need for Catherine

to ride with you,' he said. 'My pony is big enough and I am as strong as you. Why can she not ride with me?'

John laughed. 'What do you say, Catherine?' he asked. 'Stephen speaks truly. He is a strong boy. Will you ride behind him for the rest of the journey?'

She nodded and a broad smile lit up the boy's face. His beloved Catherine would ride behind him! He would guard her with his life! The switch was soon effected and John watched proudly as they rode ahead. He felt strangely content as they approached Heron and he greeted Elizabeth warmly as she hurried out to meet them. His fears for Anne were temporarily forgotten.

That night the fire was lit with a great cheer from the crowd which grew steadily larger as the tinners' children drifted into the gardens. They came shyly at first, but with growing enjoyment as the welcome darkness hid their initial embarrassment and they found friends and neighbours. Martha had anticipated such a crowd and had prepared a large basket of washed and halved parnips. These, already partially boiled, were speared on sticks, rubbed with pigs' fat and thrust into the fire so that the air was soon full of the sweet smell of parsnips. Chestnuts were plentiful and provided a source of amusement as they popped out of their skins and the fire. Retter was there and Joseph Tucker with Blanche. Andrew looked in briefly but was unable to stay long, and Martha noticed with amusement how Blanche ran to him as he arrived and taking his hand, pulled him nearer to the fire. She noticed Elizabeth, too, and saw her eyes, large and luminous in the firelight and the cheekbones more finely drawn. It seemed to her experienced eye that she laughed more readily tonight and sought her husband among the crowd more eagerly than of late.

'The mistress looks bonny tonight,' she told Jacob. 'I'll wager the Queen's not the only one to delight her husband today. You mark my words, there's more to celebrate tonight than Prince Arthur.'

And Jacob, having a healthy respect for her intuition, stared at Elizabeth, and had no doubt that Martha was right.

'Now then Eric,' Martha called. 'Where are you with that ale? Not drinking it I hope for I'll clout you one if you are.'

'Small chance of that!' he cried. ''Tis all I can do to carry the stuff.' Poor Eric was indeed struggling. 'I'm laden like a pack-horse and me arm's aching like the very devil!'

Instructed by Martha to 'bring along the ale and wine when tis hot' he now carried two pitchers in each hand and there was a stoppered leatherjack under each arm. He came gingerly down the steps for the bonfire, for safety's sake, had been lit by the river. A row of burning torches marked the water's edge so that none should venture too near. Now willing hands relieved Eric of his burden and he was despatched to the kitchen once more to fetch the remainder. Della kept an eye on the twins and Catherine stayed with Elizabeth but Stephen dogged her heels.

Andrew swallowed the last mouthful of the parsnip Blanche had cooked for him and told her he must go.

'So soon?' she protested. 'But you are only just come.'

'I must go nonetheless,' he said, 'and my thanks for the parsnip. Twas cooked to perfection.'

He made his excuses and found Elizabeth. She had sent a note earlier asking him to call at the house. He saw that her face shone in the firelight and suspected what she had to say to him.

'Oh Andrew,' she cried, taking his two hands in hers. 'I must tell you that our prayers have been answered. I am at last with child and so happy. I have not told John but will do so tonight. But thank you for your prayers and interventions. They were not in vain.'

He kissed her warmly and she said, 'So you will be an uncle at long last. How does it feel?'

'Fearful! How does it feel to be a mother-in-waiting?'

She laughed. 'Intoxicating,' she said. 'I have no need of spiced ale. I am already drunk with joy. Burn a candle for me tomorrow in thanksgiving and I will send Blanche with the money. It will be the last time we shall trouble you.'

'Until the next time.'

'Ah, don't speak of it. Let me survive this one and then I may try again.'

He made his farewells and Blanche, waiting her opportunity, escorted him to the road and waved him on his way.

'Until tomorrow,' he said.

'Am I to come tomorrow?'

He nodded and the radiance of her smile in the moonlight troubled him for a moment but was soon forgotten.

John stood in the firelight with a sleepy Catherine in his arms. Elizabeth stood beside him peeling chestnuts which she fed into his mouth. Seeing Della nearby, she called her.

'The little ones are weary,' she said. 'Will you take them all and put them to bed. I will be along directly.'

She watched them go and then slipped a hand into John's.

'Will you walk with me to the water's edge?' she asked. ''Tis so hot here.'

As soon as they stood apart from prying eyes, she became suddenly nervous and stared back at the fire at a loss for words. She had waited so long for this moment and now she could scarcely bring herself to speak of it. He watched her and grew anxious in his turn.

What troubled her? 'Oh, John, you know what we wanted . . . .' Surprised, she found she was trembling and her voice little more than a whisper. He couldn't hear what she said, and fearfully he gripped her arm.

'What do you say?' he demanded roughly. 'Speak up for pity's sake!'

'The baby,' she stammered. 'I'm with child. Oh John!'

'With child?' he repeated dazedly. 'You are with child you say?'

She nodded and tears rolled down her cheeks. Hardly daring to believe what he heard, he took hold of her hand.

'Why do you weep?' he asked. 'Tell me why.'

'I think I am afraid,' she sobbed. 'I am afraid to die.'

He pulled her into his arms and she clung to him.

'You will not die,' he said softly. 'I will not let that happen again.'

CHAPTER TWELVE

1487

Lydia Harper straightened her back carefully and smoothed the front of her blue gown, tweaking the folds so that they hung to her satisfaction. She hummed softly as she tucked a stray hair under the small beaded cap and, picking up a small hand mirror, peered short-sightedly at her reflection, careful not to show her teeth which, with age, had become discoloured and unattractive. For a moment she closed her eyes and imagined herself beautiful once more, then sighed and faced her reflection again.

'Lydia Harper,' she whispered, 'you are a vain hussy! Such preparations and all for your brother. Anyone would believe a lover at the least! Such folly and at your age!'

But in spite of her protestations, she gave herself up briefly to memories of her youth when John, aged six, had told her in all seriousness that she was 'more bonny than an angel'! He had adored all his sisters but it was to Lydia that he gave his devotion. She was now fifty-two and her sight failing rapidly and her health troubled her. But for today she was that bonny girl again, in heart, if not in body for John was on his way. She patted her cheeks to redden them, and ran her hands down her body considering its shape for the first time for months. She had put on weight but not disproportionately so. Her bosom remained firm and the flesh pale enough. Only her legs had grown ugly, flabby and veined with blue. But those he would not see. There was a knocking at the door and she ran excitedly to the window. Her house looked out across the cathedral precincts, although her view was obscured by the row of chestnuts that separated the cathedral from the road. She

216

leaned out and immediately recognized John's smiling face.

'Oh, come through,' she cried and withdrew her head as he led his mount through the entrance at the side of the house. She was down the stairs as fast as safety would allow and running to the back door flung it open.

'John! Oh, my dear!'

Glad to be free of John's restraining hand, the horse tossed his head while John held out his hands to his sister, then pulled her gently towards him until she was held in a bear-like hug. Unbidden tears sprang to her eyes but she stepped back and blinking them away, screwed up her face in an effort to focus her sight. He noted the grey-white pupils and his heart sank. She had made light of the affliction in her letters, but now he saw that it was to spare him grief. She would soon be blind.

'You look so good,' she told him. 'So — so wholesome! I could eat you. Oh come into the house. No, wait. Philip!'

She called again and a young boy appeared at the window of the house that shared the courtyard.

'Take my brother's horse,' she told him and John tossed him a coin.

He followed her into the house and was soon comfortably installed by the fire, for although it was April the sun had declined to shine and a cool wind blew from the east. He saw with dismay how her hands groped for the decanter as she poured him some wine and then hesitantly cut a slice of venison pie.

'You like venison?' she asked.

'Have you forgot?' he teased. 'I am the brother that eats everything and refuses nothing. I haven't changed.'

She laughed, carried the food in and set it beside him, then arranged herself in the chair opposite.

'You are looking well,' he lied. 'Will you never grow any older? At this rate we will soon be of an age you and I!'

'John! John! How you flatter me, but how I love it,' she

said. 'But what news of home. How is the mother-to-be?'

'Very anxious,' he said, his mouth full of pie. 'And very large.'

Lydia smiled. 'Poor Elizabeth,' she said. 'She has waited so long. Tis such an agony of waiting for the first born. I can still recall . . . But she is well and in good spirits? And what think the other babes of the news? No, don't stop eating. The answers will wait, I daresay . . . Tis so good to see you.'

He paused between mouthfuls to sip the wine appreciatively.

'And John, your husband?' he asked. 'How does he enjoy his retirement?'

'You would scarce notice he is retired,' she laughed. 'He does too much and I wish he wouldn't. But he was ever thus and does not take kindly to my scolding! He works with the choristers, now, in the cathedral.'

'He always was fond of music.'

'Aye, and clever. He wrote a chant in honour of Prince Arthur and twas very well received. The abbot at Buckfast pleaded that he might have a copy made, he rated it so highly.'

'And his sketching?' asked John. 'Does he find time still for that?'

A proud smile lit up her clouded eyes as she nodded.

'Oh, he does indeed. Let me show you, these he did only last week. The son of a friend, see.'

She produced some rough drawings from a chest beneath the window and handed them to John for his approval.

'A bonny child,' said John. 'Who is he?'

'Tis little Leonard,' she told him, 'the son of Samuel and Alison Polegate, good friends of ours for many years. He is in shipping and often across the channel. They live on the other side of the town. Three sons, they have, and Leonard the oldest. But see, such large eyes, the lad has, and that rosebud mouth. Indeed, bonny lad,'

John looked at the sketch thoughtfully. 'How old is the boy?' he asked. 'I must look to Catherine's future before too long. Would you vouch for the family?'

'Indeed I would,' she cried, surprised and pleased by the unexpected turn of events. 'You shall talk to my husband when he comes home.'

He offered her the sketch but she shook her head.

'Keep it,' she said. 'Show it to Elizabeth.'

He nodded his thanks.

'And your lads?' he asked. 'Is Alan betrothed yet?'

'Soon will be, I trust,' she answered, 'and the other four happy. And Alan has a good job now. He's clerk to the Treasurer, would you believe. I can still scarce credit he is grown up and so tall . . . . All he has to do is cross the green and he's at his place of work!' She pointed towards the cathedral where the Treasurer's house, built against the North tower, was just visible through the trees.

'But Elizabeth,' she prompted, 'and the babes.'

'They would not thank you to call them babes!' said John. 'Stephen is eight, Catherine nine and the twins seven.'

'And still inseparable?'

'Aye. Never apart.

'And soon it will be five! And are you happy, John? Master of Heron, it sounds strange to me still. To me you are "young John" with scraped knees always in mischief. Always being beat but for all the good it did. Are you happy, John? You and Elizabeth?'

'Aye, and Elizabeth is radiant.'

'She is old to bear a first child, you know. You must take care of her.'

'I know. But she was desperate for a child of her own, Lydia. It has been the one sorrow in her life so far.'

'But you have four children.'

'They are not hers. She loves them but they are Bet's and mine.'

'Poor Elizabeth. But hark at me! Why poor Elizabeth.

She is with child and will soon have a babe of her own. You must send me word at once. How long now?'

'Another month.'

'Twill soon pass. And thanks be she does not carry through the heat of summer. Alan was born in September and it was such a summer. The streams dried up and in the Dart the fish died and floated on the water. Oh, that was a summer, that was.'

John pushed away the trencher and poured himself another goblet of wine.

'And you, Lydia,' he said gently. 'You must speak to me of your sight and with truth. What says the doctor?'

She was silent and he put out a hand and tilted her head.

'These eyes,' he repeated. 'What hope, Lydia?'

'Little enough hope, but the doctor is a good man. He has logic and astronomy.'

'But what remedies does he offer? And are you obedient to his instructions?'

She shrugged lightly without meeting his gaze. 'He does his best. He is a good man and aye, I am obedient. He lets blood.'

'From which vein?'

'The mediana.'

He nodded. 'And what more?'

'I must apply egg whites when I sleep and plasters.'

'And this helps?'

'I daresay. And must nightly and first thing plunge cold water into my eyes. This to clear the cloudiness.'

'And does it?'

She hesitated. 'Who can tell?' she said simply and they were both silent.

'He is a good man,' she said again. 'He attended many noble men.'

'And cures them?'

'They say he doth delay the blindness marvellously.'

'Then I am content. If you are satisfied with him I am content. But if not, then I will seek out another.'

She shook her head, smiling. 'If the stars are favourable I shall see. If not . . . .'

'And you have been on pilgrimage?'

'Aye, to Our Lady in Walsingham. We have done all that can be done. I am content.'

'Why then,' said John in lighter tone, 'we will speak no more of such matters. You shall tell me your news.'

She brightened visibly as the dread subject was dismissed and jumped to her feet.

'I have had a letter from Edward. About another battle. I will fetch it for you.'

'Another?'

'Aye at Stoke, so he tells.'

'And how went it?'

'For the King.'

She hurried out of the room and hurried upstairs. She returned with it and had thrown a light shawl across her shoulders.

'Quite an old woman,' she laughed. 'I feel the cold in my back.'

'Some wine, perhaps to warm you. I saw that you did not drink.'

'No. I have had gout in my knee. I tell you, I am grown suddenly old.' Her lips trembled and she looked at him for reassurance.

He smiled. 'You know you are beautiful to me,' he said. 'Why, even the brightest angel has the occasional twinge! Tis chilly on those clouds and I warrant they need a shawl when the night days are cool.'

'John! Oh you are as impudent as ever. But I believe you. And here, read me the letter. It came a week since and I forget it.'

He opened the roll and turned so that the light fell on to it. 'Such scrawl!' he laughed. 'Edward never did like putting pen to paper! But now . . . .

God's greeting be with you all in that wild country you call Devon. He never forgave you for staying South! We have received no tidings of you this past six months and therefore trust all is well with you and prosperous.

Our health is good but I have trouble with a stone but tis now abating and I am in hope of a cure without recourse to surgery. Heard you the rumours regarding a counterfeit Warwick newly crowned in Ireland and declared Edward the Sixth? The King denied it mightily and moved his army North where the two contenders did meet at Stoke on sixteenth of June with fearful casualties for the Pretender and himself captured. Now rumour has it that mercenaries were brought from Germany and fought a good fight but the Irish were half naked and quickly slain. John de la Pole is killed and many other good men which shall lie heavy on the conscience of the Duchess of Burgundy who, tis said, fed the attempt by such hatred as she has for Henry Tudor.

But enough of fighting. One day, perchance, I shall write you a letter that has nought of war among its pages! How is the weather in those parts? For ourselves we have seen more rain than for many a year and the rivers are impassable but falling a little since yesterday. The sweat has broke out in the town but we have escaped so far by the blessing of God and hope to continue in his mercy. And now I bid you farewell and so on and so on.

'I look forward to his letters,' said Lydia, 'and yet they fill me with guilt for I detest the task and ever delay answering hoping Jo my husband will need to do so and I can but add a postscript! It strains my eyes to but enough of that,' she said hastily.

John rolled up the letter and handed it to her. 'So,' he said, 'what shall we do with the remainder of the day. Your brother is at your command. Where shall we go?'

She clapped her hands together like an excited child and

222

thought hard. Then, sighing, she said, 'I would like to see the river again. Shall we walk along the river bank and look at the boats?'

'And throw pebbles into the water?' he suggested. 'And drop sticks and race them under the bridge the way we used to do? And you shall pretend to throw me in and I shall scream!'

She laughed affectionately and catching his hand, raised it to her lips and kissed it.

'And when I cannot see, what then?' she whispered and fear leapt across her face making it ugly.

'Why then,' he told her, 'we shall walk together and I shall "see" it for you, and it will be so much better. The boats will be larger, the water smoother, the sailors more handsome. You will wonder why you ever relied on your own eyes when mine bring you such beauty.' He kissed her gently. 'So no more of such talk. Away and find a mantle and let's be off.'

But as she scurried upstairs he sighed and his thoughts were heavy with regret.

Elizabeth closed the lid of the chest and resting her hands on it, pushed herself upright. The old hound watching, rose to his feet and his tail wagged hopefully. She smiled and shook her head.

'I'm feared the master is away visiting,' she told him. 'Poor Rufus, there'll be no hawking today.'

He blinked and something in the tone of her voice sobered him and he stretched languidly before preparing to follow her downstairs. Elizabeth went down slowly, one hand placed on the banister, the other in the small of her back where the now familiar ache troubled her. From the hall came the chanting of Latin verbs and she glanced in at the doorway. Stephen and the twins sat along one side of the table, heads bent low over their papers and Father

Marryat, catching sight of her, smiled briefly and raised a hand in greeting.

She put a finger to her lips so that they should remain unaware of her presence, but Rufus hurried forward to greet the old priest and thus created a diversion which the boys seized upon, sliding from their beach and rolling under the table to fondle the dog.

'Boys!' cried Father Marryat in shocked tones. 'I do not recall saying you might leave your seats! Return to your studies at once.'

Elizabeth called Rufus to her side and he ran across the hall scattering the freshly strewn rushes in his haste.

'Forgive me, Father,' Elizabeth smiled. 'I did not intend to disturb the lesson.'

The three boys turned to her appealingly as they resumed their seats, but she hardened her heart and smiled instead at Catherine who sat by the window, tracing the words in a large Bible that lay uncomfortably across her knees.

Taking the dog, she left the little group to their studies and made her way to the kitchen where Martha was plucking a duck.

There were feathers everywhere and Rufus sprang forward, snapping excitedly at those that floated around his head.

'I'm not having that animal in my kitchen,' grumbled Martha who was out of sorts with a sick headache. 'Out with you. Shoo! Stole a carcase, he did, not two days since and me scarcely turned my back! But sit you down here now.'

She chased him out with much hand clapping then pulled a stool from under the table, and hovered anxiously as her mistress lowered herself on to it.

'Oh,' said Elizabeth, 'that's more comfortable. At least it will be so for a matter of minutes. If I am standing I want to sit and if sitting, why then I'm anxious to stand and stretch my legs. I think I may take a walk presently.'

Martha watched her as her fingers resumed their task,

snatching tufts of feathers from the still warm body of a wild duck.

'Is he still kicking?' she asked with a real curiosity. She had never married and had no experience of child-bearing. All the time she had been with Daniel Heron there had been no children until now. The whole process of reproduction fascinated her and she felt both thrilled and anxious as the time drew nearer. She was determined the child should be a boy.

'I think he or she is taking dancing lessons and will dance his way into the world. Elizabeth laughed. 'How will you prepare this duck?'

'I thought to hash it with claret wine and butter and a few shallots.' replied Martha 'I think the master will favour that, if he is come home in time.'

'Oh, he will be home before dark,' said Elizabeth. 'At least he promised so. Tis strange, but I did not want him to go today although tis not far and Lydia needs him. He is her favourite, and her sight is troubling her these past months though nothing that will not cure, she says. And yet I did not want him to go.' She sighed deeply.

'Why, tis no distance,' Martha reassured her. She had finished the plucking and now reached for a small chopper and severed the head with a quick sure blow. 'A ten mile at the most. And the master rides like the devil! He will be home before dark if he has vowed so. And we will have supper ready and you will have a pleasant evening together.'

Elizabeth nodded and stood up, easing her back. 'Only a few weeks more and I shall see my feet again,' she joked. 'I have forgot how it is to be without — this.' She patted her swollen belly. 'Nine months is a long time.'

'But seems longer when you are sickly,' said Martha. 'All that vomiting! The fathers have a better time of it.'

'But John has suffered my ill humour,' said Elizabeth, 'and the doctor's fees. Oh, Rufus, are you back again? Such

225

persistence! I will take you for a short walk, then, for I swear you are as restless as I am without John.'

'Will Father Marryat stay for "four hours"?' asked Martha.

'Most likely. He likes to talk and he has a great liking for your pastry, Martha. Set it out in the hall as soon as the lesson is at an end and send the children to fetch me. Come, then, foolish old dog. We will walk awhile.'

It was as she descended the steps to the river that the accident happened. Somehow Rufus, impatient to be past, pushed through between her and the wall so that she lost her balance. Her fingers scrabbled for a hold, but the stone wall was still wet from the rains and with a short cry of fear, she slipped off the steps and fell the five or six feet into the garden below. As she went down, her head struck the steps and for a while she lay unconscious among the damp grass and shrubs while Rufus whined uneasily, sensing disaster. His whining gave way to barking and he scratched at her arm in an effort to rouse her. When this proved unavailing, he left her and slunk guiltily back into the kitchen and hid himself under the table.

'Out of there!' cried Martha wrathfully. 'Don't think as I haven't noticed you. Out you go and don't come back.'

She poked at him with a besom, but to her surprise he growled warningly and she hesitated.

'Now what's got into him?' she muttered. 'And where's the mistress? That was a mighty short walk even in her condition . . . Where's your mistress, you stupid animal, eh? Or are you sulking?'

He growled again and her eyes narrowed. She stepped outside and looked for Elizabeth but saw and heard nothing. With a shrug of her shoulders, she was about to dismiss her suspicions, but she took one more look at Rufus and saw that he trembled.

'Oh, sweet Heaven,' she whispered. 'Now what . . . ' She

226

ran out into the garden shouting for Jacob who appeared, spade in hand, to see what was wrong.

'The mistress!' shouted Martha. 'She was walking in the garden. Did you see which way she went?'

'Towards the river,' he answered and together they ran across the grass and through the orchard. They found her where Rufus had left her. She was just opening her eyes and blood oozed from the cut on her head. She retched violently, but brought nothing up. Gasping and weeping with fright, she clung to Martha while Jacob ran for Eric and Father Marryat to help carry her. She tried to stand, but her right leg pained her; she suddenly screamed with a sharp pain that stabbed through her body.

'Oh, the babe!' she sobbed hysterically. 'The babe! Sweet Mary, not the babe!' Tears streamed from her eyes as she and Martha clung together. Then a second contraction seized her, and Martha put aside her own fears in an effort to calm the hysterical woman in her arms.

'You mustn't weep,' she urged her, stroking her hair and wiping away the tears. 'Think of the little one and calm yourself.'

'But if it comes,' cried Elizabeth. 'I am so feared without John. Tis coming, I know it! Aah!'

She clamped a hand over her mouth to still the scream that rose to her lips, and was aware suddenly of the panic in Martha's eyes.

'Oh, Martha, don't look so,' she beseeched her. 'You frighten me more. Send to John, for pity's sake. Send Eric to fetch him home. Oh, dear God! Sweet mother of Christ!'

The three men arrived and together they lifted her. Eric took her feet, Jacob and Father Marryat an arm each; they carried her carefully back into the house and upstairs to her chamber where they laid her on the bed, exhausted.

'The midwife!' cried Martha as another pain racked Elizabeth. She gave Eric a push that sent him flying from the room. 'Don't stand there. Fetch the midwife and quick;

Mistress Bewley from next the almshouses. Run, you dolt!'

Eric hustled down the stairs and out of the front door. Martha, Jacob and the priest stood awkwardly at the end of the bed at a loss to know what to do. Martha put her hand to her head willing herself to think straight. Elizabeth raised her head: 'Is Eric gone to Exeter?' she asked.

'Why no, ma'am,' said Martha guiltily. 'He is gone for the midwife, but Jacob shall ride to Exeter.'

Jacob looked unhappy with this suggestion and Elizabeth would not consider it.

'He will be too slow. Send him to find Joseph and ask if we may borrow one of his men to take the message. Someone who rides well. Pray for me, Father, and for the babe lest . . . .'

She was interrupted by another spasm, which brought a faint gleam of perspiration to her face and neck.

'Should it be like this, I wonder,' she muttered to herself. 'If so then I can bear it better. But if the birth is unnatural . . . Why then I cannot . . . Martha! I beg you. Don't gape so! Should we not have hot water and linens ready? Go see to it and leave me to myself. Oh Catherine!' she said suddenly. 'Little one. Mama is well. I have a pain. That is all.'

The little girl stood in the doorway, her eyes wide and troubled. Hurriedly, Martha took her hand and lead her downstairs where the other children waited impatiently for 'four hours' which was partly laid in the hall.

'Your mama is resting, my pet' Martha told her. 'She has bumped her head but will soon be recovered. You shall see her later.'

'Is she having the babe?' asked Catherine and Martha, after the initial shock, recalled that the little girl was probably more familiar with such an occurrence than she was herself. 'And I warrant she could comfort me a sight better than I might her' she pondered and was relieved to find Della in the kitchen, returned from the market. She

228

was stroking Rufus who stood with his head in her lap, while she drank a mug of ale and filled her mouth with currants.

'Out!' she bellowed and Rufus fled.

Della looked at her distraught face in surprise. 'What ails everyone?' she asked. 'I have just passed Jacob who ran like one possessed and was so short of breath he could not speak!'

'You may well ask,' said Martha, snatching up the currants. 'The mistress has had a bad tumble and gone into her pains and screaming with it, poor soul. Take Cathy into the hall and give the babes their meal. I must get hot water and . . . .'

'Is the midwife come?'

'Not yet but sent for, the master also. Keep the children from their mother lest they be frightened.'

Della hesitated. 'Should I go up to the mistress.' she suggested hopefully. 'To let her know I'm come back?'

'I'll tell her you're back. You do what you're told,' snapped Martha and began to fill the largest pan that hung above the fire.

Within the hour the midwife arrived and Della seized her chance to lead her up to Elizabeth's chamber. The old woman bustled in with a cheerful smile and sent Father Marryat on his way, for which he was secretly thankful, although he promised to look in later and see how matters progressed. She set down the birthing stool and opened her bag. From it she drew a leather bottle and a small wooden beaker, into which she poured a measure of liquid.

'There we are, my dear,' she said. 'Drink that and you'll be greatly eased. No, every last drop. Tis unpleasant I know but twill ease the pains. That's well done. And now I'll see how the babe does.'

She closed the chamber door and took a lidded pot from the bag. It was full of white grease and she rubbed this over her hands. 'Now lie back and think on other matters,' she advised, 'while I examine you.'

She waited for the next contraction to pass, then slid her fingers into Elizabeth's body.

'No, no don't tighten up,' she said, 'breathe deep, and again . . . . Why tis fine, fine, nothing to fear my dear, but twill be a while yet. Briskly she wiped the grease from her hands, then proceeded to examine her externally; pressing and probing with her head on one side and a reassuring smile on her face. The draught which she had given Elizabeth began to take effect and a strange feeling of unreality crept over her. She watched the old woman curiously, as though in a dream; but the pains when they came were as fierce as ever, and grew more frequent until the dream-like feeling took on a nightmarish quality. The pain increased, her leg throbbed from the fall and her mind wandered.

John did not come. They kept from her the fact that he also had sent a message — that he would return early next morning. John Harper was kept away unexpectedly on business and Lydia was alone. The two messengers crossed each other *en route* but Joseph's man would reach Exeter by six o'clock and John was expected home by eight.

Elizabeth lay on the bed, her hand clutching Della's while the midwife sat spinning and humming to herself. She examined Elizabeth again, declared the head well down and gave Elizabeth a second draught of the mixture. Martha popped in and out and Father Marryat returned to pray for her, but did not stay for a sick man lay dying and 'his need is greater'.

Another hour passed and the contractions gave way to the next stage. She was bearing down and the pain was worse than anything she had ever imagined. She wept for John and for herself and for the small being who waited to be born; and still the old woman spun, flicking the spindle with deft movements, coaxing the wool into thread, humming interminably and tonelessly until the whole scene blurred in Elizabeth's mind.

Then suddenly they were moving her on to the stool, the

230

last fierce thrusts sent the child head first into the midwives waiting hands and it was done.

Half-an-hour later the child, a boy, lay in Elizabeth's arms, and Della stood proudly by. The midwife had tidied matters, then left. The wet nurse would arrive in the morning and the doctor would call. The children had been in to see and admire their new brother and Elizabeth's joy was almost complete. If only John would come!

Della held the sleeping child for a while and Martha's face wore a permanent grin.

'All's well that ends well!' she repeated and recounted every detail to anyone who would listen, until Eric begged her to stop for it made him feel bad.

'*You* feel bad!' cried Martha. 'Then how think you the mistress felt? Bad's a poor sort of word for her sufferings, bless the poor soul. But there, God the sweet Virgin has seen fit to preserve them and no wonder; for she's a good woman and the master be an honest and upright man. But thank the Lord I'm never likely to bear a child for I warrant I'd never survive. No, and don't want to put the matter to the test neither.'

'You'd need a husband first,' said Jacob greatly daring, for they had supped of wine in celebration and his head was not used to such excesses.

Eric giggled. 'Aye and where'd you find such a one?' he asked.

But Martha refused to be ruffled. 'I've had me chances,' she told them, 'but I turned them down. Lumber myself with a useless old fellow, I should think not.'

Della joined them then, flopping on to a stool with a heartfelt sigh. 'Oh the pet,' she crooned. 'The little pet. And so much hair — dark it is, like the mistress was as a babe, and him so good, bless him. Fast sleep with his hands tight shut like this . . .' she held her fists to her chest. 'And I held him for a spell. Not a murmur!'

'Well then,' said Jacob. 'What's she calling him. John I reckon, after his father.'

But Della shook her head. 'I think twill be Thomas. So good he is, hasn't cried since he was born. Not one cry has he made!'

'Here's to him then,' said Eric hopefully raising his empty goblet, but Martha snorted.

'No more wine for you, young Eric,' she said. 'Oh, I do wish the master would come home. What's keeping the man? Doesn't he want to see his own son? And the mistress fretting, I'll warrant, to show off the babe.'

Upstairs, Elizabeth held the baby in her arms and couldn't bear to take her eyes from the still, small form. She watched the tiny fingers open and close and saw the eyelids flicker. He was too tiny, so frail! Her arm ached, but she would not move it for fear of disturbing his sleep. She didn't want him to wake and cry, yet she wanted to comfort and soothe him back to sleep. She knew he couldn't focus yet but she longed to see him again with his eyes open, blue like John's. They were all blue, the midwife said, when first born. Thomas Kendal . . . .

She bent her head and kissed the fine dark hair on top of his head. The head was slightly elongated due to the early birth, but that was quite common and would soon return to the normal shape.

'Dear little head,' she whispered. 'I love it the way it is. You are quite perfect, little one, and so dear to me.'

Closing her eyes, she gave herself up to the rich contentment which filled her body and soul. 'Oh John!' she thought. 'Come soon I beg you. Come and see the son we have given each other!'

But unobserved, the tiny fingers uncurled for the last time. The strain of the premature birth proved too heavy for the tiny heart and it fluttered suddenly, missed a beat and stopped. The small mouth drooped. Five minutes later, as John rode up to the house in a flurry of hoofbeats, Elizabeth began to scream.

232

Much later, John sat alone on the steps staring out over the dark garden. Rufus found him and laid his head on his master's shoulder. Without turning his head, John said quietly: 'You have cost me my son,' and drawing his dagger drew the dog's head down, held the blade to his throat. But his hand trembled and Rufus wriggled in the unusually fierce grasp, whining anxiously. John let his hand fall.

'I cannot do it!' he muttered but Elizabeth's screams still rang in his ears. Abruptly he stood up and went back into the house. 'Take the hound,' he told a startled Martha. 'Tell Eric to get rid of it.'

Martha's eyes opened wide and round with shock. 'Kill it, sir?' she gasped.

'No,' he said. 'I know well enough twas the will of God — bid Eric find it a new master. This one cannot bear the sight of it.'

CHAPTER THIRTEEN

'Keep close or we shall lose each other. I have never seen such a press of people!'

Elizabeth didn't need telling twice. She clung to John's hand as to a life-line and followed him blindly through the thousands of people who thronged the streets for the Queen's coronation. It was nearly two years since the wedding of the red and white roses and over a year since Prince Arthur was born. The battle at Stoke had settled Henry more firmly on the throne, and the people welcomed his wife, Elizabeth of York as their Queen, and turned out on to the streets to demonstrate their loyalty. The loss of the youngest Kendal son had thrown Elizabeth into a severe depression from which she was just beginning to emerge. John had written to Mark privately, warning him of her changed appearance and asking for an invitation to London. He hoped that Mark's cheerful company and the general excitement, might help restore her spirits where a succession of the doctor's potions and philtres had failed. Mark had been only too willing to help in any way that he could. He was still a bachelor, still being pursued by the determined Ella who was a lively girl, and did her best to keep Elizabeth's thoughts from past sorrows.

Twenty-fourth of November was the date set for the coronation but today, the twenty-third, the Queen was travelling from Greenwich to the Tower and the journey drew huge crowds to the riverside.

'We're going to be late,' wailed Ella, as Mark towed her through the crowd. 'You should have thought less about your belly and more about our entertainment! I'll wager we shall see nothing but the last ship's wake, by the time we reach the water!'

'Cease your scolding,' said Mark. 'We are not wed yet.'

'Nor like to be!' she retorted. 'So slow, this one,' she told Elizabeth, laughing. 'I never knew a man prevaricate as this one does. One of these days I shall drag him by his ear to the church door. He will be too old, else!'

'Mark too old!' cried John. 'That I cannot imagine! Mark will . . . . Ah!'

Stumbling over something, he glanced down to see the legs of a drunken reveller. The man lay half hidden by a stack of fish baskets, happily oblivious to the succession of people who tripped over him, cursing. But they had reached the water at last and in spite of Ella's dire predictions to the contrary, were in good time to see the Thames at its most regal. The sun glistened on the water between the large and small craft that dotted its surface. The Queen, her mother-in-law, and the cream of the nobility, stood in the royal barge which fluttered with banners and streamers.

'Oh, there's the Queen herself, God bless her,' cried Ella pointing. They saw the slim figure of the young woman sitting alone, her long fair hair cascading down her back like pale silk. The sumptuous clothes of her companions quite overshadowed the fluttering bunting, as the sound of music came to them across the water.

'She looks very beautiful,' said Elizabeth.

John tightened his arm around her. 'Of the two Elizabeth's, I swear I have the best bargain,' he said gallantly and was rewarded by a smile.

'That was sweetly said,' said Ella, poking Mark in the ribs. 'You do not pay me such compliments, sir. Am I your best bargain?'

'I would say "Aye" if I dared,' said Mark, 'but I should do penance for a lie after!'

'Oh, such sauce, this one,' she cried. 'I swear when he asks for my hand I shall refuse him.'

'Do I have your word on that?' asked Mark, which made even Elizabeth laugh and Ella admitted herself 'beat'.

The Guilds had also turned out in force to escort the Queen, their barges decorated in a dazzling variety of themes suitable to the occasion. One, in honour of the King, portrayed the Welsh Dragon, a huge red monster with spiked tail and jaws which belched most realistic flames and smoke. Each one bore the arms and badges of its particular craft, but all judged the goldsmiths barge the finest on the river. It was hung with cloth of gold; golden streamers and tassels sparkling with samples of the goldsmith's craft.

'And did you make all that yourself?' teased Elizabeth.

'I had a prentice help me,' said Mark, grinning.

'He will have us believe he made the Queen's crown next!'

With such amiable banter to occupy their wits, and a fine spectacle to delight their eyes, they passed a most enjoyable hour. When it was all over, they wandered home by a roundabout route to see some of the street decorations, which had been put up for the procession the following day.

They arrived tired but happy at Mark's small house in Cheapside.

'And now to eat,' he said. 'What say we send out to the cookshop for mutton and rolls, and a flagon of their best wine. Those in favour raise your hand.'

It was unanimous.

The following day, Mark was up early and out of the house on business of his own, but John and Elizabeth enjoyed the luxury of a late rising. Refreshed by Mark and Ella's company, Elizabeth was in better spirits and John was pleased to note her eagerness to talk over the previous day's activities.

'And Ella,' she said, 'I wonder Mark does not wed her. She is fond of him and him of her. They are two of a kind.'

'I daresay she will win him before long,' said John. 'I know how it tis when a woman makes up her mind!'

She laughed. 'Now what do you mean by that, I wonder? Do you refer to me?'

'If the cap fits . . . .'

'But you don't regret it?'

'Not for a minute'. He kissed her. 'Forgive me, Elizabeth. You have been wretched these past weeks and I fear I haven't helped you as well as I might.'

'There was nothing you could do,' she said. 'Nothing anyone could do, and you grieved also. We drew apart and should have come together. But John, we know now I can bear a child. We will have another.'

It was the first time she had spoken so positively and John, unsure what to say, and reluctant to say the wrong thing, remained silent. Wrapped in her own thoughts, she was unaware of the passage of time and he waited patiently. There had been no lovemaking since the baby's death and his body cried out for hers. But Elizabeth had lain beside him night after night, passive and defeated and his passion had cooled for want of response.

'John . . . .'

'Aye. What is it?'

'Make love to me.'

'Now?'

'Why not? If we are quick . . . .'

But they were not quick enough. Within minutes Mark and Ella arrived and shouting up the stairs, warned them to hurry and leave their bed. ''Tis time to eat,' cried Mark. 'Either a late breakfast or an early dinner. Whatever you will.'

And Ella, less discreet, called, 'Never take a woman on an empty belly!'

John cursed good-humouredly and Elizabeth laughed.

237

'She is irrepressible.'

'Mayhap she is right,' said John. 'I am hungry. It is later than I thought. Will you be here tonight?'

'Where else? I shall be here, awaiting my lord's pleasure.'

'Then I shall look forward to that sweet body.'

'Poor John. I daresay you have almost forgotten how it is.'

'But you shall refresh my memory,' he told her, 'and other parts'.

She kissed him. 'The London air makes you cheeky,' she said. 'Now do as Mark bids and get up.'

The streets along which the Royal procession would pass had been swept clear of rubbish and woe betide any who threw any slops on to its newly sanded surface. The streets were hung with tapestries ranging from the large elaborate Guild creations, to the smaller ones owned by individuals. Lining the route were the members of the various crafts, resplendent in their multicoloured liveries. Groups of young choristers chattered excitedly, eagerly waiting for the Queen to pass, and the signal from their teachers to sing their well rehearsed offerings in their brightest voices. From the Tower to St Paul's, the streets were aglow with colour and buzzing with the sound of voices. Commemorating the great occasion, the souvenir sellers did a roaring trade; carved figures, sketches of the Queen, embroidered initials, painted miniatures, badges of cloth and painted wood, ribbons in the Queen's colours, red and white roses made of silk, even lavender bags over printed with the capital 'E'.

Elizabeth bought three embossed purses for the boys, with the King and Queen's initials intertwined. Red and white silk roses would please the girls and there was a selection of trinkets for the servants.

'And Andrew!' she cried. 'What shall I buy him, and should we remember Retter?'

John took her arm firmly and steered her away from further temptation. 'You will buy for the whole of Ashburton at this rate,' he cried but while he hesitated, the sound of the approaching horses sent them scurrying for a good position at the edge of the street from which to watch the proceedings.

It was a breathtaking spectacle. The King, naturally a prudent man, knew the importance of pomp and ceremony at such a time. The common people, no less than foreign dignitaries, must be impressed with the stature of the new monarch. The coronation of his young and beautiful wife was the ideal opportunity. It was also the best possible time to establish the unity between the Houses of Lancaster and Tudor, and to emphasize the insignifiance of the recent attempt on the part of the Pretender, to usurp the throne. England was at peace. England and Wales shared a monarch. The warring factions were temporarily subdued. Long live the King and Queen. God bless Henry and Elizabeth!

Mounted nobles and civic dignitaries swept past in glittering array. Bagpipes, clarions, drum, trumpets, viols, sackbutts all came and went in a confusion of overlapping music. The crowd roared itself hoarse, as the royal litter came into view drawn by white horses in perfectly matched pairs, their harnesses gleaming and jingling with gold. The Queen wore a slim circle of gold on her long fair hair, her kirtle and over-mantle were of white cloth of gold, trimmed with fur. The litter was also covered in cloth of gold and white; the effect of such purity made splendid contrast with the brilliance and colour on all sides which surrounded her.

Elizabeth watched surreptitiously as Ella wiped away a tear. So, under that brash exterior she hid a sensitive heart. Her own eyes were moist as she watched the slim pale figure carried past, the eyes large, the expression vulnerable. The higher borne, the further to fall.

'See here comes her sister, Cecily,' said Ella.

239

'And Margaret, her cousin, and her mother-in-law,' said Mark 'But you notice her own mother is not among them.'

'Why not?' asked Elizabeth.

'Elizabeth Woodville is out of favour,' said Mark. 'And has long since been banished to a nunnery. They say she was intriguing with the Pretender before Stoke.'

'And is it possible?'

He shrugged. 'Anything is possible in this day and age,' he said. 'John will tell you. Tis hard to find an honest man in the Government of the country.'

John nudged him. 'This is not the time nor place to say so,' he said. 'Keep your voice down or we shall see you hanging at Tyburn for such treasonable talk.'

'Me, hanged?' cried Mark. 'One of their best goldsmiths? Who would fashion their gold plate if I were hanged? Have no fear on that score. No, no, you may rest assured I am indispensable. Their Majesties need me!'

Ella groaned. 'Tis his modesty that attracts me. Tis a virtue I never could resist.'

When at last the procession came to an end and the ceremony within the Abbey commenced, the crowd turned its attention to lesser amusements, to the gratification and profit of the countless jugglers, musicians, and pedlars who swelled the crowd, having journeyed to London for the day. Minstrels sang on every corner of the beauties and wisdom of the new Queen; or rendered spicy ballads on the ever popular theme of love. Tumblers walked on their hands (at considerable risk from the thronging feet) or strutted on stilts. Astrologers extracted coins from the gullible, by garbled horoscopes designed to please.

Ella listened entranced, as she was told her stars were most aptly placed in the Heavens and the portents were good. She would live long, gain riches and wed before the New Year and despite Mark's groans, she considered her money well spent. Friars were busy selling indulgencies to young men and maids who wished pardon for their 'sins' and even a dentist was discovered tucked away from the main stream of people, pulling teeth with a minimum dexterity and maximum speed.

'How are your teeth?' Elizabeth asked, but John assured her they were reasonably sound and he intended to keep them as long as possible, and recommended her to do the same.

There were the usual motley selection of beggars, some with hideous infirmities, both real and invented and cut-purses excelled themselves, judging from the frequent complaints to be heard from irate or distressed victims. Food was to be had in infinite variety on every street. Apples, oranges and nuts, pies, flans and pasties; roasted chestnuts and salted cob nuts and a bewildering choice of home-made sweetmeats from fudge to candy. Fresh milk, ale and wines washed it all down with a grand disregard for the digestion. The ill-effects might come with the dawn but the London crowds intended to enjoy their day.

'We must not eat too well,' Mark ventured. 'We are dining tonight with Nathan and his wife.'

They found a spare patch of grass and sank down exhausted to finish the nuts and raisins John had bought and drink Mark's wine.

'I wonder how old Morton does?' said John. 'Droning on, I don't doubt. These ceremonies go on for ever.'

'Old Morton!' said Mark. 'Do I hear aright? Do you speak of our new Archbishop? Fie on you for a knave, sir.'

'No doubt he is working up an appetite for tonight's banquet,' said Elizabeth.

'He will need it. The list of dishes is long as my arm. Carp in foil, pike in Latimer sauce, Marchpane Royal, Castles of Jelly in . . . .'

'Stop,' begged Elizabeth. 'I think I will be ill if I hear another word.' 'She needs more wine,' cried Ella, snatching the flagon from Mark's hands. 'She is still sober.'

Laughingly, and protesting half-heartedly, Elizabeth took another mouthful and winked at John.

'I shall be fit for nothing tonight,' she whispered.

Grinning, he leaned towards her. 'I daresay I am in worse shape. Lay me on the bed and I doubt I shall be able to raise even my head!'

They leaned together, giggling at the thought of the forthcoming disaster and Ella and Mark pummelled them, demanding to share the joke. Which only made them laugh the more.

'We need more wine,' said Mark. 'These two are merrier than we are. That will not do. Pull them to their feet, Ella. We must . . . . '

But a fanfare of trumpets announcing the end of the coronation interrupted him and hurriedly they all scrambled up and made for the Abbey to watch the Queen leave. As she appeared a frenzy of renewed cheering filled the air and the bells added their clamour to the glory of England's new Queen.

In contrast, their evening with the old goldsmith and his wife was a relaxed occasion. They chatted happily of times past and Elizabeth learned much about her husband's former life. They spoke of politics, religion, philosophy and love. Nathan played the viola and they sang in harmony. They talked and sang until the candles burned down one by one, and they were hard put to stifle their yawns from one another!

'If we do not say "good-night" soon we shall be in darkness,' said Mark as the penultimate candle flickered and died. There was a round of general agreement, and having expressed their thanks and bid their farewells the four friends found themselves outside in the chill night air. Mark gave John his key and walked Ella home. John and Elizabeth let themselves into the house and made their way

242

upstairs. As soon as the door closed, he took Elizabeth in his arms and kissed her.

'So you are not so weary?' she whispered.

'No, I am not at all weary. And if you are, I promise I shall give you new energy.'

'I am not tired,' she answered.

He lit the candle and held it aloft so that he might see her more clearly and then set it on the shelf.

'You were happy today,' he said softly. 'I cannot recall when you have looked that way. I could not bear to take my eyes from you.'

'I know. I felt them even when I did not see them. And you, you were different. You were a prentice again. It is Mark's influence. Together you rolled back the years. I saw you as a lad for the first time.'

He laughed and unfastening her mantle, slipped it from her shoulders. She shivered in the cold without its comforting warmth, for the chill November air had penetrated the unheated bedroom. John patted the bed and nodded with satisfaction.

'He has put in a warm stone,' he marvelled. 'He is a most considerate host. It will be cooling, but the chill will be off the sheets. Let me undress you.'

As his hands moved over her body gently, fumbling with the fastening of her clothes, she watched his face and wondered at her change of mood. She felt different here in London, away from the household cares and the children's loving but demanding ways. The afternoon had been a revelation to her. It was as if, after all these years, she had tasted the girlhood that had never been hers. She had been so young when she married Daniel, and had fallen immediately into the role of wife to an old man. Then, after his death, she had lived, a fiercely independent life with all the responsibilities of Heron and the realization of her ambitions. Her brief courtship by John had begun a period of adjustment as his wife and mother to four children. Joy there had been in plenty, but laughter? The carefree laughter and follies of youth untrammelled by responsibility? She thought not. Yet today, for a few hours, she had tasted a heady freedom and unfamiliar delights.

'I was a girl again today,' she said curiously. 'Did you know you had a child wife for an afternoon.'

He nodded, removing her hose and carefully lifting her into the bed which as promised, was still warm.

'Ella did that for you,' he told her. 'Her vitality is infectious.'

'It was so good. The spectacle, the company, the joy.'

'You will not need that warm stone' he assured her. 'I will warm you from head to toe with my loving. I have never loved a child wife and am looking forward to it.'

'And I have never lain with a prentice,' she said. 'What does a callow youth know of pleasing a woman?'

'I served a long apprenticeship,' he told her, climbing into bed. 'Now, I want to curl myself around your beautiful smooth back, and later, God willing, I shall prove myself a true craftsman.'

CHAPTER FOURTEEN

1488

The long shadow followed the sacrist along the cold cloisters and wavered in the light of his torch. The monk's feet, clad in night boots made no sound, as he moved from torch to torch lighting all those along the route which the brethren would shortly be taking on their way to Matins. It was nearly midnight and the air blowing across the open courtyard cut through the thick cloth of his habit as though through cotton.

He shivered and with his spare hand drew the hood closer around his face. His expression was blank, his mind still numb, as he struggled to retrieve the remains of his dream which proved more elusive than usual. He began to cough as the cold air irritated his lungs and his hand shook spilling hot pitch from the torch on to the flagstones. He knelt guiltily and rubbed them away with the hem of this cloak until, satisfied, he resumed his journey. Ahead of him in the chapel one of the novices was already busy, setting candles by the chancel step where he and his three fellows would sit. They did not yet know the psalms by heart and would need some light. Neither man spoke out merely acknowledging each other with a brief nod of the head.

When all their preparations were complete the sacrist returned to the dormitory and took up a little bell. Another burst of coughing racked his thin frame, as he moved briskly between the cubicles ringing his bell to rouse the sleepers for the midnight office.

Andrew opened his eyes and groaned inwardly. He rolled obediently out of bed and hastily pulled on the rest of his clothes in an effort to retain what little body heat he had. The dormitory was large and draughty and there was no

245

heating. Around him he heard the muffled sounds of men waking, dressing and making their beds. No one spoke between Compline and Prime, the hours of greater silence between seven at night and seven next morning. As soon as each was ready, he seated himself at the end of his bed and waited.

The tolling of the bell was the signal and as it began its sonorous call, a young monk appeared carrying a lighted lantern and led the brethren, six at a time, to the chapel. Matins commenced with the bell's silence. The Pater, Ave and Creed were recited and then the psalms. These had been learnt by heart by the monks and thus most of the chapel was unlit. Andrew fixed his gaze on the altar and tried to concentrate, but the familiar Latin required no great feats of memory and his mind strayed.

The Priory was expecting a small party of travellers the next day and he wondered if he would be among those chosen to share the meal. If so, there would be lively conversation and a richer menu than that enjoyed by the less fortunate brethren in the refectory. How long was it since he had been chosen? Nearly a year, he was sure, for the visitors had brought a brace of hare for the pot, and they had all remarked on its winter coat. But if he did share their table, he must keep a guard on his tongue and pretend ignorance of worldly affairs. It would not do to reveal the extent of his meetings with Elizabeth or the frequent scraps of information he gleaned from little Blanche. Life at the Priory was one of prayer and seclusion and it pricked his conscience that his contacts with the outside world afforded him such pleasure.

With an effort Andrew focussed his eyes once more on the altar and sang more lustily as penance for his neglect, until a glance from the abbot suggested that he now erred too far in the other direction.

When the psalms ended the bell tolled again for the commencement of High Mass.

Brother Bartholemew was coughing again and Andrew

frowned his concern. Since his own entry into the Priory, none of the brethren had died. Now all feared for Brother Bartholemew. He was an old man, older even than the abbot, and was lately taken with a consumption. Already he ate alone in the infirmary, a special diet which included meat to strengthen his wasted body. Soon, it was whispered, he would be relieved of all further duties and would spend his days and nights there under the care of Brother Jonathan. Now the first reader approached the lectern and Andrew's flagging interest revived briefly.

Brother Gregory was no reader. He gave equal weight to each word, intoning them like a dirge, robbing the phrases of shape or form. And his hand wandered frequently to his mouth so that the muffled words were lost to his hearers. Andrew was critical of the standard of reading. His own turn would come next week and he would surprise them all with the passion of his oratory. Hastily, he asked forgiveness for such vanity and made an effort to listen to the rendering; but before long the small faces of his nephews floated before him, as they had looked at him shyly a day or two earlier. William had found a bird's nest and offered it as gift which Andrew, at a nod from Elizabeth, had accepted. Matthew with nothing to give, had sung a song for him: When the snow doth fall And doth hide all ... There he had faltered in confusion and no amount of coaxing could produce the rest of the verse.

Andrew smiled at the recollection. That one had John's eyes, thought Andrew, but none of his strength. But at last the servers had come in from the sacristy with incense and Matins was over for another day. The monks rose to their feet with ill disguised eagerness. The bell was already tolling for Lauds and the brief interval gave them time to retire to the nearby common room, where a fire was kept burning to warm them after their cold vigil. Silently, they huddled round the burning logs, some nodding and smiling their 'good mornings' to each other, others grim and

247

unresponsive. Cheered by the warmth, they returned to the chapel to await the next Office.

Andrew, hiding a yawn, clasped his hands in prayer and closing his eyes comforted himself with the knowledge that after Lauds they could all retire to bed for the second half of their night's rest.

Blanche pressed her fingers into the sand pot so that the pale yellow grains forced their way under her nails, and stared at the sheet in front of her. She had written only two lines but had been at the task for nearly an hour. Idly she sprinkled sand over the dry ink and blew it away again. Then, she sighed deeply and turned to look out over the garden.

A light fall of snow had softened the bare branches of the oaks and blurred the edges of the paths. Eight rounded bee-hives stood like a row of frosted cakes, beyond them the pond had frozen over and several ducks wandered disconsolately across its blind grey surface. The sky was yellow with the threat of more snow and the air, heavy and still.

May the blessing of God come to you with this note the which I pray you read without wrath. I — How could she continue the letter. With the truth perhaps. Or with a more general observation so that he read on a little further. Or with a further request that he should not be angry with her. *I dare to hope that . . .* No. Better not use the word *dare* or he will be alarmed . . . *I have hopes that . . . .* That was not true. She had no hope. None at all. She had her dreams and fantasies but no hope . . . . She dipped the quill into the ink and let a droplet fall into the sand pot. Then another . . . .

Joseph looked into the room and she hastily threw her arms across the sheet so that he would not read it.

'I thought you would be at Heron,' he said, surprised.

'No. I am here.'

He laughed. 'My eyes tell me that, and writing! Pigs will fly next!'

'I do write sometimes,' she said indignantly.

''Tis a rare sight. Father Marryat declares you have a strange antipathy for work.'

'The lessons bore me. Father Marryat's voice is like a . . . .'

'That will do, Blanche. That is no way to speak of a reverend gentleman.'

'He is not reverend — nor a gentleman. He sang us a song once that was . . . .'

'Blanche! I will hear none of your tales. Father Marryat is a good teacher. And please do not drop ink into the sand. I have spoke of it before.'

She threw down the pen and scowled. 'I do nought right seemingly,' she said.

'But the fault lies in yourself,' he persisted, 'for you are so often out of humour these days. No one may speak to reprove you but you sulk. What are you writing?'

''Tis nothing.' She snatched it up before he could ask to see it and jumping to her feet, made to leave the room.

'Blanche!' he said irritably. 'Remain where you are until I have spoken with you. Perchance we should consider your future and arrange for your betrothal. 'Tis time you were thinking on the matter.'

'I should like to be wed,' she said. 'But where is the man for me?' 'Not far from here,' she added silently, 'yet forever out of reach.'

Joseph walked past her to the window, looked out without really seeing and sighed.

'I have always hoped you would wed into Heron,' he told her, 'but I approached John and he was reluctant.'

'They are all too young,' she said with some truth.

He shrugged. 'There is plenty of time and they will grow up. You would do well as mistress of Heron.'

'That I will never be,' she whispered to herself, but his sharp ears caught her words and his irritation increased.

'What are you muttering child? You know the trick annoys me. Speak up if you have something to say.'

'I could not love any of the Heron boys,' she said defiantly. 'They are but children. When I wed I would choose a man!'

'*You* will not choose at all,' said Joseph losing patience with his sullen daughter. 'You will wed the man *I* choose and there will be no gain saying it. Children, indeed! You are no more than a child yourself!'

'Then why must I wed at all if I am but . . . . Ah!'

Joseph struck her. 'You hold your tongue,' he said. 'Don't dare to tell me when and whom you will marry! I will do the telling. Such insolence does you no credit. If you displease me you must suffer for it and mayhap you will learn respect for those in authority over you . . . now finish your writing, I am in no mood to hear complaints from Father Marryat.'

He strode from the room, leaving Blanche tearful but unrepentant. So he assumed she was working. Let him think so. How angry he would be if he knew the truth of it. The thought gave her great satisfaction and she wiped her tears, sniffed and picked up the quill once more. So he thought her a child, did he? She would disprove him. She dipped it into the ink, deliberately shook it in the sand and dipped it again . . . .

May the blessing of God come with this note the which I pray you read wihout wrath. Forgive me, I beseech you if what I write causes you distress but I may no longer hide my feelings which perchance are known to you without word from me having been revealed in my eyes. I do most dearly — No . . . . *You are most dear —* No, no. Too blunt by far. *I fear I am in love with you—*

But she didn't fear it. She knew it and revelled in it. Her whole being throbbed with it and her world revolved around it. She sighed again and waited for inspiration, giving herself up meantime to her favourite fantasy. Closing her eyes, she imagined the young monk walking in the Priory garden, alone and pensive, tormented by thought of her and the wild dreams that nightly racked his sleep. Suddenly, looking up, he saw her at the far end of the garden, a slim virginal figure in a heavy white gown, her hair loose, her hands outstretched to him. He whispered her name but remained motionless, wrestling with his conscience, until the sight of her drove all other considerations from his mind and he moved towards her. She whispered his name and ran towards him on feet that trod air . . . and then she was in his arms and his lips were against hers and he was no longer a monk but as other men and she was no child, but a sensuous woman in the thrall of emotions too strong for her . . . .

'Oh Andrew,' she whispered despairingly. 'How will I find the words? How will I ever tell you? Oh, my love, will you ever hold me, touch me, care for me? And if you did, would you ever forgive me?'

Her tears flowed afresh and she gave herself up to the luxury of her passionate grief . . . .

'I love you she wrote. That is the truth of it. You fill my waking hours and comfort my lonely nights. The very mention of your name peals in the air like a bell and the sight of you is like wine and goes to my head. I pray you do not laugh at me and never hate me. That would kill me . . . . Do not fear, Andrew. I know you have made vows and I would not have you break faith with God, but let me love you. Without you the world is a cold empty place and I am lost in it. We need not speak of this. Tis enough for me that you know and are not angry with me . . . There I have done. I shall bring this when I next visit you, for Elizabeth and run from you while you read it. Think kindly on me. Blanche.'

Laying down the quill, she sanded the last few lines and

shook the letter clean. Then she read and re-read what she had written before rolling it up. She slipped it inside the sleeve of her gown so that she might take it to her chamber without fear of discovery. Once there, she pushed it hurriedly into her coffer and throwing herself on to the bed, gave herself up to imagining how Andrew would react when he read it.

Elizabeth read the letter through without a word, but her hands trembled. She looked up at Joseph and her face was troubled.

'How did you come by this?' she asked.

They stood together in his hall where she had come at his urgent request.

'My maid found it in the girl's chest and thought I should see it. Twas well she did.'

'Indeed . . . poor Blanche.'

'Poor Blanche,' he cried indignantly. 'Is that all you can say?' Elizabeth smiled faintly.

'I doubt a man would understand the pain and ecstacy behind this little note.'

'Little note, indeed. In God's name, Elizabeth, you take this very light. My daughter writing thus, and to a monk. How could he encourage a young girl to write, or to think, in such a manner. I find it scandalous, Elizabeth, and am shocked that you are unimpressed.'

'Encouragement?' echoed Elizabeth. 'I read nought of encouragement in those words.' She scanned the letter again and shook her head. 'Tis clear to me that my brother is unaware of her — affection . . . See here . . . *Forgive me I beseech you if what I write causes you distress but I can no longer hide my feelings* . . . So she has obviously hidden them thus far. I doubt he knows the way she feels. No doubt he may have been astonished had he received the letter. I believe you treat it too seriously, Joseph.'

252

'And I that you deal with it lightly. How think you the Prior would deal with it?'

'The Prior!'

'Should it fall into his hands, I darcsay he would deal with it very soberly and your brother . . . .'

'If it should fall into his hands? What mean you by such a remark, Joseph?'

'I do not care to think of your brother, a man of God, allowing a young girl to . . . .'

'Allowing? You choose your words most damnably, Joseph. I believe he has done nothing. Tis a girlish adoration, nothing more and Andrew is the innocent object of her misguided feelings. If you make more than this from the matter, then you do so from your choice, or design. And why have you sent for me secretly? Why did you not come openly when John was home?'

They faced each other angrily, Elizabeth more shaken than she would admit. For his part, Joseph was surprised that she had read his mind so accurately and felt guilty at the blackmail he was hoping to perpetrate. He was making more of the matter than it merited, but hoped thus to further a scheme close to his heart. Elizabeth turned and walked away from him, her thoughts racing ahead of the conversation. Joseph watched her nervously. He did not underestimate her, knowing her to be a shrewd and intelligent woman. She faced him suddenly and her expression was cold.

'I see it,' she said. 'You will refrain from showing the letter to the Prior if we agree to a certain request. No doubt the recurring one that your daughter should marry Stephen.'

He had the grace to look embarrassed. 'I was thinking along that way,' he admitted. 'I do not deny it nor am I ashamed. A match between our two families would be ideal. You thought so yourself once.'

As he hoped, this last reference to their own near marriage softened her heart. She admired the way he had taken his defeat with dignity. He had borne her no ill will, for which she was grateful. He was a good man and she still retained a certain affection for him. She smiled, suddenly.

'Aye,' she agreed. 'I thought the match ideal then and I would still favour it. But John has set his heart against Stephen marrying outside the family. Why do you not suggest that your son marries our Catherine when she is of age?' She regarded him keenly.

He laughed but made no answer.

'Because you wish him to marry within your family!'

'Aye.'

'Do not look so, Joseph,' she said. 'We all fight for our children's best interests. But I pray you, do no more with the letter and speak with John on the marriage question whenever you will.'

'Andrew?'

She sighed. 'I would like to show him the letter,' she said. 'I think he must be aware of her feelings so that he does not unwittingly, "feed the flame". Would you agree?'

He nodded. 'And what of John?'

'He must be told, although it does not bear on him directly as it does me. And do not punish the girl for her folly, I beg you. Tis part of her growing up.'

'But I must tax her with it.'

'Oh yes. She must know that you have found the letter. I have probably fostered the situation myself, by sending her so frequently to the Priory on . . . .'

She realized suddenly that she had said more than she needed.

'*You* sent her to him?' Joseph repeated.

It was her turn to be discomfited.

'Only with money — for prayers,' she said.

'Frequently, you say?'

He looked at her curiously and she hesitated.

'Elizabeth?' He was waiting for an answer.

'In confidence, Joseph . . . .'

254

He nodded.

She looked him squarely in the eyes. 'Prayers for a child,' she whispered and saw by his expression that he had not expected that answer.

'Oh . . . forgive me,' he said. 'I should not have pressed you for an explanation.'

'You could not have known.'

'You will bear another?' He said awkwardly.

'I hope so,' she said.

She handed him the letter and as he took it their hands touched, whether accidentally or not she did not know. Slowly she raised her eyes. 'Elizabeth . . . ' he began but she held up her hand.

'No, Joseph,' she said. 'Please don't.'

'I still love you,' he said, his voice low. 'I have no right to speak of it but . . . . '

'Joseph . . . Dear Joseph, please . . . . '

'Are you happy, Elizabeth?' he asked. 'Is John the right man for you?'

'Yes Joseph. He is. I love him dearly.'

For a moment they were both silent and then she sighed deeply.

'It grieves me that you do not choose another wife,' she told him.

'I do not marry because I cannot find another Elizabeth!' he said and smiled faintly.

'But are you not lonely?' she asked gently.

'Yes,' he replied. 'I am lonely at times. I won't pretend otherwise. But if you are ever alone and need me . . . I want to be free.'

Elizabeth saw the love in the dark eyes and lowered her own. 'You are too generous,' she whispered.

He looked at her and his heart was heavy with unspoken thoughts and undeclared desires. He knew what the loss of her child had meant and suffered for her. A terrible guilt burdened him too, and he now spoke of it impulsively.

'Your child,' he told her wretchedly, 'when you were

with child I was tormented with jealousy. Can you forgive me? I despised myself, yet . . . . '

She held up a hand to forestall him. 'Please Joseph,' she begged. 'Do not speak of it further but believe me, I understand and do not bear you any ill will.'

'But when you lost the boy . . . . '

'Twas the will of God,' she said simply. 'There is none to blame. Even poor Rufus . . . . But no. We will not dwell on past sorrows.'

'Then you do forgive me, Elizabeth?'

'You have done me no wrong, Joseph, nor ever will. Of that I am convinced. You are a good man. I am fortunate to have your friendship which I hold most dear. Now we have said all that must be said,' she told him. 'We must consider Blanche now.'

He drew a deep breath.

'Aye,' he agreed. 'We must think on her.'

'I will speak to my brother,' said Elizabeth, 'and you must speak to Blanche'

'And will you tell John?' he asked.

Elizabeth nodded. 'I think he must be told. And now I must leave you. God be with you until tomorrow.'

He watched her go and was filled with the familiar longing: 'Dear heart,' he whispered silently, 'I am growing older yet still cherish the thought of you. Will you ever be mine, Elizabeth? Will you ever be mine?'

CHAPTER FIFTEEN

It was cold in the little wood and quiet, as though the very air had been frozen into silence. Andrew shivered and pushed his hands further into his sleeves. His hood protected his head but his face was exposed to the raw chill air and he blinked his eyes to warm them. Brittle frosted leaves, cracked under his feet and he sighed deeply. Twenty minutes on his knees in the chapel had done nothing to ease his troubled mind and he had asked permission to leave the Priory for one hour 'to walk and meditate'. Half of that time had passed already. Elizabeth had shown him Blanche's letter and it had filled him with a great disquiet. He wondered if he was in any way to blame for Blanche's predicament, or had fostered in her mind a false impression of his feelings towards her? He did not think so. Indeed, he was aware of no feelings towards her, and yet he enjoyed her visits. Her innocent spirit gladdened his heart and her bright freshness excited his eye. The quick graceful movements of her hands and the vivacity of her small pointed face framed in smooth fair hair . . . . Dear Father in Heaven! Why was he extolling such virtues? She was nothing but a child! A pretty child, no more than that . . . yet Elizabeth had called her a 'half child, half woman'. He stopped abruptly and stared ahead unseeingly, trying to visualize the girl. Was she almost a woman and did he know that in his heart? He conjured up an image of how he had seen her on her last visit, head thrown back in laughter, recounting a trick that she and Catherine had played on Stephen earlier in the day . . . . A powdering of snow floated down from the branches above him and glancing up, he saw a squirrel outlined against the yellow sky as it leapt into a neighbouring tree.

'You should be asleep,' he admonished. 'These are lean times for small creatures.'

The squirrel landed with a further scattering of snow and ran quickly to the top of the tree before leaping into the next.

Without moving, Andrew watched until it was out of sight, then he sighed again and walked on. There had been an intensity about her face, something of which he had been dimly aware. Frowning, he pulled a rosehip from a briar and threw it at an oak blasted by lightning. The small red missile dropped into the hollow and he nodded in self congratulation. The briar glowed with crimson berries and he plucked a handful and looked at them nestling in the palm of his hand like jewels. The words of an old song hovered at the back of his mind: Lips red as cherries Or bright briar berries – But lips were not bright red. They were small and pink and so vulnerable — and when she smiled her teeth gleamed, white and even like the petals of a daisy . . . and the skin of her face was pale and delicately bloomed and her eyes were blue under the pale fringe of lashes . . . He began to throw the hips one at a time into the stricken tree. When they had all gone, he crossed over to the tree and looked into the hollow to retrieve them. Behind him, the leaves crackled and a voice said, 'Whatever are you about, Andrew?'

It was Blanche! Startled, he could think of nothing coherent to say, but began to stammer an explanation while he felt the colour rush into his face. She faced him squarely and he saw that her eyes were red-rimmed from weeping. She wore no cloak and her face and hands were blue with cold as she watched him, her face expressionless. Then, interrupting him she said, 'Papa beat me.'

'Oh, no.'

She nodded. 'And locked me in my chamber.'

'Then how are you come here . . . and why?'

'I climbed from the window,' she said, pride mingled with defiance in her tone.

258

'Blanche!'

'Tis no matter . . . They found my letter. Have they told you?'

'Aye,' he answered. 'I have seen Elizabeth and she told me . . . I wanted to help you but . . . . ' He left the sentence unfinished and made a helpless gesture with his hands. 'How can I tell you how sorry I am?'

'Sorry?' she repeated. 'I am sorry that they read my letter but that is all. Are you angry that I love you?'

'Don't, I beg you!' he cried. 'You must not speak that way. Tis folly and they will beat you again.'

'Tis no matter,' she said. But her lips trembled and he thought how he had remembered her, radiant and carefree and he, Andrew, had brought her to this distressing pass. He closed the distance between them and her eyes filled with tears.

'I'm so cold,' she whispered. 'My hands and face . . . .'

He made an exclamation of annoyance. 'I am so thoughtless,' he said. 'Forgive me,' and he unfastened his cloak and wrapped it round her shoulders, pulling the hood up so that it fell over her head hiding most of her face.

'Where are you?' he teased but she remained unsmiling.

'Don't treat me as a child,' she said. 'Mayhap I was a child yesterday but today I am grown suddenly into a woman.'

He shook his head gently but she insisted 'I am! I am! What do you know of me? How can you say?'

'Little Blanchette,' he said soothingly 'Come. We will sit for a moment and talk.'

He held out his hand but she declined to take it.

'I am not a little one,' she said. 'And my name is Blanche.'

'Blanche, then. Come.'

She took his hand and he led the way to a fallen tree trunk and lifted her on to it.

'Firstly, I beg a smile,' he said. 'That poor sad face is

259

more than I can bear. Will you not smile for me, to show that I am forgiven?'

'Forgiven for what?' she asked sharply and he hesitated before replying, aware that by his choice of that word he was acknowledging his own blame.

'I have been at fault,' he said. 'I have allowed you to — to love me and . . . .'

'No!' she broke in harshly. 'I loved you of my own accord. You did not know. No one knew.'

'I should have guessed.'

'How could you?' she said. 'You are but a monk in all truth and you cannot know the ways of women.'

He sat down beside her on the tree and considered her last remark. Did he know 'the ways of women'? What were these secret 'ways'? He had entered the Priory as a young boy and before that time had known no women save his mother and sister Elizabeth. He had been and still was reserved and solitary, lacking self-confidence. Now his lack of experience left him at the mercy of his emotions and his confusion grew as he looked at the small waif-like figure beside him.

'Tis of no consequence that you do not love me,' she said. 'Only say that I may love you, for indeed I can do nothing else.' He lowered his eyes, unable to meet the anguish in hers.

'But you must marry . . . . ' he began, then faltered into silence at the look on her face.

'Why have you come here?' she asked suddenly.

'To think.'

'To think on me?'

He nodded without speaking.

'And will you be punished if they find us together?'

'Tis very probable.'

'Will they beat you also?'

'I don't know — or care,' he told her. 'But I must make matters clear to you. I am unworthy of your love and can never be more to you than a friend.'

260

'Then you do not love me?'

He thought carefully, aware of the importance to her of his answer. 'I see you as a child and I love you,' he said at last, 'but if you are a woman then I must not.'

She smiled faintly. 'How will you know if I am woman or child?' she asked.

He shook his head despairingly and after a moment she slid sadly from the tree and unwrapped his cloak.

'My thanks,' she said and he took it from her. 'Now I must go back. I came in hopes of a glimpse of you but see, Heaven has smiled on me and I have sat with you and spoke of love.'

'Don't speak this way!' he cried. 'Such devotion frightens me. I do not deserve it, nor can I return it.'

She looked at him and there were tears in her eyes. 'Andrew, will you kiss me "goodbye"?' she asked. 'As a brother kisses a sister . . . You *are* a brother,' she told him and he smiled at the pun and leaning forward, kissed her lightly on the top of her head. But as he moved back her arms went round his neck and she pulled him towards her. He almost fell, but managed to steady himself as her mouth met his in a fierce kiss. Sensations swept through his body and he was returning the kiss, matching her passion. Then she pulled away.

'That is how you know,' she whispered, 'that I am no longer a child!'

Turning, she ran from him, darting recklessly through the trees, her long fair hair floating behind her. When she had gone, Andrew closed his eyes in a desperate bid to shut out the memory of the kiss. He was suddenly lonely, for the first time in his life.

There was a tap at the door that Blanche heard, but did not acknowledge. Then another, and Elizabeth's voice.

'Blanche, tis Elizabeth and I would speak with you.'

The girl remained silent, kneeling on the floor, her face

hidden in her hands. She heard her father's voice but he spoke in low tones and she could not catch the meaning.

'Go away,' she whispered, but against her wishes the door opened and Elizabeth entered the room alone. She closed the door quietly behind her, then turned to face Blanche and was horrified at the change in her.

'Oh, Blanche!' she cried. 'My dearest child!'

Blanche did not look at her. Her face remained hidden but the hunched shoulders and tangled hair partly confirmed what Joseph had told her.

'Blanche, look at me, I beg you. Dear Heaven, what is become of you! Blanche!'

Kneeling beside the girl she gently prised the hands from the face. Blanche looked at her without interest. Her face was thin and pale, dark shadows circling her eyes. The pressure of her fingers had left blotchy marks on her cheeks. Shocked, Elizabeth held out her hands appealing.

'Please,' she begged, 'I cannot bear to see you like this, come so low. Your father told me but I would not believe it. Take my hands. Stand up, I beseech you and talk with me awhile. This must not go on.'

The girl only stared at her, but tears welled up in the blue eyes and slid down the grimy cheeks. She had not washed for a week and she had not eaten. She had not spoken except to refuse a betrothal with William Kendal. Joseph had pleaded, argued, threatened and punished her. She refused to leave her chamber and was now losing weight rapidly; her strength was failing and her self-imposed solitude made her thoughts wander so that her mind was becoming confused.

'Blanche! Look at me!' Elizabeth pleaded. 'You must not do this to yourself, and to your father. He loves you dearly and — don't shake your head so. I tell you he loves you and desires only what is best for you. Now give me your hands, and rise from the floor. I will not take no for an answer so do as I say . . . Blanche!'

262

The girl remained where she was, ignoring the hands outstretched to help her. Elizabeth turned to the window exasperated and at a loss to know what to say to this stubborn, yet pathetic, girl. After a moment or two, she turned back and crossing the room, sat on the floor beside Blanche placing her arm round her shoulders. The girl shuddered, but made no attempt to push her away.

'Your father tells me you are not eating,' Elizabeth began. 'That will not do. The twins ask for you every day and Catherine also. I have told them you have a fever but they miss you. Will you not say "Yes" to William — and come back to us?'

Slowly, Blanche shook her head and her gaze began to wander listlessly round the small room.

'And why are the shutters half closed?' Elizabeth persisted. 'Outside the sun is shining and the snow sparkles like jewels. Will you not even look at it?'

Blanche turned to her suddenly. 'I want to die,' she said. 'If I cannot wed Andrew, then I will never wed. If I do not eat I will die and I will wait for him in Heaven.'

'In Heaven!' cried Elizabeth. 'Child, if you kill yourself you will not go to Heaven but Hell. And Andrew will go to Heaven.'

'But not if he has sinned,' cried Blanche, shaken out of her silence. 'Not if he has broken his vows. He kissed me on the lips!'

Elizabeth shook her head gently. ''Twas you kissed him,' she said. 'I have spoken with Andrew.'

'You have spoke with him? How was he? How did he look? Did he speak well of me?'

Elizabeth hesitated. 'He spoke kindly of you,' she said. 'He is distressed that you will not eat.'

'Tell him I will die,' said Blanche, 'for love of him.'

'Blanche! Would you break his heart? The poor man is wretched enough and prays daily for God's forgiveness; though I know not what wrong he has done for this was none of his doing.'

'I will die for him,' the girl repeated.

Elizabeth sighed. 'Listen to me, Blanche, and think on what I say. Andrew is my brother and I love him dearly. You are Joseph's daughter and I love you also. I cannot bear to see you both suffering so, and your father, he, too, grieves for you and is at his wits end. You know you can never wed Andrew, for he is wedded to Christ. So why will you not agree to a betrothal with William?'

'He is but a child! I would wed a man.'

'But he will grow to be a man!' cried Elizabeth. 'When you are twenty-one years he will be seventeen. He will be a man then, and a fine man. I swear it.'

Blanche did not answer. Instead she pulled herself up with difficulty, and sat on the chest. She sighed deeply and said simply, 'Andrew would not wish it.'

Elizabeth gasped, 'Tis not true! Andrew approves the match most heartedly.'

'He cannot!'

'I tell you he does!'

'I don't believe you,' whispered Blanche. 'Unless I hear it from his own lips . . . No, tis not true. He loves me.'

'No, Blanche.'

'I believe he does.'

'Oh, Sweet Heaven . . . Blanche. Andrew loves me as a sister, he loves you as a sister. He is a man of God and cannot love you in any other way.'

'He is still a man,' whispered Blanche. 'And I will not be betrothed to anyone else unless I hear from him that he truly does not want me.'

Elizabeth sat on the bed and faced her squarely. Taking both her hands in her own, she said, 'If I can arrange a meeting between you, and he tells you he will never wed, will you agree to William, and eat and speak and be yourself again?'

Blanche stared at her. 'Meet him again? How can that be? Papa will never . . . .'

Elizabeth held up her hand. 'I said "if" I can arrange it. I make no promises. But what do you say?'

A radiant smile lit up the haggard face as Blanche nodded. 'I will agree if only to see him again. Aye, I do agree, Elizabeth, but let it be soon . . . But if he tells me he does want me, then I will never wed another.'

Elizabeth nodded, satisfied. 'Then I must go,' she said. 'And think how it can be managed. Oh, Blanche, tis so good to see a smile on that face. I will tell your father you are a little happier and will eat some gruel. Oh yes, you must eat. That is part of the bargain. Farewell, for the present. I will see you again.'

She stood up and leaving the room, hurried to report her progress to Joseph.

Alone once more, Blanche, trance-like for several minutes, slid suddenly from the chest to the floor and opened the lid. She took out a small mirror and looked at herself in it. 'Sweet Mother of God!' she whispered. 'He must not see me like this!' and searching among the clothes, she found her hair brush and began to brush her hair with long rhythmic strokes.

The small guest hall was full. Two tableboards had been set up for the expected party of travellers but they had proved greater than anticipated and Thomas and Will, the servants, were hard put to push a way between the backs of the visitors as they lolled at ease. A fire blazed at one end of the room and heat came also from the burning torches in the wall and the circle of candles in their pewter frame which hung above the table to light the proceedings. Four of the brethren sat with the guests and Andrew, to his unconcealed delight, was one of them. They had eaten well: duck, capon, trout and a venison pasty with cheese, nuts and a custard. Wine was plentiful and now, as they sat replete, the talk flowed and the mood was relaxed and pleasant.

Opposite Andrew was the wife of a wealthy silk mercer, an arrogant but handsome woman with milk-white hands but whose face was blemished by pock marks. Next to her, her husband — a portly man in his late years whose eyes strayed constantly to the woman on Andrew's left. She it seemed, was his ward and barely twenty years of age. She had no looks, but a confident manner for one so young and a wit that put her guardian into fits of laughter and called forth from his wife warning looks to curb her tongue. Further down the table, Brother Gregory spoke with a nun who was on her way to London on the first step of her pilgrimage to Canterbury — the first time she had left the convent since she entered it as a girl. She was middle-aged and ruddy-faced from work in the fields. She sat now, her face flushed with wine and excitement, as Brother Gregory told a tale of his own pilgrimage many years earlier. The abbot at the end of the table, reached for the jug and refilled his neighbour's goblet before doing the same with his own. He looked weary, Andrew thought. He was nearly seventy years and needed his sleep. Beside Andrew, on his right-hand, a wealthy farmer reached to the platter in the centre of the table and pulled scraps of flesh from the duck's carcase and dropped them on to the rushes at his feet for his two spaniels who wriggled to snap them up.

'Do you have any family?' he asked Andrew for the third time. Andrew kept his face straight with an effort and replied that the brethren were his family.

'Any other family?' he persisted and belched loudly.

'I have a sister who lives nearby and her children.'

'By what name does she go?'

'Kendal,' Andrew told him. 'They live at Heron close by.'

'No mother and father?'

'No.'

'Three brothers I've got and four sisters,' he told Andrew, 'and care for none of 'em! Mealy-mouthed lot. If I never set eyes on them again, twill be too soon. And my wife — ugh! Old harridan that one. Dried up stringy old harridan . . . And her sister likewise. Harridans both on 'em . . . I envy you. Do you hear me? I envy the likes of you . . .' He stared morosely at Andrew and blinked his eyes blearily. 'No-one to scold you and spend your money. No one to . . . .'

'Hark at him!' interrupted the girl on Andrew's left. 'Cease your moping, you foolish old man. You've a woman to warm your bed and cook for you. Think yourself fortunate. Tis your wife I grieve for with such a miserable husband! Lord preserve me from such a union, I say.'

She smiled radiantly at Andrew who was by far the most attractive man at the table, but he looked away, confused by her attention. Brother Gregory caught his eye and winked briefly, before returning his attention once more to the nun who was now regaling him with a list of the faults of the abbess.

'So little she does allow us for vestments that we go nigh threadbare!' she told him. 'And the bell tower is like to fall at any time and kill us all! Not a penny will she spend without urgent cause and this in the name of thrift. Thrift? Tis not so much a virtue with her but a disease of the mind! We pray daily for a change of heart but to no avail.'

Brother Gregory nodded, sympathetically, as she paused for breath and cracked another walnut. She poked the kernel free and popped it into her mouth.

'I intend to be home by the end of the week,' she told him, 'for the Bishop's visit is due and we are all decided we must speak with him on the matter. Would you not appeal for help if so provoked? The Bishop is a fair man and will pay heed to our complaints. When he came last, we told him of the scant fire we were allowed and that oftimes it went out altogether. Imagine that if you can!'

'Dear me! Dear me!' exclaimed Brother Gregory as he handed her the contents of the walnut he had just cracked as a small compensation for the wrongs she suffered. Pleased by this gesture, she relapsed momentarily into silence and he was able to launch into his own account of how difficult it was to lift turnips when the ground was so hard.

A great roar of laughter came from the far end of the table and Andrew found himself wishing he had more humorous neighbours, but then chided himself for his ingratitude. He had eaten and supped well. He was warm. At that moment, the servant Thomas tapped him on the shoulder and whispered in his ear that Elizabeth craved a word with him.

'She awaits in the cloister,' said Thomas, 'and the young girl is with her.'

At his words, Andrew's heart began to race and he hoped fervently that his confusion was not evident. Excusing himself from the table he asked permission from the abbott to leave the hall. The abbott nodded, too tired to notice the emotion in the young man's eyes. Thankfully, Andrew left the hall and made his way to the cloisters. The two women moved towards him. He took Elizabeth's outstretched hands and put them to his lips. To Blanche he gave an awkward bow and dared not meet her glance. He had no cloak and shivered in the cold still air.

'We will not keep you unduly,' said Elizabeth, 'but Blanche would speak with you. Tis of the utmost importance, Andrew. I beg you think carefully before you answer.'

Andrew's heart sank at her words, while his spirits soared at the sight of Blanche's pale face as she stared up at him in the moonlight.

Blanche hesistated then turned to Elizabeth. 'I beg you leave us a moment,' she said. 'What I have to say, will not be easy for me. For either of us.'

Elizabeth hesitated then nodded.

'But I will not be out of sight,' she told them. 'But out of hearing. Make haste for fear we are seen.'

She moved to the far end of the path and waited, stamping her feet to keep warm. Beyond the small gate, she heard the jingle of harness where Eric waited with the horses for their return.

'Tis good to see you,' said Andrew then wished the words unsaid. He must guard his tongue, for this young girl might read into his words something that was not there.

Blanche looked into his eyes, unable in the darkness to read his expression.

'We kissed last time we met,' she said, surprising him by her directness. 'To me it twas a . . .' she paused, searching for the right word, ' . . . twas a revelation. What was it for you?'

For a second he closed his eyes. Her words recalled the exquisite pain that had flooded his body at the touch of her lips and the tightness of her arms around his neck.

'Did you feel nothing?' she asked, wonderingly for his silence seemed interminable.

'No,' he said. 'I did feel . . . I felt a physical joy that I had not known before.'

'And are you glad?'

'I have tried to forget it,' he said. 'Such pleasures are not for us. Our delight is in God's work and God's word.'

'And does God's word give you such delight?' she persisted desperately.

'I believe so,' he said. 'Blanche, I would not hurt you in any way. I know you feel for me a kind of love.'

'And you? What do you feel for me?'

He thought carefully. 'A love of one being for another,' he said.

'That means nothing,' she said sharply. 'You hide your meaning in such phrases. I must know, Andrew. I love only *you*. I love you as a woman loves a man. I want you. I want to lie with you. I want to be your wife! Now will you also speak openly that I may understand?'

'As God is my witness,' he said, 'I shall try . . . I enjoy the sight of you. Your beauty dazzles my eyes. There is no harm in that for me. God puts beauty into the world for our enjoyment. I enjoy your company. Your youthful chatter pleases and amuses me . . . no, let me finish. Your kiss awoke in me a need that all men have for a woman, but a need that monks have put aside. The memory of that moment torments me and makes me guilty. Fills me with guilt . . . .'

'You need not stay a monk,' she cried. 'Tis possible to leave the brethren. Others have done it. Others have . . . .'

'I do not want to leave them,' he replied firmly. 'That is my dilemma. I have known no other life since I was a boy. I know little of the world and do not care to. I am safe here. I belong here. Do not ask me to leave, Blanche. For me, it would be a mistake.'

She turned away so that he might not see the hurt in her eyes.

'They want me to wed William,' she said, her voice flat.

'Twould be a good match,' he said.

'So you would approve?' She turned to face him again, her voice cool but ringed with a desperation. He nodded.

'Say it then, Andrew,' she said. 'Say that you do not want me.'

'Do not ask it of me,' he said. 'I have no wish to hurt you.'

'Say it,' she insisted. 'Without those words I shall never wed William, nor any other.'

He swallowed and made an effort to steady his voice.

'I do not want you in that way, Blanchette.'

'No!' The word was a scream and her small hand came up to strike his face.

'I am not Blanchette!' she hissed. 'No longer a child! Are you blind as well as fearful? Very well, Andrew. You have said it. I will wed William when he comes of age. And you and I will not meet again!'

Turning, she ran past Elizabeth towards the horses and he watched as the gate swung to behind her and the shadow of the trees hid her from his sight.

He turned to Elizabeth helplessly. 'I did not mean to hurt her,' he said. 'She would hear it . . . .'

Elizabeth squeezed his arm. 'Tis well it is done,' she told him. 'She will recover. Her anger is easier than her grief. Tis the only way we have to deal with our rejections. I must go with her,' she said, 'and you must rest easy in your mind. Twas no light matter, but tis done with and best forgot. I see you share the pleasures of the Guest Hall tonight.'

He sighed. 'Aye,' he said, heavily. 'But now I fear I shall find its heady delights more than I can bear.'

They made their farewells and parted. He remained where he was, listening to the sound of the hoofbeats until they faded into the night. Then he went to the chapel which was in darkness and kneeling, began to pray.

CHAPTER SIXTEEN

1494

Elizabeth listened wearily as the familiar argument developed between John and Stephen. Why was the boy so
intractable, she wondered for the hundredth time. Now
John's eyes flashed dangerously and she saw that his
patience was nearly at an end.

'You show no interest in the mine,' John cried. 'You
argue against your law studies.'

'Because I have no interest,' said Stephen. 'I do not care
to spend my days tunnelling through dark earth like a mole.
I like to see the sunlight.'

'You saw precious little of it this morning,' John reminded him. 'You did not stir til after nine.'

'My head pained me and I . . . .'

'You drank too heavily last night,' said John. ''Twas wine
that caused you pain and no one to blame but yourself.
Drinking and carousing until the early hours, with those
feckless creatures you call friends!'

'We were enjoying ourselves,' said Stephen, controlling
his voice with an effort. 'Were you never young? Did you
never enjoy a drink with friends?'

'Aye — in moderation, but I worked hard and deserved
to play. You do nothing but wait for Heron to fall into your
lap like a gift from Heaven.'

He turned away and stared angrily out of the window.
'All that you can see will be yours,' he told Stephen. 'A
thriving prosperous land rich in tin. Land that your mother
and I have striven for. Tis your inheritance and yet you will
not work for it.'

'Because I do not want it,' cried Stephen and Elizabeth
rose angrily to her feet but let him continue. 'Mama worked

for Heron because she loved it. You worked as a goldsmith because you loved the work and were talented. Why cannot I work at something I love so that my heart can be in it? I want to farm. I do not want to mine for tin. I have told you a thousand times.'

'Dear God!' cried Elizabeth desparingly. 'Why, Stephen, why? Why scratch a living from the turf and a handful of sheep when you can go take the rich ore from below the turf? We are miners, not farmers!'

John turned and glanced at Elizabeth. Her face was pale and she twisted her fingers nervously. He knew how the constant clashes of temperament distressed her and, crossing the room put an arm around her shoulder.

'Leave us,' he whispered. 'Let me speak with him alone. You look tired and should walk in the garden while the sun still shines.'

She made as though to protest, but was glad when he insisted. Stephen watched her go thankfully. It was difficult for him to speak his mind freely when his mother was present. With John he could talk almost as one man to another, for he felt at fifteen years he was almost adult. In his own mind he was a man as determined about his life as John had been before him. His dark head sat on his shoulders with the same arrogance as John's and the blue eyes were equally cold.

'How do you expect to farm?' John asked him, making a fresh effort to speak reasonably and without anger. 'You have no money to buy sheep and know nothing of them. How will you hire a shepherd? Have you considered?'

'Heron could give me the money,' said Stephen. 'I am the first-born son and it owes me something.'

'Give you the money!' shouted John, his good intentions thrown to the winds. 'Bleed Heron to set you up as a farmer? Is that your plan? You may be the first-born and you should inherit — but you inherit the mine.'

'I do not want it!' Stephen cried, bringing his fist down against the tableboard so that it shuddered and rocked. 'If

273

you will not give me the money, then lend it and I will repay you.'

'The Kendals are not money-lenders!'

'And I am not a miner!'

'You speak the truth, by God, for you are nothing! Do you hear me? Nothing. And without Heron you will remain nothing! In God's name, Stephen, do not provoke me too far. You drift through life without a care, drinking, gambling . . . .'

'I throw a few dice, that is all.'

'You are not betrothed nor will consider any of the marriage contracts we propose for you.'

'I do not wish to wed yet.'

They faced each other, John white with rage, Stephen trembling but determined.

'We go round in circles,' said John grimly. 'There is no point in further argument. You will inherit Heron as we have planned for you. You will go to London and study law as we have planned for you. And you will marry whoever we choose for — Wait! You will . . . .'

But he was too late. The boy had gone.

They rode slowly through the dripping countryside. It had rained without pause for ten days but now the wind had veered and the drenched land enjoyed a welcome respite. Everywhere echoed with the sound of water trickling down every rock face, dropping from the boughs above their heads, oozing from the rough turf below them as the horses' hooves left a trail of small hollows which filled with water before the riders were out of sight. Eric, riding beside Elizabeth, glanced curiously at his mistress but said nothing. For him, it was a long awaited outing and Elizabeth's preoccupation cast only a small shadow on his pleasure. Ahead of them a lark rose suddenly, trilling its way upward, and the bird on her wrist stirred eagerly at the sound.

'Not yet, little one. Not yet,' murmured Elizabeth fondly and Eric laughed.

'She's raring to be away,' he said, 'and wondering why she's been perched so long.'

Elizabeth nodded. 'She may be difficult to retake,' she said. 'We must see she doesn't go into cover for twill be a wet task today to retrieve her even with Jasper's nose.'

The spaniel, hearing his name, glanced up, then resumed his meanderings. He too was pleased to be out and about though the heavy rain had washed away many of his favourite scents and his snufflings among the sodden undergrowth brought little reward.

The merlin, inside her hood, blinked at the sound of Elizabeth's voice. Already there was an understanding between bird and mistress. Although Elizabeth had only owned her for five months, her training had progressed without too many problems and the sport, new to Elizabeth, afforded her exercise and a new interest. She had plenty of time to spare now that the children were growing up. Too much time and too little company, she thought regretfully. John's absorption with business and mining took up most of his time and they were rarely together. She sighed deeply, and glanced at the bird perched on the leather gauntlet on her left arm.

'You grow heavy, Amber,' she chided her. 'Lack of exercise makes you fat. We shall see what this afternoon's sport brings you in the way of a quarry. I trust you will prove less heavy on the way home!'

'I believe Jasper is grown heavy too,' said Eric, 'for he's a lazy animal when all's said, and would sleep by the fire all day now that the days grow colder.'

'He grows old,' said Elizabeth, 'and was ever a fine-weather dog!'

The black and white spaniel had been bought to replace Rufus and was now nearly eight years old. John had not trained him for hawking, being used to the older dog, but Elizabeth found him satisfactory. As a puppy he had helped to fill the void in her life when her baby died and there was a bond of affection between them. She sighed again. But I still have my family, she reminded herself. Catherine now seventeen, was betrothed to Leonard Polegate in Exeter. She lived with his family and would be married when Leonard was of age. Meanwhile, she divided her time between his family and her Aunt Lydia, now virtually blind. And Matthew had grown into a likeable young man, Thoughtful and considerate, but so shy. So different from William who was full of charm and confidence, bold in the extreme. And Stephen. Poor, angry Stephen. She shook her head and Eric looked up, thinking that she spoke. Elizabeth noted his glance and smiled ruefully.

'My mind strays,' she told him, 'but I think we may soon call a halt. Tis fairly open here and we should not lose her.'

They reigned in the horses and looked about them. The moor sloped away as far as the eye could see. To their right, a mile or two away, was a small copse of stunted hawthorns. Elizabeth hesitated.

'She will work downwind,' she said. 'I think we must go higher up. A quarter of a mile should suffice.' She stroked the bird's neat back, taking her usual delight in the dark wings and tail, and lightly speckled breast.

'We shall soon have that hood off, my pet,' she told her. 'And you will be off like an arrow from a bow! And mind that you return for I shall miss you if you go astray. I should miss my bonny Amber, indeed I should.'

Eric hid a smile. It amused him to hear her speak so lovingly to a bird and the softness in her tone was rare these days. She had grown harder with the passing years and did not speak to tenderly to any but the bird and dog. Yet who save Blanche spoke tenderly to her? He shrugged. He would waste no time on Elizabeth's problems. He had plenty of his own, for he had a wife now, having wed Della the previous year and her tongue grew sharp already at his expense. She was with child and sickly and her cheerful spirits had deserted her. With a jerk he brought his thoughts back to the present for they had stopped once more and Elizabeth was waiting for him.

Hurriedly, he slipped from his horse and tethered it to a heavy boulder. Then, he whistled the dog and set off in the direction indicated by Elizabeth. Jasper, sensing his excitement, made a great display, leaping among the low brackens and nosing rapidly through the heather. Eric swung his arms and hallooed until, almost under his feet, a lark rose twittering with alarm and began its ascent. Immediately, Elizabeth slipped the hood from the merlin's head and freed it from the leash. The bird's beady eye picked up the flight of the lark and chattering excitedly she launched herself from the gauntlet and swooped in pursuit. Elizabeth shaded her eyes as she watched the hawk rise, the strong wings beating the air, the small head thrust determinedly forward.

'She'll have it!' cried Eric, his excitement overcoming his discretion. 'See how she goes . . . Ah, she's a rare sight. I'd not be that lark for a bag of silver!'

Elizabeth didn't answer and he felt reproved and fell silent in his turn. Together they watched the aerial dance that was taking place as the two birds pitted their wings against each other. The lark, singing its alarm, lifted itself higher and still higher into the grey sky until it was no more than a dot. Round it the merlin pursued its own swooping flight, circling round and round, gaining height steadily. Suddenly the dot blended with the clouds and was lost to view. The merlin hovered uncertainly.

'She's lost it. I never would have thought it,' Eric frowned his disappointment as Elizabeth nodded.

'Aye, so she has,' she said. 'Out of condition I daresay, from lack of exercise.'

Taking the lure from the saddlebag, she swung it expertly, letting out the cord gradually until it described an arc which could be seen from the height at which the hawk flew. She dropped like a stone and seized the lure – a leather weight with feathers in the likeness of a bird. Before the bird could discover the deception, Elizabeth walked up to it and kneeling steadily, offered a morsel of sheep's heart on the palm of her glove. Willingly, the merlin forsook the lure and stepping on to her wrist once more, began to tear at the meat with her powerful beak. Deftly Elizabeth secured the leash and stood up. She looked around, hesitating.

'We'll try again,' she said. 'A hundred yards hence. And did you lose your lark, my pretty?' she crooned, stroking the bird. 'Never fret. We shall find you another and now that your wings are restored you shall take it this time.'

As she spoke, she replaced the hood over the bird's head and walked on, leaving Eric to bring the horses.

Jasper ran ahead and within minutes, had put up another lark. Off came the hood and away went the hawk. The lark took fright. Suddenly silent it veered to the right with the hawk close behind, then suddenly changed direction again and began to rise. But the first flight had been a mistake. Despite its striving, the small bird was unable to gain height fast enough. The merlin swooped upward, circling closer and closer, until it was above its quarry.

'Now!' cried Elizabeth, her attention rivetted on the dark shape which plummetted downwards.

'She stoops!' cried Eric. 'She has it!' and he threw his cap in the air by way of celebration. Elizabeth laughed, but her own satisfaction was evident. Eric whistled Jasper who came unwillingly. It would not do for the dog to disturb Amber who now on the ground broke into the dead lark, tearing at its feathers. Should anything startle it, the merlin would 'carry' — withdrawing her prey to some inaccessible spot. While Eric held the dog, Elizabeth moved smoothly forward and once again offered the bird a small piece of meat on her glove. After a moment's hesitation, the merlin obeyed her training and returned to Elizabeth's wrist where she was rewarded with a suitable morsel of meat.

Too large a reward and she would be reluctant to fly

again. Too small, and she would resent the loss of her lark.

'Will you enter her again?' asked Eric hopefully, but Elizabeth looked up at the sky. Large, heavy clouds were rolling in and she shook her head.

'I dislike these clouds,' she told him. 'We have some way to go and may still get caught in a storm. I think we must return, even though we disappoint Amber. But you have enjoyed your outing, my pet?'

Eric helped his mistress to remount and then swung himself up on to his own horse. They turned the mounts and began the journey home. The merlin at Elizabeth's wrist, now unhooded, watched the passing landscape with small movements of her head.

Eric glanced anxiously at his mistress. They had a few miles to go and he liked to talk. But she was quiet of late and if he did not initiate a conversation, he would be left to his own thoughts while she withdrew into hers.

'I think she missed her companion,' he remarked cheerfully. 'She does not like to hunt alone.'

Elizabeth considered his remark as he had hoped she would.

'Mayhap,' she said. 'A cast is better sport than a single bird, but Jupiter suffers from a pain and has had a scouring pill these last two days. Next week I trust we may fly them both.'

'And after partridge?' he asked enthusiastically. Elizabeth laughed. 'I swear you are become as keen as I am. A few more weeks and we may well fly her after partridge.'

'And the master, will he join you?' Eric pursued.

A shadow crossed Elizabeth's face. ''Tis possible,' she said. 'But I think not. The master is fully occupied these days and has little mind for hawking.'

'Master Stephen then?' the boy persisted.

'Master Stephen? I cannot say,' she answered. 'He will

279

be leaving for London soon and must make preparations.'

It had been decided after the last bitter argument, that Stephen should join Joseph Tucker's son Jo, who already had lodgings in London and hopefully might exert a favourable influence on him. Jo, too, was learning law in preparation for the time when he would replace Joseph as master of Maudesly. But would Stephen ever take his rightful place in Heron? She doubted it. Details of the previous day's quarrel revolved in Elizabeth's mind and she rode thoughtfully, a frown on her face, the bird on her wrist forgotten. The first raindrops pattered down and Eric cursed.

'We'd best make haste,' he urged. 'We're in for a storm.'

'A storm?'

'Aye,' he insisted. 'Did you not see the lightning — ah, here comes the thunder. What did I say now?'

'You spoke truly,' cried Elizabeth. 'We must indeed make haste.' And spurring their horses, they galloped, heads down, across the moor towards Heron.

The rain continued throughout the night. It fell on to ground so saturated it could absorb no more and the fresh rain ran along the surface until it found crevices in the rock. Silently it flowed down the smooth sides of the granite, finally reaching a layer of softer, more permeable material and began a new horizontal course. Dropping occasionally, it was fed from other sources and swelled in volume until it gurgled and spluttered through the underground courses, worn by water through countless ages. It dropped again down a natural 'chimney' in the rock, and gathered speed until there was more water than the normal course could take and the surplus found its way through a new split. This led into a small cavern from which there was no ready exit. The water level rose in the cavern and the weight of it pressed increasingly against the thin rock wall that separated the cavern from the shaft in which John stood.

He and Old William were the only men in the shaft for it was Sunday. John had decided to inspect the progress made in the attempt to connect this, the fourth 'spoke of the wheel' to the perpendicular shaft which was its hub. William, a few yards further back, was complaining of the quality of the latest timbers which shored the roof of the tunnel when his ears picked up an absence of sound and he paused, listening, his head on one side. Alerted, John listened also. Water was no longer trickling into the cavern which was brimming with two thousand gallons of water. The two men looked at one another uneasily. The existence of the cavern was not known to them, but they sensed impending danger.

'Out!' cried William but even as he spoke the rock wall collapsed on to him, killing him instantly. As the shattered rock filled the tunnel, the water swirled backwards hurling John like a twig against the far end of the tunnel. Then it washed backwards towards the rockfall and forced its way between the fallen rocks and William's mangled body to flow along the tunnel and out on to the hillside. With it went the timbers newly torn from the roof of the tunnel, to be tossed like so much kindling wood among the bracken on the hillside. The roar of its passage was heard faintly more than a mile away and many who heard it wondered for a moment. The only man who might have recognized the sound was Will Retter and he was attending the parliament on Crockern Tor nearly eight miles away.

Elizabeth, on hearing it, raised her eyes from the ledger in which she was writing, added some figures in her head, then bent to continue her calculations. The rain had ceased and she wondered whether or not to fly the merlin again, but did not relish another solitary outing. She had suggested that John might accompany her. It was Sunday, she pointed out, and a day of rest, but he had arranged to inspect the mine with one of the men as guide and would be away for several hours. So she busied herself with the household accounts, a task which gave her no pleasure.

And Della was with child! The news, an hour earlier, had taken her by surprise. She had had no time in which to compose her expression and the pain had showed in her eyes and the faltering congratulations. Della had not stayed. She grieved for her mistress and sympathized with her distress. Now Elizabeth's thoughts returned to the girl. She would make a very feckless mother, she thought, then reproached herself for her spite. The figures in the page floated before her eyes as tears brimmed up in them, but she brushed them away angrily. Jealous of a serving girl! It was preposterous! She stabbed the quill into the ink and resumed her accounts . . . She supposed she would have to replace the girl eventually. How long did they continue working? A few months more, surely. And Eric was to be a father! She smiled wanly at the idea. To her he was still a cheerful lad, a loyal and cheerful lad. He would not be leaving them. There were hoofbeats outside and she hurried to the window. Joseph was dismounting as Eric ran forward to take charge of his mount. Glad of the excuse, Elizabeth abandoned the accounts and hurried downstairs. She opened the door and he laughed, his hand raised to the bell.

'Such service!' he teased. 'To answer the bell before it has been rung!' His smile changed to a look of concern as he saw the remains of tears on her cheeks and knew that she had been weeping.

'Twas nothing,' she told him. 'Come in and welcome. I am alone as you see. John is at the mine; Stephen is in . . .' she shrugged helplessly. 'I don't know where he is. And the twins are practising.'

'I saw them at the butts as I rode up,' he said. 'William has a good eye and a strong right arm.'

'And Matthew?' she prompted.

'Matthew? Ah, he's not an archer, that one!' he laughed, 'though he looks fiercely at it and draws with a will!'

282

She led the way into the hall where a few logs smouldered redly. Seizing another, she tossed it into the fire, dislodging the others in a shower of sparks and ash. It began to smoke and they moved back a little.

'The wood is wet,' she grumbled. 'And small wonder this weather. I dare swear there is no dry wood to be had in all the West Country!' She rubbed at an ink spot on her finger.

'Have I saved you from the accounts?' he asked and she smiled.

'I do not need a very large excuse,' she said. 'I find them boring, yet usually they interest me. I think the fault lies within myself. I am restless today and do not know what ails me.'

'You have been weeping,' he said gently.

''Twas nothing,' she assured him. 'Della is with child. She told me this morning.' She turned her face away, and spoke lightly, but he was not deceived.

'Your turn will come again,' he said.

'If it should be God's will,' she said.

She drew a long deep breath, turning towards the fire as though to take comfort from its warmth. Now the logs blazed more fiercely. Joseph looked at the slim back and saw the dejected slope of her shoulders.

'What brings you to Heron?' she asked, turning to face him and smiling with an assumed cheerfulness which did not deceive him for an instant.

Joseph bit back the words he wanted to say. How could he tell her that he came to Heron whenever he could find a ready excuse, just to see her again. To hear her voice and warm himself in her smile. If she had noticed his frequent visits she made no mention of the fact. And John, did he wonder at all?

Rapidly he searched his mind for the excuse which brought him on this present occasion.

'John told me he was thinking of selling his bay,' he said, 'and I heard this morning of a likely buyer — the blacksmith to the west of the town has had his mare stolen. Gipsies he reckons, but the beast has been gone for a week and will no doubt be at a horse fair by now half-way across the country!'

'Did you mention the bay to him?' she asked.

'Aye, and he's interested and would like to come up and see it.'

'I'll tell John,' she said. 'He will be pleased and will, I'm certain, approach the smith. Will you take a drink of wine while you are here?'

He was on the point of accepting the offer when a further clatter of hoofbeats drew them to the window. A riderless horse stood outside, tossing his head while his rider, breathless and dishevelled, burst suddenly into the room mumbling incoherently. Elizabeth gazed at him in dismay, sensing that his news whatever it was, would not be welcome. 'Speak slow, for pity's sake!' she cried. 'You tangle your words so! Start again and speak slow.'

His lips worked soundlessly for a moment and his eyes darted nervously round the large hall. Then he began again. 'The workings,' he said. 'The water in the workings!'

His words, clear at last, shocked her into a fearful awareness.

'Tis the workings!' he told them. 'The new shaft. The rocks have fallen in . . . flooded it were, and the props all higgledy . . . .'

'The workings?' echoed Joseph. 'The Heron workings? Speak man.'

'Aye, the Heron workings.'

'And John, my husband?' faltered Elizabeth. 'What news of him?'

'None can say, ma'am,' he told her. 'Tis just now discovered and Tom Liddle is gone through the tunnel to see what he can find. Some say the Master and Old William was meaning to go along today.'

'They did go,' said Elizabeth, her heart heavy as lead. 'What caused the fall? Is it known?' she asked.

'The water, most like,' the man told them.

'Will Retter!' cried Elizabeth. 'He's the man for us now! Send word to him.'

'But he's a long ways off,' he said. 'Crockern Tor, that's where he is.'

'Dear God!' cried Elizabeth. 'The man speaks truly. Retter is gone to attend the parliament.'

'Then we must fetch him home if needs be,' said Joseph. 'But for the present we'll ride to the mine and see the situation for ourselves.'

Five minutes later, they were dismounting at the entrance to the new shaft. A group of tinners were there before them, shaking their heads and speaking in hushed voices. Elizabeth felt frozen with a terrible apprehension.

'Was anyone in the tunnel when it happened?' she asked.

One of the men nodded. 'Reckon so,' he said. 'Old William never turned up for his dinner. Never late for that, he weren't. So his old wife sent her grandson to find him and he found all this.' With a sweeping movement of his hand, he indicated the newly deposited mud at the entrance to the tunnel, the scattered splintered props, and jagged freshly broken boulders.

'Has anyone been along to see if . . . ' Joseph didn't finish the sentence. They shook their heads, a trifle shamefaced.

'Might be another fall, see,' one of them muttered.

Joseph turned to Elizabeth. 'I'd best take a look,' he said but she clung to him, oblivious of the surprised and embarrassed stares of the tinner.

'I beg you not to go in there,' she cried. 'The men are right. There may be another fall. Must I lose you both,' she added in a whisper, while her eyes pleaded with him to remain.

'I must go,' he said. 'Wait here — and do not let any follow. Do not despair. There is still hope.'

'After this!' she pointed to the debris and he shrugged. His own feeling was that no one could have survived either the rock fall or the pressure of the water, but without another word he ducked into the mouth of the shaft and began to make his way through the rubble. Outside the small group of tinners grew in number as word spread of the disaster. Old William's wife arrived and Elizabeth took her hand wordlessly.

'There's still hope,' she said without conviction.

'My William's dead,' said the old woman as though Elizabeth hadn't spoken.

'Oh no!' cried Elizabeth. 'You mustn't speak that way. We must—'

'He's dead,' she repeated and there was no emotion in the voice, only finality. She crossed herself and Elizabeth shuddered. 'Passed me it did and touched my face,' said the old woman.

'I don't understand.'

'His spirit passed me,' said the old woman. 'Cold as ice it was across my face . . . My William — he's dead.'

Before Elizabeth could answer, they heard Joseph returning, his face ashen.

'Tell her tis so,' the old woman prompted him. 'Tell her my William's dead.'

'We don't know,' he said.

Ignoring him, the old woman turned and walked towards her daughter who had now arrived. Elizabeth met Joseph's eyes and he shook his head.

'Tis bad,' he told her. 'Very bad. The tunnel is blocked completely but for what distance I cannot say. There is no sign of John. Turning to the tinners,' he asked, 'Does that tunnel connect with the main shaft?'

'Not yet,' one of them replied. 'But twasn't far off, so Retter reckoned.'

'At least there's no more water,' said Joseph. 'I think another fall is unlikely but we cannot be certain. If either

man is still alive, every moment is vital. There is no time
to ride for Retter. We must act now....'

When John regained consciousness, he opened his eyes to
find himself in darkness. His head throbbed violently, so
that the slightest movement made him cry out. He had no
way of knowing how long he had lain there. He remembered Old William's cry of 'Out!' and being swept off his
feet but no more. He tried to pierce the darkness, blinking
and rubbing his eyes but saw no chink of light anywhere,
no lightening of the intense blackness.

'William!'

His voice frightened him, sounding unfamiliar in its
hoarseness. No more than a croak. He called again but with
no result. He tried to recall where William had been when
the rock fell. Could he possibly have escaped that torrent
of water?

'William!' he cried again. God's nails! Were they trapped
like rats behind a wall of rock? If only he could see....

Warily, he lifted his right arm and felt his head. There
was a gash of some size from which blood still oozed. He
could move his left arm, also his right leg, but the left leg
... Leaning forward, he felt for his left leg and it was there,
but there was no feeling at all. He leaned back. The effort
of these small explorations exhausted him and he felt a
sweat break out on his forehead.

'Fear,' he said aloud and found his voice was comfort-
ingly familiar once more. 'William!' he called again, but the
silence mocked him. Perhaps the old tinner had been swept
to safety and was even now raising the alarm. He wanted
to think so, but his common-sense told him that it was
unlikely. 'Highly unlikely,' he said to himself. He felt
light-headed as if slightly drunk and it was not unpleasant.

'I am not cast down,' he said and grinned. He was aware
suddenly of a pain in his neck and turned his head, trying

287

to ease it. 'So . . . my neck cannot be broke!' he told himself hazily.

No, it cannot be broke . . . His breathing grew louder, more rhythmic . . . He was falling asleep . . . He jerked his head up. That wouldn't do. He must stay awake. Must hear when the rescuers came to find him and dig him out . . . His head lolled but he jerked himself upright again. And if they didn't . . . . If they didn't come for him? He listened but heard nothing but the drip, drip, drip, of the confounded water and a sonorous breathing that must be his own . . . . And then the drips were raindrops, beating against the fine windows of his boyhood home, and he traced them with a stubby finger as they ran from red to yellow and from yellow to green . . . He must not snore, he told himself. He must sleep quietly or he would disturb Bet . . . She would awake and, grumbling, push him over on to his side so that his mouth closed . . . It disturbed her . . . His snoring . . . He listened anxiously but his breathing was relaxed and quiet . . . .

'Now I'm wide awake!' she grumbled and turning, snuggled against him complaining that she was cold.

He took her into his arms. The tousled curls tickled his chest and her small fists were indeed cold. He became aware of the rest of her body curled against his own and kissed the top of her head . . . Poor Bet! Poor little Bet! How they had despised her . . . Small and helpless as a churchmouse — and as poor as one! She brought no dowry but an illegitimate child and a body covered in bruises. Pregnant by a brutish lover, she had run sick and trembling into the shop to hide. And John had fought for her. His first fight . . . He felt again the yielding flesh of the man's face and heard the crack of his own rib under the man's fist. And when it was over and Mark found him, bloody and defeated, the girl had gone. But the following day she had come in, shyly, to thank him. John had wed her against all advice to the contrary. His parents had been furious . . . *I can scarce believe that you intend to wed such a girl. She can bring*

288

you nothing. Union with this girl would be the height of folly and we can never give our blessing to it. You must put the idea from you or expect to incur our severe displeasure. He saw again his mother's strong, well-formed handwriting and felt the roll crumple in his hand as he tossed it from him, cursing. He had never taken Bet home. None of his family had ever met her. Catherine was born, a small blonde child, always smiling and immediately Bet had fallen pregnant again. She had laughed at his dismay.

'What — are you a rabbit?' He had teased and she had promised him a warren full of baby rabbits. And after Stephen came the twins and she had died .... 'Bet,' he whispered into the darkness. 'Don't leave me here alone ....' But she had gone and he lay in the darkness sobbing. Still the water dripped until he closed his eyes and then the sun came out and the tall grass had closed over his head as he waited for the birds to see his tame owl which now perched sedately at one end of the perch, blinking in the unfamiliar light. And a thrush had come to investigate and flew into the trap. The net folded over him and he ran forward and took the fluttering bird in his hand ....

'William!' he called again but there was no answer and then his first-born, Stephen, lay in his arms, his face blue and wrinkled, screaming his distaste for the world, his fists pummelling the air. John had laughed at him. 'Is that all you can do?' Bet cried with mock indignation. 'I give you your first son and you laugh! Small thanks indeed for all my efforts. I shall not give you another.'

And he had thrown back his head and laughed with joy at the wriggling, yelling child in his arms. Then handing the babe to the midwife, kneeled and kissed his wife who lay flushed and exhausted. He had stroked the small firm breasts and rosy nipples with gentle fingers. 'And must I now share these with another man?' he asked, and she had blushed for fear the midwife overheard ....

When he opened his eyes, his head ached less, but his left leg pained him below the knee. 'So I still have a whole leg,' he thought and wondered at the time it took them to find him. The temperature in the tunnel was very low and now great shivers shook his frame and his teeth chattered. The darkness seemed to press on him, weighing him down with its intensity. He wondered how long he had slept and how long he had been down there. An hour? A day? It could not be so long . . . .

He must keep warm, he told himself. Must keep moving. 'Keep moving,' he muttered. 'Keep awake until they come — until they call. They will think me dead, else . . . .' Slowly, he moved his head from side to side then eased his shoulders away from the cold rock surface against which he was propped. The ground beneath him was damp but very smooth; washed clean by the force of the water so that no small pebbles or gravel remained. His fingers groped in the darkness, finding nothing. He blew on his hands to warm them, but the simple exertion tired him and he fell back against the side of the shaft and closed his eyes. The dripping of the water grew louder, hypnotic in its regularity. Clenching and unclenching his fingers, he felt the billet of yew, pliant in his hands and steadied it for the axe blow. It split cleanly into two sister halves, revealing the pale pristine heartwood. Drawing his knife, he began to shave one half, tillering it from time to time to encourage the curve. His brother, nodded approvingly.

'You do well for a beginner,' he told him. 'We shall make an archer of you yet!'

John glowed inwardly at the words but said nothing. Gently, lovingly he worked on the two halves of the bow until he was satisfied and showed the boy how to fashion the two halves into one with a 'fish tail' and then it was ready for sanding . . . . The white sapwood gleamed like ivory and the plied flax was taut against his fingers. The arrow rested lightly on his left hand, tipped with iron and flighted with goose feathers. Leaning on the bow, he steadied it — and the arrow sped on its way to drive, quivering with shock, into the heart of the target.

'A fine shot!' cried his brother, clapping his hands. 'You have a good eye and a steady arm! The accursed French will do well to stay on friendly terms with us now!'

John's heart burst with pride and he reached over his shoulder for a second arrow . . . . The sound of voices filtered into his consciousness and he opened his mouth to cry out. He could make no sound. He was no longer propped against the rock wall, but had slipped down and lay sprawled on his back. Somewhere he could hear voices. Somewhere he could hear the grating sound of rocks being moved but it came from all round him and above him. Or was it inside his head? Old William was coming to find him. Old William was not dead and was coming towards him. He saw him, holding out his hands to pull John to his feet but the fingers were without flesh and the face was without eyes! John hid his face in his hands and whimpered, 'No, William . . . no . . . .'

Raising his voice, Joseph addressed the crowd gathered about the mouth of the tunnel.

'I'll speak plainly,' he told them. 'I cannot tell how far the fall extends nor do I know the cause of it, though I'd hazard a guess twas a build up of the water which still runs as you can see for yourself.' They looked silently at the water which trickled past their feet to disappear into the sodden turf beyond them.

'Tis possible the danger from the water is now past but by no means certain. I'm asking for men to help me but if you've a family, you'd best stand aside.

The men muttered among themselves, then one stepped forward.

'I've a mind to help,' he cried, 'and having a wife won't stop me.'

'She will that!' cried a young woman, heavy with child, who pushed her way forward. 'You'll not leave me a widow, Henry, while there's single men as is willing!'

'She's right,' Elizabeth intervened as fresh argument broke out. 'We want no tragedies, take him home girl — and let us see who remains that we can make a start.'

Eight men stepped forward, the rest withdrew to their homes, unwilling to stand idly by while their friends took risks.

'We'll need fresh torches,' Joseph told them. 'You, Thomas, see how many you can collect and set them up along the walls of the shaft. I see the small wagon is useless now. We must form a chain to pass back the rock while you, James, see if the wagon can be restored. We will need it for some of the large rocks can scarce be handled by men's hands . . . .' He broke off and met Elizabeth's gaze.

'What can I do?' she asked.

'Go back to Heron,' he said. 'This is no place for a woman. I will send news of . . . .'

She shook her head.

'I shall stay,' she said, 'so do not waste your breath on argument. This mine is Heron and I am Heron. I will not be sent away.' Her eyes flashed defiantly and the body was drawn up straight and tall.

He smiled. 'Then you stay,' he told her. 'And take your place with the men.'

Thomas had already left in search of torches and James crouched over the damaged wagon, which was normally hauled to and fro along the shaft to bring out the hewn rock and tin bearing ore. While they waited impatiently for the torches, Elizabeth spoke with Joseph, her voice low.

'Joseph, what chance is there? I beg you speak truthfully.'

'Little chance,' he said. 'The water must surely have drowned them if by some miracle they escaped the rock fall. I could hear nothing. No groaning, no tapping, no sign of life.'

'They might be stunned.'

''Tis possible.'

'But you do not think so.'

'I fear the worst, Elizabeth. We are . . . Ah, Thomas, well done. Now set them at intervals and we can make a start. Move with as little sound as possible. Then we will hear them if they cry out.'

An hour later, Elizabeth ached all over. The muscles in her back screamed with each new effort. Her hands were sore and bleeding from the rough granite and her feet were cold and wet. Her eyes, too, were strained from the unaccustomed gloom and her head throbbed. And they had found nothing. Had heard nothing. Her fear grew that John was indeed dead. Joseph was right. There was little chance that anyone could have survived such an accident. She straightened up, a hand to her back, supporting herself with her free hand against the wall. The man beside her looked at her with concern.

'You should take a rest, ma'am,' he said.

'And shall you rest?' she asked.

The man shook his head.

'Then nor shall I,' she retorted.

A cry went up suddenly from further along the shaft, and they all turned in hope and fear towards the sound.

There was a quick exchange of lowered voices at the rock fall.

'What is it?' cried Elizabeth.

''Tis the old man,' they told her.

Joseph came down to her, his face haggard in the flickering gloom. ''Tis the old man,' he said. 'They are still freeing him—'

'And is he—'

'Aye. Dead. Killed outright I shouldn't wonder for what we can reach of him is crushed like matchwood—'

'Dear God!'

'I'm sorry.'

She swayed and would have fallen but for his arm. He hesitated.

'Take her outside,' he told the nearest man, but she opened her eyes and would not go. They freed Old

293

William's body and Elizabeth watched, stricken, as he was carried past the line of silent tinners who crossed themselves and muttered a prayer for the safe passage of his soul. Next time it would be John, broken and lifeless. She would never again see the thin mouth drawn down in the grim little smile or the hard glint in the blue eyes.

'But did you love me?' she whispered.

She had been so sure of herself, so confident that she would make him happy. She had offered him so much, her love, her body, Heron. All she had, in fact, to offer any man. But had she robbed him of his pride? Should he have remained a goldsmith, to rise through his own efforts? Did he unconsciously resent the fact that Heron was not his except by marriage? Was it bitter to him that she was mistress of Heron before he was master? So long ago the future had looked so bright! 'Where did it go wrong?' she whispered.

Still the jagged rocks passed through her torn fingers but she no longer felt anything physical. The agony in her mind outweighed everything else.

On the hillside, the light faded from the sky and those who still remained gave up and went home. But still the men laboured. Finally, the wagon was restored to working order. Joseph called a halt.

'We are not all needed now,' he said. 'No more than three can work at the rockfall for lack of space and only two are wanted to haul out the wagon and unload.'

'I will stay,' said Elizabeth. 'While there is still hope.'

'There is very little hope,' said Joseph gently. 'We may find him but I doubt we shall find him alive. Won't you go home and wait there? You are exhausted, and push yourself too far.'

'I shall stay until you find him,' she said and he marvelled as he had done once before at the strength of her will.

After some discussion, four of the men left on the understanding that they would replace those who stayed if John had not been found by first light in the morning.

294

'Go to Heron,' Elizabeth told one of them. 'Tell Martha we are still working and bid her bring food and drink.'

He nodded and they left. Joseph organized the remaining rescuers into a team: two at the rock fall, one loading the rock into the wagon, the remainder hauling it free of the shaft and returning it empty. One or two of the torches had burned out and they had to manage with the light that remained. Another hour passed and suddenly the cavern was revealed beside the shaft. Joseph climbed into it and worked his way round to try and by pass the rock fall. The collapse of the wall had weakened the roof of the shaft and that too had fallen.

'What chance is there?' Elizabeth asked him as he crawled through the cavern.

''Tis hard to say,' said Joseph. 'If he is under the rubble, then I doubt if he could live. But there may be a gap between the end of the fall and the furthermost point of the shaft. If there is a gap and if he is in it, there may be a chance for him.'

'He does not seem to call,' she said. 'If he called, would we hear him?'

'Aye. The sound would travel between the rock fragments. He may be unconscious.'

'You will not give up, Joseph,' she begged. 'Make me vow that you will not give up! Not knowing . . .'

He put an arm round her briefly and whispered, 'I will never give up. We shall find him, I swear it.'

Before they could resume, Martha and Eric arrived with hot broth, bread and cold mutton. They called a brief halt while the men sank down, taking the welcome food eagerly. Elizabeth leaned back against the hard rock wall, her eyes closed, snatching great bites from the mutton. Joseph had a few words with Martha who was shocked to see the state of her mistress.

'Ma'am!' cried Martha. 'You must come away. This is no place for you! Eric will take your place and you must . . . .'

'Aye, that I will!' cried Eric eagerly, but Elizabeth shook her head without even opening her eyes.

'Don't scold me, Martha,' she said, 'or I shall weep like a child. Let me be. At least I am near him.'

Martha shrugged. She knew better than to pursue the matter.

'I would like to stay,' Eric persisted. 'Another pair of strong arms cannot come amiss!'

Joseph smiled at his enthusiasm. 'You can stay if you've a mind, but first bring fresh torches,' he said, and Eric hurried away, proud to be of service at such a time.

After some deliberation, Joseph decided there was little to be gained in the short term by searching the rubble for John's body if he was in fact dead. Butter to establish whether or not a gap existed at the end of the shaft in which he might still be alive. They therefore began work at the far end of the cavern. Every few moments they paused to shout John's name and wait for any response. Eric returned with fresh torches and then joined the small band of rescuers, replacing one of the men who collapsed with exhaustion and was forced to rest.

It was nearly midnight before one of Joseph's shouts unexpectedly elicited a reply! At the sound, they all froze, straining their ears to hear whether it was repeated.

'John! John!' shouted Joseph, cupping his hands to his mouth. 'Do you hear us?'

Faintly — so faintly — came an answering, 'Aye'.

'Dear God!' whispered Elizabeth, almost afraid to believe it.

'Don't give up!' shouted Joseph. 'Keep shouting so we'll know where you are!'

Buoyed by fresh enthusiasm, Elizabeth and the men struggled on. They had no more cries to guide them, however, for John had slipped into unconsciousness again; but they worked towards the sound as best they could until at last a rock did not reveal more rocks but a space and they knew they were through.

'We've done it!' cried Joseph.

He moved carefully lest a rock, carelessly dislodged, should fall on to John and do him further injury. Taking a torch, he stepped down into the shaft and found John lying there unconscious, and with a broken leg. Elizabeth, scrambling through after him, gave a cry that was part grief, part joy. For a second her eyes met Joseph's in mute gratitude, then she was kneeling beside her husband, and cradling his head in her arms.

The small cottage stood at the end of the track. It had a single sloping roof of turf. A pile of newly chopped wood lay against the end wall next to the door. A water butt stood at the corner, and beside that a broom and a rake. The cottage had been home for nearly fifty years to Old William and his wife, Marion. Elizabeth drew a deep breath then rapped on the door, noting the rusting hinges and gaps at the lower edge where the wood had rotted.

'Who's there?'

'Elizabeth Kendal.'

'Come you in.'

She lifted the latch and the door swung lop-sidedly, on one hinge.

'He were going to fix that,' said Marion, staring up at Elizabeth, dry-eyed. She sat alone beside the ashes of a fire. 'That crazy door, he used to call it and he were always going to fix it. Always going to, but never did — and now he's dead and never will.' Her voice was matter-of-fact, without a trace of emotion.

'I came to offer my sympathies . . . . ' began Elizabeth.

'D'you want to see him?' interrupted the old woman. 'D'you want to pay your last respects, like?'

She peered up, her eyes bright and bird-like, her head tilted on one side.

Elizabeth repressed a shudder and nodded. Not to see the body would be an insult.

'I've got him over here,' said Marion getting to her feet with an alacrity surprising in one so old. She led the way to the far end of the room which mercifully for Elizabeth was very dark.

The dead man lay under a blanket. Only his face showed as a pale oval.

'Lost an arm, he has,' she told Elizabeth. 'Ripped off by the rocks, they reckoned. Tore right off his body and can't be found. We'll have to bury him without his arm, seemingly.'

Elizabeth crossed herself and moved her lips hurriedly in prayer for the dead man's soul. The woman's garrulous words and the smell of the cottage made her queasy. As her eyes became accustomed to the gloom, she made out a row of garments strung across one corner of the room to dry. A leg of smoked pork and several branches of dried herbs hung from the roof, alongside a large pan and a string of onions. The truckle bed on which the old man's body lay, was the only piece of furniture apart from the two stools. The smell of stale wood smoke hung in the air and the floor was covered in droppings from the two hens that pecked in the straw under their feet.

'He was a good man, your husband,' said Elizabeth, lamely.

'Oh, aye, he were that,' the old woman agreed. 'He were a good old man but now he's dead.'

She settled herself on the stool once more and motioned for Elizabeth to sit on the other one. She did so, gathering her skirts together and lowering herself carefully in hopes of avoiding the worst of the mess underfoot.

'Your daughter,' she suggested, 'Will she not sit with you? You shouldn't be alone.'

'Alone? I'm not alone. I've got William's body.'

Elizabeth stared at her perplexed. She had come expecting to cope with grief but this passive acceptance bewildered her.

'His soul will be on its way to Heaven by now,' said Marion.

'Oh – – aye' agreed Elizabeth. 'I have asked Father Marryat to pray for his soul.'

'Tis all done then, seemingly . . . And they found your man, they tell me.'

Elizabeth bowed her head, 'Aye,' she said. 'God has been merciful to me.'

'Not dead then, yours?'

'No, though they say tis a miracle he is not. What will you do now?'

'How d'you mean?'

'How will you live? With your daughter?'

'Not that one!' said Marion disparagingly. 'I never could live with that one. Not never. Oh no!'

'Then how . . . . ?'

'Tis no matter.'

'But . . . .'

'Tis no matter,' repeated the old woman, more firmly.

'I have brought you this,' said Elizabeth, holding out a small purse full of silver.

'Thank you kindly,' said Marion but made no attempt to take the money. Elizabeth dropped it into her lap and the old woman nodded.

'The back of his head,' she began again, 'twas broke open by a rock. There's a hole in the back of his head as big as my fist. I could show you.' She held up her hand, tightly clenched, and Elizabeth shook her head hastily.

'I shall need a new girl soon,' Elizabeth said hurriedly changing the subject. 'My maid is with child. I thought mayhap your granddaughter . . . .'

'Oh?'

'She could do the work, if she'd a mind to.'

'She'd like that, right enough.'

299

'Shall you speak of it to her, then? The money would help you.'

'Aye.'

Suddenly Marion kicked out with her foot as one of the chickens came within range and sent it fluttering and squawking towards the door.

'He were going to fix that door,' Marion told her again, 'but now he won't. Still, no matter now.'

She stared blankly ahead and seemed indifferent to Elizabeth's presence.

'I'll send Eric to mend it,' said Elizabeth. She felt guilty that John had been spared while Marion's husband had died.

'He had such arms when he were a lad,' continued Marion. 'I warrant you never saw such arms on a lad so young. Wrestling, that's what made his arms the way they was. He told me that himself. Tis wrestling, Marion, he told me . . . such arms he had . . . .'

Elizabeth looked at her properly for the first time and was ashamed. The withered face was brown as a nut from years of hard work in the fields at harvesting time and days spent on their own plot, while her husband hacked tin from the earth with those proud arms of his! Was she really indifferent to his death — so unaffected, so acquiescent? The eyes glistened darkly below heavy lids and the skin was drawn tight across the cheekbones. There was no spare flesh. Most of the teeth were missing and those that remained were worn and brown. Only her ears were still beautiful; small and rounded, finely shaped.

The hen now squeezed back under the derelict door and resumed its nervous search for food.

'Wrestle with anyone, he would,' the old woman went on. 'No matter how big the lad was, he'd take 'un on for joy of wrestling. He was a rare one for a fight, was William. Not that he'd always win neither. Broken nose, broken teeth! He never minded such things . . . But he'd mind losing that arm.'

300

Without warning she began to sob, short painful gasps half stifled, torn from her reluctantly. Tears ran down the hollow cheeks and fell on to the coarse stuff of her gown.

Elizabeth reached out her hand and timidly patted the bony shoulder as the tears came into her own eyes for pity of it all. But the old woman paid her no heed and after a few minutes Elizabeth decided she should leave her alone with her grief. The woman's family should be with her. Closing the door awkwardly behind her, she looked around. Eric waited further down the track with her horse. As she moved towards him, William's daughter appeared from another cottage and approached her.

'Your mother is distressed,' Elizabeth told her. 'But I can offer no comfort. She seems unaware of me.'

'Aye,' she answered. 'She has been so for nearly a year now and is troubled with her mind.'

'I left some silver —'

'Tis very kind, ma'am, and I thank you for it.'

'And your daughter. I shall soon need a new maid and will consider her if you are willing.'

The woman's tired face lit up.

'More than willing!' she cried. 'And God bless you, ma'am.'

Eric arrived with the horses and helped Elizabeth into the saddle. She looked down. 'We shall pray for his soul,' she said.

The following day, Marion was dead also. She died peacefully in her sleep, and the old man and his wife were buried together. Two days later, Elizabeth held the inventory of their goods and read it slowly:

Inventory of William Foster, tinner, and his wife, Marion, of Ashburton, sixth of October, 3, 1494.
A hatchet prysed at 8d. Sundry implyments at 4s. 0d.
A bedsted and sheets 4s. 6d. Pair of pillows 1s. 4d.
Too hens at 1s. 0d. A crocke and sundry pans 1s. 8d.

Two stooles, a rayke, broom and water butt 3s. 10d.
Wearring apparel at 10s. 0d. Fyrewood at 1s. 0d.
Summa total is £1 9s. 0d.

She read it through again, changed the nine shillings to a
seven, and carefully added her own signature.

CHAPTER SEVENTEEN

1495

John laid down his quill as Elizabeth entered the room.

'Do I disturb you?' she asked.

'I am thankful for an excuse to stop,' he said. 'This heat is unbearable. The shutters are wide but there is no breeze.'

'Then shall we walk in the garden?' she asked. Standing behind him she slid her arms over his shoulders and leaning forward, kissed his hair. He laughed.

'I am too easily tempted,' he said. 'Who will check the returns if I do not?'

'You will do them later — in the cool of the evening.'

Standing, he stretched luxuriously and she took his hand.

'We shall walk down to the river,' she told him, 'and I shall bore you with such small items that your weary head will need to struggle no more!'

'I ate too heartily at dinner,' he said wearily.

'Or drank too heartily!'

He laughed. 'Your teasing is too near the truth,' he said. 'My poor head longs for its pillow.'

'Then why did you not rest?'

He shrugged. 'There is much to be done.'

In the orchard the air was heavy with the sound of bees and somewhere a woodpecker drilled into a tree.

'And how is Blanche behaving herself?' asked John.

Since her betrothal, Blanche had moved into the Heron household — into Catherine's room. Catherine, betrothed to Leonard Polegate, was in Exeter.

'She seems content,' said Elizabeth, 'and is obedient at all times.'

'And your brother Andrew — does she speak of him still?'

'Never. That ended long ago,' Elizabeth replied.

'I hope so.'

Elizabeth paused and pulled down a branch of the nearest apple tree to examine the newly formed fruit.

'Such a crop!' she cried. 'There is scarce room for them all. See here.'

As he walked towards her, Elizabeth was suddenly aware of his limp. His broken leg had mended too rapidly and would never be straight. It pained him in the cold weather and too much walking tired him. To Elizabeth, the sight of his uneven gait was a constant reminder of the disaster. He had suffered greatly from the accident, with a fever that persisted for several weeks and alarmed even the doctor. Elizabeth had nursed him back to health and their relationship had regained much of the early fervour. He looked at the cluster of small green apples and then glanced up at the rest of the branches.

'Mayhap Jacob will thin them,' he said. 'I will speak to him later. The lack of winds in the spring has preserved too many blossoms.'

Under the trees, the leaves dappled the sunlight and cast a welcome shade. John sat leaning against a tree and Elizabeth sat beside him, his arm thrown casually about her shoulders. He picked a twig from the grass and rolled it idly between his fingers, his thoughts wandering.

Without looking at Elizabeth, he said suddenly: 'Tucker still loves you. Did you know?'

'I think he does,' she said quietly.

'Does he tell you so?' he persisted.

'I see it in his eyes.'

He was silent again, then sighed.

'I thought I had lost you — last year,' he said. 'I didn't know what to do and I did nothing . . . It was cowardly of me.'

304

Elizabeth's fingers plucked at the grass around her, cutting the soft green blades with her nails.

'I thought I had lost you,' she said. 'Those hours at the mine ... and then afterwards. You spoke often in your sleep during the fever ... of Bet. Only of Bet ... I wondered how much I meant to you and was afraid to ask.'

'Poor Bet. How can you fear that poor little ghost?' he said.

'But I do! For whenever she is in your thoughts — where am I?'

Flicking away the twig, he stood up and held out his hands to her, pulling her to her feet.

'Say that you love me, Elizabeth.'

'I do,' she said, 'and dearly ... Do you regret anything?'

He shook his head.

'Not giving up your work in London?' she insisted, 'nor settling in the West?'

He shook his head again. 'I love you. I always will. To be with you is all to me. Where, is of no matter.'

'Then I am content, John.'

He took her hand and led her down the steps to the river and they stood side by side watching the smooth clear water. Below, the mullet swam lazily among the green strands of weed and on the surface tiny white flowers filled the air with their almond perfume.

'Soon the twins will be gone to London,' said Elizabeth. 'We shall miss them.'

'Aye . . . William is enamoured of his new horse, I hear.'

'The black cob? Twill suit him well. He needs a horse with a spirit to match his own.'

'I have written to Mark,' she said, 'to keep us well informed of their progress.'

'And you think they will make good craftsmen?' she asked.

He laughed. 'I hope they will do well enough! William is full of enthusiasm. He will do well, at least. And young Blanche is a comely girl. She will make him a good wife.'

'I'll see to it that she does,' said Elizabeth.

'We must make negotiations for Matthew. We should consider these friends of Mark — the Swaynes? They have three daughters?'

'Aye,' said Elizabeth. 'But the elder girl is already wed and the second betrothed.'

'So only the youngest is still unspoken for? I must go to London and speak on the matter. By all accounts they are a well-established family with a successful ship building business in Rye, Sussex. A little further on from Hastings.'

'Bet would be proud of her twins,' Elizabeth said softly.

John looked at her gratefully.

'I like to think so,' he said.

Martha, her face beaded with sweat, ladled vegetables from the pot into a broad bowl.

'Give that bird another turn,' she told Izzie and the girl moved reluctantly towards the fire.

'Don't hurry yourself!' said Martha sarcastically. 'Why Della could move twice as fast as you. You want to stir yourself, you lazy lump.'

The 'lazy lump' put out a tongue at Martha's unsuspecting back.

'Tis too hot to move any faster,' she grumbled glancing at Jacob for his support, but he carefully avoided any involvement in the argument. He sat on the back step rubbing goose grease into John's boots.

Izzie, Old William's granddaughter, reached forward and gave the spit a turn or two, then returned to the cooler side of the kitchen. As she did so, someone darted past the back door but was brought to a standstill by Martha's strident tones.

'Oy! You!' she yelled. 'Not another step until I clap eyes on you. In here and let's be seeing you.'

Joseph Tucker's young stable lad presented himself at the door, cursing her vigilance. He had wanted to deliver the news to the family himself. He came slowly into the kitchen and winked boldly at Izzie.

'We'll have less of that if you don't mind!' said Martha. 'And what might you be wanting?'

'The master said I was to tell Mistress Elizabeth and Master John — as we've players coming this evening and you're all welcome.' He grinned round delightedly, proud of his news.

Even Jacob pricked up his ears at the news, while Izzie cried her delight aloud and leapt to her feet, looking at Martha appealingly.

'Oh!' said Martha. 'So you can move fast when you've a mind! Up in a flash when there's owt that pleases you but when I say "Turn the bird" tis "Oh ma'am" and its too hot for you. You'll not be seeing any players, my girl, so don't think it.'

Izzie let out a wail and the lad, seeing his chance, tried to slip out of the back door but Martha arrested him.

'No, you don't,' she bellowed. 'I'll tell the mistress your message when I'm ready and you shall hear what they say to it. So sit yourself down.'

And she resisted the temptation to go straight to Elizabeth but seized the duck from the spit and placed it upon the vegetables. Jacob glanced over his shoulder. 'And who are they?' he asked.

'Eight of them, there are, come straight from the fair at Tavistock and not stopping here more than a night or two but must then on to . . . .'

'What's their haste?' demanded Jacob. 'Consciences pricking? Those players are more often rogues than not.

307

You want to look to your silver and plate with players in the house!'

'The master says they may bide,' said the lad indignantly, for Jacob's comment cast a slur on Joseph's good judgement. 'And they look straight enough — I've seen 'em with my own eyes!'

'Oh, you have!' cried Martha. 'And they *look* straight enough. Well, if they *look* straight its no matter if they steal the silver.' She sniffed disparagingly and lifted the dinner. 'Open the door for me, you useless lump,' she told Izzie and, hopeful of a last minute change of heart, the girl leapt to her feet and rushed to go her bidding.

'And don't think to sweeten me,' Martha added as she swept past and the girl relapsed into a sulk which a wink from Tucker's lad did nothing to dispel.

Elizabeth, John and Blanche sat at the table as Martha bustled in full of her tidings.

'Players?' said Elizabeth. 'Oh, how splendid. Do you recall the ones that came here last year, John? But they were only four. These are eight you say?'

'That's right,' said Martha, beaming. 'The lad says they look straight enough.'

'Straight or crooked, I've a mind to see them,' cried Blanche. 'May we?'

John nodded. 'I've a mind to see them myself,' he said. 'Tell Tucker we accept with pleasure. Did the lad say at what hour?'

Martha couldn't recall but said she would send word before long.

'Shall you like to come, Martha?' asked Elizabeth. 'And a few more of you. Joseph has room and to spare. Twill be an outing for all of us.'

'Thank you, ma'am,' said Martha gratefully and hurried back to the kitchen with her own good news.

Promptly at six o'clock, the audience assembled in Joseph's large hall. A semi-circle of benches and stools were arranged at one end of the room before a makeshift stage.

This area was outlined by rods laid across the rushes on the floor. Joseph and his visitors from Heron filled the front row and most of the servants of both establishments crowded behind them. Blanche sat with William, though Elizabeth thought they took little interest in each other.

Joseph's three hounds sprawled in front of them, ears pricked, sensing something unusual was about to happen. William tossed one of them a walnut that he could not crack and received a reproachful look from the brown eyes for falsely raising his hopes.

'You should not offer them nuts,' said Blanche. 'He may break his tooth.'

William opened and closed his fingers and thumb to represent Blanche's nagging.

'And we are scarce betrothed!' he added which earned him a kick on the shin from Blanche.

Joseph raised his eyebrows and turned to Elizabeth. 'Such unseemly behaviour,' he said, 'from a young woman recently betrothed! You must see to it that she behaves more decorously.'

'They find it hard to think of each other in that way,' said Elizabeth. 'They have played as children all their lives and now they must act as lovers! But I persevere. We shall make a lady of your Blanche, never fear.'

The dogs leapt to their feet, barking furiously, as the first of the players sprang into the room and turned a somersault across the stage. He wore a devil's mask which terrified the dogs and sent them scurrying for safety under the feet of the audience.

'My lords and ladies and — ' He paused to survey the servants, 'and assorted vermin!'

There was a loud outcry and much laughter at his words and he darted back, hands held protectively to his face. 'No, no! I see I have offended. Let me say then assorted rubbish — Oh, that does not please them either. I see we have a pernickety audience here tonight and must be on our mettle. I know, I'll sing you a ballad of love and of war —

and if you don't like it, I'll sing it no — Ooh, what a foul smell!' He held his nose and rolled his eyes in mock disgust. 'I swear tis the foulest smell I have ever smelled. I think you have a dead fowl hidden about you, eh madam?'

And stopping before Blanche, he reached under the hem of her dress and drew forth a cloth chicken to which a few feathers had been sewn . . . .

Blanche screamed as the bird was tossed over his shoulder to be caught by a second player who entered carrying a lute. Another followed with a viol. They began to play as the first man somersaulted his way out. He returned almost immediately to snatch up the bird and carry it out, rocking it as though it were a baby. The musicians struck up a tune and two others ran into the room on to the stage and began to juggle with oranges tossed to them by a fourth. The music quickened and the juggling became more skilful and finally drew a round of applause from the audience as they tossed the fruit among them and bowing, ran outside, leaving one of them to recite —

> 'And now pay heed to what we say
> There is a moral to this play
> A tale I tell of love and hate
> A soldier bold and his fair mate . . .

There followed a 'true' tale, indifferently acted, concerning a young wife whose husband is away at the wars who gives way to the wiles of another. There was a fearsome scene in which the usuper was poisoned and writhed about on the floor in agony while confessing his misdeeds and asking for forgiveness. This was greatly overacted but brought forth cries of pity and not a few tears from the more susceptible members of the audience; but happily he made a sudden and miraculous recovery. He then put the young wife from him forever and decided to find a new love. Running among the 'assorted vermin', he ended up in Izzie's lap to her pretended embarrassment and the delight of everyone else.

A performing dog was then put through his paces followed by a tumbler who walked on his hands and balanced a stool on his feet. All eight players then ran into the room and began an elaborate mime in which they suffered acutely from hunger and thirst and Joseph, laughing, took the hint and everyone was invited to share in the refreshments.

Ale and wine were brought in, also biscuits and various sweetmeats. The players were now without their masks and Blanche found herself next to one of them. He was slimly built, with a bright complexion accentuated by a mop of red hair. His grey eyes were humorous and she noticed, with some surprise, that the hand holding his goblet was well-shaped and well-manicured. She watched him with interest as he spoke with Matthew and was taken aback when he turned suddenly towards her and raised his drink in a toast.

'To la belle demoiselle' he said softly so that only she heard the words.

'I thank you,' she said. The grey eyes stared straight into hers and she found herself unable to look away.

'So beautiful and yet unwed!' he said.

'I am bethrothed.'

He spoke quietly and she did likewise.

'And this most fortunate gentleman — is he with us tonight?' he asked.

Still their eyes met and their conversation was whispered.

'He is to your left,' she said.

'In the blue doublet?'

She nodded and he raised his eyebrows in surprise.

'He is but a boy and you are a woman.'

The grey eyes were steady, his gaze direct. Blanche said nothing, but her eyes did not leave his face.

311

Slowly he raised the goblet to his lips and drank the remains of his wine.

'I see the future in your eyes,' he whispered. 'And your pretty palm will tell me more . . . Would you learn what the future holds in store?'

She nodded.

'I will be in the garden,' he told her, 'after The Maiden's Lament. Shall you be there?'

'I have no silver about me,' she stammered.

'But I see a dainty jewel at your throat.'

Blanche wore a small topaz on a fine gold chain. It had been given to her by her grandmother on her fourteenth birthday. She hesitated, then nodded. She would pretend it was lost. She had other such pieces.

He laughed aloud suddenly, as though at a joke, and she saw that Elizabeth approached them.

'Come, Blanche,' she said. 'The performing dog has a litter of pups and we may see them if you've a mind.'

Blanche excused herself and followed Elizabeth into the driveway where the players cart waited, piled high with baskets and props of all descriptions. In a corner, the little poodle lay with five mewling pups. The player who had accompanied them, dropped one of them into Blanche's hand and she felt the tiny heartbeat speed up as it sensed the separation from its mother. The eyes were just opening — mere slits revealing a dark liquid blue and the tiny feet were like those of a mole, pink and delicate. The body was warm and smelt of milk.

'Are these her first pups?' Elizabeth asked, but he said they were her second.

'And will they be poodles?'

'Who can tell!' he laughed. 'The bitch has a great many admirers. But a mongrel learns just as easily as a poodle. We shall keep them all.'

He handed a pup to Elizabeth, but the mother became uneasy and began to whine for the two that were missing.

'See how your mother cares for you,' Blanche told the puppy. 'She cries for your return.'

Kissing the small creature, she set it gently back against the mother and watched as it foraged blindly for milk. Then, Izzie ran out of the house to say the performance was about to continue and they all hurried back inside the house.

After a few more conjuring tricks, the red-haired youth sang them The Maiden's Lament — a very bawdy ballad about the exploits of a young woman who couldn't find a man to satisfy her. His audience, now flushed from the wine and more relaxed, joined in the chorus with abandon but Blanche, though she mouthed the words, was unaware of what they sang. Her mind was filled with her assignation and the knowledge she hoped to gain from it. As the song ended, the young man's eyes met hers for a second and then he was bowing his way out, modestly refusing an encore. Blanche rose to her feet and ran out of the room as naturally as she could. No one appeared to notice her departure. If they did, they showed no interest and she breathed a sigh of relief as she hurried out of the front door. She waited on the far side of the cart pretending to look at the pups. Should anyone follow her, she would complain of the heat and express a need for fresh air. For a moment, she thought the young man was not going to appear, but then he came running down the steps to join her.

'Ah, this is where you are hiding!' he laughed. 'And how did you like my song?'

'I scarce heard it — I'm sorry.'

'Tut, tut, I have sung my heart out in vain. But mayhap was too naughty for such dainty ears.'

'Please,' she said, 'I beg you hurry. I am afraid we will be disturbed or I shall be missed. Where shall we go?'

'Where? Let me see . . . .'

His grey eyes travelled over the garden and lit upon a oak tree some twenty yards away. Taking her hand, he ran across the grass and round behind the tree.

313

'Now,' he commanded. 'Give me your hand. My, what slender fingers and such pale skin....'

'What do you see?'

'Nothing. I see nothing.'

'But you said—'

'You are too hasty, my sweet demoiselle,' he said. 'You are uneasy and I cannot see . . . Look into my eyes and breathe deeply . . . relax . . . let me look into your eyes that I may interpret more easily . . . such pretty eyes they are, but they have known sorrow—'

He waited and she nodded.

' — and a great longing...'

'Aye,' she whispered.

'But the palm awaits.'

He lowered his eyes to her hand and began wordlessly to trace the lines in her palm. As his finger moved, he pursed his lips and frowned.

'What do you see?' she asked breathlessly, but he shook his head and continued his exploration of her hand.

'I beg you — ' said Blanche.

'I see it . . . wait . . . ayè, here's a long life. A very long life . . . and children . . . and here's wealth — I see wealth, gold, silver pieces...'

'And — my husband?' she asked.

He stared at the pale hand that lay in his own and sighed deeply. 'Here is a husband who is not a husband . . . tis strange . . . and here is good health and —'

'Please!' she insisted. 'Tell me of the one who is husband and not husband. How can this be? I do not understand.'

'Sweet demoiselle,' he said, 'I can only tell what I see...'

He stared at the lines again then shook his head regretfully. 'But mayhap your eyes will speak to me again. Look deeply into mine . . . that boy within the house — he is not your husband . . . he is not the one who shares your life—'

'No? Then who — '

'Open your heart to me with your eyes . . . ' he whispered. 'I see clear into your heart . . . there is another in your life . . . '

'Aye . . . ' Blanche whispered.

'That is where your heart lies yet here — ' he turned his attention to her palm, ' — your lives cross but briefly. Tis very strange. These two lines meet and separate . . . '

'Separate? No, no, that cannot be!' she cried. 'Show me!'

Carefully his finger traced for her the crossing of two lines and then he paused again, puzzled.

'And here's another!' he said. 'Clear and strong — and yet a fourth! I swear I have never seen so strange a hand!'

Impressed, in spite of himself, he stared at her and she met his gaze, confused, half-frightened.

'I don't understand,' she whispered and her voice trembled. 'Are you certain — of what you say?'

'Oh yes, demoiselle. Quite certain — and that is all I can tell you.'

'Oh . . . ' she sighed heavily. 'Then I must pay you.'

She reached behind her neck to the fastening of the chain.

'You tremble. Allow me to help you.'

His arms went round her neck and his fingers fumbled for the catch. His face was very near her own and she could smell the wine upon his breath. Imperceptibly his lips came closer to hers.

'No!' she whispered.

'Who will you tell?' he mocked gently. As his lips brushed hers, the chain and topaz swung from his fingers.

'And now I must go,' he told her. 'My audience will grow restive. Shall you return to the performance?'

Blanche hesitated, then shook her head.

He shrugged lightly, turned and ran back across the grass

315

towards the house. At the door he turned and gave a light mocking wave, then he was gone.

Weakly, she leaned back against the oak, her thoughts chaotic. Such a strange power he had! And could see so much! And what did he see that he did not tell? Unaware of her direction, she began to walk towards the river. So, she would not wed William. Was he the husband that was not husband? Is that what he meant — that they were betrothed but would not wed? And if not William, then it must be Andrew . . . but, no, that could not be. That could never be! And he spoke of a third and fourth! He could not mean it. He jested with her — and yet he had seemed in earnest. His gaze was direct. Strangely compelling: she remembered the touch of his lips and shuddered as though in revulsion. At the mercy of her thoughts, she pushed her way through the brambles regardless of the thorns that reached for the skirt of her gown. Already some of the berries were reddening. She tugged one from its stem. It was hard and she rolled it in her fingers as she walked.

As she neared the river, she could hear the weir — the water rushing smoothly in the familiar muffled roar. Soon, she stood beside the lower reach where the water fell boiling and tumbling in a white froth that curled angrily, greedily, sucking down any unwary leaf or twig that ventured on to its surface. She tossed in the blackberry and it disappeared without trace. This part of the river had terrified her as a girl. The noise had dulled her senses and the churning water had reduced her to insignificance. One day she had brought little Catherine down to show her this impressive sight — to share the feeling of awe. But Catherine had declared it 'bonny' and clapped her hands to her ears and laughed. Earlier still, she and Jo had stood where she stood now, watching the trout leap at the weir, hurling themselves from water into air in a desperate instinctive attempt to move up river. Time and time again they would fall short and be swept down into the maelstrom only to try again. And those that made the leap successfully would dart forward, flashing silvery in the green water, to reach the calm depths of the pool before swimming up river to the next weir a few miles further. –

What had he meant, that youth — 'a husband who is not a husband'? Gold and silver, she would have, and children. But whose children would they be? And four men in her life! Was he a charlatan? No. She did not seriously consider the idea. And William would not be her husband . . . Who, then, would William wed? She reproached herself for not asking these questions, but the truth was she had been afraid. Either of the youth himself or of his strange power. Or had she been reluctant to hear his answers? Yet he had been well paid for his vision. The loss of her topaz pricked her conscience, but she shrugged. It was hers to give. She climbed the bank where it rose steeply alongside the weir, walking under the tall trees which hid her from the sun. Here in spring they had gathered primroses and violets and bound them into posies — the fragrant blue blossoms in the centre, the soft creamy yellow surrounding them. Her mother had been alive then and had carried the posies home and put them in water. Once, she and Jo had cast their posies into the slow pool of water then hurried downstream to watch them fall over the weir to their destruction. One of the posies had survived and they had argued over its ownership. She smiled at the recollection and saw herself again, stamping a defiant foot, her voice shrill.

The pool above the weir extended for nearly a quarter of a mile, slow and calm. Trees grew right down to the water's edge except for a few grassy areas much beloved by picnickers. Blanche picked her way through the trees, a child again, cherishing memories which had lain dormant for many years and now sprang to mind, crisp and clear . . . Gradually, she became aware of another voice, singing thinly above the water. As she did so, she almost tripped, stepping on to a sandal. At her feet, two sandals and a dark garment had been neatly arranged. A cord wound neatly into a coil was laid upon the folded habit. One of the monks was bathing — swimming alone and singing to himself! She smiled at the picture thus conjured and peered through the trees to the river, careful to make no sound. Halfway across, she saw a blond tonsured head rise from the water, then a hand came up to wipe the eyes clear. The head then went down again and a narrow back curved out of the water, buttocks tapering into long pale legs as the feet slid under the green surface with scarcely a ripple.

'Andrew!' she whispered.

She watched him unobserved for a long time. He swam well and with obvious delight. Faint snatches of his song reached her, but she recognized none of it. Unaware of her presence, he was completely relaxed, pausing at intervals to look up into the sky, a smile on his face and once his lips moved silently as if in prayer. Did he give thanks, she wondered, for the beauty of the moment — or for life itself? Almost she envied him. On the far side, a squirrel ran across the bough of an ash then scrambled up the smooth trunk and out of sight. He trod water, watching it, then dived down again. The lean body moved below the water, out of sight. Frowning, she searched for him, but he surfaced suddenly on the far side and pulling himself out of the water, flung himself on to the grass, momentarily exhausted. With the toe of her left shoe, she eased off her right and stepped on to the grass. Without taking her eyes off the man on the far bank, she took off her left shoe. With a deft flick, she removed the net which confined her hair. Then she reached down, took hold of the skirt of her gown and pulled it up and over her head in one smooth movement. It fell on to the neatly folded habit in careless folds. Her kirtle followed it. She stood quite naked and the filtered sun warmed her body. She waited in full view of the opposite bank. Andrew sat up at last, rubbed briefly at the grass on his elbows and sprang to his feet. Arms outstretched, hands together as if in prayer, he poised himself on the edge, toes gripping the turf. As he bent his head to dive, he saw her. His weight was already forward and be regained his balance with difficulty. Even at a distance of thirty feet, she observed the shock on his face. For a moment, they stared across the intervening water until he remembered his own nakedness and plunged hastily into the river. The dive was a poor one. He bent his legs as he entered the water and sent up a considerable spray. He surfaced midway and trod water, staring at her helplessly, completely at a loss to know what to do or say. Now that he had seen her she too, was disconcerted and hesitated. His eyes travelled slowly over her body, up to the long blonde hair and sweet face, then down again. She stepped into the water and waded towards him. Only when she was out of her depth did she begin to swim.

'No!' he whispered as she drew near. 'No, Blanche . . . Dear Lord!' and he made ineffectual movements with his hands through the water as if to push her away from him.

'Why not?' she asked lightly, although any other man would have noted the tremble in her voice.

'The pool is free to all,' she told him.

'Please!' he mumbled.

His feet had found a boulder on which to stand and he now waited waist high in the river, while she swam round him in circles, a mocking smile playing about her lips.

'Aren't you going to swim again?' she asked. 'Shall I join you on that rock?'

'This is folly,' he said wretchedly. 'We may be seen.'

She glanced quickly up and down both banks.

'There is no one here but us.'

'I must go back . . .' he said.

'I shall not stop you.'

She rolled over in the water and swam lazily to and fro between the boulder on which he stood and the bank where his clothes lay.

Suddenly he plunged into the water and tried to pass her, but she caught hold of his foot. Doubling up, he took hold of her fingers and tried to prise them free. Her face was close to his and he saw the laughter in her eyes and the small white teeth between the parted lips. Her long fair hair floated round him, and clung to his shoulder.

'Stay a while,' she begged. 'Swim with me! No one will know. Then I will allow you to dress unobserved as is proper and will trouble you no more.'

'You must not . . . you must let me go . . . ' he stammered and, wrenching himself free, turned to make his escape. She swam alongside and laughed wickedly.

'Then I shall help you dress,' she told him and laughed aloud at his obvious dismay.

He reached shallower water, waded so far then stopped, embarrassed.

'Please, Blanche, stop this foolishness,' he said. 'I beg you, leave me be. I dare not . . . .'

His reluctance hurt her more than she would admit.

'I think you dare,' she said, 'but you do not want to swim with me.'

He didn't answer and she looked down at the water, unwilling to admit defeat, unsure how to finish what she had started.

'Only tell me,' she said, the laughter had left her voice. 'Only tell me you do not want to swim with me and I will "leave you be".'

'Blanche . . . .'

'Tell me!'

He also was silent. Glancing at his face she saw that the dismay had given way to indecision.

'I cannot say that!' he said quietly.

She held out her hands.

'Then swim with me,' she invited but still he hesitated, ignoring the outstretched hands which offered him such forbidden ectasy. She moved towards him until she stood so close her nipples nearly touched his chest and he was aware of one of her feet touching his. Droplets of water from her wet hair dripped on to her breasts. Her shoulders gleamed in the sunlight and the long fair lashes were spikey above the blue eyes . . .

Half ashamed, she stood her ground defiantly, her emotions veering wildly with each passing second that passed between them. Above everything, she saw the cool grey eyes of her 'fortune teller' and the words echoed in her mind — 'the boy — he is not the one who shares your life . . . and here is a husband who is not a husband—'

'Andrew,' she faltered. 'Swim with me!'

Her longing had become three words. His heart hammered against his ribs. Suddenly, she reached forward and very gently stroked the blond hairs that curled on his chest. The movement was instinctive and he knew that she no longer considered what she did. He gave a short muffled cry. Kneeling, he kissed each gleaming thigh and slid slowly, effortlessly into the water and began to swim. She followed him and reaching him, floated against him, letting her hands flow over his long body.

He turned as her hands slid from his feet and seizing her hair, pulled her towards him, then drew back, watching the long strands hang in the water like silver weed. He pressed her shoulder with a fingertip and she drifted away from him. She lay on her back floating, drifting, like a pale reed. Diving, he swam up beneath her and caught her round the waist, pulling her gently under then releasing her.

She surfaced to find him some distance away, floating face downwards, arms outstretched in front of him. Lazily, she swam towards him and under him, so that her hair touched him, making him dart away like a fish that senses danger. He swam upriver and she waited, turning and rolling in the water, until he returned and, taking her in his arms, swam with her unprotesting form; holding her close then letting her drift away but never, never quite losing contact with her soft, yielding body . . . .

'I'm cold,' she said at last and he carried her to the bank, feeling her grow heavy in his arms and on his conscience.

321

But it was too late to regret. He lowered her to the ground, lay down beside her, and drew her into his arms, breathlessly kissing the wet face and shoulders, his body hopelessly aroused, his senses overwhelming him. There was nothing in the world for him save her white flesh, the soft limbs, her lips, teeth, breasts. She saw that he had closed his eyes and pulled him down on to her body.

She wanted to say 'I love you', but dared not interrupt the moment for which she had waited so long. He entered her fiercely, with a cry of pain which should have been hers, then his teeth bit into her shoulders and neck with an intensity which frightened her and brought a sob to her throat.

'I'm sorry . . . I'm sorry . . .' he whispered, and repeated the words, over and over, faster and faster, as he brought his body at last to a long gasping moment of satisfaction his tears flowing on to her face.

Afterwards they dressed quietly, respectably, concerned with their privacy. She squeezed water from her hair and it fell like tears on to the crushed grass where they had lain. She stood, ready to leave, and looked down at him. He sat on the grass and struggled with trembling hands to fasten his sandal.

'Shall you confess?' she asked wretchedly.

He nodded.

She looked out at the still river, its surface unruffled. There was a blankness in her mind that did nothing to ease their parting.

'Shall you be punished?'

'I hope so.'

Still he fumbled with his sandal and she knelt to fasten it for him. He stood up and their eyes met. Blanche sighed deeply as she read in his face the misery in his soul.

'I'm sorry,' she whispered. 'Twas *I* seduced *you*.'

'The world has seduced us both,' he whispered and as

though at a signal, they turned from each other and walked away from the deed.

Across the channel a small fleet was making preparations to sail to England. The purpose of this journey was to carry the latest pretender to the English throne to claim his heritage. This time it was Perkin Warbeck, son of a Jew from Tournai, now accepted by Margaret of Burgundy as the Duke of York, son of Edward Plantaganet and miraculously 'escaped' from the Tower. Credence for this story was given by the fact that Sir William Stanley supported the young man's claims, and had as recently as February been executed for his part in the treason.

Many loyal Yorkists had crossed the channel to join the young pretender, among them Alan Courtenay of Exeter; who had thrown up his promising career with the Treasurer to fight for the cause in which his cousin, had died at Bosworth.

Warbeck's attempt was made and proved abortive. His ships sailed with the tide and made good time, fetching up off the Kentish coast outside Deal. Perkin Warbeck wisely forbore to go ashore and was forced to watch the carnage from a safe distance, as King Henry's loyal Kentishmen cut through his Yorkist followers like a scythe through corn. A hundred of his supporters died and many more were taken prisoner — the English to be hanged — (Alan Courtenay among them) — the foreigners to be ransomed and returned to Flanders. The pretender himself withdrew and hastily set sail for Scotland with what remained of his army. His story was not quite finished although the sands were running out for him.

Elizabeth, fretting at the window, gave a cry as she saw the little group of horsemen turn into the driveway. She ran out of the house followed by John. Lydia, sat silent, her face impassive, while greetings were exchanged. Still badly shocked, she looked thin and terribly pale. John's heart sank, seeing the change in her since his visit a few months' earlier.

Reaching up, he said gently, 'Allow me to help you, Lydia. I would that your coming was for happier reasons.'

Lifting her down, he felt her body, limp and uncaring. There was a vague expression in her eyes as though she expected to find herself elsewhere. Jacob came out and helped to carry and begs and trunks.

'Catherine!' cried Elizabeth. 'I swear you are grown taller. What do they feed you on in Exeter that we lack at Heron!'

The girl had asked the Polegate's permission to ride with her aunt, since Lydia's health was poor and her husband felt a woman companion might be necessary or at least a comfort to her on the journey. Catherine too, had been distressed by the death of her cousin. She had grown fond of the young man, admiring his zest for life and constantly amused by his ready wit. Now she embraced her mother and turned to greet Blanche who ran to meet them from the stables.

'Tis good to see you,' said Catherine, 'though tis a sad homecoming. And where are the twins?'

'Out hawking,' said Blanche. 'Or, I should say that Matthew hawks. William enjoys his new horse, a fine black cob that is his pride and joy. Stephen is in London as you know. But come. Martha is bursting to see you and has made a pan of spiced biscuits in your honour. We must not let them waste.'

They moved indoors into the cool hall where Martha and Izzie hovered eagerly waiting to greet them.

Lydia, expressing fatigue, was put to bed where she fell at once into a deep sleep. Her husband and Catherine refreshed themselves downstairs, with biscuits and ale.

'Lydia looks very frail,' said Elizabeth.

324

'She has taken it very hard,' said her husband. 'We are all saddened beyond measure. Such a waste to die in such an inglorious rout. Had Richard carried the day, why, he would not have died in vain. They say Richard did not set foot on English soil! 'Tis hard to believe. 'Tis hard to believe that a Plantaganet should not lead his men, inspire his followers . . . .' He shook his head wearily and sighed. 'I am at a loss — he went on, 'rumour has it that Richard is not all he seems. That there is deception and we are duped . . . . I cannot believe that.'

Such a rumour had indeed reached Heron; but Elizabeth and John had decided not to speak of it for fear of adding to the bereaved parents' pain.

'There are always such rumours,' said Elizabeth. 'We set no credence by them here.'

The old man looked up gratefully. 'I would not believe it,' he repeated. 'But Lydia causes me much anxiety. She scarce seems to take in what has happened and I fear to speak of it. She is so strange . . .'

'How — strange?' asked Elizabeth, glancing uneasily at her husband. The old man frowned. 'She rarely speaks,' he said slowly. 'And when she does it is of other matters. She does not speak of the boy. Will not speak his name . . . She has not wept and looks unnatural.'

'No doubt the shock,' said Elizabeth.

'Oh, 'tis the shock I know that. But this lack of grief . . . I swear 'tis unnatural in a woman. There was no want of love between them. She doted on him. I was quite jealous! I would wish that otherwise.'

'We are all jealous of our sons,' said John. 'And the women envy their daughters! 'Tis normal. Do not reproach yourself.'

The old man sighed. 'What can we do?' he asked helplessly. 'We cannot undo what has gone, but remorse adds to our grief.'

Elizabeth hesitated then rose to her feet.

'Let us speak of it another time,' she said gently. 'I wish

325

you would cast your expert eye over my merlin? She is sickly and I fear she has the falling sickness. You were always well versed in these matters and I would trust your opinion.'

He rose readily to his feet, glad of a diversion however obvious, and followed Elizabeth to the far end of the hall where the hawks were perched.

'If tis the falling sickness,' he began, 'then wash her meat in the juice of asterion — a few drops of pellitary of Spain in her ears and nares ...'

Later that evening, Elizabeth sat with Lydia in her chamber. A small fire burned in the hearth for the old woman complained of the cold, although it was July and the weather was clement. She sat propped against the pillows while Elizabeth sat by the window, catching the last of the light for her sewing. The two men and the young people made music below — faintly the sound of Catherine's treble and Blanche's lute came to their ears.

'You have not eaten yet,' Elizabeth chided her sister-in-law. 'You must not neglect your health. I will ask Martha to coddle an egg for you before you settle for the night. You will not sleep on an empty stomach.'

'I am well enough,' Lydia replied. The failing eyes stared straight ahead.

'I am working on a pair of pillowslips for Catherine,' said Elizabeth. 'I can scarce believe she will soon be wed!'

'Leonard is a nice enough lad,' Lydia commented.

'Your husband looks very fit.'

'Aye, he's rarely sick,' she said tonelessly.

Elizabeth laid down her sewing and looked at the old woman anxiously. The head was steady, the eyes staring, but the fingers moved constantly, touching and exploring the other fingers, feeling the nails and knuckles.

'Do you still play the spinet?' Elizabeth asked her, but Lydia shook her head.

'I cannot see the music,' she said and Elizabeth cursed

her own stupidity. 'John tells me you had a beautiful fine soprano voice,' she ventured, 'When you . . . .'

'When I was younger? Aye, I had a fine voice — but not now. I cannot sing any more. The tone goes if you do not practise . . . and the breathing . . . .'

Elizabeth resumed her sewing, trying not to see the restless fingers on the coverlet.

'Exter is a fine city,' she said. 'Catherine writes of its splendours.'

'She is a good girl,' said Lydia. 'A daughter is a great comfort to a woman.'

There was a silence while Elizabeth snipped the silk and rethreaded the needle.

'A daughter doesn't die,' said Lydia suddenly, her voice flat. She turned her head slowly until she faced Elizabeth. 'They don't die,' she said again. 'My son is dead, you know. Did you know that? Did you know that Alan is dead?'

'Aye – I know,' said Elizabeth. 'Tis a great loss, to lose a son.'

'Alan, my son, is dead . . . killed . . . did you know?'

'I did.'

'They told me he was dead — and I couldn't weep! Can you believe that? I wanted to, but couldn't . . . The tears wouldn't flow. My son is dead and I can't weep for him. Tis a terrible thing to have no tears. To have no tears for a dead son!'

Elizabeth struggled to keep back her own tears but failed. With a choked cry, she threw down her sewing and knelt beside the bed, clasping the restless fingers, but Lydia continued, 'You are fortunate, Elizabeth. You have no sons of your own. None that are part of you . . . .'

'But John's sons are my sons,' she protested, 'Stephen and William and —'

Lydia shook her head, a faint smile on her face, a bemused look in her eyes.

'They are not of your flesh,' she said. 'They are not of your body.'

'I had a son that was of my flesh,' whispered Elizabeth. 'I lost my little son.'

'Aye. He was part of you.'

'But so are my other sons. They are!'

'God forbid you may lose another.'

'Oh, don't speak of it!' cried Elizabeth. 'But we speak of your grief. We weep for your son. I don't want to speak of mine — to remember . . . For pity's sake! Why do you do this to me, Lydia?'

'Someone must weep,' said Lydia wonderingly, 'when a son dies . . . They hanged him you know — like a criminal. All of them . . . hanged. When I close my eyes I see him swinging there . . . turning slowly round and round. I hurt inside, but I still can't weep . . . .'

Elizabeth turned toward the window.

'Please,' she begged. 'Try to rest now.'

Obediently Lydia closed her dry eyes and went to sleep.

CHAPTER EIGHTEEN

The old monk woke suddenly confused and Blanche stared down at him, as he lay half hidden by the lilac bush. The neglected shears lay beside him and the green smell of cut grass hung in the warm air. Blanche drew back full of apologies for she had stumbled over him.

'I did not see you,' she said. 'Forgive my clumsiness.'

Brother Gregory sat up and she reached out a helping hand as he struggled to his feet.

'Tis I should beg your forgiveness,' he said. 'One does not expect to fall over sleeping bodies.'

She smiled and he thought enviously that youth had such a bloom to it.

'I hope I have not hurt you?' she asked.

'No, not at all. Your arrival is most timely. I might have been discovered by eyes less kind . . . But what brings you here?'

A faint colour touched her cheeks.

'I wish to see Brother Andrew,' she said. 'I have a letter for him.'

His eyes widened as he picked up the shears.

'Brother Andrew? But . . . .'

'Tis from Elizabeth Kendal,' she lied. 'The letter is from Elizabeth.'

She thought he looked at her curiously and prayed he could not hear the beating of her heart.

'But Brother Andrew is already on his way,' he told her. 'He has been gone these last ten days. I am surprised you . . . .'

'Gone?' she cried. 'Gone where? He did not . . . .'

She stopped abruptly, aware that her distress must be obvious to him if she continued.

'Why, he is gone on pilgrimage to the shrine of Compostela in Spain. I do not envy him the journey at this time of year. All that heat.'

She was staring at him, her eyes dark with shock.

'To visit Compostela! But for how long?'

He shrugged. ''Tis usual for such a journey to last fifteen weeks or more. The abbot last year was away for twenty all told, but he met with many hazards on the way poor man . . . . The plague was broke out in Bordeaux and many of his party fell sick. Some men died, God rest their souls.'

'Sweet Heaven!'

He looked at her curiously.

'And his sister did not know of this pilgrimage?' he asked. 'That is most odd . . . and yet we were all a little surprised I think. He is a very young man still and older brethren expected to go before him. But there, who are we to question the abbott's wisdom in such matters. But tis strange he did not tell his sister! I don't understand it at all.'

He snipped idly at a nettle while he spoke so that prying eyes could see him working.

'And he has been gone ten days?'

'Aye, ten or eleven.'

'Then where should he be by this time? Do you know?'

He scratched his nose thoughtfully and considered. 'Why, he will head for the port of Soulac above Bordeaux but it all depends when he embarks from England. There was no passage booked for him so—'

'Why not?'

He shrugged again. 'A good question but I cannot give you a good answer. Mayhap he went hurriedly and . . . . ' He frowned. 'Now that I think on it, his going was a hurried business. He spoke of it one day and was gone the next, with scarce time to make provision. Scarce time even to sew on his red cross! Aye, now I think on it, t'was very strange.'

330

'Then I — then Elizabeth is too late,' said Blanche. 'We cannot reach him . . . Sixteen weeks he will be gone!'

'You might send the letter,' the old monk suggested. 'Send it with another and the letter may catch up with him. We expect pilgrims in our guest house tomorrow night bound for Galicia. They will cover the same ground. Leave the letter in my keeping and I will see that it finds good hands.'

She thought desperately, then handed it to him.

'I beseech you not to speak of this matter. I — Elizabeth wishes it to be most secret!'

'The letter will be safe with me,' he said, and his look was kindly.

'I will find a discreet bearer for it, never fear.'

'Thank you,' she said, and had to be content. She decided to wait, either for word from him or his return.

But the fateful letter did not reach Andrew. It went no further than Orleans where the discreet bearer was attacked and robbed. The torn letter was scattered to the four winds and Blanche waited in vain for an answer.

Alice Cozen's home was no more than a hut built against the side of the hill. It had no window save a small hole knocked in the wall but it was cleaner than Blanche expected.

'Sit you down,' commanded the old woman.

'Thank you,' said Blanche. 'I want to —'

'Who sent you to me?' she wanted to know, her voice sharp.

'Who sent me? Oh, twas Izzie Foster, Old William's grand daughter. She . . . . '

'I know her.'

Blanche sat bolt upright.

'I think I'm with child,' she blurted out. 'At least — that is I'm sure I am.'

She swallowed and kept her eyes in her lap.

'Oh, aye,' said Alice. 'What makes you so sure?'

'I . . . my terms are late.'

'That could be fear. It does strange things to a woman's body, fear does.'

'And my breasts are heavier,' Blanche continued. 'Not much, but I cannot pretend to myself tis otherwise.'

Alice looked at her shrewdly; her eye was practised. The girl's face was drawn, the eyes lustrous and she had the air of one who listened inwardly.

'Aye, you are with child,' she said.

'But I am not sickly,' cried Blanche. Now she had convinced the woman she strove to reverse the diagnosis. 'I suffer no queasiness.'

'When did it happen? Do you know?'

'July.'

'July! And tis now November. You should have come earlier.'

Blanche had waited desperately until the time of Andrew's expected return from Spain, but there had been no word and he did not return. She did not even know if he lived! She could wait no longer. Izzie's elder sister had once aborted a child and Blanche had approached Izzie, paying dearly for the information and her silence. Alice Cozen was respected for her knowledge of herbs and their properties. She practised no magic and it was rare that her clients died.

'November!' she echoed. 'You have left it very late. You should have come earlier. Why did you wait? You are not wed, I see.'

'No . . . .'

'And your name?'

Blanche shook her head. 'My name is of no importance,' she said, 'But I am betrothed.'

'To the father of the child?'

'No.'

The word was almost a whisper. 'The father does not know. He is abroad, on business . . . . The man to whom

I am betrothed must not know. No one must know. All I ask is that you tell me what to do. I cannot have the child! I dare not!'

'You may have to,' said Alice. 'You have waited too long but I will try. You have money?'

Blanche shook her head. 'My jewels,' she said and handed the woman a small cloth purse. Alice tipped the contents into the palm of her hand and tried not to show her satisfaction. She would be amply paid if the child was aborted and generously paid if it was not! Without further argument, she crossed to a corner of the room and unstoppered a small bottle. She poured a few drops into a small bowl, added water and handed it to Blanche.

''Tis unpleasant,' she said. 'Drink it.'

It was vile! Blanche sipped it and screwed up her face in disgust.

'Swallow it down,' commanded Alice impatiently. 'You waste precious time.'

Blanche closed her eyes and emptied the bowl then fell to gasping and spluttering.

The woman took the bowl from her and indicated a door at the far end of the room.

'Lie outside there,' she said. 'Take this to cover yourself. Twill work in about an hour and you must call me if you need help.'

'Help?' queried Blanche, a terrible cold fear numbing her mind.

'Aye . . . . I shall hear you.'

The door led to a small yard in which a pile of freshly cut bracken served as a bed. A gnarled hawthorn grew low over the bracken and a small coloured bird hung in a cage from a hook in the wall of the hut. For a moment, Blanche looked around, then she sank to her knees on the bracken, drawing the blanket which Alice had given her round her shoulders.

'Oh Andrew,' she whispered wretchedly. 'Forgive me.'

She tried not to think — to make her mind blank.

Time passed, cramps developed in her abdomen and grew steadily worse, leaving her pale and shivering. Once when the pain was very bad, she called Alice who came and looked at her.

'Not yet!' she said and left her alone again. The pains began to tear at her body and the sweat ran from her as she tossed restlessly on the bracken, praying to God to witness her distress. 'Punish me, sweet Heaven' she begged, 'but spare Andrew I beseech you. Keep him in Thy safe keeping wherever he may be for he has done no wrong. Twas I that sinned! I can bear any punishment if you will be merciful unto him . . . .'

The pain continued for nearly an hour and then she noticed that the cramps grew less fierce.

Alice shrugged. 'You are too late,' she said. 'Tis as I thought. You should have come a month ago.'

Weakly, Blanche put a shaking hand to her face, to wipe away the sweat.

'Then should I not drink more of it?' she asked innocently. 'Mayhap if I . . . .'

'Another dose will kill you,' Alice told her, bluntly. 'There is no more to be done. The child cannot be loosed. Tis too late.'

She brought her cold water to drink but Blanche shook her head.

'I would like to die,' she whispered but Alice snorted indignantly.

'Not in my yard you don't!' she said firmly. 'You've paid for my help and you've had it. Now you must go.'

Blanche shook her head again but the woman dragged her to her feet.

'Is there nothing else I can do . . . . ?' Blanche began.

'Nothing . . . . Now I've the fire to mend. Be on your way and speak of this to no one.'

She smiled fondly at the bird, then went back into the hut and closed the door.

Blanche waited until the trembling in her body ceased, then stumbled back along the path towards Heron.

When she came in sight of the house she stopped, unable to face the prospect of meeting anyone who might comment on her distraught appearance. Where could she hide — have time to think? She would go to the stables. There was a roomy loft above the horses stalls where they had often played as children and where Eric had once slept. No one would find her there and she could rest. Eric was nowhere to be seen. Probably in the kitchen boasting of his new son she thought. It required a tremendous effort to climb the ricketty ladder into the loft, but once up there its familiarity enfolded her like welcoming arms and she threw herself on to the sweet hay with a gasp of thankfulness. For a moment, she closed her eyes but reluctantly opened them again. She could not afford the luxury of sleep. Oblivion, however brief, would only prolong her misery. She would pray for guidance. Instinctively, her fingers went to the gold cross she frequently wore at her throat but it was missing. Alice Cozen had it! Then she must pray without it. Kneeling, she put her hands together and closed her eyes.

'Sweet Mary, Mother of God, look down on me with compassion, I pray you. I am not worthy of your love — I do confess it . . . . I have sinned most grievously and I do not rail against my punishment. I only beg for guidance, to know what to do. I confess I have sinned against this day but the child is not destroyed and mayhap tis the will of God . . . . I do not know what I should do, nor who to ask for help save only you, Sweet Mother of God, who does protect all women and forgive their sins if they do truly repent. Do not punish the child, I beseech you. Show me what I must do to keep him in righteousness that he may not suffer for my wickedness . . . . '

She froze as foosteps passed below and Eric came into the stable. He whistled a few bars of a song now grown familiar. It was *The Maiden's Lament* and had been on his lips ever since the players visit. He sang and whistled it from dawn 'til dusk until they had grown exasperated and begged him learn another! He now broke into song tunelessly but with obvious enjoyment!

> 'My husband is both old and grey
> And sleeps abed when I would play
> But the miller's lad with me did lie
> With nonny ho, anonny heigh . . . . '

He whistled it again and Blanche clapped her hands to her ears to shut out the sound. She had no wish to recall that day. She sat thus for some time, trying to shut out not only the unwelcome song, but all the pains, fears and remorse which crowded in, filling her mind with a blackness which threatened to overwhelm her. When she listened again, there was silence below and she resumed her prayer. Her voice, no more than a whisper, trembled.

'Dear Mother of God, pity my child who has done no wrong. His father is a good man and was without sin until — until . . . Oh God! How can I regret that I gave him such joy, only that for him it was a sin but he now makes pilgrimage for penance and I pray you preserve him from all dangers along the way and bring him to a state of grace in Thy sight that he may return safely to tell me I am forgiven. And what must I do? Who must I tell? Help me, I pray . . . . '

William lowered his head to the pillow with a groan and Matthew, not yet undressed, laughed.

'I warned you,' he said, 'but no, you must needs continue! How much did you lose?'

'More than I can afford! My head. There is a pounding. I think the wine was sour.'

'Twas not the quality that bedevils you but the quantity,' he chortled. 'Your eyes are bigger than your belly!'

There was a knock at the door. He looked enquiringly at William who shrugged. Blanche stood outside.

'I must speak with William,' she whispered. 'Is he awake?'

'With William? At this hour? You should be abed.'

''Tis most urgent, Matthew. Will you wake him and say I am here.'

'I will, but he'll take it very unkindly. He has drunk too well and his head hurts.'

'Please ask him if he will come to my chamber.'

'Wait here.'

He closed the door but was back directly.

'He is awake — barely and bids you come to him. He says he will not leave the comfort of his bed.'

She went into the room where William sat up in the large bed which slept both boys.

'What are you about, Blanche?' he said irritably. 'Twill not look well if you are found here.'

'I must speak with you,' she said. 'We can speak more privately in my chamber if you . . . .'

'I'm hanged if I will stir from my bed. What can you want to say that Matthew cannot hear?'

The two boys stared at her curiously and she looked at the two faces as though for the first time. The soft light from the candle hid the difference in their colouring and accentuated the similarities.

They both had the high Kendal cheekbones, thin mouth and strong jawline. William was like his father, Matthew less so. She wondered when they had relinquished their boyhood? She had the sensation that her presence in their room was no more than a childish prank. Now reality was softened by the darkness — but in the cold light of morning . . . .

'Blanche! Are you deaf as well as dumb!' cried William. 'I ask why you have come?'

'I — we must be alone,' she protested. 'When you hear what I . . . .'

The boys exchanged glances. Matthew perplexed, William exasperated.

'Please, Blanche,' said William. 'Tell me what brings you here or save it until morning. I am in no mood for games.'

'Perhaps I should wait elsewhere,' said Matthew, but William would not hear of it.

'Stay where you are,' he said, sharply. 'If Blanche will not speak out, then she must leave us to our slumbers. What are these urgent tidings? Tell me at once.'

Such arrogance, thought Blanche wearily. He is a true Kendal.

'I think you will regret your insistence,' she said quietly.

'Let me be the judge of that,' he replied.

She looked appealingly at Matthew who made as if to move, but William cursed and he hesitated.

Blanche's own temper was rising in the face of William's obduracy.

'I ask you once more,' she said, but he sprang suddenly from the bed and slapped her across the face.

'Enough of your games!' he cried. 'Say what you have to say or leave us.'

A red mark was appearing from his blow, but the rest of her face had gone terribly white. Her eyes reflecting the candlelight, seemed enormous.

'I'm with child, William,' she said, simply.

The silence was almost tangible. She was aware of two pairs of eyes. William breathed heavily. His eyes never left her face.

'With child?' he said foolishly. 'You are with child?'

'I am,' she confirmed.

Her momentary anger had evaporated and she was suddenly very frightened. Her mouth felt dry and the palms of her hands were clammy.

'By Christ's wounds!' he whispered, then shook his head unable to go on.

Blanche was frightened, yet strangely calm. She found herself wondering if he would pretend to the world that the child was his, or admit that he had been cuckolded. Perhaps he would kill her.

Matthew turned to his brother reproachfully. 'You struck her!' he said. 'She carries your child and yet you struck her!'

'*My* child!' cried William, startled out of his doze. ''Tis not *my* child she carries. She has not known any seed of mine! Aye, I struck her and I will do so again!'

He lunged towards her, his body gleaming naked in the candlelight. She tried to dodge the blow, but his fist caught the edge of her mouth and drew blood. She stumbled backwards against the door but did not fall.

'William!' cried Matthew. 'In God's name! She says she is with child. Calm yourself before you do her worse harm.'

He flung himself between Blanche and William, his hands held up in a conciliatory gesture.

'Please, William,' begged Blanche. 'Will you hear me out? I know I . . . . '

'Listen to her, Will,' said Matthew. ''Tis only fair to . . . . '

'Fair! You ask me to be fair,' cried William. 'My betrothed comes into my chamber to tell me she is — is with child by . . . . ' He stopped suddenly. 'Aye,' he said slowly. 'With child by whom? Let us hear who has got you with child, then I may kill him with all possible despatch.'

He pushed Matthew to one side and caught hold of Blanche's hair. 'Who must I kill?' he asked, his tone ominous. 'Tell me whose child you carry . . . . Tell me or by Christ I shall beat the truth from you!' He slapped her again until Matthew once more pulled them apart. 'Take your hands from me!' cried William. 'This is not your fight and tis no business of yours. The slut shall tell me who wrongs me and I shall kill him. Aye, and delight in the killing!'

'No, no!' cried Blanche. 'You must not speak so wildly.' She collapsed sobbing on to the floor while Matthew fought to keep William away from her.

'Stop, I beg you,' she cried. 'Leave him, Matthew, I implore you. If he must kill, then let him kill me. I would die rather than tell him what he wants to know. For pity's sake, stop fighting! You will rouse the whole house!'

William tore himself free and flung himself face down on to the bed. 'Tell me who it is,' he said quietly. 'I think I have a right to know.'

'Forgive me,' Blanche whispered, 'but I cannot tell you that.'

'Then there is nothing more to be said.' His voice trembled and she looked at him with compassion. He lay across the bed, his body shaking with the beginnings of tears.

'I pray God you will find it in your heart to forgive me,' she said.

'I never will,' he said weeping silently.

She looked at Matthew who stood by helplessly.

'Will you comfort him,' she asked and he nodded.

'But you,' he said, 'you are hurt. Someone must see to your mouth. I will send Martha to you.'

'No! She must not see me like this. She will tell Mama.'

'Someone must care for you.'

'Then send Izzie.'

William looked up suddenly, his face tearful, vulnerable. 'Will he wed you this man?'

She shook her head silently.

'Then you carry a bastard,' said William triumphantly, 'for I shall not give him a name. And you will never now be mistress of Heron. Our betrothal is ended and I shall ask for new negotiations to be started on my behalf.'

Dear God, thought Blanche wonderingly. He looks and speaks like a defiant child. Poor boy, he is so young to be hurt in this way. How will I ever atone for all this misery?

And must my poor child do penance for me, to be born a bastard and suffer for my sin? Oh, why do I weep? Tears will not undo the wrong. Oh, Andrew! My dearest love. Tis better you do not know how low I have fallen . . . . She closed the door quietly behind her and re-crossed the passage to her own room. A few minutes later, Izzie knocked on the door and came in, wide-eyed, to minister to Blanche's various hurts. Instructed by Matthew to ask no questions, she dabbed away in silence until she could stand the suspense no longer.

'Did Alice — you know, ma'am?' she burst out. 'Did she do it?'

'No,' said Blanche. 'She tried but twas too late. The child would not be loosed.'

'Oh, ma'am! What will you do now?' she asked but was regarded by a shrug.

'Aren't you going to be wed, then ma'am?'

'I don't know . . . . I would rather not speak of it,' said Blanche, 'I'm so weary. I am sick at heart and cannot think straight.'

'I've brought you a sleeping draught,' said Izzie. 'Master Matthew said you was to have one. The green bottle, he said on the top shelf. Is this it?'

She produced a small bottle and offered it for Blanche's inspection. Blanche sniffed at its contents and nodded. 'Aye, that's it. Bring me some water to drink it in – and my thanks.'

She swallowed the draught and climbed into bed. Izzie tucked the coverlet round her and clucked sympathetically.

'I'll pray for you,' she said and departed, leaving Blanche alone with her fears.

John slammed his fist down on the tableboard so that the dishes rattled and Elizabeth's wine jumped in its goblet.

'No! No!' he shouted. 'How many more times must I say

it. Blanche Tucker shall never marry into Heron. No one shall foist a bastard on to my son. He shall father his own heirs! If I have said it once, I have said it a dozen times.'

'No one is foisting a child on to him,' said Elizabeth. 'Matthew has offered to wed her. He wants to wed the girl. Tis not the same thing at all. Tis certain that he . . . . '

'There is but one thing certain. They will not wed whether Matthew wishes it or no. The girl is pregnant. She refuses to name the father. It could be — why, the stable lad! A bastard is shame enough. An un-named bastard for Heron — never!'

Angrily they stared at each other across the remains of the meal. Neither of them had any appetite. John poured himself more wine and Elizabeth wondered if she dare pursue the matter. It did not seem a very propitious time. The more they spoke of it, the angrier John became. Blanche had confessed to them earlier in the day and was now with Father Marryat who heard her confession. John had flown instantly into a towering rage. Elizabeth had been shocked and dismayed. Joseph Tucker was out of the county so was still unaware of what had happened, otherwise Blanche would have been banished at John's command. Elizabeth had argued that they dare not send her home to an empty house with only the servants. In her present mood of desperation, there was no knowing what folly she might commit. Now John downed his wine in two massive gulps and threw down the goblet.

'Mayhap – ' Elizabeth began. 'I wonder could it be Matthew's child?'

John stared at her. 'Matthew's? Then why should he not confess if he wants to wed her?'

'Because it would hurt William more if it was Matthew's child . . . . His own brother . . . . '

John sighed wearily and rested his head on his hands.

'If tis Matthew's own child, then she must wed the boy. If the child is a Kendal she shall stay with Heron . . . . I wonder if you are right? The matter is bad enough but that fact would better it . . . Oh God's blood! We never should have agreed to the betrothal. Twas at Tucker's insistence, you may recall and now she cuckolds my son! Hell and damnation!'

Elizabeth looked at him with compassion. His pride suffered. He could more easily bear loss of fortune than loss of face.

'Joseph Tucker saved your life not so long ago,' she said quietly. 'You did not curse him then. And he may well rail at *us* for our neglect. Blanche was betrothed to our son and in our care.'

'You mean she makes a fool of my son and we are to blame!' cried John. 'I mistrust your tongue. It has a way with truth like a knife turning in a wound. Are we, then, to grovel to Joseph Tucker? Is that what you would have me do?'

'No,' said Elizabeth. 'There need be no grovelling. There is blame on both sides and I wish we might look for a solution instead of fighting among ourselves. If she is to wed Matthew, then the sooner . . . . '

'She may not wed Matthew!' and his fist came down again. 'Don't think I am fooled, Elizabeth. I understand your reason for this pleading on her behalf. I know you better than you know yourself. You want the child here. You have none of your own and would find solace in the bastard! My children have not been enough for you, but you must have more. You want a child and do not care whose! But I care. I do not choose to feed and clothe the off-spring of God knows what . . . . And what of Stephen, Catherine and William? Are their children to be cousins to this brat?'

Elizabeth rose to her feet, the colour draining from her face, but he went on.

'And should we set a precedent? Shall Catherine present us next with a child out of wedlock – and Stephen bring home a pregnant wife . . . . '

With a wild cry, Elizabeth snatched up an earthenware dish and dashed it to the floor, and followed it with the flagon still half full of wine. Her eyes blazed and her body trembled and she controlled herself with an effort.

'Your precious Catherine would have been a bastard but for you,' she cried. 'Bet, your own wife, was no better than Blanche! Or had you forgot!'

His head went back slowly and he closed his eyes. A small muscle jumped in his neck. Eventually, he straightened his head and looked at her.

'Aye,' he said, 'I had forgot!'

Martha stood by the kitchen table, a hare in one hand, a chopper in the other. She laid the hare on the chopping board and deftly removed the feet. Then she took a knife and slit open the belly.

'Ugh!' cried Blanche wrinkling her nose in distate.

''Tis no use to say "Ugh" if you've a meal to cook,' Martha told her. 'And you'll not be able to serve it with the fur on. So you mind now and watch how I slide my fingers under the skin and ease it off — see how it slides off. Here, you have a try. Go on. It won't bite you.' Reluctantly, Blanche moved round the table and took the partly skinned hare from Martha's capable hands. She pushed her fingers under the skin and eased it from the pale pink flesh.

'That's the way,' said Martha, 'but now let me finish it or twill be bedtime afore you've finished. You write it down in your roll.'

Blanche's household roll had been started when she was first betrothed to William. Recipes for toothpaste and complexion water jostled with remedies for the flux and charms for a long life. Now she was to marry Matthew she applied herself urgently to extending her knowledge of household matters. She sat at the far end of the table and noted down the recipe for Hare in Onions.

'Young Master Matthew loves this dinner,' said Martha.

'Or it can be made with a coney. There's little to choose between them but for the size, though some say the coney has more delicate flavour . . . . So, flay the hare, make it clean, hack it into lumps and seethe in water with salt.'

She tossed the seasoned joints into a pan of water which hung above the fire.

'Now tis pepper and saffron with a little ground bread, and temper it with ale. Then take . . . .'

'I cannot write it fast enough!' cried Blanche. 'I'm lost . . . ground — er — bread — temper — it — with — ale.'

'Tis to be hoped you can cook faster than you can write!' said Martha. 'Now mince the onions with the parsley and watch that you don't weep for the onion is sorrowful stuff, and this last is to seethe by itself and later to dress the cooked hare.'

Blanche wrote industriously while Martha wiped the table clean and then she stood up, easing her back with one hand.

'I felt a tiny flutter this morning,' she told Martha. 'Twas here.'

She placed a hand low down on her right side. 'Twas like a moth fluttering its wings.'

'Why then, tis the babe starting to move,' said Martha. 'Did you tell Master Matthew?'

'I haven't seen him. He rode into Exeter with William at first light. Oh, here he is come looking for me!'

Matthew came into the kitchen and Blanche flew into his arms.

Regardless of Martha's presence, he kissed her fondly.

'Martha has been cooking one of your favourite dinners,' said Blanche 'and I have added it to my roll.' She waved the roll of paper at him and he smiled.

'And I have brought you a gift,' he said. 'So will you walk with me awhile?'

'Oh, I will!' she cried, and Martha watched them go with

a lump in her throat and a conviction that Matthew was the finest young man she had ever set eyes on!

Matthew led Blanche into the hall and stood with her before the fire which crackled and spat with burning apple wood. He handed her a small package and she opened it to find a small ring delicately wrought in gold.

'Tis a way of saying I love you,' he said, and taking it from her, tried it on her fingers until he found the right one.

'Oh Matthew,' she cried, 'how am I to show that *I* love *you*?'

'You do not love me yet,' he said gently. 'I know your heart is elsewhere, but I will make you love me in time.'

'But why?' she said as he wiped her tears. 'Why are you so good to me? Tis like a ray of sunlight in the dark, but I do not understand.'

He lifted the beringed finger to his lips and kissed it. 'Tis very simple,' he said. 'I have loved you ever since I was a boy. I thought you would wed Stephen because he was the oldest, but then it was to be William. I never thought to ask for you. I knew you did not love me . . . but see, Fate has been kind to me and we are together. When I saw William strike you that night, I prayed he wouldn't change his mind and wed you inspite of — this.'

He laid a hand gently across Blanche's curving belly. She looked down at the hand then up into his eyes.

'I want to tell you about the child,' she said, 'but do you care to know? I don't want you to imagine anything unclean. Would the knowledge hurt you?'

He shook his head.

'Nothing will alter my love for you,' he said. 'Tell it if you wish.'

She took a deep breath.

'The father is Andrew,' she whispered. 'Andrew Sheldyke'.

'Aye . . . I thought it must be,' he said steadily.

'How did you know?'

'It could be no one else. And he has gone away so suddenly on pilgrimage.'

'Does everyone know?' she asked soberly.

'No one speaks of it to me.'

'And now that you know?'

'I am glad because he is the one man who cannot take you away from me. You see I am very selfish.'

'You will not hate him when — if — he comes home.'

'I do not hate easily,' said Matthew. ''Tis through him that you are to wed me and not William. The child will be handsome and I shall give you many more. We will have a fine family!'

She sighed. 'I love you more with each passing minute,' she told him. 'Before long I shall be besotted!'

'I shall look forward to that,' he laughed and gently, tenderly, took her into his arms.

CHAPTER NINETEEN

Andrew stood at the ship's side looking towards England.
He was tanned from months under a Spanish sun, and had
lost a lot of weight. Three weeks with a fever and a later
bout of food poisoning had taken their toll on his health.
A beard softened the hollow cheeks and made him look
older. His hair was bleached white by the sun. Even the red
cross on his tunic had faded to orange. A small scallop shell
from the Galician beach — the pilgrims 'token' — was
stitched to his sleeve. A small bowl hung at his waist.

He looked frail, but spiritually he had gained a new
strength. No longer bowed by shame and guilt, he had
purged his sin in the sight of the Lord. He had made his
peace with God and was coming home to ask Blanche's
forgiveness and to make what reparation he could. His
sudden departure had been at the abbot's command. He
was forbidden to write to England and Blanche's letter had
never reached him. He did not know that she was pregnant
but realized there was a possibility.

For nearly six months he had made his own way in the
world, without friends and with little money. Poverty,
hunger and disease held no more fears for him. He had
known them all. He had travelled alone and defenceless
among foreigners. Fear had taught him to trust no one. For
the first time in his life, he had to fight for his survival and
the ordeal had strengthened him immeasurably. The shy,
withdrawn youth was no more. A new self-reliant man had
taken his place.

'Tis a grand sight, that!' said the man beside him.

'Aye,' Andrew agreed. 'And only six months since I bade
it farewell. I can scarce believe it. It seems I have been away
a year or more!'

The man who spoke to him was a merchant by the name

348

of Chappel. He had made his recent pilgrimage to give thanks for the deliverance of his eldest daughter from a consumption. They had met at Soulac on the return journey and had shared a room at an inn while waiting a passage to England.

'As soon as I am home my eldest son is away to Rome,' said Chappel. 'My poor wife complains that she is always waiting on news from somewhere! I have promised her she shall go to Canterbury next Easter.'

The captain joined them, leaning over the side and watching the water curling away from the bows.

'So,' he said, 'one from Compostela and one from Rome. I reckon tis time I went on pilgrimage. I've lost count of the pilgrims I've carried, yet never been myself except to London to the blessed Edward the Confessor. Now that's a sight to dazzle your eyes that is. Silver and gold and jewels! You take my word on it. But Spain, never. France, never. But I'll make the journey one day.'

Andrew and Chappel exchanged amused smiles. The captain had been extremely surly throughout the trip, but was obviously now hopeful of an extra monetary reward at the end of the voyage. He would be disappointed, Andrew thought, unless the merchant had money to spare. Andrew had left money in Soulac to cover his passage home. He would have to walk from Plymouth and beg his food.

'Take a swig on that halliard!' roared the captain suddenly and a small wiry man sprang forward and tugged on a rope that criss-crossed a dozen others, snaking upwards among the curving sails.

'A tidy sight better than last week's crossing,' he told them. 'Ah, that was terrible! We could scarce keep a footing on the deck. I tell you, twas one of the worst trips I've . . . .'

He broke off to dart forward and seize the arm of the mate who stood in the forecastle, a hand to his eye to keep out the sun.

'Yonder!' he cried. 'See there — breaking water . . . Reef ahead! Is the anchor ready for letting go?'

'Aye, sir.'

Andrew and Chappel strained their eyes for a glimpse of the 'breaking water', but could see nothing unusual among the rolling waves which stretched endlessly ahead.

'His eyes are sharper than mine,' Andrew commented.

There was a tightness in his stomach which was partly hunger. He had not eaten the dry biscuits which were offered at first light and did not trust the water. He thought longingly of the small brown loaves at the Priory in their white napkins, the rich bean soup, soft cheese and red beets in creamy sauce. Never again would he deem such fare simple! Behind him, the activity of the crew increased; bare feet ran to and fro, orders were shouted and repeated, and anyone not involved crowded to the side, squinting into the sun for a first sight of land.

'Land ho!' came the cry from above, but still Andrew could not see it.

And then it came like a thin grey smudge across the sky.

'Where d'you reckon we are?' the mate asked the captain.

'Tis likely Prawle Point,' he said, 'but we might be further east . . . . No. Tis Prawle Point. We'll make for Plymouth.'

The mate cupped huge hands to his mouth and bellowed, 'Bring her round!' The timbers creaked and the deck heaved as the ship turned on to its new course. Unconsciously Andrew straightened his back. He was home!

The abbot rose to his feet as Elizabeth was shown into the room.

Andrew, beside him, rose also. Elizabeth caught her

350

breath at the sight of him. He was changed. Not only in looks but in bearing.

'Good morrow, my dear lady,' said the abbot and held out a hand in greeting.

'And to you, Father,' she replied. 'I trust you are as fit as you look.'

The old man smiled, pleased with the compliment. He was over seventy, but looked younger. Occasionally he still worked in the gardens or walked to the river to watch the fish being brought out.

'We are pleased to welcome back Brother Andrew,' he said and smiled at the young monk.

'I am touched by your generosity, Father,' said Andrew and he meant it.

'You see that travel in a foreign land has done him no harm,' said the abbot 'On the contrary, he has returned from Santiago de Compostela in a state of grace.'

Elizabeth's eyes met Andrew's, but neither spoke. The old man smiled.

'And now I must leave you alone,' he said. 'I have to speak with the sacrist and no doubt you have much to say to one another. I will be back directly.'

He nodded to them and left the room. Brother and sister moved towards each other. Elizabeth looked up at him and he kissed her lightly on the cheek.

'You are so changed!' she said. 'Was it very bad? What happened that you were gone so long? I began to doubt that you would ever return!'

'Twas hard,' he said. 'Very hard. But I was thankful for that. But Blanche — the abbot tells me she is with child.'

'She carries your child, Andrew. There is no doubt of it. Has Father told you all? I scarce know where to start.'

'Start with your forgiveness, Elizabeth,' he said quietly. 'I pray you can find it in your heart to do so. I have most truly repented and have been forgiven in the sight of God.'

351

'I forgive you,' she said. 'But Blanche will not forgive you. She declares there is nothing to forgive, that it twas her own wilfulness and you were not to blame. She will not hear a word spoke against you.'

'Not even that I left her alone when I should have given her support? That was the hardest part — leaving so suddenly — but the abbot would consider nothing else. I could not even tell you, but trusted you would be told in due course.'

'She tried to loose the child — did you know that?'

'Dear God!'

'She had left it too late.'

Andrew stared past her out of the window, his face grave.

'That poor girl,' he whispered.

'But let me tell you before the abbot returns' said Elizabeth. 'Do you know that she is wed to Matthew? Twas the strangest thing how Fate has worked for him. Matthew is saying that he has always loved her — and yet never spoke of it! And now he is as proud as a peacock with his new wife.'

'They are already wed?'

'Aye. It had to be a hasty affair. She is only three months off her time!'

'And Blanche. How does she feel about Matthew?'

'She is content and thinks herself fortunate! William would have none of her when he knew. Took it very hard . . . he struck her about the face, but Matthew intervened for her.'

He swung round suddenly to face her.

'I have asked myself a thousand times,' he cried. 'How did I let it happen? I did not think myself capable of such feelings! Such terrible weakness! To take a woman! To disregard my vows so easily! I have so despised myself . . . .'

'You must not think too harshly of yourself,' said Elizabeth. 'The blame is shared.'

352

'But Blanche is only a child.'

'She is also a woman,' Elizabeth reminded him, 'and you are a man for all your vows.'

'How does Matthew speak of me?' he asked. 'Ill, I daresay.'

'He does not mention your name.'

'And is Blanche well?'

'Very well. She is become very earnest and dutiful and spins and sews for the babe . . . . Oh, Andrew!' she cried. 'Do you never think you might have shared the child? Your own flesh and blood? A Sheldyke child!'

Slowly he shook his head. 'I have tried,' he said. 'I have tried to — to feel something for the child but I cannot. Something is lacking. It almost frightens me. I want to feel, but there is nothing in my heart!'

Elizabeth sighed.

'Mayhap tis as well,' she said. 'Joseph was enraged. Blanche went home for a few days while the matter was discussed, but we had to bring her back to Heron. I feared the news would kill him. He looked so pale and his hands trembled, he could scarcely speak for the beating in his heart. The doctor gave him a draught to soothe his mind and calm his body.'

He sighed heavily.

'Is Matthew home?' Andrew asked, but she shook her head.

'Both boys are in London at their apprenticeship. They will be home at Easter, but Matthew will come home whenever the child arrives. But how is it here for you? Does anyone speak of the matter — beyond the abbot, I mean?'

'Tis never mentioned,' he said.

'Do they know?'

'I cannot tell. I believe some will have guessed.'

'It cannot be easy for you,' she said.

'I don't ask that it should be,' he said.

353

Elizabeth remained silent, and almost wished the abbot would return.

'And John — how did he take the news?' Andrew asked. 'I pray there is no coldness between you two because of me.'

Elizabeth shrugged. 'He was against the marriage with Matthew. He didn't want any alliance with Blanche. But I reminded him that . . . no, we need not speak on it. Suffice it to say that he changed his mind and let them wed. He is happy enough, I think. Tis all better than we might have expected.'

She took his hands in hers and looked at the roughened palms and broken nails. He laughed at the expression on her face.

'A man does not come home from pilgrimage with beautiful hands!' he told her. 'These hands have chopped wood, emptied slops, lit fires, fought off thieves, caught lice . . . .'

'Stop!' cried Elizabeth. 'Enough. I am convinced. But let us talk about the journey. I scarce know how to begin. Is Spain very beautiful — and France?'

He nodded and took a small pebble from his pocket and held it between finger and thumb.

'Tis from the beach at Santiago,' he said, 'and has been hallowed at the shrine itself. I brought it for Blanche but now I wonder — will you have it?'

Elizabeth hesistated, then took the small brown stone in her hand.

'My thanks,' she said. 'One day I will give it to the child.'

Blanche's child was due later in the month and preparations were under way. As fast as Blanche spun the wool, Elizabeth wove it into a blanket or shawl. John listened to the repetitive sound of the shuttle, but his thoughts were miles away. Elizabeth finally drew the shuttle towards her, tightened up the thread and then laid it down. She rubbed her eyes tiredly.

'Did you conclude the business this afternoon?' she asked.

John glanced up enquiringly.

'The marriage settlement?' she repeated. 'Is it concluded?'

'Aye.'

'Was Joseph satisfied also?'

'He appeared so. We are bound to convey land to Matthew within six weeks.'

'To what value?' she asked.

'Twenty-five pounds. He wanted forty, but I argued for twenty-five now, and more at my death.'

'And then what?'

'Most likely another forty-five in trust for Matthew's male heirs, provided Matthew is properly governed to me as he should be.'

'He should be satisfied!' she said. 'I trust we have done as well out of the bargain.'

'We have done very well. The bargaining power was in our hands in the circumstances. Tucker will settle three hundred pounds on her also.'

'Three hundred! We have indeed done well!' cried Elizabeth.

'To be paid on the first of next month. What do you think of the settlement?'

Elizabeth smiled. 'I am well pleased. My congratulations. You have done well, John.'

She picked up the shuttle and resumed her work.

'There is to be a new bell in the Priory tower,' she said. 'Did you know? They say the old one is cracked and the new one is to be larger.'

'I have thought it cracked for some time now.'

'Robert Martin is coming from Exon and has been asked for a price.'

'Twill not be cheap, I'll warrant,' said John. 'Don't you

355

want to know from whom they will purchase the extra tin?' asked Elizabeth. 'I thought that question would have tumbled to your lips!'

'Heron, I trust.'

''Tis Heron.'

'He has not spoke with me,' said John.

'He spoke with me a week ago,' she said. 'Robert Martin was one of Daniel's friends. He declares he would buy from none other! They will want fifteen pounds of white tin from us, and a hundred pounds of copper from the brazier at Totnes.'

'Then you have the matter well in hand,' said John briefly and Elizabeth regretted her careless words. John still did not care for her to negotiate Heron business alone, and yet it still came so naturally to her. She rarely gave it a second thought.

''Twas a small enough matter,' she said hastily. 'I thought you would not mind.'

''Tis of no consequence,' he said. 'Now I wish to finish my letter.'

He is in a strange mood this last week she thought and it puzzles me. I cannot for the life of me see the reason, unless it is the marriage settlement. Yet that is settled most satisfactorily and without my help! She continued her weaving, watching him from the corner of her eye. She noticed another strange thing. He did not write.

The quill was poised over the paper but did not move across it. A brittle silence existed between them and she really did not know why. Later, she tried again.

'They are casting the bell in the Priory grounds,' she said. 'I thought we might watch them take down the old one. They make a little ceremony of it and the abbot has invited us to attend.'

'When will that be?' he asked.

'On Tuesday next, late in the morning.'

'I shall be in Cornwall at Godolphin's,' he said. 'You will have to go alone.'

Elizabeth stared at him, surprised.

'But you were there only a week since! I think you will soon spend more time in Cornwall than you do in Devon!'

'You always survive my absences,' he said. 'You are most competent.'

And to Elizabeth's consternation, he laid down the pen and strode out of the room without another word.

As the old Ashburton bell rang out for the last time, John stood outside the gaol in Tavistock. He sat his horse nervously as he waited for the young woman who two weeks earlier had been committed on his word. Now he had secured the girl's release but almost wished the charitable deed undone. Time passed and his nervousness grew. Why should he concern himself with the wretched girl, he argued silently. She was one of hundreds of such girls, and he would get no thanks for his action. He would go. Forget her — but no sooner had the decision been made than the prison door swung open and the small figure of Jennet Raikes was pushed out on to the street. She stumbled, sprawling. John slid hurriedly from his horse to go to her assistance, but she was quickly on her feet again.

'You watch yourself, you baggage,' shouted the gaoler. 'Or you'll be back in here again and by Christ's blood I'll have you then!'

The girl ignored him, and brushed herself down as the door clanged shut again. She looked up startled as John's shadow fell across her.

'You again,' she said curtly.

'I wanted to help you,' he said.

'Help me?' she laughed shortly. 'What, you!'

'You put yourself in. You stole the purse.'

''Twas you named me,' she spat and began to walk down the street. John followed but she rounded on him angrily. 'Leave me be,' she cried.

357

'I want to help you,' said John uncomfortably aware of the curious looks they were receiving from passers-by.

'I told you. I don't want your dratted help.'

'Whether you want it or not . . . .'

She snapped, 'I don't want help from the likes of you.'

Her tone was sharp but her voice shook slightly and John caught her by the arm and swung her round to face him. Her bright golden hair was dirty and there were tears in the green eyes. He shook his head despairingly.

'Listen,' he said. 'You stole from a friend of mine and I saw you. What kind of friend would I have been to let you go free.'

'He'd plenty enough,' she said and wrenching herself free, she walked on. The streets grew narrower and dirtier and John's horse, disliking the confined space, whinnied nervously. John had to tug at the bridle to coax it further.

'I would like to help you,' he tried again. 'Will you accept some money?'

'I don't want naught from you — just leave me be, for God's sake, and give over following me.'

John watched the girl picking her way ahead of him through the refuse like a cat across stepping stones. Her feet were bare, her gown faded and patched, and her arms, bent to raise her hem from the mud, were thin.

She stopped suddenly at the side door of a shabby baker's shop and turned on him furiously. 'Well, now you know where I live,' she cried. 'And much good may it do you! You sent me food in prison. I asked naught of it.' And she was gone before he could protest further, slamming the door in his face.

He stood uncertainly listening to her footsteps on the stairs then recalled her feet were bare. Dear God! Those little bare feet of hers. He shook his head, bemused. What spell had the wretched girl cast on him that he, John Kendal, should stand thus defeated and in such a mean street? The girl was right. He had been instrumental in her original committal, but had done his best to make amends. They owed each other nothing. The incident was closed. It had been a foolish weakness on his part to visit her in the gaol. He had been ashamed of his folly and told no one, not even Elizabeth. Now the girl was free, he could forget her. He turned away, awkwardly backing his horse in the narrow street and began to retrace his journey. *Jen – net, Jen – net.* Even the horse's hooves seemed to tap out her name. Damnation! He would have to go back.

He went up the bare wooden stairs and tapping on the first door, received no answer. Pushing it open, he saw the girl, face downward on the bed, sobbing uncontrollably. Her skirt was dishevelled and he saw the thin ankles and dirty feet. One arm was curled protectively around her head and the other lay across the bed cover, the fingers clenched into a small grimy fist. A terrible pity welled up in him as he watched her, waiting for her to turn, but she seemed unaware of his presence. He took a sovereign from his purse and laid it on top of the small coffer that stood beside the bed. Then he left, closing the door quietly behind him.

He was nearly at Godolphin's when the truth came to him. The unfortunate girl reminded him of Bet! With that knowledge he made up his mind that on his next visit to Godolphin's he would call on her briefly, to reassure himself of her well-being. It was to prove a most fateful decision.

The spot chosen for the casting was the drying ground on the far side of the Priory. A circle had been marked out and dug to a depth of five feet. Further over, against the high garden wall, a chimney had been built of brick and clay and in it the old bell and the new tin and copper would be melted down. The charcoal had been delivered and lay in sacks against the wall until such time as it was needed. The mould had been prepared in the centre of this – a bell-shaped mass liberally smeared with wax and oil.

'Is that mould of earth?' Elizabeth asked but the abbot shook his head.

'Tis a delightful mixture,' he told her. 'Sifted earth and horse dung! Aye, you may take my word on it. I am become an expert on the casting of bells. Poor Master Martin is tired of all my questions, I am sure, but too courteous to send me on my way!'

Elizabeth and Della stood with him, watching the activity in the bell tower. Della carried her young son on her hip. His thumb was in his mouth and he slept throughout the proceedings. The priest of the Ashburton church was present as well as the Portreeve and other local dignitaries. The various brethren appeared from time to time, whenever they could find a convenient moment to slip away from their labours. Master Martin and two of his men were in the tower deciding how best to dismantle the old bell.

'They are going to break it up,' the abbot told them, 'and lower the pieces 'Tis a sad day for the old bell which has served us faithfully for twenty-nine years. It bears an inscription, "The lords Servant" and it has, been exactly that . . . . Ah, here is your brother escaped from the accounts! I am telling your sister,' he informed Andrew, 'we are become experts on this noble art.'

Andrew laughed and greeted Elizabeth and Della, and the abbot excused himself and wandered away to speak with the Portreeve.

'And how are all at Heron?' Andrew asked carefully avoiding any names for Della's benefit.

'All well, I thank you,' said Elizabeth. 'We all wait on the great day when this young man has a new playmate!'

The 'young man' on Della's hip had opened his eyes and now fixed Andrew with a long stare.

'He grows more like you, Della,' said Andrew.

'Poor little mite!' she exclaimed. 'With this nose and chin of mine he will never be handsome!'

A loud clanging from above made them all turn to the tower once more. One of the novices hurried out with a tray of goblets, followed by Brother Gregory with a flagon of Bordeaux wine. Everyone was given a goblet which was hastily filled. They looked towards the abbot who raised his glass towards the bell tower.

'To the passing of a faithful friend,' he said, 'and to his resurrection in the new bell. May he ring the hours for us for many years to come!'

They all raised their goblets and drank to his toast. The abbot turned to Brother Gregory.

'Take up a drink to Master Martin,' he said, 'and for his men. We mustn't forget our master craftsman. That would not do at all.'

The clanging continued to the accompaniment of a few oaths, and eventually they started to lower the fragments of the old bell. One of the men came down and collected each piece, untying it from the rope and carrying it to the furnace. The rope was pulled up again and the process repeated. It was a slow business.

Della looked at Andrew and thought how he had aged. Izzie's silence, so dearly bought, had not lasted and it was known that Andrew had fathered Blanche's child. She wondered how he could ask so coolly after the health of 'all at Heron'. He had never so much as set eyes on Blanche since his return from Spain. Had not spoken with her either as far as any could tell. Della didn't know whether this was the abbot's ruling or a sense of discretion on the part of all concerned. This was the first time she had seen him and was at a loss for something to say. 'Was Spain very hot?' she asked so that she broke the silence between them. 'Aye, and in France, also,' he said, 'but cooler by the time I left Santiago.'

'Is the shrine very beautiful?' she asked, reassured by his composure.

'Incredibly beautiful,' he told her. 'The body of St James lies in a marble tomb raised high above the altar. Tis lit by

361

many torches and tis surrounded by perfumes! What more can I say? It defies description.'

'And would you go again?' she asked.

Elizabeth waited curiously for his answer.

'Not to Compostela,' he told her. 'I would go to the Holy Land if twere ever possible. I spoke with many palmers at Soulac newly returned from Jerusalem, and they say tis most wonderful to see the Holy sepulchre and Mount Sinai. But I doubt I will ever be so fortunate. Among all the brethren, only the abbot has been to Jerusalem.'

Della's son was becoming restive and she stood him down, but held his hand tightly so that he shouldn't wander. There was a cheer as the last of the bell was lowered and Master Martin joined them, impatient for the arrival of the tin and copper which was already a day late. Just then, Eric ran up to Elizabeth, a huge grin on his face. She looked at him, startled.

'You have a granddaughter!' he cried exultantly. 'Twas all over in . . . .'

She stared at him. 'A granddaughter! So soon? It cannot be! And me not there! Oh, Eric!'

She was already running for her horse, looking for the abbot as she ran. He was nowhere to be seen and she grumbled under her breath. Della and Eric ran alongside, the child in Eric's arms.

'Why didn't you fetch me?' demanded Elizabeth. 'I can't believe it!'

'I was sent to bring the midwife — and Martha was with Mistress Blanche — and Izzie boiling up water and carting it upstairs. Twas a right old tangle, I can tell you! Who was to come and fetch you?'

'Go back and make my apologies to the abbot,' she told him, 'for my sudden departure.'

A sudden thought struck her. 'They are both well?'

'Both blooming.'

'Heaven be praised!' said Elizabeth. 'Then I will ride on. You bring Della with you; she can ride behind you. And

362

has Matthew been sent for from London? And does John know?'

'The master's in Cornwall,' he reminded her. 'And no word has gone yet to Master Matthew so far as I know.'

She turned her horse without waiting to hear more and took a short cut cantering across the moor towards Heron while Andrew, forgotten, went into the chapel to give thanks for Blanche's safe delivery.

As Elizabeth ran into the house, Martha ran down the stairs, her face wreathed in smiles and bubbling over with details of the excitement.

'Twas all over in an hour!' she cried, stumbling up the stairs again behind her mistress. 'Can't be yet, I told her, but she says it must be — she had these cramps so strong. No, I tells her, tis indigestion most like but she wouldn't have it. Told me to run and find you, then shouts for me to come back! I didn't know my head from my heels and that's the truth on it!'

The midwife met them at the top of the stairs. 'I've left a lass starting her pains at the far end of Ashburton,' she told them, 'so I daresn't stay longer. All's well with mother and daughter and so quick I can hardly credit it. I've known a second child be born that quick, but never a first! A brave little mother that one. Made no fuss at all. Master Matthew can be proud of his little family. But I mustn't stop. I'll call in later if I'm able or else twill have to be tomorrow.'

And she was gone. Elizabeth and Martha went into the bedchamber where Blanche sat propped up in bed with a small bundle beside her. Her face glowed with joy and Elizabeth's heart went out to her. She kissed her cheek and Blanche held up the baby for her.

'Smile at your grandmother, Sophie,' said Blanche but the dark eyes wandered vaguely and the tiny mouth puckered.

'My dear girl,' said Elizabeth. 'I am so pleased for you.

363

And to happen so quickly! The midwife said you were very brave. Oh, she's a bonny little girl. Does Joseph . . . .'

She was about to ask if he knew, but Blanche forestalled the question. 'He has gone to Exeter,' she said, 'but Izzie has left word for him. Oh, Elizabeth, what will Matt think of her? Won't he be proud! Little Sophie Kendal! I'm so happy I can scarce believe it. And when I think . . . .'

'When you think what?' said Elizabeth.

'That I — I nearly ended her life!'

'Tis well that you didn't,' said Elizabeth gently. 'Your little Sophie will be greatly loved.'

Blanche was sleeping when Matthew tiptoed into the room to take a look at his new daughter. The baby lay in a small wooden crib beside the bed and though silent, was wide awake and staring vacantly about her. Her lashes were fair and there was a soft down on her head.

'And ears like little shells,' whispered Matthew. 'You are a bonny little lass, Sophie. I swear there is none finer in the whole of the West Country!'

Blanche still slept and he sat beside her waiting patiently until she awoke. She did at last and stared at him in disbelief.

'Matthew!' she cried. 'You've come so soon. Oh, tis so good to see you!' She held out her arms to him and he moved into the warmth of her embrace.

'Did you hear how quick it was?' she asked him proudly. 'Why I never knew such impatience! That little girl of ours could scarce wait to be out in the world. The midwife was barely in time. Oh, let me kiss you, my dearest Matt! I count myself so fortunate. A loving husband and a healthy daughter.'

'And I a father and husband,' said Matthew, 'when four months ago I was nothing . . . I would not change places with any other.'

'Amen to that!' said Blanche. 'Now let me show you her tiny hands they are perfect. Give her to me, and I will unbind some of the swaddling. You can see naught but her

364

face . . . . Come to your Mama, little one . . . There, such dainty fingers . . . and look at her legs, Matt — and see how they kick! She is so strong. When I feed her she tugs at me . . . .'

'You do not suckle her yourself?' asked Matthew surprised.

'Only until they have found a wet nurse. Oh, but she's so greedy for her milk! Now, Matt, you must hold her. Go to your Papa, Sophie. Everyone says she is like me.. What do you think?'

Blanche had decided that no one should see any other likeness in the child. Both she and Andrew were fair so it would not be difficult.

'She has your long lashes,' he agreed. 'See, she doesn't weep. Not even a murmur.'

'She has nought to weep for,' said Blanche. 'Heaven has smiled on her. Is William with you?'

'No. He will be home at Easter — but sends his congratulations.'

'Give me the babe,' said Blanche,' 'and I will wrap her against the draughts. Elizabeth will scold me if she finds her thus. She is like a broody hen with this little chick of ours.'

Matthew waited until the child was safely back in her crib then took Blanche's hand.

'I have something to tell you,' he said. 'I beg you to understand.'

'What is it?' she cried, alarmed, the joy fading from her eyes, to be replaced with fear.

'Tis nothing to fear,' he said hastily. 'But Andrew is downstairs.

He waits in the hall to see the babe. No, don't say anything. Let me finish . . . I asked him to come. Tis not natural that a man should not see his own daughter. I spoke with him at the Priory on my way in.'

'Oh, Matt!' she began but he put a finger to her lips.

'I ask him in today, but I have told him I do not wish him

365

calling to see you while I am in London. I am afeard . . . .'

'Afeard?'

'No, not of that,' he said. 'I do not want . . . .'

He stopped again and turned away, so that she could not see his face. 'I fear that Sophie will know Andrew better than she will know me,' he said. 'I daresay that is a selfish.'

'No, Matt, tis right and proper,' cried Blanche. 'Come to me, I beg you and do not look so woebegone! You are right. I had thought on it, too, and would have spoken by and by.'

She took him into her arms once more and kissed the dark head that lay against her breast.

'Blanche, Blanche . . . ' he murmured. 'I could not bear to lose either of you.'

'Rest assured you will not,' she told him. 'You and Sophie are all that I wish for in the world!'

She took his face in her hands and smiled.

'Rest easy in your mind,' she said. 'I swear to you by all that's holy that Matt Kendal is my dear Lord and master . . . 'til death do us part — oh, Matt.'

There were sudden tears in her own eyes as they clung together.

'I have told him he can see the babe now, while I am with you,' said Matthew 'then tis done with. He will be an uncle, no more than that. Do you despise me?'

She shook her head.

'I have such respect for you,' she said. 'You are more to me in my eyes than any other man, now and forever.'

'You will see each other occasionally, I know. That is inevitable.'

'He will be no more to me than Brother Gregory,' said Blanche, 'and he shall be Uncle Andrew to Sophie.'

He laughed, albeit a trifle shakily.

'Then I'll call him up', he said.

Andrew told Elizabeth later that he had felt nothing for the child.

'And, strangely, nothing for Blanche,' he said. 'Tis as though my absence has removed from my mind all that went before. I was conscious of an emptiness, a loss, mayhap. I looked on that scrap of humanity that is my own flesh and blood and felt only a curiosity . . . . A moment's passion so long ago — and now this child. Tis somehow sudden.'

'Twas scarcely sudden to Blanche,' said Elizabeth and her tone was sharper than she intended. 'But there, if you felt nothing then her loss is easier for you to bear. I have promised Matthew that you will not visit regularly while he is away. Tis hard for him to be in London, but his apprenticeship is less than half done. He is young still and must learn a trade. He will not inherit Heron so must earn a living, and John is eager for them to follow in his footsteps. So . . . we shall see less of you but you will be in my thoughts.'

'Forgive me, Elizabeth,' he said. 'I disappoint you, I know. I feel of so little worth. I am fallen very low in your eyes.'

He sighed heavily, and she could not think how she could, with honesty, reassure him.

'Tis not a perfect world,' she said. 'We are all far from noble. With God's help we must make what we can of ourselves. The past is done. For the present, it looks well enough. Pray God we have seen the last of sorrow. Go back to your brethren. You must find happiness in your own way.'

The day for casting the bell was finally decided and timed for the evening, by which time the furnace would be at the correct temperature, having been burning all day. The shell of the mould was in position, clamped over the core; leaving a gap between the two moulds into which the molten metal would flow to form the bell. A channel of baked clay had been built connecting the furnace to the bell mould. At the appropriate time, the molten metal would be released from the furnace and would flow into the mould. It had been announced that silver would improve the tone of the bell and various people donated articles.

Joseph had contributed a pair of silver candlesticks and Elizabeth had tossed a silver brooch into the molten metal. From time to time, Master Martin or one of his men would stir the metal with a long pole thrust into a hole left specifically for that purpose. Most of the brethren were present, as well as the dignitaries who had attended the breaking up of the old bell. Blanche had contributed a handful of silver coins, but was not present at the casting.

Joseph stood with his son Joe who had taken a week's leave from his studies to visit his father. Joseph's health was causing some concern. Since the shock of Blanche's pregnancy, he had grown noticeably weaker. His heart had suffered and, despite frequent bleedings, was now easily tired. He had not ridden for the past two weeks and had risen later in the mornings. He now felt an increasing urgency to conclude negotiations for his son's marriage and see him established at Maudesly.

'I thought the choir was to sing,' said Joe.

'Perhaps tis later,' said Joseph, 'When the metal flows into the cast. I saw you speak with Father Marryat. What was it he threw into the bell?'

'A small chalice. He asked after Blanche and the babe. He was most concerned that she bawled at the baptism.'

'He is a foolish old man,' said Joseph. 'Don't all children bawl at such a time. Is Elizabeth here?'

'Aye.'

'And John?'

'No . . . he is still away.'

'No,' thought Joseph. He would not be present. No doubt detained on business in Tavistock! Was Elizabeth deaf to the rumours or did she merely pretend ignorance? It was said that he did not go to Cornwall as often as he claimed but broke his journey in Tavistock, though for, what purpose none could say. He sighed heavily. What could he, Joseph, do about it? On what pretext could he intervene, and to what purpose? And yet it grieved him to stand idly by unable to help her. Suddenly, he saw her walking across the grass towards him and hastily aware that he frowned, composed his features into a smile. She was no longer a young woman, but she was still beautiful even though the years had softened the contours of her face and emphasized a sadness in her eyes.

She wore a mantle of dark red and the winter sunlight reflected the colour into her cheeks. As always, her fingers strayed to her hair, tucking up the fine strands under her head-dress in that delicate, familiar way that he found so touching.

'I have parted with a well-loved brooch,' she told him laughing. 'If the tone does not please me, I have told the Father I shall ask for its return! Have you stood by the furnace? The heat is tremendous. Oh, here come the choir. Then tis almost time.'

Eight of the brethren lined up beside the bell pit and at a sign began to sing '*Laudate Dominum* at which the rest of the crowd fell silent. There was a fine mist drifting across the ground and the light had all but faded from the sky.

Suddenly, after a cry of warning from Master Martin, the molten metal leapt from the furnace and splashed into the trough below. Sparks flew and the fierce red glow lit the faces of the spectators as a cheer went up from crowd and choir alike. Elizabeth turned to Joseph in her excitement, her eyes gleaming.

'What a sight!' she cried. 'I would not have missed it for the world.' Then turned once more to watch the narrow trail of living metal as it flowed into the prepared cast.

Master Martin controlled the flow, wiping the sweat from his face with the back of his sleeve and closing his eyes to protect them from the heat and glare. All eyes were on the red hot stream. Above them, startled, the birds flew from the ivy and wheeled over their heads. The glowing metal set the darkening sky alight and Joseph moved slightly closer to Elizabeth so that their shoulders brushed each other, but if she was aware of it, she gave no sign. She turned to him again, laughing with excitement and her face was framed, by the soft white folds of her head-dress. He wanted to take her in his arms and kiss her. He longed to protect her from the pain and distress which he felt sure was to come.

Elizabeth sat at the window brushing her hair with slow even strokes. Her eyes were large with fear, a small knot of misery locked in her throat. She had not eaten all day and her stomach craved food, but the thought of it made her nauseous. She looked out over the shadowy garden and tried to think calmly. Tried to subdue the terrible panic that rose within her. John had not come home. He had left, promising to return in three days, but now four, days had passed and still he had not returned. It was becoming a familiar occurrence. It was rare nowadays that he did come home when she expected him.

'Where are you, John?' she whispered.

She did not ask but tried to behave normally, seeing to his comforts. Speaking lightly of the children, always loving. In her heart she pitied him. He was obviously wretched, growing irritable with the servants, tossing restlessly at nights while sleep eluded him.

Poor John....

She laid down the brush and leaned her forehead on the cool stone of the window ledge. There was a tap at the door and Martha came in.

'I've brought you mulled wine,' she said, 'and a slice of that saffron cake. No! Don't tell me you cannot eat. Tis no way to go on. You'll mar your health.'

She had set down the tray and now eyed Elizabeth severely. She knows, thought Elizabeth and felt that the shame must show in her face. She does not comment on John's absence as she used to do. I wonder what they know? More than me, mayhap. And so they pity me!

'Thank you, Martha,' she said.

She strove to find a casual comment, but her mind was not functioning normally and she lowered her eyes, avoiding the expression on Martha's face.

'Now you jump into that bed,' said Martha. 'Sitting by the window like that, in this weather! You'll catch a chill and then where will we be?'

She turned back the coverlet and slid her hand under the sheets.

'Tut! The pan's half cold. I'll put some fresh coals in for you. Lucky I haven't raked out the fire as yet.'

She pulled the copper pan from between the sheets and bustled out of the room.

Elizabeth sighed. Taking up the goblet, she sipped at the warm spicy liquid, holding the goblet in both hands, glad of its comforting warmth. And Joseph—what did he know of John's whereabouts, she wondered? He called at the house more frequently and she found it hard to discourage him. Did he come out of kindness? Did he still love her? She thought of him and realized suddenly how much he had aged in the past year. He had lost weight and did not ride so frequently. Poor Joseph . . . . She took a bite from the cake. In her present state of mind it was tasteless, but she did not want to disappoint Martha. How they must gossip in the kitchen! Dear God. Is it come to this that even my servants pity me! Oh, John, John! Where are you? You will come back to me in body but not in spirit. Your thoughts and desires will be elsewhere. What must I do? Sweet Mother of God, help me to be patient. I will wait if only he will love me again.'

She fell to her knees before the window, oblivious of the

371

goblet still in her hands and was still there when Martha returned.

'Now then, that'll keep you warm until the early hours,' she said. 'So finish off that wine and into bed, my child ... That's it. Now old Martha shall tuck you up. You forget all your troubles and off to sleep. Tomorrow is another day.'

Elizabeth tried to smile but her lips trembled. She dared not speak. Please do not speak kindly, she begged silently. I cannot bear it. When the old woman had gone, she lay straight and still on her side of the large bed aware of the cold, emptiness of the other half.

The wine was affecting her, making her light-headed but pleasantly so. She closed her eyes and tried to think on happier topics: the players at Maudesley, Blanche's child, casting the bell at the Priory....

But the wine had been too strongly spiced and when she slept her dreams were dark and fearful. She wandered through a dark pine forest lost and stumbling as the brambles caught at her legs, tearing the skin painlessly. Lying among the pine needles was a goblet, encrusted with mud. As she brushed at it, the caked mud fell away and there were jewels set into its rim. She must show it to John!

But she was alone among the trees which rustled now and creaked in the rising wind, whipping the pine needles into the air, driving them against her skin. Then, above the wind, another sound, a terrible roaring and a bear appeared walking on its hindlegs. It was large and shaggy and suddenly it was John and he was holding out his arms to embrace her. She ran into his arms, but they tightened round her in a grip of iron which squeezed the breath from her body and his eyes were cold and full of hate.

CHAPTER TWENTY

1497

In retrospect, the next year was, for the West Country, the lull before the storm. There were no major alarms but throughout the region, discontent was rife among most of the tinners at the high level of taxation imposed on them by the King. There were constant small breaches of the peace. Horses and cattle were stolen, feuds between neighbours continued to provoke assaults of one kind or another. On several occasions desperate tinners broke into churches, stealing the silver and even kidnapping various people with whom they had a real or imagined grievance over mining rights. But such occurrences were merely an extension of everyday life and aroused little excitement except to those personally involved.

Heron continued to flourish and Retter's influence in the neighbourhood grew daily but he remained single; a dour, silent man who delighted in the company of William and Matthew on their frequent visits home. Stephen was still a problem. He caused great concern to John and Elizabeth, growing sullen and morose and although he outgrew his dissolute friends, he did not replace them. When he was home he spent most of his time alone on the moor, often staying away for days and nights at a time. He steadfastly refused to agree to a betrothal and showed no interest in Heron or its future prosperity. When pressed, he declared his wish to be a farmer and although Elizabeth was not unwilling, John was adamant. They knew he would never make a lawyer — he had no real ability and no liking for the profession. It was obvious he must not be allowed to drift, but it was difficult to take positive action in the face of his continued lack of interest. He came home early in

April and John once more broached the subject of his future. He finally left Ashburton on the eleventh of April with scarcely a 'goodbye' for any of them and his going cast a gloom over the entire household.

'Four hours' that afternoon was a subdued meal. Martha, bringing in the bread and soft cheese, made no effort to disguise her disapproval at what she considered his banishment.

'Reckon a small loaf will do you this afternoon,' she said pointedly. 'With the best appetite gone.' Elizabeth looked at John anxiously, but he let the comment pass.

'If t'will make you feel better, Martha, I will eat for two!' William offered, but she refused to be mollified and withdrew coldly to fetch in the ale and a dish of junket. They cut the bread in silence and spread it thickly with the creamy white cheese.

'He should be nearing Salisbury by now,' said Matthew, 'and will change his horse.'

'And sleep the night, I hope,' said Elizabeth.

'If he has wits enough,' said John.

'He will surely not ride on alone,' Elizabeth protested anxiously. 'The rest of the party is to rest overnight, for they are being joined by two more on the morrow.'

'Don't fret on his behalf,' said John. 'He is eighteen years of age now and must fend for himself.'

'Aye,' William agreed. 'Why, the Prideaux lad from the village has gone with Daubeny and hopes to fight Richard and the Scots before he is much older. He is but seventeen and meagre with it. You could put him in a pint pot and lose him!'

Elizabeth laughed. 'He was ever a hot head, that lad,' she said, 'and nothing pleases him, but he must run off and find himself a war instead of learning his father's business.'

'We've a mind to ride into Cornwall,' William continued. 'Flamank is speaking at Bodmin and the smith, Michael Joseph, is riding up from St Keverne. It should be a lively meeting.'

Blanche pulled a wry face. 'Holy Katharine!' she protested. 'You two boys are no sooner on Heron soil than you would up and leave again. I shall tell Sophie her father is become a vagrant.'

Elizabeth laughed, but the men pretended deafness.

'Go if you've a mind to,' John said. 'I hear he speaks well, but when all's said and done they are but rabble rousers.'

'That may be so,' said William, 'but there is some justice in their cause and their claims are reasonable.'

Matthew nodded soberly. 'There is great hardship,' he said, 'and it worsens daily. Many of the tinners are near to starving. They cannot pay the taxes and ought to be excused.'

'Tis true,' said Blanche. 'The Pinner woman has lost her newborn babe they say she had no milk to suckle it . . . and I saw the youngest Cadwolley boy begging in the market and more whose names I didn't know. The January tax has brought them very low.'

'And for what?' said John. 'To keep out the Scots? We have no fear of the Scots here in the West. I say let the North pay tax for their own protection. We have problems of our own. Marauding neighbours, marauding foreigners in the channel. God's truth! There's no end to them.'

Elizabeth nodded, now only half listening, her thoughts reverting to Stephen who had looked so very young and vulnerable as he rode off. He was so like his father. The same tight jaw, the same trick of turning down the corners of his mouth. She cut herself another slice of bread and Matthew passed the cheese bowl.

'This Flamank,' said Matthew, 'is well spoken of as an honest man. He has spoke at several towns and draws large crowds. They say he urges no violence, but urges that we appeal direct to the King.'

'Aye, for the removal of Mortan and Bray,' said William. 'This tax is their brainchild and the King would be well rid of them.'

'Go by all means,' said John. 'It can do no harm to know what's being said. A proper appeal, legally designed, may move the King to think again. Who knows?'

Elizabeth sighed. He spoke so rarely of the county's affairs — or even of Heron's affairs. A few years earlier he would have ridden with the twins. Now he showed little interest. He was withdrawn, aloof and the love between them had grown cold. She knew in her heart that his affections were with another, but was helpless in the face of such knowledge. John would not leave her. Marriage was forever. Yet she almost wished it were possible. His attitude towards her was one of reluctant acceptance. Heron was his and she was part of Heron. She never spoke to him of the reason for his coldness. She feared his answer. For the first time in her life, Elizabeth knew what it was to be afraid; afraid and helpless in the face of an unknown threat.

But now the twins looked at each other with ill-concealed delight. They had not expected to gain approval for their trip so easily and, as soon as the meal was finished, they returned to a favourite spot in the orchard to make plans.

Mid-morning, two days later, the two boys set off for Launceston where they broke their journey. They stayed overnight, rising early the next morning to breakfast and ride on, reaching Bodmin in the early afternoon. The common where the meeting was to be held, was already crowded with men. A few horses were tethered to trees but many more had been retained by their riders; for it had rained heavily in the night and the ground was very wet. Now the sun shone warmly, the spirits of the men rose with the temperature and there was a feeling of camaraderie among them which conveyed itself instantly to William and Matthew, as they led their mounts in search of a convenient space. Occasionally, they called a greeting to someone they recognized from their own area, but mostly the crowd was made up of Cornishmen. Neither Flamank nor the smith had arrived and the men chatted good-humouredly among themselves while they waited, patiently resisting most of the efforts of the local populace who were quick to realize the financial possibilities of so many visitors.

Bakers, ale wives, pedlars, minstrels — they descended from miles around to try their luck with the captive 'market'. Individually the men had very little to spend. It was their poverty that drew them to hear what the lawyer and smith had to say. But small amounts in large numbers provided an unexpected source of income to those who hawked their wares and a steady trade flourished.

A sudden ragged cheer heralded the arrival of Michael Joseph.

He galloped into the field on an enormous black shire horse, holding one massive clenched fist above his head in a gesture of defiance; which inspired even the meekest among his audience to scramble to their feet and swell the cheer to an enthusiastic roar of welcome. He reined in with a flourish so that his horse reared and his nearest supporters scattered in alarm.

'Cornishmen! Fellows!' he cried. 'Greetings and God be with you.'

Resting the reins in his lap, he held up both his hands in a wide gesture of friendship and the crowd roared anew. He wasted no time.

'Sit yourselves down and listen.' They did so. 'I'm nobbut a plain man,' he began. Someone in the front of the crowd shouted, 'We're all plain men,' and there was a great shout of 'Aye'.

The smith pointed to his grizzled face and said, 'Well, mebbe I'm plainer than most;' A roar of laughter. 'But I've eyes in me head and wits, too, and I can see what's going on and I don't like it.' Another shout — 'No, more do we!'

William looked about him as the exchange continued. He recognized a few faces — Calwodeley, Whalley, Tresithney, Retallack. Cornishmen, restless men, their natural rebellious spirits now fed by a new resentment and about to be fired with a new fervour. He looked at the sea of faces turned towards the speaker. There were very few blond heads among the hundreds of small dark-eyed men. Few soft hands among the many grimy, calloused ones that negligently held bill hook or staff or the occasional bow. They were not armed for war, but merely carried a means of defence against the ever present risk from cut-throats and thieves who were a common hazard to all who travelled the highways. The crowd were mostly tinners, farm labourers, seafarers, artisans of all trades; but a large number of unemployed swelled the ranks. They were poor and they were desperate. Since no one else would champion their cause, they must take it upon themselves.

'Who's going to help the likes of us?' demanded the smith.

'No one!' came the answer.

'We are all God fearing men,' he cried. 'We're hardworking men. We ask nothing but to earn enough to keep our wives and little 'uns. Food for their bellies, clothes for their backs and a bit of fire in winter. Is that too much to ask'

A roar of denial.

'Do you want to see your kids starve?'

'No!'

'Or barefoot in the snow?'

'No!'

His speech was simple, his appeal direct, for Michael Joseph spoke as one of them. He was a blacksmith, he worked with his hands, he was poor. He wept with them, laughed with them, shared their hopes and fears. He was of the people and when he finished they rose to their feet and cheered; not only for him but for themselves.

'They love the man,' said William, and Matthew smiled.

'Wouldn't you?' he asked.

378

Thomas Flamank was quite a different proposition. The son of an old Cornish family, his father, Richard Flamank, was a district commissioner, one of the men responsible for collecting the very taxes against which the men were protesting. The smith described himself as a plain man. Thomas Flamank was a plausible one, and years of study and experience as a lawyer fitted him for the role he now elected to play, as spokesman for the under-privileged against the establishment. He rode up and greeted Michael Joseph who, observing his approach, had timed his speech to end with his arrival in front of the crowd.

For a while the two men chatted together while the rest spoke animatedly among themselves. Then it was the lawyer's turn. He was a smooth, persuasive speaker — where the smith had roared, he lowered his voice and the men strained their ears to catch every word. He spoke quietly but his well-trained voice carried a surprising distance. Those that couldn't hear shuffled nearer. No one shouted 'Speak up!' Not to Thomas Flamank. It was very simple, he told them. The Government had never intended such a burden of taxation to fall on the tinners. The King did not wish it. The country was not at war. A few Scotsmen raiding across the northern borders hardly constituted a major threat to the security of the realm. So who was responsible for the parlous state in which the West Country found itself?

Two men, Cardinal Morton and Sir Reginald Bray, two of the King's financial advisers. If Parliament had granted the King £160,000 it was at their instigation. Whether such a large amount was necessary was a moot point. Even if it were, it had never been intended that such a large proportion of the new tax should fall on poor men. It should be raised by loans from the wealthy and contributions from the Church. The collectors in Cornwall were altogether too eager and interpreted their instructions too literally and with great harshness. Wasn't the provost of Penrhyn a case in point? Here a low murmur spread through his listeners.

Sir John Oby, the provost referred to, was hated in the area. It was rumoured that he took excessive taxes and that much of the money found its way into his own coffer. The King must be told that his loyal subjects were being exploited by ruthless men. He would want to know.

Flamank spoke with conviction and a quiet passion. They should go to the King and put their grievance to him. They meant no harm to anyone and there would be no violence. They would not go in anger: they had no quarrel with the King, but to demand the redress of a wrong. Morton and Bray must go! They would walk to London and all who cared to should join them along the way.

'We have nothing to lose and much to gain,' he ended. 'Who will come with us?'

The field rose as one man, and William and Matthew were cheering with the rest. A mood of sweet exhilaration seized them all. They slapped each other on the back and threw their caps into the air. A great load was lifted from their weary shoulders. The smith and the lawyer would lead them to London. Incredibly, within the hour, they were on the move.

Those on horseback moved at the speed of those on foot, but the weather favoured them. They were in high spirits and covered a considerable distance each day. They met with sympathy wherever they went and were fed and cared for. Men joined them at every stop, hundreds in a day as word spread of their purpose. It was a popular cause. They crossed from Cornwall into Devon and Somerset where more recruits came forward — not only working men but some of yeomen stock — John Tolle of Lamerton, John Broke of Doddebroke, Warwick of Plymouth and Fader of Suttecombe. The hundreds became thousands, but still they moved peacefully enough. Songs were sung, jokes told and retold. Friendships were struck up in minutes and as quickly forgotten. The amorphous mass wound its way through the midsummer countryside, fording rivers, skirting quarries, scaling hills, filling the highways for miles at a time and overflowing into the fields and woods.

It was at Taunton that the first blood was spilled. The provost of Penrhyn heard with dismay that his name had been mentioned at the Bodmin rally and he deemed it prudent to remove himself from the area as quickly as possible. Unfortunately, he moved in the wrong direction. Had he fled west he would probably have been safe. Instead he fled east and took refuge in Taunton. Word reached him there, that the men were on the move towards London, but, under-estimating the speed at which the marchers moved, he was still there when the smith and lawyer led their followers into the town. The townspeople made hurried preparations to receive them.

Food had been donated — bread, ale, cheese, cold meats and ale in vast quantities for the men who would sleep rough that night. Many would be given free lodging. The streets were lined with well-wishers and at every window curious faces peered out to view the phenomenon of a peaceable army. Traffic came to a standstill as thousands of men filled the streets.

A few angry incidents resulted as both pleasure and business were interrupted and delayed by the influx. Matthew and William, riding at the front of the column, were offered accommodation by an elderly couple who lived over a shop overlooking the market square. They accepted gratefully.

Matthew, never so strong as his twin, had suffered from the sun and was weary from lack of sleep. Two straw pallets had been laid on the floor of the parlour and he threw himself down on to one of them with a groan of exhaustion. William looked at him exasperated.

'And are you going to rest long?' he asked. 'They say Oby is hiding hereabouts and there's a move to search him out. I've no mind to miss such sport.'

'You call that sport?' asked Matthew. 'You can do little if you find the man.'

William laughed. 'We can frighten the wits out of the wretch! And some even talk of taking him to London with us. The King might care to hear his excuses at first hand. I'd like to see that thieving little snake wriggle!'

'You tell me of it tomorrow then,' said Matthew, easing off his boots. 'Me — I'll settle for a good sleep.'

William rubbed the sweat from his face with a towel thoughtfully provided by their hosts. 'And won't you eat?' he asked.

His brother shook his head.

'I am even too weary for that,' he confessed. 'Leave me be, William. Go out and enjoy your hunting.'

He turned on to his side and closed his eyes. Seconds later he was asleep.

He awoke suddenly some time later and abruptly sat up, his senses alerted though for what he didn't know. The room was darker, it must be early evening. He became aware of a commotion in the street outside and crossed to the window. The market place was full of men and, some on foot, some mounted, milled about in disorder. Voices were raised, but he couldn't catch what was being said. Probably a clash between local lads and the marchers, he thought. There had been a few such incidents along the way, when the local girls found the newcomers more exciting than their regular swains! He was turning away from the window when the door burst open and their host rushed in and past him to look out of the window at the scene.

'Tis the man from Penrhyn,' he told Matthew. 'Seems he led them a fair old dance, but they finally caught him. Paraded him through the streets on a horse and everyone jeering. See there — that must be him. I'd not like to be in his place, whatever he's guilty of. He looks right flustered as well he might.'

'Poor wretch,' said Matthew. 'I'm not saying he doesn't

deserve it. There's been some shady dealings and in the name of the King, but he's got friends in high places and none dare touch him. He's a cold pitiless man but I'd still . . . .'

'See there!' interrupted his host. 'Behind him! Tis your brother, surely. If not, tis very like him.'

'Aye, tis William,' said Matthew. 'I should have known he'd be there. He's a hot head on his shoulders, that one!'

There was a sudden roar from the crowd and the provost was pulled from his horse, the men instantly closing around him.

'I think I'll go out there,' said Matthew uneasily. He pulled on his boots and hurried outside and began to push his way through the crowd towards the spot where he had last seen his brother. Now he realized how ugly the crowd had become.

There were cries of, 'Put him in the stocks!' and even, 'Flog and hang the bastard!'

Someone fell against Matthew and he felt a searing across his cheek, as a naked dagger caught him an unintentional blow. He felt the warm blood flow down his face and neck and the next few moments took on a nightmarish quality.

'William!' he shouted. 'No! No! Don't do it.'

Ahead of him he caught a glimpse of the provost's pale face and terrified expression, then a hand clutched at the man's hair and jerked him out of sight.

'Let him be,' shouted Matthew, but no one heeded his lone cry for clemency. Now all around him staves were raised, knives were unsheathed, a chanting began for the provost's blood.

'Kill him! Kill him!'

It happened in slow motion, right before Matthew's horrified eyes. The man's jerkin was ripped off, a blade swung up and down, and another. Staves thudded against the fragile skull. A bill hook clawed at the thin neck, partly

383

severing it. The man slid to the ground and Matthew, stumbling, was thrown forward on to the body; then he was dragged away again so that the murderers might finish their work unimpeded. Now an axe fell, and the head rolled free of the body, blood spurting on to the legs of those nearest to it.

Matthew's senses reeled and a merciful darkness swept over him, blotting out what followed. He lay unconscious under the feet of the crowd, and it was only William's presence that saved him from being trampled to death. Cursing, he sheathed his dagger and dragged his brother to his feet. With the help of another, he managed to keep him upright as the crowd surged backwards and forwards.

Then suddenly it was all over. Their rage spent, the sacrifice made, the marchers suddenly withdrew. Some exultant, some dismayed, all shocked. Within seconds, the square was empty of life. One dismembered corpse remained, bleeding silently into the dust.

'There was no need for it,' Matthew repeated. 'No need.'

'There was every need, Matt, and you know it.'

Matthew lay on his pallet while William turned from the window and faced his brother angrily. 'Just because it was not to your liking, you deem it unnecessary. Nobody enjoys killing a man but . . . . '

'Oh, but they did!' Matthew protested. 'That's what sickens me. They *did* enjoy it. It was writ large on their faces — and all eyes gleaming with grim satisfaction!'

'Rot! Your imagination has run away with you. He was a thief and a cheat and he got no more than he deserved.'

'No one deserves to die that way. No one,' said Matthew. 'It was savage . . . brutal . . . . Dear God, it turns my guts to remember it. I think the scene will be with me for ever.'

384

He put his hands over his bruised face and moaned softly. William looked at him with distaste.

'Lord, what a milksop you are become,' he said. 'You talk like a woman. And to swoon that way! I was ashamed to call you brother.'

'Do you think I am proud of your part in the deed?'

'I care not.'

'I would not have your conscience,' said Matthew.

'You are never like to.'

'Indeed I hope not. War is one thing. Murder's another.'

''Twas not murder!' shouted William.

'What name would you call it by?'

'What name? Why, retribution, if it must have a name. What does it matter? The wretch is dead and none will weep for him.'

'Not even his wife and children if he has any?'

'Grown rich and comfortable on his dishonest pickings! Oh, Matt. Must we fight over a miserable provost? I swear I do not relish the rest of the journey if you are to continue this way. You will . . . . '

'I am not going to London.'

There was a moment's silence.

'Not going?'

William looked at him in disbelief. 'Not going to London — and all on account of a tuppenny provost! Sweet Heavens, what ails you, Matt?'

'I am sick at heart . . . . This was a peaceful march, do you recall the words. No harm to any man, he said. That's what Flamank told us. Yet already we have killed a man. And we are still miles from London. What will it be at Wells? A couple more killings — and at Salisbury a dozen mayhap? And will we still be welcome at each town and fed and sheltered like brothers? News travels fast. More likely they will shrink from us. Bar their doors and close their shutters!'

There was more than a grain of truth in what he said and

385

William was momentarily chastened; but before he could answer there was a tap at the door.

'Pray enter,' said Matthew, and Mistress Allen came in with an assortment of bottles on a tray.

'Now I won't hear "Nay,"' she said to Matthew, 'for what your poor wife would say if she should see you in this state, black and blue from head to toe t'would break her heart — your face cut and a tooth broke! I've chervil water to break up the blood and bishops-weed and honey to take away the colour. So inside and outside we shall soon have you fair as a peach and none any the wiser.'

She began to dab the sticky lotion on to Matthew's face, ignoring his protests.

'They say a man was killed. Is that right?'

Matthew nodded.

'There now. Who'd have thought it,' she said without surprise. 'We live in dangerous times and that's a fact. Do they know who did it?'

'No,' said Matthew quickly. ''Twas not one man but many.'

'Tut, tut! There's a terrible thing. Terrible . . .' she said. 'Now you drink this and never mind the flavour. Always wrinkled up his nose, my son did, when he was a lad. Poison, he used to call it and it does have an unfortunate flavour I grant you but . . . .'

There was a brisk knocking on the street door and William looked at his brother. 'That's them,' he said. 'They are ready to go. Will you change your mind?'

'No.'

'If you decide later you could catch us up by . . . .'

'I'll not be coming to London, William.'

'You must please your self.'

'Go to London in this state,' exclaimed Mistress Allen. 'With nigh on every bone broken in your body! I should think not.'

But Matthew's eyes were on William.

'I'll be on my way then,' said William and his eyes met Matthews's in an unspoken appeal.

'I shan't speak of your part in it,' Matthew said. 'Twould only grieve the womenfolk.'

'My thanks.'

'And William — God be with you.'

'Aye — and you. I'll see you anon.'

He turned away abruptly and they heard him go downstairs.

There were greetings and a shout of laughter. The street door, slamming behind him, separated the brothers for the first time in their lives.

CHAPTER TWENTY-ONE

When the news reached the King of the rebels progress he was both surprised and alarmed. Somehow a small localized grievance had become a rebellion to be reckoned with. Henry asked for further information and was told that the numbers were growing daily. The men had left Taunton and passed through Wells, where they had been joined by Lord Audley.

This last item was disturbing, for Audley had a private quarrel with the King and obviously saw the situation as an opportunity to settle old scores. His accession to leadership of the rebellion subtly altered the venture — in the eyes of the King if not the eyes of the rebels — for Lord Audley was of the old nobility and a force to be reckoned with.

His alignment with their cause was perhaps less fortunate for the Cornishmen than they imagined for his presence alarmed the King and prompted him to consider serious defensive measures. More than ten thousand now moved towards London, and it was the King's duty to ensure the protection of the townspeople. From Henry's point of view, it couldn't have happened at a worse time, for he was already preparing to repulse a possible invasion from the Scots. The eight thousand men already preparing for war with the Scots were now retained in London under Lord Daubeney's command.

A smaller force under the Earl of Surrey was despatched northwards, with instructions to take only defensive measures, until Daubeney's main force was free to reinforce them there.

Unaware of the reception being planned for them, the rebels moved on peaceably enough through Salisbury and Winchester, gathering recruits, on through Sussex and finally reached Kent. Here they met with a set back. The

Kentish men were disappointingly loyal to King Henry, so the rebels turned west again towards Farnham. From there, they passed through Guildford, Banstead Down and reached Blackheath on the sixteenth of June where they made camp on a hill overlooking London across the river.

Lord Daubeney's force, now waited at St George's Field and the King joined them there with his own army, making a satisfying total of twenty-five thousand men.

William, dismounted, and held a flagon of wine to his lips. Beside him John Lattimer pointed excitedly.

'The River Thames!' he said. 'London's own river. I never thought to see it so soon.'

'But you did reckon to see it then?' said William. He wiped the flagon's neck with his sleeve and passed it to his friend who drank noisily before replying.

'Oh, aye,' he said. 'I'd have seen it sooner or later. Where's your brother? I've not seen him since Taunton.'

William flushed slightly. 'He was injured,' he said. 'He slipped and fell in the market place and was near crushed to death! He wasn't fit to walk, so I bade him stay and go home when he was recovered. He didn't care to give up but there was no other way.'

He thought this version a reasonable approximation of the truth and John appeared satisfied. The two men looked at the river for a while longer then made themselves comfortable. Camping overnight had become a way of life and they were soon settled with their saddles for pillows and their cloaks for blankets. They sprawled completely at ease, their heads close together so they might talk with some degree of privacy. The same matter was disturbing both of them.

'Did you hear of last night's doings?' asked John, his voice low.

'Aye, but twas abortive, thank the Lord,' said William. 'Why, what a shame if it had come to nought after all we've been through. Twas a bad business.'

The previous night, news had reached the rebels of the large numbers amassing against them and for the first time it became clear to them that the King no longer viewed them as loyal and misused Cornishmen with a just grievance. Suddenly he saw them as dangerous insurgents. It was not a pleasant thought and some of them had grown uneasy, and decided to seek the King's pardon, for he spoke of treason and rebellion and even a confrontation.

'I can understand that some of our men are timid,' said William, 'and many have no stomach for a battle. But to sue for a pardon! God's life! A pardon for what? What are we guilty of?'

'We *have* killed his provost,' John reminded him but William dismissed the idea as of no significance.

'An unfortunate accident,' he said. 'There was an argument and tempers flared. A pity, I grant you, but hardly a crime. No, tis the offer to betray our leaders that sickens me. After all they have done for us! Sweet Heaven! To offer them up like pawns in a game of chess! That takes some believing.'

His friend was silent. It was the painful truth that some among them had gone secretly to Daubeney's camp with 'panic terms' — an offer that Audley, Flamank and the smith would be 'surrendered' in return for a general pardon and a safe passage home for the rest of the rebels. The offer had been turned down.

'It was a false move,' said William. 'It showed the King we are divided in our cause.'

His friend nodded. 'Tis said we lost a lot of men last night,' he said. 'They crept away like whipped dogs, with their tails between their legs! Nigh on a thousand, I'm told.'

'I don't believe it!' William exclaimed. 'I heard four hundred. Yet more will go tonight I'll wager.'

'Can you blame them?' asked John. 'They have wives and children and they did not come for war. They came in peace and now believe they were misled.'

'How can they think so!' cried William. 'Is it our fault that the King takes arms against us?'

'Try telling my wife that,' laughed John. 'If I am killed I doubt she will take much comfort from it!'

'So, you have a wife? You did not speak of her before. How long have you been wed?' asked William.

'Nigh on a year — and Sarah is big with child already.'

'That sounds like a boast!' laughed William.

'And why not,' said John. 'I never was a man to waste time, but must needs get on with the job. You should find yourself a wife and settle down. There's nothing like it, I'm telling you.'

A shadow crossed William's face and he laughed shortly. 'Let's drink to that,' he said, and held the flagon aloft between them. 'Here's to life and a willing woman!'

He drank quickly and handed it to John, who took a mouthful then held it aloft in his turn.

'And here's to tomorrow,' John toasted.

'Tomorrow!' echoed William and his gaze travelled over the darkening field which swarmed with men and hummed with the murmur of their voices.

Already fires were lit for the air was chill. They glowed like jewels against the dark ground and sweetened the air with wood smoke.

'Aye,' whispered John. 'Tomorrow.'

By the next morning their numbers were sadly depleted; but those that remained were in reasonable spirits and eager to come to grips with the opposition. Tension was high all that day, but no move was made by either side.

In the evening, the rebels held a conference of war and archers and guns were sent to hold the bridge at Deptford Strand. Apart from this, there was virtually no plan of action for the battle; for their leaders were not skilled in warfare and great reliance was placed in the Lord's intervention on the side of the just. The King, meanwhile, planned his campaign. At dawn, the Earls of Oxford, Essex and Suffolk would take their men and surround the hill on which the rebels were camped. The bridge under Deptford Strand would be taken by spearmen led by Sir Humphrey Stanley and Daubeny's force would follow across the river as soon as possible. As archers, both John and William were at the bridge, delighted to be in the forefront of the action. The night passed quietly enough but they slept little.

At first light, they were alerted by sounds behind them and peered anxiously through the mist. Hoofbeats, the clash of steel and the shouts of battle hung in the air. 'They are on all sides!' said John. 'All round the hill.'

'And in front of us!' shouted William exultantly and his first arrow sped on its way.

'Jesus!' cried John and his followed.

Ahead of them Stanley's spearmen appeared out of the mist, walking steadily towards them in grim rows. The rebel guns exploded into life and clouds of acrid powder hung in the still air. A number of the advancing men fell beneath the feet of those who followed them, but then another volley of long Cornish arrows added to the confusion.

'I hit one!' cried William 'I swear I did!'

He snatched another arrow from his quiver and released it. Stanley's men were well disciplined and continued to advance, despite the intermittent havoc wrought by the guns and the rain of arrows, some of which fell on them from above and others from in front. Now some of the spearmen had set foot on the bridge and were attacking the gunners. From behind William, a group of rebels rushed to their aid, swords drawn, and were immediately engaged in heavy fighting.

They were ill-prepared, wearing no protective clothing except such makeshift armour as they had been able to devise, but they struggled bravely against overwhelming odds. William sent another arrow into the advancing men, but by then the two sides were so mingled that it was impossible to carry on. More of Stanley's men gained the bridge and finally his standard drew near, carried aloft by one of his horsemen.

'Too close,' cried William for the nearest spearmen were now only yards away and it was not possible to loose their arrows at such short distance.

Glancing around, he saw that most of the archers had already withdrawn a matter of twenty yards and, choosing their moment, he and John ducked their heads and made a run for it.

'Just in time', grinned John. 'It was getting too hot for my liking. When you can see the whites of their eyes, they're too close! I wish I knew what was going on further back. There's a devilish lot of noise. Here they come again!'

A group of spearmen burst through the mêlée and rushed towards them. One of John's arrows sank into a shoulder, William's into an eye. Then he was knocked sideways by a passing horse; as Daubeny charged across the bridge at the head of the main force. The cavalry thundered past behind him, scattering their own men and the rebels with complete indifference.

'You're hit!' said John and William was surprised to find that he had indeed received a gash across his ear and temple. Now it began to sting and blood trickled down his cheek, but it was a superficial wound and merely served to inspire in him a desire for revenge. Now swordsmen appeared on the bridge and William, throwing caution to the wind, stood boldly in front of one and sent an arrow straight into his heart. The man dropped his sword and clutched at the arrow trying to jerk it free. He stumbled, his mouth open, eyes rolling, and pitched forward at William's feet. Snatching out his dagger, he leant down and dispatched him. But more swordsmen replaced him in ever increasing numbers, and the Cornishmen were forced to give ground until none remained on the bridge except the dead and dying.

William looked round for John who beckoned him towards the fighting which was taking place to their right.

'They have taken Daubeney!' he shouted and the two men raced across the grass towards a solitary horseman surrounded by men on foot. Before they reached him, however, the mounted man broke away from his captors and raced towards a corner of the field, where his forces were to be seen in vastly superior numbers.

'God's wounds! They have let him go!' cried William. 'What a prize to slip away!'

He hesitated, wondering which way to turn. Everywhere the rebels were losing ground. It would soon be over.

'Damnation,' muttered John. 'It goes against us.'

A horseman appeared suddenly from among the nearest group of fighting men and galloped past in retreat. William looked at his friend in disbelief.

'The smith!' he whispered. 'I don't believe it!'

The two men threw themselves to one side as a group of the King's cavalry thundered past in pursuit. A roar went up from the King's men, and moments later word passed among the rebels 'Flamank is taken!'

Many of the rebels, sadly discouraged, began to flee the field; others threw down their weapons and gave themselves up. A minority fought on, but there was no longer any hope.

While John and William wondered what to do, a number of men broke away from a bitter engagement halfway up the hill.

As they moved towards them John cried. 'The man in the centre — tis Audley!'

It was. Fierce fighting broke out and William and John were swept into it. The bows were useless at close quarters and they threw them down and used their daggers. There were shouts from elsewhere on the field as others realized the importance of the struggle taking place, and men converged on them from all directions. The air shuddered with the sound of steel on steel and the cries of the wounded. Someone tried to pull Audley from his horse and John wrestled with him. One of Stanley's horsemen now intervened and, bringing up his sword, prepared to bring it down on John's skull.

'Would you then!' grunted William and he threw himself forward. At the same time Audley's horse sprang suddenly sideways. William, falling under it, received a blow from the horse's hoof which split his head open. Minutes later he was dead.

John stood at the window and stared unseeingly across the garden. Elizabeth sat at the table, the letter from Mark Lessor unrolled beside her. Her eyes were red from weeping.

'Matthew had no right to leave him!' John said harshly. 'He should have brought him back with him from Taunton.'

'Don't speak that way, John,' Elizabeth begged him. 'You know William would never heed Matthew. Nothing and no one would have persuaded him to turn back. Matthew is suffering enough. Don't add to his burden, for pity's sake.'

'Where is he?'

'He took a horse and rode off. He needs to be on his own.'

'He *is* on his own,' said John bitterly and tears sprang anew in Elizabeth's eyes. She longed to take him in her arms comfort him but earlier, when she had tried, he had brushed her away impatiently. Now, when they desperately needed each other, there was half a room between them. John, proud as ever, would not admit his need for consolation.

'I wish we could have brought him home,' she said. 'I

would like to think he was near us. It grieves me that he must lie in a common grave.'

'Is it too late?' asked John. 'Will you read the letter again? I have scarce taken in anything but his death.'

She hesitated. 'Will you not read it yourself?' she asked.

'No, you read it from the beginning.'

'Oh no John! Not all of it.'

'Please Elizabeth.'

She blinked back her tears, picked up the letter and reluctantly began to read the terrible news.

Greetings to you my dear friend John and to Elizabeth, also, from your friend Mark Lessor, this day of June 1497. I write with heavy heart of grievous tidings but I know not when you will hear account of the matter. King Henry's forces did lately engage with rebels from Cornwall and the West Countries who marched on London in great numbers, some say nigh on ten thousand, but I know not if this be true. You will know William was amongst them. At Deptford Strand there were killed eight of Lord Stanley's men, but of the Cornishmen around two hundred souls. Many more are taken as prisoners. William, God rest his soul, is among those killed. I could scarce believe it, but did search for him and saw his body with my own eyes. His head was broke and he must have died on the instant which is to lighten your grief. He lay in a grave with his fellow and there I said prayers for him as did many others for pity of it all.

Of the leaders Flamank, the lawyer, died quietly. Not so the smith. Tis said he fled to Greenwich but was pursued and taken there. He was dragged through the streets on a hurdle and boasted to all, showing no remorse but vanity throughout and was hanged at Tyburn. Lord Audley was drawn through the city also in paper armour as befits his downfall and was beheaded on Tower Hill. I tell you all this that you may rest content that such men have met their rightful punishment that would corrupt the minds of innocent men to rise against the King. The smith and the lawyer's heads are both set up in the city for all to mock at, but the Lord Audley is buried in the church of Blackfriars within Ludgate, though for my part he was as guilty as his two fellows being a Lord and like to know better.

And now I conclude this letter which for my life I would rather not have written remembering as yesterday William's birth and not expecting to learn so soon of his untimely passing. I commit you, John, to the loving care of your wife Elizabeth and pray you both to visit me when your mourning is done. In sorrow this day.'

Neither of them spoke as Elizabeth laid down the letter. She crossed the room to stand beside him and slipped her hand into his. She squeezed it, but he made no sign that he noticed.

'Don't keep a distance between us,' she begged. 'I want to help you and I need help, too.'

'He was not your son,' said John tonelessly and she drew her breath sharply at the pain of his words.

'He was like a son to me, John,' she said and her voice trembled in spite of her efforts to remain calm. 'He was barely four when you came here and I have loved him ever since. That is a lot of love. I cannot believe I will not see him . . . .'

She buried her face against the silk of his sleeve, clinging to him, willing him to soften his heart and turn to her.

'John, I beg you,' she sobbed. 'Take me in your arms and comfort me. Let us comfort each other.'

'He is gone and there's an end to it,' said John.

He tried to release himself from her clasp, but she fought against his hands until he held her wrists and kept her at arm's length.

397

'Why do you weep?' he asked tonelessly. 'Can you bring him back?'

'Oh John,' cried Elizabeth. 'What is the matter with you? Let the tears flow for the lad that is your own flesh and blood. Do not be ashamed to show that you love him!'

'Loved,' he corrected her yet again and there was an agony of bitterness in his voice.

'*Don't* say that!' she pleaded. 'I know he is dead. I know his life is ended. It is hard enough for us to bear. Why must you make it harder?' At that moment they were suddenly aware of a sound behind them and turned to find Martha in the doorway. Her eyes puffy, her fingers twisting and fumbling at her apron.

'Master Tucker is here,' she said, 'and tis nearly "four hours." Will you eat a little?'

Elizabeth looked at John and he shook his head.

'No thank you, Martha,' she said. 'Perhaps later . . . and shall Joseph come in, John?'

'Aye, show him in,' said John, 'but I shall ride out.'

'Let me come with you!' she cried.

He shook his head. 'I must be alone. Forgive me,' and with that he strode past her out of the room.

The two women looked at each other, helplessly.

'He doesn't mean to hurt you, ma'am,' said Martha seeing the misery in Elizabeth's face. 'He's taken it so hard.'

'I know . . . .'

Joseph Tucker came into the room and Elizabeth turned to him. He stood for a moment searching for the right words then, finding none, held out his arms. Elizabeth, after a moment's hesitation, moved into them and gave herself up to the luxury of weeping, while he stroked her hair and clumsily murmuring the words of comfort which John had been unable to speak. Martha retired to the kitchen where she cut herself a slice of saffron cake and left it uneaten; as she stared unseeingly into the hearth and sifted through her memories for glimpses of the lad they would never see again.

That night, Elizabeth lay in the fourposter bed, wide awake, her ears straining to catch the sound of John's return. It was nearly three o'clock and Matthew was not home either. She had left the bed curtains undrawn and the door ajar so that she could hear Della in the next room and would feel less alone. She lay in dark misery and thought angrily of her body, despising its flatness, hating its refusal to grow John another child. Such a darkness and warmth within her could surely succour one more child before she was too old. If only she could offer him one more heir. If only . . . She sighed deeply. But would that comfort him, she wondered? Does one child ever compensate for the loss of another? Suppose she were pregnant and he didn't care. Suppose, after all this time he didn't want her to bear him a child. She went cold at the thought. He never spoke of it these days — but was that to spare her feelings? To spare her shame? What was wrong with her body that it was so unreceptive to his seed?

Suddenly she sat up in bed, her heart racing. Della had spoken one day about a mandrake root; an old 'remedy' against childlessness. 'They say the mandrake only grows neath a gibbet,' the girl had told her. 'The life stuff drops from the corpse as it rots and feeds the plants. It won't grow nowhere else and you must find the right root, ma'am,' she had said giggling. ''Tis no use else. Only a man shaped root will do.'

Elizabeth had been puzzled. 'Man shaped?' she repeated.

'You know, ma'am' Della giggled again. 'Two roots so.' She held out two fingers. 'Like his legs.'

'I see,' said Elizabeth. 'A double root.'

'And more, ma'am!' she winked at Elizabeth, exasperated by her slowness. 'Two joined roots for his legs and in the middle — a wee bit more!'

She would try Della's remedy. She would go, now, to the gibbet outside the town and search for the precious root. Or was it too late? The plant should be gathered at midnight? Did the time really matter? It was the root itself that was important. If she went now John need never know. It was such agony to lie passive and lonely in the large bed, the expedition would relieve her feeling of helplessness.

Slipping to her knees beside the bed, she closed her eyes and prayed hurriedly. 'Look down on me sweet Mother of God, and help protect me from all the rigours of the night. Bless my purpose, I pray you, that I may bear a child. Amen.'

Five minutes later, she was letting herself out of the house. She ran to the stables and saddled one of the horses. The others stirred curiously at the light of her lantern and Eric put his sleepy head over the edge of the loft.

'Go back to sleep,' she told him, but he protested he must come with her 'wheresover it be'.

But Elizabeth was adamant. For the remedy to work she must go alone. He was not entirely convinced but, while he hesitated, she rode out of the yard a great deal more nervous than she would admit even to herself.

It was a beautiful night. A large moon hung above her and stars pierced the dark sky. A soft breeze rustled the trees on either side of the highway and stirred her hair which fell freely to her shoulders. She wore a riding cloak over her kirtle but her feet were bare — so hurriedly had she made her departure from the safety of her bed.

She rode at a walking pace, soothed by the darkness which flowed around her, enveloping her making her feel invisible under the vast sky. Her nervousness faded. It was as though she no longer had substance and was therefore no longer vulnerable. Suddenly, a great calm filled her spirit! She was convinced her mission would be graced with success. She would find the root. 'And it will help me' she told herself, whispering into the darkness. She felt tranquil.

Even the staccato fluttering of a bat did not alarm her. An owl hooted and was answered and she smiled . . . .

She was nearly at the crossroads where the gibbet stood, when a small night creature — a rabbit or a stoat, perhaps — ran in front of her horse causing it to rear in fright, casting her to the ground. She lay there, crumpled and breathless, while the palfrey hesitated close by; then turned and cantered away into the darkness.

Shocked and bruised she sat up slowly, feeling herself for broken bones. There were none, but her fall had shattered her new-found calm. Now, her heart raced and she was suddenly prey to many nameless fears. Alone in the darkness, barefoot and without a mount, she would be an easy victim for a cut-throat. Her hand was bleeding, presumably cut or grazed in the fall. Fortunately, she could not see properly by the light of the moon and need not know the extent of her injuries until later. Her lantern lay on its side in the grass, the light extinguished. Ahead of her, she made out the shape of the gibbet, its outline stark against the curve of the hill, its grim burden swinging and creaking in its chains. It was a thief who hung there, his body shrivelled and cold, his eyes pecked dry by marauding birds. Elizabeth shuddered at the sombre spectacle. She pulled her cloak tighter, pulling the large collar protectively about her face, shrinking into its welcome warmth; for the shock had robbed her body of heat and left her shivering. She stared up at the wooden structure and its pitiful captive.

'Under that "thing" the mandrake plant should grow,' she told herself. 'I need but a few leaves and a root. Twill take but a moment . . . .'

She moved forward a few paces, one hand to her ribs which ached abominably, aware also that her left ankle pained her when she put her full weight on it. Underneath the body she hesitated once more, then fell to her knees averting her gaze from the feet which were no more than bones. Feeling among the grass, her fingers found leaves. 'No, not these,' she muttered. 'They are too small and rough. Della said large leaves and smooth . . . . Oh, for the lantern. A curse on the rabbit or whatever it was . . . . Ah, what's this?' Her exploratory fingers had discovered a small clump of large leaves. 'Smooth and broad! These are they, I dare swear it! So . . . a few leaves more . . . and now a root . . . .'

She scrabbled at the soil trying to loosen the root of the plant. Gradually, she worked it free and was on the point of wrenching it from the ground in triumph when the sound of hoofbeats came to her ears. She froze with fear, her heart thumping painfully. Where could she hide? There was no cover. Terrified, she decided they were coming her way. How many of them, she wondered. Twas no lone rider but she reckoned at least two.

'Sweet Mother of Christ, help me!' she begged. With no means of defending herself and nowhere to hide, her plight was serious. A blind panic seized her. Hardly knowing what she did, she wrenched out the mandrake root. As it came free, she lost her balance and toppled against the corpse. The bony feet brushed her cheek and at the same moment the horsemen clattered into view. In spite of herself, she let out a thin, high scream of terror and immediately they reined in, only yards away.

Scrambling to her feet she began to run but they pursued her. She tripped, stumbled, righted herself and somehow ran on. Aware that she could never outstrip them, she turned aside from the track and forced a way through the stunted bush that edged the highway. Scratched and sobbing for breath, she glanced back. Unable to persuade the horses to follow, they had ridden further down the track, seeking a gap in the vegetation. They found one and were upon her in a matter of seconds. A hand reached down and grasped her hair. Her head was pulled round and she faced her captor. 'Elizabeth!' he cried.

Fear and shock had robbed her of speech and she could only stare up into the beloved face of her husband. She turned and saw that the second rider was Matthew, and that

402

he held the reins of her own horse. Opening her mouth to explain, she found herself unable to put the words into any kind of sequence and shaking her head, held out the precious leaves and root in a pathetic plea for understanding.

'In God's name!' cried John and he sprang from his horse in time to catch her as she swayed forward. As she lost consciousness, her last thought was that she was in his arms at last.

CHAPTER TWENTY-TWO

Blanche looked up at her husband and laughed.

'You will wear out that letter,' she teased him. 'I swear you have read it ten times if not more!'

He smiled. ''Tis come all the way from Yorkshire,' he said. 'If I read it but once then twas hardly worth the journey.' He shook his head. 'So this new Richard of York is in Scotland now and he and King James like two birds in a nest! The King has even given him a wife, the Lady Catherine Gordon. I cannot but believe the man must be genuine. Why else would the King of Scotland be honouring him in this way?'

Blanche sat little Sophie on her knees and, holding her hands, gave her a 'ride', bumping her up and down until she laughed with excitement.

'King Henry or King Richard — what does it matter? Whoever sits on the throne there will still be battles to fight. We shall still be taxed to pay for them.'

Matthew referred to the letter again.

'It seems,' he said, 'that Richard and his fleet have set sail for Cornwall and mean to hold the West Country against Henry.'

'And we in Devon are becoming anxious,' said Blanche. 'Papa says the Earl of Devon is raising an army and will garrison them in Exeter. I warrant Catherine will enjoy the excitement. Whoops! Down she goes!' She parted her knees to let Sophie slide between them much to the child's delight.

'You will over excite her,' said Matthew. 'She will never sleep tonight.'

'But she loves it,' said Blanche. 'Here, go to your Papa, Sophie and let me rest, you are too heavy for me, little tub of lard!'

The child was certainly plump, but looked the picture of robust health with podgy, rosy cheeks and a dimpled chin. Her eyes were as blue as cornflowers and her blonde hair hung straight and fine to her shoulders.

She was the image of Andrew but by tacit agreement it was never mentioned. Matthew took the little girl and raised her above his head, where she kicked and squealed with obvious enjoyment. Blanche picked up the letter and scanned it again.

'And another cousin is gone with Richard,' she said. ''Tis to be hoped he is spared. The Kendals have given enough sons in that cause. I think I would have kept the lad at home.'

'You might have tried,' said Matthew. 'The lad ran off — like Lydia's Alan — and then what is to be done? Some young men must be always fighting or they are not happy. They enjoy the taste of battle.'

A shadow crept into his eyes and Blanche knew that his thoughts were with William. His twin's death had had a profound effect on him. All his life Matthew had leaned unknowingly against William. Had drawn strength from him, taken a lead from him. Suddenly the prop was knocked away and he stood alone in the world. He was quieter, blaming himself still for not preventing William's death. No one could convince him otherwise and he lived with the remorse. 'I still sense William,' he told Blanche one day. 'Still hear his voice and not only at night. He is still with me. I feel that if I turn quickly enough I shall see him. Often the bed creaks when I am still, as though he climbs in beside me. He cannot be gone away for we are part of each other.'

He had turned to Blanche to assuage his loneliness. She had stroked his head and kissed away the tears and hoped that as the months passed he would grow stronger. And he had.

'You will not go, Matthew,' she asked. 'To Exeter?'

'To enlist?' he questioned. 'No, rest assured. I have no

stomach for it. They may beat their drums and unfurl their banners. I shall be deaf and blind to them! But if Richard takes Exeter, why then he will command the West Country. And Henry will come post haste. Oh, there will be no end to it!'

Blanche held out her arms for their daughter, and Matthew returned her.

As she went to leave the room, she paused at the door and turning back, said 'I think your mother is unwell. Do you not notice a change in her? Her face is thinner and her eyes are large in her face. How old is she, Matt?'

He shrugged. 'More than forty,' he said. 'Mayhap nearer fifty. I do not know.'

'As old as that? Then I am mistaken. She has that look about her — I thought she was with child.'

Elizabeth was with child. At forty-eight years she was pregnant for the second time and eleven years after her first child. She was happy and frightened. Forty-eight years old. Almost an old woman, almost too late — but she was with child and the ridiculous feeling of triumph persisted through the worst moments of panic. She told no one, not even John. She feared the surprised looks, the anxious mutterings, the dire warnings. She knew exactly how it would be. They would discuss her in her absence, and would follow her anxiously with their eyes and they would steal her joy. She decided to say nothing until she must. It amused her to remember how, indirectly, the mandrake root had worked its charm. The child had been conceived that night from their love-making — a desperate attempt to alleviate their separate griefs. They had come together frantically, silently — an oasis of passion in a desert of misery. The next day, John had ridden out with the hawk and she had prepared the root, grating it finely, adding honey and water, simmering it until it was a thick syrupy jelly. It was not unpleasant. She poured it into a small bottle, placed the stopper securely and hid it. She drank a spoonful each night on retiring to bed and it was soon gone. Ironically, there had never been an opportunity to test its potency, for John's indifference returned and they did not make love again.

Weeks passed. Again and again Elizabeth decided to tell John about the child, but each time she hesitated, finding an excuse for not doing so. But at last, she determined to break the news and waited until one night as they lay in bed together, the candles extinguished, the house still. He lay beside her, pretending sleep, facing away from her.

'John, are you awake?' she asked, although she knew by his breathing that he was. He made a slight sound, almost a grunt, but gave no other answer.

'I must talk with you. John, wake up, I beg you.'

She touched his shoulder and he gave a twitch and said.

'What do you say? What is it? I was sleeping.'

'I must talk with you, John.'

'Let it wait until the morrow,' he replied. 'I have had a long day and am weary.'

'I'm sorry, John,' she said, 'but twill not wait longer. And I believe you will find it pleasant hearing.'

Sighing heavily, he rolled on to his back and turned his head towards her. She could see his profile outlined against the light from the window.

'We are going to have another child, John,' she said. 'In March of next year.'

'A child? At your age? Tis not possible!' he gasped.

'But tis so, John. I have seen the doctor.'

'You are pleased, then,' he said.

'I am. And you, John? Surely you are pleased. We have waited a long time.'

'Too long, perhaps,' he said soberly.

A panic rose within her but she fought it back.

'But better a son now than never,' she said lightly. 'I feel certain twill be a son. Say you are pleased, my love, or else you take away my joy.'

'It will be good to have a son,' he said, choosing his words carefully. 'Aye, I am pleased.'

'You hide your joy, then,' she said, her tone sharpened by her bitter disappointment. 'Something troubles you, John. Can you not tell me?'

He shook his head.

'Have I wronged you in some way?' she asked.

'No, never. Tis not of your doing.'

'Then whose?' she asked.

He shook his head again and turned, pulling her clumsily towards him. Kissing her lightly on the forehead he told her. 'Enough of this. You are with child and I am delighted. We must take good care of you.'

'But are you happy?' she begged. 'You speak the words, but I hear no happiness in your voice. Oh, John, I fear lately that you do not love me. You stay away. I miss your company. I speak to you and you are far away — where I know not.' She faltered, 'But if you truly love me then I'm content.'

He listened to the little speech without a word and she waited anxiously for reassurance.

'My heart is heavy,' he said at last. 'I don't deny it. I have — certain regrets. I must think on them and act as I see fit.'

'But let me help you!' Elizabeth cried.

'No, that's not the way,' he said. 'Trust me, I beg you. The problem is of my own making. I must find a solution, and will, I promise you.'

'Tell me. Let me help you!'

'I can tell you nothing!' he cried and his tone grew suddenly harsh. 'I say we will speak no more of it.'

She longed to say 'I love you', but the words died on her lips and her heart ached with misery for the estrangement between them. As she lay in the darkness later, listening to his breathing as he slept, she clutched desperately at the

408

thought of the child within her. Another woman, she feared, had robbed her of her husband's love. But no one could rob her of his child.

Blanche reached the church door and hesitated, with her hand on the latch. She glanced behind her to reassure herself that she was not observed. Then she lifted the latch and pushed open the door. It swung back creaking, and she closed it behind her. It was darker inside the church than outside and, as she waited for her eyes to adapt to the change, there was a sound to her left and Father Marryat hurried towards her, a finger to his lips to silence her greeting. He pointed and Blanche saw Elizabeth kneeling before the altar. The old man shrugged despairingly.

'Tis so every day,' he whispered. 'I thought you should know. Hour upon hour, kneeling thus, her eyes on the Virgin Mary.'

'Is she praying?' asked Blanche, keeping her voice low.

'Her lips are still,' he said, 'but she may pray inwardly in her heart. She looks so strange and when I would speak with her, she looks at me as if a stranger. What ails her?'

Blanche sighed heavily.

'I cannot say, Father. She will tell no one.'

'Not even her husband?'

'He shows little concern,' she said reluctantly. 'There is a constraint between them these last few weeks.'

Suddenly Elizabeth stood up and they moved hurriedly back into the shadows. She rubbed at her knees and then stared around the church as though surprised to find herself there. Her face was drawn, her expression haggard. The once beautiful hair, free of a restraining head-dress, hung loosely across her shoulders and with her right hand she fingered the lace at the neck of her gown. For a moment, she stared straight at them but without recognition, and

409

then walked heavily to the side of the church and slid down to a sitting position on the floor, her knees pulled up, her head resting upon them.

'Let us leave her. You have seen enough,' whispered the old priest and Blanche followed him back into the wintry sunshine outside.

'She looks so thin,' said the old priest. 'Is she ill?'

'She does not eat,' said Blanche. 'Martha grumbles and coaxes and cooks her favourite recipe to tempt her appetite, but she takes scarcely a mouthful and the rest grows cold upon the trencher.'

'And you say she is six months gone with child?' said Father Marryat. 'She does not show it. Are you certain of it?'

'Quite certain,' she told him. 'The doctor has examined her.'

'But at her age — is it wise?'

Blanche shrugged helplessly. 'She has wanted another child ever since her son died, but I think we all doubted she would have one now.'

'And her husband — is he not pleased?'

'He will not speak of it. He is rarely at Heron these past weeks. When he is home they are rarely together.'

She hesitated, then blurted out, 'I too begin to fear for her mind, Father. She looks so ill at ease and she takes no interest in Sophie whom she adores. I plan the menus now. Retter deals with much of the accounting for the mine. I hoped you might speak to her, Father. You are not the family and she might confide in you.'

'But I have tried to talk to her,' he protested. 'Every morning I pause and smile and bid her "Good morrow". She smiles briefly but then falls to staring again, and later she moves and sits leaning against the wall, as you saw. 'Tis unnatural. There is no doubt she suffers grievously. You must surely ask the doctor to call again.'

'I will do so, Father,' said Blanche, 'but I doubt she will

see him . . . I wish that Matt was home, or even Stephen.'

'Speak to your father,' said the old man. 'He might be of help. He has a wise head on those broad shoulders. But now try to take her home with you. We will go together and try and rouse her. And do not look so unhappy. She is in God's house here, and no harm shall come to her. But she must eat or how will the child thrive? Come.'

They went back into the church and Elizabeth turned at their approach.

'Ah, my dear Elizabeth,' said Father Marryat, holding out a hand. 'Come along, my dear. Take my hand, that's it, and up you come. Tis cold in here and you'd best be off with your daughter-in-law who is come to fetch you — that's the way . . . .'

Carefully, Elizabeth stood up, brushed down her clothes and smiled faintly at Blanche who put an arm round her shoulders.

'Sophie is asking for you,' said Blanche brightly, 'and sends me to fetch you. She says you have promised her a pomander and she grows impatient.'

Elizabeth's smile deepened. 'Oh, the pomander!' she said. 'Yes, I did speak of it. I shall make her one with cloves and an orange. I forgot . . . .'

'That young Sophie is as bright as a button!' exclaimed Father Marryat.

He opened the door and Blanche and Elizabeth stepped out into the sunshine.

'Will you come to Heron,' Blanche asked him. 'You are welcome to join us for supper this evening.'

But the old man shook his head. 'I am eating with the abbot,' he said. 'He has guests and I am invited to join them. One of them comes from my home town and we shall have much to talk about. But I will call in tomorrow, if I may.'

'Please do,' said Blanche. 'Now we must be on our way. God be with you, Father, and thank you.'

'God's blessing on you both,' he said. 'I will pray for you.'

The old man watched the two women make their way along the path and out of the churchyard, and his heart was filled with pity for the once proud and beautiful Elizabeth.

CHAPTER TWENTY-THREE

1497 EXETER

'Aunt! Where are you?'

The door of the small house slammed behind Catherine as she dropped her basket full of shopping on to the kitchen floor and called again.

'Aunt! I have news. The whole town is abuzz with it. Oh, there you are.'

Lydia looked towards her but saw only the shadow of a person. Catherine took her hand and knelt beside her.

'There is an army outside Exeter, Aunt!' she told her excitedly. 'An army – they say there are thousands of men. Tis Prince Richard, not dead after all but escaped and . . . .'

'Child, wait a while,' begged Lydia. 'Start again, I beseech you. You say there is an army – outside Exeter?'

'Aye, tis true. I have spoke with Leonard and have seen. They are camped outside the walls. Inside they are digging . . . .'

'Digging? What are they digging, this army? I do not understand.'

'Aunt!' she cried. 'There are thousands of soldiers drawn up outside the walls, at the North and East Gates. Tis Prince Richard come to claim the throne . . . .'

'Prince Richard, Duke of York? But he's dead, child. Murdered, they say, in the Tower, poor little . . . .'

'But he is not murdered, Aunt!' cried Catherine. 'That's what I am telling you. He is alive and claims back the throne from the Welshman!'

'And Leonard is helping him, you say? Your Leonard?'

The girl laughed. 'He is not my Leonard yet, Aunt, though he will be soon, I warrant. But no, he is helping to defend the town, under Edgecombe. Sir Thomas Trenchard is here also and Carew and their companies. And they have closed the town gates and posterns and pile up faggots to fire against them.'

Lydia paled. 'Oh Cathy, child. Stay with me until my husband comes. I fear to be alone. Oh, that I had my sight! Do the Polegates know you are with me? Can you stay awhile?'

'Of course, Aunt. I told them I would spend the day with you.'

'Then lock the door, while there is yet time,' she cried, 'and close the shutters. Why doesn't John come home? Will he have heard, think you?'

'Indeed he will, Aunt — everyone has heard!'

'Then go and find him, child,' said Lydia fearfully. 'Go and find him. I will bolt the doors after you and you must knock three times on your return that I may know tis you. Make haste, I beg you. I shall not rest easy until he is home. Run, child.'

'I have left the basket in the kitchen . . . . '

'Forget the basket, child, and go fetch my husband!'

Outside, the streets were filled with hurrying people criss-crossing the town in all directions. Many carried bags of provisions to lay in against a long siege; others were on their way to the market for the same purpose. Wagons and carts trundled along carrying brushwood and logs to be piled against the gates which were all securely closed, bolted and locked to the dismay of those citizens wishing to flee the town before the siege began. Soldiers were everywhere, most on foot but others on horseback, and the air rang with the shout of orders and the jingle of harness. Frightened women searched for their children who roamed the streets wide-eyed, enjoying the excitement. They had been released early from their lessons so they might rejoin their families while there was still time.

Catherine pushed a way through the crowd, and crossed the road then made her way across the grass towards the cathedral. Her uncle would normally be rehearsing the choir at this time, but where he would be in the present emergency, she could not guess but determined to ask anyone who knew him. She ducked under the low boughs of the chestnut and out into the sunlight on the far side. Ahead of her was the Treasurer's house built against the North Tower and already the windows were shuttered and barred. The Treasurer himself stood outside, in earnest consultation with one of Trenchard's men.

'Have you seen my uncle?' Catherine asked him.

He paused to consider, then shook his head briefly and resumed his conversation. She pulled open the heavy door and entered the cathedral and her heart sank. It was filled with people seeking sanctuary within its walls. People who lived alone and were afraid; families from immediately inside the town walls; the homeless who had nowhere else to go. Children, pets and possessions filled the aisles and Catherine despaired of finding a way through. As she hesitated, a cry went up at the other end of the aisle and the rumour spread rapidly.

'They demand our surrender! They call on us to lay down our arms!'

Uproar followed this news and a woman near to Catherine fell to her knees in fervent prayer: 'Dear Lord, deliver us — spare Thy people who have committed no sin and punish our adversary.'

A small boy scrambled over the bundles of bedding and tripping, sprawled at Catherine's feet, wailing for his mother. She tried to pick him up, but at the sight of her unfamiliar face, he redoubled his screams and she hastily withdrew from the chaos within the church to the comparative quiet of the chaos without.

'Cathy! I'm here, child!'

It was her uncle, red and perspiring with anxiety. As he

415

bustled up to her, his chest heaved and he was sadly out of breath.

'Oh, Saints preserve us all!' he cried. 'What a to-do. I must be in two places at once it seems and now they are moving against us at the North Gate. Thousands of them and many Cornishmen and they say their bowmen are deadly, so be off the streets, child and . . . . '

'Aunt is asking for you,' she interrupted quickly. 'She begs you to come home at once.'

'By and by, tell your aunt. I have things to do . . . . '

'But are we to fight alone?' asked Catherine. 'Is no help coming to Exeter? I do not understand what it is all about.'

'Why child, no one rightly understands,' he said. 'Richard is alive and claiming the throne.' He shrugged expressively. 'Who are we to ask the why's and wherefores? But we have sent down messages over the walls to ask for reinforcements. What is that?'

A dull thud echoed through the warm September air, followed by another and another. Catherine felt a prickling of fear. Her eyes met those of her uncle and she saw that the pupils of his eyes were dilated.

'They are battering the North Gate!' he gasped. 'Make haste and return to your aunt. Tell her I will be fifteen minutes — no more. I must look in on my sister. Go home, child.'

Catherine needed no second telling, but picked up her skirts and ran. Everywhere the pace had quickened. Carts were abandoned as people ran for shelter. The first flight of arrows came whining through the air and there were cries as they found their targets. The battering continued. The men abandoned their digging and retired behind improvised ramparts made with the soil thrown up from the trenches. An urchin ran past triumphantly brandishing an arrow tipped with blood and Catherine shuddered.

So there were casulties already! She sped across the grass

and ducked under the chestnut tree where she collided with Peter Wolford, a friend of her aunt's.

'Forgive me,' she gasped. 'I trust I have done you no hurt. I was not looking ahead . . . .'

'No bones broken,' he said, 'but you should not be out at such a time.'

'I am on my way to my aunt,' she said, 'but was sent to fetch my uncle home. But what news?'

He shrugged. 'They attack the North Gate,' he said, 'but are ill-equipped with little armour and weapons. Mercifully, they have no siege engines or guns, nothing save bows and they will not serve at close quarters. We must try and resist them until help comes — if it does! Did you ever hear the like. What a predicament and all out of the blue. Yet someone must have known what was afoot, for you cannot move six thousand men unnoticed! Tis preposterous!'

'Six thousand!' cried Catherine. 'So many? I heard four or five.'

He shook his head. 'I have seen them. All of six thousand or I'm a Dutchman — and I'm not! But tis no time for gossip. Hurry home and sit tight and once your uncle is home, bolt your doors and keep them bolted. I must away.'

And he hurried off, leaving Catherine to cross the road and run to the door. She found it already closed and she hammered on it to no avail, until she suddenly remembered the agreed three knocks and was promptly admitted.

'Oh!' cried Lydia. 'My heart is thumping fit to burst from my ribs! Why did you hammer so, child? I did not know who it could be.'

'And feared the worst,' Catherine added. 'Poor Aunt, forgive me, I forgot.'

She put an arm round the frail shoulders and hugged her.

'Come into the parlour,' said Catherine, 'and I shall pour us a goblet of wine to soothe our fright. And Uncle will be home within ten minutes. He only goes to call on his sister

417

and see that all is well for her husband is away .... How gloomy the house is with all the shutters closed in the middle of the day .... '

Outside the town Perkin Warbeck, the bogus Prince Richard, was suffering his first defeat at the northern gate and finally withdrew from that area to consider alternative attempts. He had an army, six thousand strong, and more than half of them were Cornishmen loyal to the Yorkist cause. At least three thousand had joined him at Bodmin after his march from Whitsand Bay where he had landed from Ireland. Now he was determined to seize control of Exeter, declare himself Richard the Fourth and wrest the throne from Henry Tudor. His attack on the North Gate having failed, he now conferred with his advisers, John Herne of London, mercer, Richard Skelton, tailor, and John Asteley, scrivener. The North Gate, standing above the river and beyond the low-lying Exe Island, was apparently impregnable. It would have to be the East Gate. They therefore reformed and attacked this gate, this time with better success. The battering rams finally broke down the gate and word spread to the dismayed inhabitants that the army was within the walls! There followed some bitter hand-to-hand fighting and the rebels forced their way to Castle Street, before the Earl of Devon brought his company from Blackfriars and resisted them fiercely. But despite their superior numbers, the Cornishmen were for the most part unused to the disciplines required for such fighting and fought bravely as individuals, but without regard to leadership or a sense of unity. They had been promised rich spoils if they took the city and they struggled optimistically against men that were better trained and better armed. Slowly they were forced to retreat the ground they had gained and in so doing, they suffered many casualties. When they were finally driven out of the town, they retired disheartened to regroup and discuss further moves, while the town rejoiced in its temporary deliverance. Bonfires were lit at strategic intervals so that the attackers could be kept under surveillance throughout the hours of darkness.

As the shouting and sound of clashing steel faded, Catherine's uncle ventured to open the upstairs shutters and look down the streets. A small group of soldiers, some with minor injuries, were making their way past.

'Is it all over?' John called to them. 'For the present at least.'

'And tomorrow?' he persisted.

'Who knows.'

John was far from reassured by this laconic answer. His nose had caught the smell of burning wood and he called again. 'What's afire? I smell burning. Have they set fire to . . . .'

'No, no, old man. Calm yourself. They've done nothing so far. Tis our own bonfires you can smell and they'll burn all night. You can rest easy but tomorrow . . . . ' He shrugged. 'Why then, lock up your jewels and your wife!'

Then, realizing the old man's age, he muttered something in an aside to his comrade and they both burst into lewd laughter that caused John to withdraw his head hurriedly and close the shutters, somewhat discomfited, but slightly reassured.

'All's well for the present,' he told them. 'We can enjoy our meal in peace and . . . .'

Lydia gave a little gasp. 'Oh, the meat?' she cried. 'Tis still at the cookhouse. These alarms have driven all thought of it from my head. Catherine, run down and fetch it for me, will you. Tis a leg of mutton, though with standing all this time, will be cold most likely.'

'Cold or hot, I care not,' said John feelingly. 'I have a great hunger and will do credit to anything set before me! So make haste, child, for pity's sake, then we will light the candles early and settle down for the evening. Perchance Catherine will read to you, Lydia, while I finish a business letter.'

The next morning, Warbeck and his followers made another assault on the North Gate, but were easily repelled with very little loss of life. They retreated to a safe distance and went into conference once more.

When they emerged, it was to announce a complete withdrawl and by midday, to the surprise and relief of the townsfolk, the Pretender and his army were moving towards Taunton and already out of sight. What Catherine did not know until the following day was that Leonard, her betrothed, had been wounded during the skirmish on Castle Hill.

She was at breakfast when Leonard's father arrived, and one look at his gaunt expression was enough to tell her that he bore grave news.

'Tis Leonard!' she cried, jumping to her feet. 'What ails him? Tell me, I beg you.'

Samuel Polegate, nodded, patting his chest. 'Tis his chest,' he told her wretchedly. 'Twas a knife thrust and the doctor cannot stay the bleeding. He is with him now.'

'Oh dear God! I must go to him,' cried Catherine. 'Aunt, do you hear? Leonard is wounded and I must go to him. In the chest you say? Then tis a serious matter. And is he conscious? Does he speak? Oh my sweet Leonard!'

And before he could reply, she had darted out of the room, and was away down the street; the front door swinging unlatched behind her. Samuel Polegate hesitated, regarding the blind woman with some embarrassment. She sat at the breakfast table crumbling a hunk of bread with nervous fingers.

'Will he die?' she asked and he nodded, then remembering her disability, spoke it aloud.

'Aye. We fear so.' His voice trembled so that Lydia held out a hand in his direction. As he took it, she said, 'I shall pray for him — for all of you. He is a fine son. You must be proud of him. Now, go and be with him. Your wife needs you. Tell Catherine I shall manage well enough until she returns.'

'My thanks,' he muttered, and taking his leave of her, hurried after Catherine back to his dying son.

Leonard Polegate lay in his bed as pale as the linen sheets, his face twisted with the pain of the wound in his lung while his breathing rattle with frothing blood. His brown hair, damp with perspiration, curled on his forehead and his eyes were large with fear.

His mother stood at the foot of the bed, a bowl of mutton gruel in her hands. Two younger boys, clutching at her skirt, stared wonderingly at their brother, silenced by their awareness of unaccustomed tragedy.

A loud knocking at the door heralded Catherine's arrival and the older boy was despatched to let her in. As she came into the room, the woman held out her arms appealingly and the girl ran into them. They clung together briefly, speechlessly, and then Catherine broke away and crossed to the bed with timid, fearful steps. Leonard turned his head with an effort and tried to smile, but small flecks of blood oozed from the corners of his mouth and she gave a cry of despair.

'Leonard! Oh my love, tis me, Cathy. I came as soon as I knew . . . Dear God, he looks so pale!'

She turned imploringly towards his mother who made a small helpless gesture with her hands and fondled the heads of the two little ones, who now clamoured for attention and the reassurance she could not give them.

'Leonard! Can you speak to me?' cried Catherine. 'Sweet heaven!'

She took his hand in hers and rubbed it passionately, as though to impart some of her own vitality through the friction of her fingers. She leaned over and kissed his face gently then turned to his mother.

'May I sit with him?' she asked and a stool was brought for her. 'Shall I feed him the gruel?' she suggested, but his mother shook her head despairingly.

'He cannot swallow,' she said. 'There is so much blood

in his throat. It makes him cough and that increases the bleeding.'

'But what has the doctor done? Can he not stop the flow?'

'He has tried everything,' said his mother, 'but with no effect — ah, here is Samuel.'

She turned to her husband who hurried into the room.

'How is he?' asked Samuel anxiously.

'The same,' she whispered.

'The Lord have mercy upon us . . . and the doctor — will he call again?'

'He says not. Oh, Samuel, he gives us no hope!'

She began to cry and he placed his finger on her lips, for fear Leonard should hear and guess the reason.

'Come,' he said. 'We will go into our chamber and pray. I have sent for the priest.'

'The priest! Oh Samuel, Samuel . . . . ' She wailed.

He led her from the room and the two little boys hesitated a moment and then followed.

Catherine fought hard to keep back the tears, while she both kissed and rubbed Leonard's lifeless hand which lay in her own.

'Leonard . . . my dearest Leonard, I love you,' she whispered helplessly. 'Don't leave me, I beg you. Don't die, my love, Oh, don't die, I beseech you.'

She felt a slight pressure on her fingers as he tried to squeeze her hand, but he was very weak. Forcing a smile, she tried to speak cheerfully.

'Did you know that Prince Richard was not Richard at all?' she asked. 'King Henry denounces him. They say he is called Warbeck and yet the King of Scotland was taken in by him and even gave him a bride. Oh, Leonard!'

With the word 'bride' carelessly uttered, her brave attempt at cheerfulness crumbled and tears filled her eyes and her lips trembled. She, Catherine, wanted to be bride to this young man; wanted to lie with him and bear his

422

children; longed to share his life. And now it would never be. The young life now flickering would soon be extinguished. She watched his eyelids droop, then close, then open again.

'Leonard?' she said frantically.

He gazed into the distance and when she repeated his name, gave no sign that he heard.

'Dear Mother of God!' she whispered terrified. 'He will die without the last rites!' and instantly she began to recite the only prayer that her dazed mind could recall — 'Hail Mary . . . .'

But at that moment, the priest arrived, and Leonard lay, eyes closed, barely breathing. As the priest moved to the bedside, Samuel took Catherine by the hand and gently led her from the room.

Perkin Warbeck, the charming Pretender and inadvertent cause of her bereavement, had reached Cullompton with his followers. Here many of them, discouraged and disillusioned, deserted him and he made his way towards Taunton with growing unease. On the twenty-first of September at dead of night, he fled with sixty chosen horsemen and headed for the south coast; but on reaching Southampton, he learned that Daubeney had sent two hundred spearmen to head him off and he took sanctuary in Beaulieu Abbey. Here he was surrounded and held until the King reached Taunton on the fourth of October. The following day Perkin Warbeck surrendered.

The cathedral close rang to the sound of the axes, as they chipped and bit their way into the broad trunks. Splinters of bark and wedges of wood flew in all directions and the surprised comments of the bystanders mingled with the curses of the workmen. Thomas Appleby rested his axe on the grass and straightened his back.

423

'God's nails! Tis heavy going,' he grumbled. 'We'll not get these down in time, King or no King, you may take my word on it!'

'There'll be summat said if we don't!' said his partner, wiping a hand across his sweating forehead.

The overseer passed them and shouted, 'Pick up those axes and use them. There's work to be done and you're being paid to do it! These are all coming down and the quicker the better so look to it.'

'Ruddy wood's like iron!' muttered Thomas. 'Twill take a month of Sundays to get through it.'

'Aye, well you've got two hours, so move yourself.'

'I tell you we'll not do it in time.'

The overseer thrust his face up to Thomas's. 'Do you want to tell the King that or shall I?' he demanded. 'He'll no doubt be by shortly to see what progress we've made.'

Sullenly, Thomas picked up his axe and swung it into the tree. His partner fell in with the rhythm and the two men worked on till the overseer moved away, then he spat scornfully. The row of trees had stood for a hundred years or more along the north side of the cathedral, screening it from the road which ran parallel to it. Now two men worked at each tree. From the row of houses immediately affected, several tenants appeared to complain of their destruction.

'King's orders,' snapped the overseer in answer.

'But why?' they persisted.

'Ask him yourself,' said the overseer. 'I do my work, I don't ask questions. King says chop them down, we chop them down. Tis simple enough.'

There was a warning shout and the first of the trees fell with a heavy thud, scattering dust, twigs and leaves. The axemen turned their attention to the smaller branches, stripping them with quick neat blows and a fire was started. The larger boughs were then taken off and horses and carts were brought in to take them away. The trunks were rolled to one side for attention at a later date when time was not so pressing. Smoke billowed from the damp wood and hung in a layer above the grass. Axe blades flashed, voices were raised, the horses whinnied and the carts creaked protestingly under the weight of the boughs.

Lydia stared sightlessly from the window. 'What is all that noise?' she asked.

John Kendal stood beside her.

'They are taking down some of the trees,' he told her. 'Lord knows why.'

'Not those beautiful trees!' cried Lydia. 'Oh, I remember them. They were glorious in the spring — so pale and green.'

'They are glorious now,' said John. 'Red and gold. But you can see the cathedral now and the Treasurer's house — and they are working on that, too. Something is happening without a doubt . . . . Ah, here comes Catherine. She may be better informed.'

'She is a dutiful girl, your Catherine,' said Lydia. 'I shall miss her visits. She spent so much time with me whenever John was away on business and she is so loving. I am grown fond of the girl and wish she would stay with me, but since Leonard's death she has no liking for Exeter.'

''Tis her own choice that she comes home,' said John. 'We are willing for her to stay with you until another betrothal can be arranged.'

His sister hurried to the door in answer to the knocking and Catherine followed her back into the room. She greeted John fondly with a kiss and thought he looked unwell. She herself looked pale, her eyes red-rimmed from grief and lack of sleep.

''Tis good to see you,' said John, 'but we all regret the reason for this meeting. Your mother sends her love and we both feel for you in your grief.'

'Thank you, Papa,' she said. 'I beg you let us speak of

other things. My heart is too heavy and my tears flow too easily. I am so weary.'

'Come sit with me,' urged Lydia quickly in an effort to change the subject, 'and tell me what goes on in the close. I hear the axes and those trees come crashing down. What is it all about? Have you heard?'

The girl moved to the window and gazed over the scene of desolation. 'Aye,' she said. 'They say the King himself has ordered their removal. He is coming here this afternoon to hear the hostages plea for pardon. He will watch from the Treasurer's house and they have knocked out a new window for that purpose.'

'But why the trees?' said Lydia, uncomprehendingly.

'They spoil his view,' said Catherine. 'The hostages will be paraded along the road outside here.'

'And will their leader be with them — this Pretender?' asked John.

Catherine shook her head.

'Tis unlikely,' she told him. 'They say he and his wife are both lodged in the Tower and like to remain so! I would he had never set foot on English soil — then my Leonard . . . .'

She turned abruptly from the window. 'What news from home?' she asked John with an attempt at brightness. 'How is Blanche and little Sophie? I confess I am looking forward to seeing them.'

Lydia got to her feet. 'I will leave you two to your talk,' she said, smiling, 'and I will see that cook has the dinner well forward. All this excitement has sharpened my appetite!'

'Are you warm enough?' John asked and Lydia nodded, pulling the shawl more tightly round her shoulders. They stood later that day at the front upstairs window. The shutters were thrown wide and they waited eagerly. She could see nothing but John, as he had once promised, would see for her. Catherine had gone out into the street to mingle with the crowds who lined the streets expectantly. The town, as victor, had taken on a slightly festive air and pedlars and friars had converged to take advantage of the crowds who had flocked in from the outlying villages and nearby towns. It was not often that the ordinary people in the West Country had the chance to see a reigning monarch.

A sudden cheer went up and Lydia clutched at John's sleeve.

'Ah, tis the King!' he told her. 'He is come to the window of the Treasurer's house and waves his hand most graciously. The people toss their hats in the air and slap each other on the back — and the voices!'

'I can hear it,' she said. 'And the King — what is he like? Can you see his face?'

There was a distance of nearly a hundred yards between them, but John had seen the King in London.

'He has a fine thoughtful face,' he told her, 'and his hair is mid-brown. An angular face, I think, but intelligent.'

'What does he wear? Can you see?'

'A velvet cap of red,' John invented, 'and a doublet of red and gold. He smiles to someone who stands beside him. Tis the Treasurer, mayhap. I do not know.'

'Are the trees all gone?'

'One or two remain at either end of the close. The stumps are so ugly.'

'A great pity,' said Lydia. 'Had I known he could have watched from here and spared the trees!'

John laughed. 'You should have offered your hospitality,' he teased. 'He might have thought himself well served with one of your venison pasties! Ah, here they come now.'

Another great roar from the crowd heralded the approach of the hostages, who shuffled along the road, herded like cattle by the King's soldiers.

'There are so many!' said John surprised. 'Over fifty . . . no, more like a hundred, and many with their hands tied

427

before them or behind their backs. And here come the leaders, no doubt, with halters of rope around their necks . . . the first of them are passing the house now. Do you hear their feet shuffling, some barefoot?'

'I hear them,' said Lydia. 'Will they all die?'

'I think not,' John told her. 'They say this Henry is a merciful man.' 'I hear the crowd hiss,' she said.

'Aye, they hiss and spit on them and some throw stones.'

''Tis no more than they deserve,' said Lydia. 'But for them poor Catherine's Leonard would be living and the date set, no doubt, for the wedding. Likely she also spits on them and jeers. I would in her shoes!'

John sighed but made no answer.

'Do you see Catherine?' she asked. He shook his head and then said, 'No.'

'You will not see her, then,' she said. 'Will you not wait a while? Where are you headed?'

John was grateful that she could not see his face. The innocent question brought a darkness to his eyes. His visit to her was a brief one. He was on his way to see Jennet for the last time and he did not look forward to the meeting, fearing her terrible grief.

'The remaining trees are full of people!' he said quickly. 'All leaning for a better view. And the King beckons — ah, the hostages are pushed forward across the grass towards the King and now the soldiers push them down on to their knees . . , . '

'To pray, think you?'

'No,' said John. 'In supplication to the King. They hold up their hands and cry out for mercy.'

'I hear them,' said Lydia. ''Tis like the moaning of beasts. I can imagine it — all those arms upstretched, like a forest of limbs.'

'In faith!' cried John. 'I do believe you see it for yourself! Your apt description puts my humble words to shame! But now the soldiers whip them and they grovel, crouched on the grass like sheep and a few are prodded, stand up — and are dragged forward by their halters till they stand below the window where the King watches. He shakes his head and gestures with his hand. I think they will hang, those men.'

'The leaders, probably,' she said.

'Aye, probably,' said John. 'They lead them away and all the others stand. The King nods his head — he will pardon them. He is most merciful.'

'I hear them cheering,' cried Lydia. 'And calling his name — Henry! Henry!'

'They are fortunate. There will be no bloodshed today.'

The soldiers moved in again, driving the prisoners back on to the road while the onlookers, less hostile now, moved back to give them space. They were led back the way they had come. Slowly the crowds dispersed. The King withdrew from the makeshift window and a curtain was drawn across. Children scrambled, shrieking, over the tree stumps and the wind, rising a little, blew flames into the smouldering bonfires. By the time Catherine returned, the close was deserted and John had already left.

CHAPTER TWENTY FOUR

Later that day John stood outside the little shop in Tavistock and knocked at the door. Behind him, his horse whinnied fretfully and he put up a hand and patted its neck. The animal moved restlessly, its hooves slipping on the rain-washed cobbles, its head shaking impatiently.

John knocked again, then put his eye to the small window, but could see nothing. Above him to his right, a window opened and an elderly woman put her head out.

'Tis no use banging,' she said. 'She's sick and like to die.'

'To die!' John's voice rang with disbelief.

'Aye. I reckon tis the plague, though the doctor said not, yet he wouldn't give it a name.'

'But she was well enough when I came last.'

'That's as may be, but she's sick enough now and I'll not nurse her for the plague jumps from one t'other and I've a family of my own to think on. Tis bad enough with the sickness almost on my doorstep, and I've a babe of two years. You'll find that bolted from inside.'

John, trying the latch, found it as she had said. He looked up at her.

'Stop your babbling!' he cried, 'and tell me if the back door is also bolted.'

'How would I know,' she said, offended by his brusque tone. 'I tell you, I've no mind to go in a house where the plague is raging. I've a family to think on and she must fend for herself — why, the ungrateful wretch. That's the thanks I get for my information.' And she closed the window with a bang.

John had disappeared through the narrow alley between the shop and the house to the left. His horse followed reluctantly, shying at the narrowness of its path and thankful to reach the small yard at the rear of the building. John tied his horse to a post and tried the back door. To his relief, it opened and he rushed in, calling 'Jennet! Tis I, John.'

Upstairs the house smelt of sickness: a blend of burnt herbs, putrid air and fear. Jennet lay sprawled across the bed which was filthy with spilt ale, urine and dried vomit. Her sunken eyes were closed and she was deathly pale except for a small crimson patch on each cheek. Around her on the bed lay long strands of her bright golden hair, and the shears were still clutched in her hand. Her head was shorn like a boy's, the once glorious hair reduced to a jagged stubble. In spite of himself, he recoiled from the stench and retreated to fling open the window. He approached her again fearfully and put his fingers to her wrist seeking a pulse. She still lived! But for how long?

Her breathing was so shallow that her chest barely moved.

'God's death!' he whispered at a loss to know where to start. He moved back to the window and gulped in the fresh air. He wanted to fetch a doctor but dared not leave her in this state. And how near was she to death? His intuition warned him that she could not live for very long. There was an unnatural sweetness in her breath. He wondered how long she had lain there, neglected, needing help. The doctor should have sent in an old nurse. There was no shortage of old women who, however ignorant, could at least change and wash the sheets and hold a bowl to her mouth, when necessary. Still he made no move towards her. The sight of the bed and its occupant disgusted him and the fact made him ashamed. The helpless creature on the bed was the same woman who had lain with him there, whispering and beseeching him. He tried to visualize her in health and could not.

'Dear God, help me,' he whispered and turned from the window. What must be done, he wondered. He would change the bedding, strip her and wash her and put her into

431

fresh linen. But first he would send out for a nurse. He ran downstairs and unbolted the front door, shouting to the first urchin who chanced by.

'There is a woman here, very sick. Go fetch an old woman who will nurse her. Go on! Why do you wait?'

The boy was about ten, ragged, dirty and barefoot. He held out a grimy hand.

'What, pay you now?' cried John. 'You'll be rewarded when you have done your errand.'

The boy grimaced horribly and waited with his hand outstretched.

'You heard me! Be on your way, you insolent puppy or you'll not get a penny!'

'And you'll not get a nurse-woman,' came the sullen rejoinder and the boy settled himself comfortably against the door of the house opposite.

'Hell fire, you deserve a pounding!' cried John, but there was no one else in sight that might run the errand in his place, so John was forced to give in. He tossed the boy three coins and the boy inspected them greedily. Then, satisfied, he ran off to spend them. The nurse-woman never arrived.

But meanwhile John had relit the fire and hung a pan of water to boil. While he waited for it, he looked in the chest at the bottom of the bed and found a clean shift which would serve to cover the sick woman. Removing the clothes she wore was an unpleasant task. They clung to her flesh, damp with the perspiration which still poured from her fever-racked body. She no longer had control of her limbs and could not help him as he struggled to slide each arm from its sleeve. She did not know him, did not even know that anyone was with her. Her conscious mind had ceased to function, her body was as limp as a rag-doll.

Having freed the arms, he tugged the gown down over her body and threw it thankfully into the far corner of the room. The cold air from the open window blew across the sweating body and great shivers seized it, making her teeth rattle.

'Oh, Jennet! God, what has become of you!' John muttered as he unfastened her white cotton kirtle and pulled it off over her lolling head. Her body, once so yielding, now lay in his arms, limbs sprawling. The flesh had fallen away from the bones and the soft roundness was now gaunt and unattractive.

'Jennet! Speak to me . . . open your eyes!'

He shook her, as though to break the stupor which claimed her, but she remained passive. He bent his head to kiss the mouth, but drew back as the parched lips neared his and concentrated all his efforts on reclothing her as quickly as possible.

When she was once more covered, he laid her on the floor while he stripped the bed and found and spread clean sheets. At last she lay, clean and still and he threw a clean blanket over her and ran out of the room and down to the yard to gulp deep breaths of fresh air into his lungs. His hands trembled. There was no food in the kitchen but he found plenty of wine and drank deeply. She was going to die. He knew it. There was nothing he could do to save her.

'That pathetic creature is not Jennet' he told himself. 'That sickly shell is nothing but a shadow . . . Where is that damned nurse. The boy has been gone an age.'

The water boiled and he took a little in a bowl and washed Jennet's face and hands, but could not bring himself to uncover her body again. That done, he carried the soiled clothes and bed linen downstairs and pushed it into a tub which he found in the yard. He dropped in a handful of soft soap and poured out the remainder of the boiling water, poking the clothes and sheets well down into the water.

'So she's dead, is she?'

He looked up. From a window in the house next door his original informant now leaned enquiringly.

'Go to hell, you miserable wretch!' he shouted. 'No, she's

433

not dead but not far off. Does that satisfy your nasty mind? Is that what you want to hear?'

The old woman bridled, 'Don't you go name-calling me,' she yelled. ''Tis no fault of mine if she dies. Twasn't me as gave her the sickness. She'd no right to come bothering me, I've my children to think on.'

'I doubt she'd bother the likes of you,' said John angrily.

'Why, you'd be wrong then,' she snapped. 'Come calling up at this very window, she did, asking me to run her errands for her. I've got a family to . . .'

'What errands?'

'Why, to fetch medicaments as the doctor had told her — and such a sight I never seen. Cut off all her hair, she had and the shears still in her hand. Lost her wits, I reckon. I didn't want no bother with the likes of her. Ask your fine gentleman friend to run your errands, I said, and she had no answer to . . .'

'You evil old witch!' shouted John, his face white with rage. He picked up a stone and flung it up at her, but it went wide of its mark and fell harmlessly to the ground. He turned blindly and stumbled inside, closing the door behind him.

'The likes of her . . . gentleman friend . . . ' Was that how it looked? Dreary and sordid. And because of him, the old crone had refused to help her. Now, she lay dying and wound never hear the words he had feared to tell her. She had been spared that. He would sit with her until she died. It was precious little but she might regain consciousness and he must not abandon her . . . He sat with Jennet through the night, drinking heavily and in the morning she was dead but John too drunk to know it. He lay beside her all the next day, until in the evening he took the sickness. His head began to ache and his temperature rose. He didn't know that he was ill until the wine's effects faded. By that time he was too weak to move. The disease followed the same pattern as hers and three days later his tethered horse, rearing wildly, frantic with hunger, alerted the old woman to the realization that all was not well.

She called a doctor but it was too late. John had died a few hours earlier. Poor little Jennet, helpless and adoring, had killed him.

It was Joseph who rode to Tavistock to identify John's body and it was Joseph who broke the news to Elizabeth.

'Oh no!' she cried. 'Not dead.'

The shock had robbed her face of all its colour. He nodded, watching her eyes for signs of emotion, any emotion that would reflect a return to normal awareness. But the tone of voice accepted the news although the words denied it.

'He will never see the child,' she said. 'After all these years. He will never see the child.'

She sounded perplexed and glanced up at Joseph, as though to assure herself that he saw the mistake John had made. He nodded, wondering how much she understood and how much he ought to tell her. So far he told her only that he had contracted a fever and died of it. With a sigh, she moved from the table to the fire and turned to face him so that she was silhouetted against the burning logs. She was so pitifully thin in spite of the child.

'Was he alone — when he died?' she asked.

'No, Elizabeth. He was—'

'With her?'

'Aye. She was dead also.'

'You saw her, Joseph?'

He nodded.

'Was she very beautiful?'

'Not any more,' he said. 'I couldn't tell.'

'I'm glad she's dead. Is that very terrible?'

Her voice surprised him, lacking the vagueness that had been so marked over the past weeks.

'Tis natural to feel so,' he said. 'She has caused you much grief.'

'And now she has died and taken John with her. I wonder if he wanted to go.' She looked at him, expecting an answer.

'No one wants to die,' he said. 'I made arrangements that John's body was to be brought home. I thought you would . . . .'

'No!' she said sharply. 'He chose to die with her. Let them be buried together. He would not wish to share a grave with me.'

'But Elizabeth!' Joseph protested, scandalized at the suggestion, 'Heron is his home! You must . . . .'

'There's nothing I *must* do,' she said, 'if I choose otherwise. He shall not lie here.'

'But where then?' stammered Joseph. 'You know they cannot be buried together.'

'He must go back to Yorkshire. To his family.'

'Elizabeth, I beg you! What will be said! Tis not seemly. He must be buried here at Heron. Believe me, Elizabeth. Nothing else is possible.'

She turned to the fire and held out her hands.

'I will not have it,' she repeated. 'His body shall never come home.'

'Elizabeth, don't speak so,' he begged. 'Such bitterness is not like you.'

'Oh, but you are wrong!' she cried passionately. 'I have been tortured these past months fearing his infidelity. Then, at least, I suffered in private. Now, by his death he humiliates me in the eyes of the world!'

He was silent, moved by her passionate plea, awed by her blazing eyes. But even as he watched, her brave words deserted her.

'Oh, Joseph, I am hurt,' she whispered. 'I am hurt so badly that all the love drains from my heart like blood from a wound . . . Help me, Joseph, help me . . . .'

She broke down, covering her face with her hands,

shaken with the ferocity of her sorrow. He turned her slowly round and sitting on the high-backed form, drew her down on to his lap so that she nestled against him like a child. He comforted her, his generous heart aching with love for her, while his own tears flowed down his face unchecked.

John's letter arrived the next morning. It had been found by the old woman who laid out the two bodies and entrusted to the next traveller passing through Ashburton. Elizabeth paid him well and stared at the letter as though at a ghost. She had not expected it. Unrolling it slowly, the familiar handwriting was like a voice from the past. Impulsively she rolled it up again, fumbling in her haste. It could only add to her pain. His last thoughts would not have been of her. She couldn't read the letter. And yet she must know what was in it. She would ask Blanche to read it. No, the girl must not be hurt any more. The scandal had done enough damage to the family already. She would ask Joseph. He was near to her and would be discreet.

Oh, dear God! Why was she so foolish. Nothing he could say in a letter could harm her more than his actions. Of course she could read the letter herself, and if necessary, destroy it. Her fingers unrolled it again and her eyes raced along the smudged and uneven script.

> Elizabeth, my dearest wife, greetings and God's blessing on you, she read, a stillness on her face at the unexpected warmth of the greeting — I pen these words in great agony of mind. The doctor has been summoned but does not come. I came to tell Jennet I would not see her again but find her in such grave distress. Her state is parlous and I cannot leave her for pity's sake but must do what I can for her well-being.

Elizabeth closed her eyes and tried to imagine her husband in a strange house, nursing a strange woman, and found it impossible. The images refused to form in her mind and she turned back to the letter. The writing now grew jerky, slanting across the page.

Thursday – she is dead. I am faint and in great pain, the pen grows heavy in my hand. I will not see my child – forgive me, Elizabeth . . . .

Here the words were smudged beyond recognition. She tried to decipher them but could not. The handwriting was so cramped and the letters so poorly formed that her eyes filled with tears at the thought of him struggling to write so near to death. At that moment, Joseph arrived and Izzie ran past her to open the front door. As soon as he saw her face he guessed the writer of the letter and she looked up and nodded.

'Where was it found?' he asked. 'I looked for a letter but found nothing.'

''Twas on the stairs,' she told him. 'The old woman found it. You may read it presently. But come into the hall and warm yourself.'

He followed her and they sat together before the fire. Elizabeth read again and he waited in silence until she should be finished. She handed him the letter. As he came to the end of it, she said simply, 'Tell them to bring him home.'

Elizabeth watched as John's body was slowly lowered into the ground. A slight mist hung in the air and the trees were red and brown. John's favourite time of year. He loved the autumn with its short days and firelight and roasted chestnuts. It was fitting that he should die in October. At a sign from Father Marryat, she dropped in her sprig of rosemary. For remembrance — aye, she would remember John and think on him with love. They had been married sixteen years, but she had first set eyes on him nearly thirty years ago on that fateful ride south. She had not looked on his body when they brought it home, not wanting to see the handsome face ravaged by disease. She remembered him astride his horse in the middle of the river, his hand outstretched to help her. His eyes had been so very blue, bold with colour. His cheekbones so prominent and covered with the young fine down, too soft to be a beard. And, oh, the mouth, that thin expressive mouth turning down into that wry smile! And now he lay there, wasted and still and the blue eyes were closed forever. A sob from beside her made her turn and she took Catherine's hand in her own and squeezed it.

Poor little Catherine. She had lost Leonard and now her father. The two men dearest to her in the world dead within the space of a month. And she was so young, so undeserving of this double twist of Fate. The rosemary fell soundlessly but the earth that followed rattled like hail on the wooden coffin. Opposite her, Blanche stood with her hand in Matthew's, Joseph on her other side. Stephen had not come home. He had sent no word and Elizabeth was hurt by his absence. Above their heads the passing bell tolled its message. Another soul fled this world – weep for it as for your own!

'Dear Lord, we beseech you to accept the soul of John Kendal into thine eternal favour . . . ' began the old priest and all heads bowed as one.

Martha sniffed loudly, dabbing at her eyes with a square of linen and Della and Eric beside her, exchanged sombre glances. Elizabeth, lifting her eyes, caught those of Matthew, steady grey eyes, dark with grief. She was glad of his presence. He was suddenly become a man — but Stephen was the head of Heron now and he was in London! Her back ached and she changed her weight slightly to ease it. The child lay curled in her womb and would never see his father and the knowledge saddened her.

'Let him find grace in they sight, O Lord . . . .'

'So now I have lost two husbands, thought Elizabeth. Daniel so weak and John so strong. She found herself wondering if Jennet Raikes had been buried and was curious about the woman who had indirectly brought about

John's death. Had she known intuitively, as women do, that she was no longer loved? Or did she die content? Woodsmoke from a bonfire drifted towards them and under their restless feet dead leaves squelched damply. The last words were spoken, the bell was silent, the gravedigger moved forward.

She did not recognize him. Old Donnell himself had died and this man had taken his place. Sighing, she thought that nothing stayed the same. Always change . . . .

'I seem to recall another such moment,' said Joseph, offering his arm as they turned to go. 'To me twas only yesterday that Daniel was being mourned.'

'Poor Daniel,' she said. 'And poor John. I hope they are at peace.'

'I think they are,' he said.

'I wonder if I did right to bury John without the presence of any of his family.'

'I think so. The circumstances are rather delicate,' he said. 'Twould cause them needless grief to learn the truth of his going. Better to write of it in a letter as you suggest, choosing the words carefully.'

'Aye, I must do that. I thank God his mother is not alive . . . . I hope I made him happy, Joseph.'

'You did,' he said.

'Then why, Joseph, why Jennet Raikes?' she cried, unaware that she raised her voice. 'I stood in church and wanted to run to the coffin and shake him by the arm, and ask. Why, John? How did it happen? Where did I fail?

He has died without answering me and now I shall never know . . . . Never be sure.'

'Shh! People are turning round. They hear you!'

'But I need to know!'

'We are not meant to know everything,' he assured her, his voice low. 'There is a place for each of us and we do our best within its boundaries. No one is perfect. We are all human and we all make mistakes. We forgive each other the hurting and we learn from it.'

440

The little procession wound its way along the path under the dripping trees. Elizabeth and Joseph walked slowly at the rear of the mourners. Matthew walked immediately ahead of them, with Catherine on one arm and Blanche on the other.

'John is fortunate,' said Elizabeth suddenly. 'He does not have to grow old. We do.'

'Does it frighten you, Elizabeth, to grow old?' Joseph asked.

'I think it does,' she said, 'When Daniel died I felt life beckoning me. I had so much courage. Now, I bury John, and I am suddenly fearful. Am I old, Joseph?'

'No,' he said. 'You are weary and you are sad and you have not eaten properly for weeks. But you are not old, Elizabeth.'

'I am twice widowed and have lost a son.'

'But you carry another! That is a reason for living, if you seek one! The answer to so many prayers.'

'I am glad and yet my joy is halved. I had hoped to share the child with John.'

Joseph stopped abruptly.

'Share it with me, Elizabeth,' he said. 'Oh, I know I speak too early! Twas my fault when Daniel died and you took me to task for it. But then you needed no one. Now I think you do. Please! Let me finish. I love you. I have waited a long time and now I want nothing more than to care for you and the child. In a few months, when the mourning is done, will you wed me, Elizabeth?'

'Yes, Joseph,' she answered. 'I should be honoured. You have my word on the matter. I think John would have wished it. In the . . . . '

'No, Elizabeth! Not because John would have wished it. Not for the child's sake.'

'But because I love you?' she asked. 'Then let me say it. I have never loved any but John. But he is dead. Give me time, Joseph, and I will learn to love you.'

CHAPTER TWENTY-FIVE

'Tis hard to believe I shall be leaving Heron,' said Elizabeth.

'Do you regret it very much?' Joseph asked her.

While she considered her answer, he looked at her as she rode beside him, the merlin on her wrist. Brightwing, his gerfalcon, rode on his own gauntlet after a distinguished afternoon's performance. Between them the two birds had taken five larks and three partridges, the latter now lay across Joseph's saddle and would be a welcome supplement to their menus in the very near future.

'I do regret it,' she said. 'I cannot pretend otherwise. 'Tis like parting with an old friend, and yet I am grown weary of late and the early joy I felt in it has gone. The family is almost flown the nest and no one needs me but this little Kendal who will leave me in the fullness of time. And he will not be a Kendal but a Tucker . . . Will Retter does not relish my interference and I do not choose to cross him. He is so competent.'

Joseph laughed. 'He is a strange fellow. He says less with each passing year,' he said. 'I never knew a man so sparing with his words.'

'Aye, he doesn't waste words. He will not use two where one will suffice!'

Her horse stumbled briefly and she steadied him with the rein. The merlin fluttered its wings in disapproval and she laughed.

'Even the bird grows old and crochetty!' she said. He will not suffer the slightest jolt without protest. No use to scold me, little one. 'Tis the horse that stumbled, not I.'

Her eyes shone, her face, how plumper, shone with health and her cheeks were flushed and rosy from the fresh air and gentle exercise. She was seven months pregnant and her mourning period was over. They would be wed within a fortnight. The banns had already announced their intention to a delighted congregation and Elizabeth now faced the prospect of life at Maudesly. They rounded the corner and Heron came into view, grey and sprawling in the wintry sunshine. The garden wrapped it protectively and the river bounded it on the eastern side where the land dropped abruptly over the granite. Elizabeth caught his look and her heart was filled with a calm joy — a peaceful way of loving that was a new experience for her. There was no fear in it, no doubts. For her now it was the right kind of loving and she cherished it.

'Why do you look at me so?' she asked, knowing the answer but wanting to hear it said.

'I am thinking how beautiful you look,' he said, 'how fortunate I am and how happy you make me.'

'You cannot guess how those gentle words soothe my wounded spirit,' she told him. 'If I look beautiful, tis because you make me so. I think the joy within me shines through with a rosy glow!'

They splashed their horses through the river and urged them up the bank on the far side.

'I still await word from Stephen,' said Elizabeth, a slight frown crossing her face. 'I have written twice and still he doesn't come.'

'He missed John's funeral,' said Joseph. 'I did not speak of it at the time, yet thought it odd.'

'Aye, and he hasn't been home to Heron since. I think I will send word to Matthew to seek him out. The truth is I am uneasy in my mind. He was always so wilful.'

Joseph nodded.

'Do you think him the right person to inherit Heron?'

'I cannot make up my mind,' she answered. 'Mayhap the responsibility will calm him — that and a sensible wife. I am in hopes of this Mary. She is no beauty but has breeding and will bring a good dowry. Twas almost settled when John died. Now, they may not relish the match. The circumstances of his death . . . .' She broke off, reluctant to finish the sentence, but he understood and nodded.

'The boy does not want Heron,' said Elizabeth. 'That is the truth of it. He wants to farm. Always, since he was a lad, he has wanted to farm! Tut! A fine home and a flourishing business and he chooses to mind sheep! I don't understand the boy at all.'

'Children are not so obedient as they once were,' said Joseph. 'When I was a boy, no one asked me what I would like to do. They told me what I would do and there was no gainsaying it.'

'You are fortunate,' said Elizabeth. 'Your Joe will be home soon and Maudesly will have both of you — and me! Twill be strange to look across the valley towards Heron.'

'And spend each day in Maudesly.'

'And eat there.'

'And sleep there!'

They looked at each other like two conspirators and moved their mounts closer. Joseph moved his left arm so that the hawk was no longer between them and they kissed.

They rode into the stableyard and the boy hurried forward to help them down and unsaddle the horses. From the spare horse box a grey put out its head, and Elizabeth looked at it sharply.

'Whose mount is that?' she asked the boy.

'Gentleman from London,' the boy informed her. 'I don't rightly recall his name.'

'A boy or a gentleman?' she cried. 'Was it Stephen?'

He shook his head, being new to Heron, since Eric had done some damage to his back which was slow to heal. 'He inna a boy,' he said.

Joseph and Elizabeth exchanged looks and hurried through the yard and into the far end of the hall, where they perched the hawks and called for Martha to take the partridges. She bustled in, her face troubled.

'Tis Master Lessor, ma'am,' she said. 'Come post-haste from London. He's with Blanche and Sophie at the bonfire.'

Jacob had raked up the dead leaves and had cut back a large mass of bracken which encroached each year on the garden from the surrounding moor. It blazed fitfully and produced a great deal of smoke, but Sophie clapped her hands and jumped up and down in her excitement. Jacob smiled as he watched her and put out a restraining hand.

'You'll jump right into the fire if you're not careful,' he told her. 'This tiddler loves a bonfire,' he told Mark proudly. 'I swear she can smell smoke a mile off.'

Mark smiled, but he appeared preoccupied and Blanche was pleased when Elizabeth and Joseph approached them. Mark had declined to tell her the reason for his unexpected visit, which fact promised ill tidings. As Elizabeth reached the bonfire, Sophie ran to greet her, tugging at her skirts and asking for chestnuts to roast in the fire. Elizabeth stroked her head absentmindedly and held out her hand to Mark in greeting.

'Come back to the house with me, Mark,' said Elizabeth but though she smiled her heart lurched uncomfortably. Joseph hesitated, unsure whether to accompany her but Elizabeth held out a hand for him also and they all walked back to the house. As soon as they were in the hall, she turned to Mark.

'Is it Stephen?' she asked and he nodded and glanced hesitantly towards Joseph.

'Speak freely in front of Joseph,' said Elizabeth. 'We are to be wed shortly.'

Mark expressed his congratulations and Joseph thanked him.

'But what of Stephen?' she asked.

He lowered his eyes so that he need not witness the shock in hers.

'He is in the Fleet prison,' he said.

445

'The Fleet!' cried Elizabeth. 'Sweet Mary, what has he done?'

'Tis a debt,' Mark told her. 'Or more truly, tis two debts.'

'I must sit down,' said Elizabeth and Mark and Joseph immediately moved to help her on to a chair.

'Please go on,' she said. 'Have you seen him? How much are those debts? Does he have money for food?'

'I gave him some,' said Mark, 'but I doubt he still has it. There are in London many thieves and his fellows are a motley assortment.'

'Then I will repay the money to you,' said Elizabeth. 'But is there more to tell?'

'He is — unwell,' said Mark. 'Forgive me, Elizabeth, I do not relish the telling, but he looks ill and very thin.'

'Oh dear God!' she cried. 'Joseph, I must go to London at once.'

Mark shook his head. 'He will not thank you for your efforts,' he warned her. 'He tells me he intends to remain there. I have tried to free him but the sum is a large one. There is also a warrant against him for assault.'

'On whose behalf?' Joseph asked.

'A Robert Garrett of Fetter Lane who accuses Stephen of striking him in the arm with a dagger during a brawl.'

'A brawl? Oh, thank God John isn't here to hear of it,' cried Elizabeth. 'He would say let the young fool take his punishment. And there may be sense in it. But if he is unwell, he may worsen and die there.'

'He is very weak and his colour is all fled. He cannot sit up but lies on a mattress.'

'They have given him a mattress then,' said Elizabeth.

'Tis more a filthy pallet than a mattress,' said Mark.

'How did you come by this news?' Joseph asked him.

'I heard it from Matthew,' he told them. 'He thought Stephen was in for some trivial matter and would not have you alarmed. I went to the Fleet and made enquiries.'

'How much money?' asked Elizabeth. 'However much it be, I must raise it and bring him out. I will not lose another. There's William gone and John, also . . . .'

'Tis nearly two hundred pounds,' said Mark, 'and you will need a bribe to get him out on the assault — another hundred may suffice.'

'Three hundred pounds!' gasped Joseph, and Elizabeth looked at Mark in horror.

'So much!' she whispered and he nodded. 'Who are his creditors?' she asked.

'Two young gentlemen with whom he gambled,' said Mark. 'They played often at dice it seems and went regularly to the cock-pit.'

They discussed the matter further over their meal and it was agreed that Elizabeth should ride back to London with Mark, taking Eric with her, and would try to secure Stephen's release. Joseph would manage Heron and Maudesly in her absence. Mark did not enjoy the prospect ahead of them. Joseph was not happy about Elizabeth travelling, although she insisted on going. Martha served them roast pork with apple and nuts and a pan of roasted parsnips. The two men and Blanche did justice to her efforts, but Elizabeth had lost her appetite.

The Fleet prison, off Fleet Street, was situated just outside London's city wall. Eastward, the prison faced the Old Bailey, but it was bounded on the west by the River Fleet which was no more than an open sewer. Much of London's filth found its way into it, and the stench in summer was a source of constant complaint by the inhabitants unfortunate enough to live in the vicinity.

Rotting garbage and untreated sewage created a health hazard of which the city council was well aware. The inmates of the Fleet prison added their disgruntled voices to the clamour and the matter was permanently 'under review', though nothing was ever actually done. Conditions inside the prison were no worse than in the other London prisons, being overcrowded, dirty and unhygenic. They were hot and airless in summer and bitterly cold in winter. A fit man might soon succumb to one of the many diseases rife at the time, a sick man would die, starve to death. Money for food and drink was not forthcoming from the prison authorities and the poor prisoners depended on the charity of the rich who, for the good of their souls, donated money for their relief and left legacies when they died. Not all this money found its way to the prisoners, however, for the gaolers were often unscrupulous men or pardoned criminals and, paid very little for their work, they subsidized their meagre earnings as best they could. The accommodation varied. A rich man could live in relative comfort in the better half of the prison. Stephen was in the other half.

He shared a mattress and blanket with a vagrant whose passport had been found to be forged. Having no home or shelter of his own, he was in no way reluctant to spend the winter in prison, trusting blindly in the Lord to secure his release when the weather improved. Stephen had scratched out his name for him on the wall next to their mattress and he was busily etching it deeper with a rusty knife for the sake of posterity. When he wasn't scratching at the wall, he was scratching himself, for he was lousier than the bedding.

'You're coughing well today,' he remarked cheerfully as Stephen was doubled up by a fit of coughing which left him exhausted and out of breath. 'You'll cough your way into your coffin if you go on like that. Exercise, that's what you need. A bit of exercise to get the damp humours out of your lungs. Walk up and down a bit. Jump about. Wave your arms. You'll do yourself no good lying there coughing. You mark my words. A bit of a walk's what you need . . . . You sure you got this name right?' he asked suspiciously as he began on the third letter. 'Seems a mighty lot of it to me.'

'You said your name was Wilberforce,' Stephen reminded him and that's what you've got.'

'I said my name was Sam Wilberforce,' said Sam. 'Is this Sam or Wilberforce?'

'Wilberforce,' replied Stephen, rolling over and trying to draw the inadequate blanket up to his chin.

'Wilberforce!' protested Sam with a comic display of dismay. 'Why not Sam? This will take till judgement day.'

'What of it?' said a pretty young woman nearby. 'You're not going anywhere so what's your hurry? Keep you out of mischief that will.'

She sat huddled against the wall with two other young women. They were all prostitutes and were also sisters. They were in the enviable position of having something to sell. Their lives were made more tolerable by the money paid them by certain gentlemen in the better half of the prison, who occasionally sought their favours. The youngest woman dangled a baby on her knee. Beyond them a group of men threw dice and squabbled for the pleasure of it; for there was no money changing hands. An old man lay sleeping against the wall curled up like a baby and a woman sat beside him endlessly combing her hair with her fingers.

'Or if not Sam, then Will,' continued Stephen's bedfellow, trying to keep the young woman's attention. 'What's wrong with Will? Nought, I swear, and tis a lot shorter than this Wilberforce you've set me.' He winked at her. 'I'll do your name next if you've a mind,' he offered gallantly, but she shook her head laughing.

At the far end of the room, several men stood waiting below the grating in the ceiling which let in light and air. From time to time, visitors to the prison dropped coins through it, although the habit was frowned on by the gaolers.

'Where's that cursed basket man,' grumbled Sam, suddenly aware of his hunger. 'I swear he comes later every day. When I wed my rich widow . . . . There were loud cries of disbelief but he ignored them. 'When I am rich I shall buy the wretched man a large and weighty timepiece, tie it round his neck and push him in the Thames!'

There was an appreciative roar of laughter. 'I shall tell him your plan,' one of the women informed him. 'No doubt he'll find you an extra large crust or a juicy bone!'

'More like the smallest,' cried Sam, 'or a bone pecked over by a flock of starlings!'

The basket man, who roamed the streets collecting unwanted scraps of food, was arriving at the gate at the same time as Elizabeth, Mark and Eric. The gaoler nodded to him and he shouldered his way past them. The gaoler scowled at Elizabeth and held up a peremptory hand.

'Which prisoner?' he asked, picking at his tooth with a filthy finger.

'Stephen Kendal,' Elizabeth replied.

'Only one visitor,' he said and held out his hand for the 'garnish' without which no door would be unlocked and no favours allowed.

Elizabeth looked at Mark in dismay as she handed him the money and he looked at it disparagingly, and thrust his hand out once more.

'The doctor's fee,' he said tersely.

'I doubt the wretch has called a doctor,' said Mark in a low voice, 'but he's a surly devil and you'd best sweeten him.'

She put another shilling into the man's palm and he stowed it in his purse without any thanks, then jerked a thumb towards another door where another man waited with an outstretched hand. Elizabeth looked at Mark.

'If Stephen is unwell,' she said, 'we may have need of lodgings in the town until he is well enough to ride. Would you find us lodgings?'

'You might stay with me and welcome,' said Mark, 'but I have only one spare bed and you will be three. But I'll search out a suitable room for you while you bargain with this "gentleman". No doubt a few more coins will secure Eric's entrance as well as your own.'

It did. Five minutes later, Eric and Elizabeth were making their way through the crowded cell, conscious of the eyes of the prisoners who stared at them with avid interest. Embarrassed, Elizabeth kept her gaze on the straw-covered ground and attempted to avoid the worst of the dirt. She ignored the hands held out to her for alms, recalling the incident with the lepers.

'I beg you stay close,' she whispered to Eric and he put an arm round her protectively and warded off the most persistent beggars. Yet she was horribly aware of the hopeless people on all sides. The nearness of their bodies was a physical burden oppressing her spirits.

'Where is Stephen?' asked Eric. 'I don't see him.'

'Is this the right cell?' said Elizabeth, anxiously. 'We had best ask.'

Eric took hold of the sleeve of one of the men and asked for Stephen Kendal. He shrugged his shoulders and pointed to his ear and then his mouth.

'Dear Lord!' cried Elizabeth. 'The poor wretch is deaf and dumb.'

A woman turned to them. 'Kendal?' she queried. 'He's over there on the bed,' and she jerked a thumb towards the far corner of the room.

'Thank you,' said Elizabeth.

Stephen struggled to sit up when he saw her, and Eric knelt quickly to help him.

His wretched condition sickened her and for a while she could only stare at him speechlessly with his hand clasped in hers.

'You shouldn't have come,' he said. 'I didn't want you to.'

'Stephen!'

'I told Mark . . . leave me here . . . let me be,' he said with an attempt at defiance which was frustrated by an outburst of coughing, which hurt him so badly, that he

451

clutched at his chest and screwed up his face in pain. Sam turned from his engraving.

'None of that now,' he said. 'How can an artist work with all that spluttering going on?'

Stephen smiled faintly. 'Mama, this is Sam Wilberforce,' he said.

Elizabeth smiled and Sam swept her an elaborate bow and indicated his work.

'When tis finished, I shall embellish it — now there's a good word — ' he said. 'I shall embellish it with hearts and flowers and what you will.'

He waved a disparaging hand around the walls. 'Aye, twill be very superior to this other poor scribble.'

Elizabeth looked at the walls where countless prisoners for years past had inscribed and super-inscribed their names, initials or marks. So many hours of pointless effort; so many wasted lives! She sighed deeply. Pray God Stephen should not be among them much longer. The grey stone walls were damp and covered higher up by a film of green slime. The ceiling was low. The window was a square opening filled with a rusting iron grid.

'And I'm Annie,' said a pretty young woman and Elizabeth smiled again. At that moment, the door opened and the basket man entered. There were cheers and catcalls and a general stampede, but the gaoler who accompanied him bellowed for silence.

'There'll be nothing for anyone until you hush your babbling,' he shouted. 'So keep back until your name's called . . . that's better. . . . '

He consulted a list and began to call out the names of the prisoners poor enough to receive the free rations. 'Edmunds, Farraday, Francis, Grimwaddy, Garret, Smith Benjamin, Smith Robert. . . . '

'Don't you get food?' asked Elizabeth.

'I won't eat it,' said Stephen. 'Tis not fit for dogs! Stale pies, mouldy loaves, trimmings of raw meat, scraps from the rich man's table ugh! I would rather starve.'

' — Turner . . . Tyburn . . . . '

Stephen glanced across at the old man who still slept against the wall. Beside him the woman, a pie in one hand, still combed her hair with the other.

'They called his name,' Stephen told her. 'They called Turner. You should wake him.'

She shook her head and bit fiercely, ravenously into the pie. The effort of speaking had almost exhausted Stephen, but he persisted.

'Shake him,' he told her. 'He must eat something.'

The woman shook her head again. 'He's not hungry,' she said between mouthfuls. 'He's sleeping.'

Sam snorted. 'Strange kind of sleeping,' he said. 'I have not seen him awake these last two days! He's dead, more like.'

Elizabeth looked at the still form uneasily.

'Take a look at him Eric,' she begged. 'He does seem very still.'

Reluctantly, Eric crossed to the old man, watched by the woman who smiled vaguely and repeated that he was sleeping and had no appetite.

Eric put out a hand and shook the bony shoulder. To his relief, the man stirred, changed position slightly but could not be woken.

''Tis probably a coma,' said Stephen indifferently. 'If so, then he is fortunate, for he will die dreaming far from this place.'

Elizabeth tried to collect her wits and return to the matter of Stephen's release. She waited until Sam had resumed his scratching then spoke to him again, her voice low.

'I will say nought now of what brought you to this,' she said, 'although it grieves me sorely. But you are ill and I will not lose another son. What did the doctor say of your sickness — and what treatment have you had?'

'I have seen no doctor,' he told her, 'and I have had no treatment. I have a chill. Tis no more than that. I have no wish to be bought out of this place. I am here under warrant — taken out by my so-called friends.'

'But surely you do not owe so much!' said Elizabeth. 'Two hundred pounds! You cannot . . . .'

'I do, Mama, and there's an end to it.'

The familiar sullen note crept into his voice despite his predicament and Elizabeth was sorely tempted to shake him.

'You prefer to rot here then,' she said.

He shrugged. 'I do not wish your interference,' he said and was again shaken with a violent bout of coughing.

'You know your father is dead?' asked Elizabeth.

'Aye. I'm sorry.'

'Sorry!' cried Elizabeth, her anxiety giving way to anger. 'You are sorry? No more than that? Does it not mean anything to you? I am shortly to be wed and will move into Maudesly so that as elder son Heron is yours. Two of your brothers are dead and you would lie there and make a third! Heron is yours whether you want it or not and . . . .'

'Matthew is welcome to it,' he said. 'He will cherish it for you.'

'Matthew is an apprentice goldsmith!' cried Elizabeth. 'He does not have the legal training that you have been given. A goldsmith is not . . . .'

'Papa was a goldsmith,' he reminded her. 'You will not argue that he did not succeed.'

Their raised voices were attracting attention and Elizabeth made an effort to speak in more moderate tones; though such scenes were not uncommon and provided an interesting escape from the normal monotony of the prisoners' days.

'Whatever you feel about Heron can be discussed later,' said Elizabeth grimly. 'My present concern is to see you removed from this place and in the care of a doctor. If tis possible, I shall settle the debt and buy you off the other charge . . . . Is it true that you stabbed this man?'

454

'Aye, tis true,' he answered. 'I would I had killed him!'

'In a brawl?'

'We had been drinking. He cheated me.'

'Dear God!'

'She rose to her feet with Eric's help and stared down at him with a mixture of anger and bewilderment. 'You cannot want to stay here,' she said. 'You cannot want to die in this miserable place and be no more to anyone than a name scratched on the wall!'

'I do not wish to settle those debts,' he said grimly. 'They were my friends and yet they cheat me. Aye, I would rather die than give either of them a penny!'

'And when they hear you have died in prison,' cried Elizabeth. 'Who is then the loser? You are as stubborn and as proud as your father but I can be stubborn also. You are John's rightful heir and he would want you at Heron. I have brought some jewellery with me and I shall realize money on it. I shall take you out of here whether you wish it or no!'

Despite his protests, Elizabeth set about securing his release. Mark introduced her to a friend of his — a dealer in gems who gave her a fair price for the two rings, the locket and the brooch. Next, he visited Robert Garrett in Fetter Lane and to her surprise, found him a reasonable young man. Faced with the immediate settlement of the debt, he agreed to withdraw the assault charge. Stanley Farrow was the second creditor and Elizabeth learned that he lived in Colman Street. He was less reasonable and inclined to be argumentative, but Elizabeth made it clear that if he did not accept settlement from her, he would never be paid so he finally agreed to the sum. After that, it was comparatively easy to 'persuade' the gaoler to release Stephen. Indeed, he had no reason to detain him further and a week after her arrival in London, Stephen was moved on a litter to the room Mark had found in Wood Street. Eric was to share the room with him while Elizabeth would lodge with Ella.

By this time, Stephen was considerably weaker and in no state to complain about his removal from the Fleet. Mark's doctor was called in and immediately bled the patient and prescribed a special diet of beef, broth and red wine, but as the days passed there was little or no improvement in his condition. The date of the wedding approached and Eric was finally despatched to Ashburton to ask Joseph to arrange a postponement, until Stephen was sufficiently recovered and able to undertake the journey to Devon.

Joseph heard the news with dismay.

'How long does Elizabeth expect to be in London then?' he asked.

Eric shrugged. 'Stephen is bled,' he said, 'but seems to grow worse instead of better. I doubt she will come home within the week. More like two, I'd say.'

Joseph was most unhappy with the situation. At the back of his mind was the memory of their last visit to London and its outcome! He did not relish the thought that Elizabeth was once more in London unattended and decided to join her. Eric, to his infinite disappointment, was told to stay at Heron while Joseph made his way to London alone.

He arrived three days later and went straight to Mark's lodgings. He was shown upstairs and found Mark, Elizabeth and Ella finishing their supper.

'Joseph!' cried Elizabeth. 'Oh how good to see you!'

She jumped up from the tableboard and ran to him and he took her into his arms and kissed her.

'I thought you may need my help,' he told her, 'and I missed you!'

'Oh, that's sweet to hear,' she said. 'Now let me see . . . you know Mark, of course, but not Ella.'

Joseph kissed her hand courteously and she glanced down at their half-completed meal.

'You will be hungry after your ride,' she suggested. 'Shall I run round to the cookhouse for more mutton?'

'I won't refuse such a kindly offer,' he said. 'I have ridden hard and it has sharpened my appetite.'

Ella stuffed the last spoonful of tart into her mouth and darted away downstairs; while Joseph unfastened his doublet and sank gratefully into the chair beside the fire, stretching out his long legs.

'Please finish your meal,' he told them. 'I am happy to rest awhile and will tell you the news from Heron while you eat.'

Blanche and Sophie were well and happy. Izzie had scalded her foot but not too seriously 'and got little sympathy from Martha' he told them, 'for she declares the girl was skylarking and deserved no less!'

'And the mines?' Elizabeth asked.

'No direct problems,' Joseph told her. 'The men from Dartmouth are agitating again. They now claim that the red soil in the water poisons the fish and rots their nets!'

Elizabeth laughed. 'They are inventive if nothing else,' she said. 'Any news of the last survey in our fourth shaft?'

'They have found little to date,' said Joseph. 'Retter thinks you will do well to abandon that one and try further over.'

'It may come to that,' she said. 'If Will advises it.'

She poured a glass of wine for him. 'At least you can join us in a drink,' she said. 'Ella will not be long. The cookhouse is only round the corner.'

'I have been urging Mark to wed the girl,' said Elizabeth. 'All these years she has waited, when she could have bettered herself elsewhere!'

'Bettered herself?' cried Mark. 'Now where could she find a better prospect than me? I tell her, patience is a virtue.'

Elizabeth laughed. 'I despair of you,' she said. 'By the time you wed you will be old and grey.'

At that moment, Ella returned and a trencher was filled with mutton and vegetables for Joseph. He fell on the food gratefully and, while he ate, Elizabeth told him of Stephen's situation and her concern for him.

'I am convinced this bleeding does him no good,' she said, 'but when I spoke on the matter with the doctor he suggests a purging draught instead. Tis such folly! To nourish him with beef and red wine and at the same time purge him! The doctor is an old fool. He has no logic worth a mention and a child has more understanding of astrology! Mark will forgive me, I know, but I have no faith in him and would rather take Stephen home and consult our own doctor.'

'I do not defend him,' said Mark. 'In truth I am so rarely sick that I daresay I have only called on him once or twice in my life. He may well be a charlatan as you suggest.'

'Ah, remind me later,' said Joseph. 'Izzie has sent a rabbit's foot for Stephen — to put under his pillow and hasten the cure. I own the thought touched me. She is a funny little thing, that Izzie.'

'Scatter-brained,' said Elizabeth, 'but her heart is kind. I will bring her with me when I move into Maudesly if you are agreeable. Oh, Joseph, I am so sorry that we must postpone the wedding.'

'I warrant Joseph is sorrier!' laughed Mark. 'But has Elizabeth told you my news?'

He looked enquiringly at Elizabeth who shook her head.

'I am buying the shop from Nathan,' he said proudly. 'He is to retire and I shall be my own master.'

'Congratulations!' cheered Joseph. 'But surely now you will need a wife. A master goldsmith does not cook his own supper — or mend his own hose!'

Ella grinned. 'He is no master with a needle,' she said, 'and will never pass muster as a cook.'

'Then he will soon become a byword,' said Elizabeth. 'A

butt for honest men, married men and an object of pity. Tis very sad.'

There was a moment's silence while Ella, Elizabeth and Joseph all looked expectantly at Mark. Then he burst into laughter.

'I see I am outnumbered,' he said with mock dismay, 'I shall have to take a wife after all. That pretty wench at the cookshop will suit me well enough . . . .'

He could go no further for Ella descended on him, fists flying demanding that he name the day or she would go straightway into a monastery.

'A convent, surely!' he teased, but Ella declared that the monks would be better company.

'I could not let you go,' he told her, 'for what have they done to deserve such a fate. No, I will wed you myself.'

Ella stared at him uncertainly. 'Are you in earnest?' she asked.

He nodded.

'And tis not a joke?'

He shook his head again. Elizabeth held her breath, but Mark suddenly dropped on to one knee.

'Will you, Ella, wed your humble servant Mark?' he asked and for once his eyes belied the bantering tone.

'Aye, Mark,' she said softly. 'I believe I will.'

She kissed him and pulled him to his feet, declaring that he looked shorter than ever on the floor.

'And here's me wanting a tall husband,' she said, 'but a few hours on the rack will help you!'

Joseph and Elizabeth congratulated them and the goblets were refilled for a toast to the happy couple.

'And now a toast to Joseph and Elizabeth!' cried Ella. 'Now if you were to stay in London longer we should have a double wedding! But here's to you both — for poor Joseph has waited for Elizabeth almost as long as I have for this wretch!'

The second toast was drunk and they discussed what to do with the rest of the evening. It was decided that they should take Joseph round to Wood Street to see how Stephen was progressing and minister to any immediate needs.

The landlady told them the doctor had not called. Joseph arranged for the stabling of his horse and then he and Elizabeth went up to Stephen's room. He was awake and looking brighter. The doctor had not called, it seemed, so he had not been bled. He had taken some broth and a little bread and honey. No one referred to the Fleet and in front of Joseph he was less sullen than he had been for some days. Suddenly Elizabeth felt less apprehensive. She had brought a custard tart which Ella had baked for him and, cutting him a large slice, was pleased to see that his interest in food was returning. Joseph stowed his spare clothes in the small chest under the window and the landlady brought up a jug of hot water and a towel. While he was washing his face and hands, Elizabeth felt the first pain. Very slight and lasting only a moment but unmistakable. She groaned inwardly. She was not ready for the child. She wanted it to be born at Heron. She wanted to be married before the child arrived. She was only in her seventh month . . . . The list of reasons against having the child was endless — but would the child understand that she thought wryly. Probably not. John's child was probably as stubborn as the rest of the Kendals she reflected.

The pain came again but she said nothing to Joseph, — it might be a false alarm. Half-an-hour later, she knew that it wasn't and could no longer hide her distress when the contractions seized her. A certain amount of panic and confusion developed. She went home with Ella and she retired to bed. Ella was marvellous company declaring that the early confinement was a godsend 'for now I am to be wed I must know what to expect if I should lose my shape for nine months and suffer the torments of hell!'

The midwife arrived soon after eight o'clock and the child, a healthy boy, was born soon after. Elizabeth looked down at their son, at the living legacy which John had left her and a sudden thought brought a smile to her lips. The child had been born ahead of time and she and Joseph were still unwed. She was still Elizabeth Kendal. 'So, John,' she whispered, 'did you want your little Luke to be a Kendal? Then you have got your own way!'

SWEET SALLY LUNN
Pamela Oldfield

Fleeing from Louis XIV's persecution of the Huguenots, young Solange Luyon arrives with her family in England. They know no-one there, except the one person most important to Solange – her father, Pierre, who mysteriously deserted his family years ago. But unable to locate him, the Luyons are forced to struggle on alone through the harsh realities of a new life.

Solange, inheriting her family's traditional baking skills, and taking the English name of Sally Lunn, moves to Bath and becomes the celebrated owner of Sally Lunn's Coffee-House. With her bright eyes and golden-yellow curls, she attracts a stream of admirers. But the path of true love is not a smooth one; it is strewn with the torment of fierce passion, voices from the past, the hurt of rejection, and the ardent attentions of Beau Nash, the handsomest dandy in England . . .

0 7474 0873 4
GENERAL FICTION

JUBILEE
Claire Rayner

THE POPPY CHRONICLES

An enthralling historical saga . . .

Mildred Amberly – suffocating in affluent Leinster
Terrace – doomed at 28 to be an old maid. Lizah 'Kid'
Harris – a Jewish boxer from London's East End – living
from one fight to the next. Worlds apart . . .

But one rainy night Mildred takes a cab across London
into Lizah's world – a world of drama, excitement and
teeming life. But if she has escaped Leinster Terrace,
Mildred can't get away from its values . . . And Lizah's
family exerts pressures of its own. The past will tear them
apart . . .

Yet out of all this conflict comes Poppy – with her
mother's strong will and her father's boundless appetite
for life. Poppy, whose first memories are of Queen
Victoria's jubilee, who will live through two world wars,
and witness a century of change . . .

0 7221 7292 3
GENERAL FICTION

☐ THIS RAVISHED LAND	PAMELA OLDFIELD	£4.99
☐ AFTER THE STORM	PAMELA OLDFIELD	£4.99
☐ WHITE WATER	PAMELA OLDFIELD	£4.99
☐ GREEN HARVEST	PAMELA OLDFIELD	£3.99
☐ SUMMER SONG	PAMELA OLDFIELD	£3.99
☐ GOLDEN TALLY	PAMELA OLDFIELD	£3.50
☐ A DUTIFUL WIFE	PAMELA OLDFIELD	£3.99
☐ SWEET SALLY LUNN	PAMELA OLDFIELD	£4.99

Warner Books now offers an exciting range of quality titles by both established and new authors. All of the books in this series are available from:
Little, Brown and Company (UK) Limited,
Cash Sales Department,
P.O. Box 11,
Falmouth,
Cornwall TR10 9EN.

Alternatively you may fax your order to the above address.
Fax No. 0326 376423.

Payments can be made as follows: cheque, postal order (payable to Little, Brown and Company) or by credit cards, Visa/Access. Do not send cash or currency. UK customers and B.F.P.O. please allow £1.00 for postage and packing for the first book, plus 50p for the second book, plus 30p for each additional book up to a maximum charge of £3.00 (7 books plus).

Overseas customers including Ireland, please allow £2.00 for postage and packing for the first book, plus £1.00 for the second book, plus 50p for each additional book.

NAME (Block Letters) ....

ADDRESS ....

....

☐ I enclose my remittance for _____

☐ I wish to pay by Access/Visa Card

Number ☐☐☐☐☐☐☐☐☐☐☐☐☐☐☐☐

Card Expiry Date ☐☐☐☐